PLACES
IN THE
DARKNESS

CHRIS
BROOKMYRE

orbit

www.orbitbooks.net

ORBIT

First published in Great Britain in 2017 by Orbit

1 3 5 7 9 10 8 6 4 2

A CIP catalogue record for this book is available from the British Library.

ISBN 978-0-356-50627-2

Typeset in Caslon by Palimpsest Book Production Limited,
Falkirk, Stirlingshire
Printed and bound in Great Britain by Clays Ltd, Elcograf S.p.A

Papers used by Orbit are from well-managed
forests and other responsible sources.

MIX
Paper from
responsible sources
FSC www.fsc.org   FSC® C104740

Orbit
An imprint of
Little, Brown Book Group
Carmelite House
50 Victoria Embankment
London EC4Y 0DZ

An Hachette UK Company
www.hachette.co.uk

www.orbitbooks.net

For Keva

PROLOGUE:

SOME ASSEMBLY REQUIRED

"Consciousness Does Not Exist," says Mehmet.

Jenna has just caught up to her lab partner as they glide along the main level-two conduit inside the Axle, his eyes betraying that his focus is not entirely fixed on his immediate environment. He is reading something on his lens.

"That sounds deep for this time of the day," Jenna replies, by way of bidding him good morning.

"No, it's the name of the lecture Maria Gonçalves is giving today. Really wish I could have seen that."

"You'll see it after you finish work. And you've seen a hundred. What's special about this one?"

"I mean seen it live. She's giving it in person."

Okay, now she gets it.

"Seriously? Wow. When did that last happen?"

"When I was in diapers, probably."

"Damn. Couldn't you have swapped your shift?"

Mehmet fixes her with a withering look.

"Yeah, like that's why I won't be there."

"Only the great and the good able to get tickets," Jenna suggests.

"Tickets? You jest. Invite only. But on the plus side, they sent me my date for getting the new Gen-4 mesh. Four weeks today."

"Way to go. I'm not even on the formal waiting list. I'm on the waiting list for the waiting list."

"How come?"

"My own stupid fault. Dragged my heels because I wasn't

convinced it would make much of a difference, but that's not what I'm hearing from the people who have got it."

"No kidding," Mehmet says, warming to the subject. "I was talking to Javier last week. He's had his a month. He says the data retrieval is night and day's difference. It's like you just instantly *know* the information."

"Yeah, I hear there's far less of a watermarking effect. You don't get that feeling like you're peering over somebody's shoulder at their worksheet. Guess I'm going to have to wait a while to experience it, though."

They reach a six-way junction, both of them changing axis with a practised light tug on a handhold. Official protocol states that personnel are supposed to come to a complete stop before proceeding, but right now there's nobody else around to bump into. That's what she loves about working in the Axle. There never is. Compared to the wheels, it's always practically deserted.

"Lateness appears to be a consistent theme for you at the moment," Mehmet says. "I thought I was going to end up on my own here today."

"Sorry. There was a problem on the static. They had a car out of commission, meaning a knock-on delay, and then the car I got from Faris was rammed."

"Little flavour of home. When the static is busy like that, close your eyes and you could be on the subway train in New York City. Just need somebody to piss on the floor a few hours before, give it that authentic smell to recreate the full effect."

Jenna yawns and stretches as they drift along the shaft.

"Late night?" Mehmet enquires.

"No, just feels like it's been a long week. Late night tonight though. Gonna tear it up."

"Got a date?"

"Only with one of those famous Sin Garden mojitos over on Mullane. Then maybe five more."

Mehmet shakes his head, a wry smile on his face.

"What? You still think I'm crazy paying those prices?" she asks.

"No. I think it's funny that somebody is getting a backhander purely for growing mint to supply those things."

"Unauthorised botanical cultivation. Can't imagine that's what the Seguridad call a jump-seat offence."

"No, but I'm sure some prick at the FNG would be able to tell you the exact expected yield in zucchini, or whatever, that they would otherwise be growing in that square footage of soil."

"And what about your social life?" she asks. "I hear you're switching phase on us."

Mehmet looks bashful.

"Yeah, this guy I've been seeing. It's getting serious. He's on Meridian."

"And you're leaving all us sweet people on Atlantic for him? It really must be love."

"I already got a lot of friends who are on Meridian phase. Been thinking of making a change for a while. This was just the final nudge, you scope me?"

Jenna fixes him with a look. He withers.

"Okay, it is love," he admits.

"Knew it."

"So what tests we running today?" he asks, conspicuously changing the subject.

Jenna smiles by way of acknowledgement. It will be a shame when he switches. She likes working with him.

The test chamber is now only a few metres ahead. The entrance is a bladed aperture at the end of the shaft, but inside it's like a giant buckyball. She and Mehmet are both in synthetic pharmacology research, based out of Wheel Two. The firm they work for has a block booking on this chamber, studying the sustained effects of microgravity on certain artificial compounds.

"That's weird," she says, reading the security status on her lens. "The chamber is open."

"It looks unambiguously closed to me," Mehmet responds, confused.

"I mean it's not locked. The team using it last can't have closed up properly. See, these are the losers and wasters you're about to throw your lot in with when you shift to Meridian."

Without the security interface requesting an access code, they don't have to stop outside. The aperture dilates in response to their proximity, so they can let their momentum carry them inside uninterrupted. Jenna executes a somersault to emphasise this fact, but as she spins upright again, she is tugged to a stop. Mehmet has grabbed the rim for purchase with one hand and taken hold of her shoulder with the other.

She looks at him by way of demanding an explanation.

Mehmet is staring into the vastness of the chamber, eyes wide: speechless, shivering, scared.

In zero-g, the gentle ballet of objects in motion can make anything look elegant.

Not this.

Glistening organs dance gently around each other in the bright expanse, like motes of dust in a shaft of sunlight. Intestines curl and twist between sections of limbs denuded of skin, muscle exposed like illustrations in an anatomy textbook. She sees an empty skull, the top sheared off. The brain has been removed, floating free amidst this carnal constellation.

Jenna is almost as much a geek as Mehmet for the work of the Neurosophy Foundation, but the one thing she never got is why they are pioneering memory erasure. She couldn't understand why anyone would want that.

She does now.

PART ONE

PART ONE

AWAKENING (I)

"There will be no children."

It is the first thought that flashes into Alice's mind as she slowly approaches consciousness, like a diver rising towards the surface. The words are prompted by a sound: that of children's voices, laughing and shrieking with delight. At first she thinks she is imagining them, but though her eyes are closed she knows the voices are coming from outside her head.

There will be no children. It is one of the things she remembers being told to expect about her first trip to Ciudad de Cielo – CdC – and yet she can hear them, clear as day. Is it a recording?

She opens her eyes. She can only see directly in front, the beige wall of the passenger capsule's interior. Her head is restrained for safety inside a protective cradle, but the brace is not there purely to hold her in position. It also houses sensors monitoring her vital signs, which it streams to her lens, superimposing the data upon her field of vision.

The standard lens system comprises one contact for each eye, transferring data to and from a circular processing unit attached to the wrist. This disc also accommodates a sensor that interprets finger gestures by way of a primary control interface. The rig is completed by a sub-vocal audio relay that integrates so seamlessly with one's hearing that Alice sometimes forgets it's an auxiliary source. It is from this that the children's laughter briefly issues once more before being cut off.

She has been asleep. Or maybe it would be more accurate to say she must have passed out. She does not know for how long. Alice has never felt so disoriented, so brain-scrambled. This must be what it feels like to have a hangover, she thinks, never having experienced one personally. She has consumed alcohol, but only in moderation, strictly within the recommended lower- and upper-limit parameters prescribed for maximum health benefit.

"Dr Blake?" says a voice, close by this time, not originating from the speakers.

A male face moves into view, the motion strangely fluid, as though gliding. It is further evidence of her wooziness. He seems to float into her field of vision like a figment from a dream. His hand is resting on the outer guard rail around her passenger cradle.

His features are Chinese, but less diluted than hers. He is about her age, either side of thirty. He is smiling, his tone gentle, his accent American.

"You lost consciousness. It sometimes happens during the ascent."

Alice searches for her voice, feeling relief when it comes online. "How long was I out?"

He smiles in a manner she interprets as intended to be reassuring.

"Precisely two hours, seventeen minutes and twenty-two seconds, but you've been monitored the whole time."

"What caused it?" she asks. She knows that a precipitate loss of consciousness sits on a spectrum bookended by simple fainting and hypoxic brain injury.

Again the patient smile.

"I'm not qualified to interpret the data, but in my experience, most of the time it's a result of cumulative exhaustion brought on by tension and anxiety over the prospect of the ascent, exacerbated if you had a long trip to reach Ocean Terminal. Don't think of it as anything more significant than that you were tired and you fell asleep."

It feels like more than that though, like coming around from anaesthetic or something. Some parts of her mind seem accessible, others clouded. She knows that the platform is one hundred and sixty thousand kilometres above the base. She knows that the ascent takes five hours and fifty-three minutes. She knows all manner of technical data regarding the elevator and its operations, but she has an altogether less crisp recollection of her trip prior to entering this capsule.

"How much longer is the climb?" Alice asks. She can see the

current time on her lens, but the formerly animated trip data field is now blank.

"The climb ended twenty minutes ago," he replies, amusement now taking over from reassurance in his tone. "Welcome to Heinlein Halfway Station."

He loosens his grip on the guard rail, which is when she understands that he was not resting on it, but holding it to prevent himself from floating away.

"The other passengers have already disembarked from the capsule. The protocol states that we leave you to come around on your own. Nobody stays out for very long once we hit the top, though you were nudging at the upper end of the scale."

He brushes his fingers against the rail, the action providing enough purchase for him to rise and drift away from her with dreamlike fluidity. It is no dream, though.

"Ladies and gentlemen, we are floating in space," he says.

She wonders why he makes this statement of the obvious, confused further by the absence of passengers who might be the other addressees. She detects a certain self-consciousness to it too.

She searches her memory for secondary levels of significance to the words and he reads her confusion in the blankness of her response.

"It's just something we say, a stupid tradition. Don't know how it started, but it kinda stuck."

Of course. The minute self-consciousness denoted that he was quoting. Like many such frivolous and pointless customs, it was observed for no greater reason than that it has been observed many times before, though its current observers could not explain its origin.

"Don't worry if you're feeling a little disoriented," he assures her. "Again, it's perfectly normal."

Alice stares at his features. She doesn't remember ever seeing this man before, though he must have been with her in the capsule.

No, she recalls. He wasn't. Nobody occupies a passenger position unnecessarily. An escort leaves you at the bottom and another meets you at the top. Every inch of storage space, every gram of weight is carefully accounted for to a precisely budgeted dollar value. The elevator massively reduced the cost of reaching geostationary orbit. Cars run constantly, as many as four simultaneously at different stages of ascent and descent, totalling twenty trips per day. The weight and volume of materials being transported over any given twenty-four-hour period exceeds the cumulative payload weight and volume the human race sent into orbit in its first five decades of space exploration. But nonetheless, nobody is assigned a passenger cradle unless their travel has a demonstrable value – which is what truly confuses her as once again laughter and high-pitched squeals of delight ring through her ears.

"I can hear children."

"Yeah, that's a common-access feed from elsewhere on the platform. You'll be sharing a shuttle with them to CdC. The family came up on an earlier car but they have been taking a tour of the platform before moving on."

"A family?"

"Tourists." He gives her a knowing look. "Every million they spend pushes us a little closer to the stars."

Alice strains to look around, but her head is snugly secured.

"If you feel you're good to go, I'll disengage your restraints. You ready?"

He means is she ready for physical movement and for microgravity, but these are merely physical considerations.

"My body seems fine, but my brain feels like it is still catching up."

"Don't worry, that's perfectly normal too. Do you need any pointers? Like who you are and what you're doing here?"

She realises that this is a joke, though it is uncomfortably close to the truth.

"Probably wouldn't hurt."

It is coming back in waves: articles and fragments of memory washed up like flotsam that she now has to assemble into coherent objects. She hopes this is all an effect of the ascent, and therefore temporary, rather than a result of being in space. Her name is Alice Blake. She is travelling to CdC on behalf of the Federation of

National Governments to replace the outgoing Principal of the Security Oversight Executive. She will be here a minimum of six months as long as she doesn't screw up; considerably less if this woolly-headedness proves chronic.

She remembers things about her journey but she isn't sure they are in the right order. The capsule. The elevator. A platform in the ocean.

Logic helps fill in the blanks between specifics like track between stations. There was a long flight in an airplane. Did she fly direct to Ocean Terminal? No. It was too small to land an aircraft that size. She was on a large passenger jet, a long-haul flight. There was a delay, a problem with hydraulics.

She remembers the docks, azure water all around the platform, sparkling in the hot sun as she climbed the gangway. She went there by boat, a hydrofoil. She remembers ships moored at other points on the hexagon, offloading cargo. The shouts of men on the vast floating docks working to prepare the payloads for the elevator, the complex tessellation of pallets and cases in the vast hold beneath the tiny passenger capsule.

There is a soft hum as restraints withdraw from around her body, the head brace folding up and back. She attempts to stand but finds she cannot: one final anchor point at the base of her spine is preventing her from moving.

"Yeah, before I uncouple the last safety bolt, I have to advise you to please let me know if you think you might throw up, in which case I'll guide you to the nearest vacuum sluice. A proportion of people get nauseous in microgravity. We still don't know why: it's been happening since the first rocket crews, though obviously what they brought up was the right stuff."

She doesn't understand what he means, how twentieth-century astronauts' vomitus could somehow be a suitable substance, though from his expression she suspects it was another joke. She does not get it, but responds with a polite smile.

"Just take it slow, see how it feels."

Alice hears the clunk of the maglock disengaging and pushes up with her palms. She recalls her briefings on this but the result is

11

still massively disproportionate to the effort. She rises instantly and at speed, shooting up past her escort before throwing out a hand to stave off impact with the ceiling.

Another childish giggle reverberates in her ears, but this time the source is her own throat.

As the sensation of drifting through the air registers around her body, she experiences the most intense endorphin rush. It is as though the weightlessness extends beyond the physical, a feeling of the purest pleasure, the simplest, most undiluted awareness of mere being. She is lost in the moment, everything beyond it divested of relevance. It only lasts a few seconds, but even as her body thrills, it is as though this purge reboots her mind. Everything comes rushing back in, the fragments assembling themselves into place, properly this time.

He guides her towards a circular hatch in the ceiling, a bladed aperture on a surface ninety degrees from the doorway by which she entered the capsule. It dilates in response to his proximity, granting access to an airlocked passage at the end of which is a second blade-locked circle. She is uncomfortably reminded of an automated device for chopping vegetables that sat in her parents' kitchen, but she obliges as he glides to one side and beckons her to pass through first.

The second aperture swishes quietly open once they are both inside and its counterpart has closed. Again he urges her upwards. She rises into a white-walled corridor, punctuated by panels of black. As she draws closer, she sees that they are not black, but transparent: there are tiny points of light in the darkness. She is looking into space. Then as she floats closer and higher, her elevation affords her a perspective directly down upon the Earth.

She gasps, quite involuntarily, looking round at him as though to say: "Are you seeing this?"

"Yeah. It never gets old."

He looks pleased but there is something knowing about his intonation, something minutely self-conscious, like when he said "we are floating in space".

She does not have enough experience of this individual to get a reliable reading on his microgestures and the subtler nuances of his speech. She can't be sure, but something seems insincere, rehearsed. She searches for a comparison. It prompts a memory of a tour guide, an attendant at a theme park. And, of course, that is all he is. This is not her liaison.

Glancing up again, away from the mesmerising sight of the glowing sphere beneath, Alice looks out into the blackness and observes that the points of light she saw were not stars. They are shuttlecraft, part of a constant traffic between here and her final destination.

"Getting like a freeway out there," her escort tells her. "Our fleet of ion shuttles are the workhorses of modern space. CdC is in an orbit seventy thousand kilometres above us, but these old faithfuls make each round trip burning less energy than it takes to drive a city block."

He beckons her along the passage, leading her upwards at a perpendicular junction. His hair moves like he is underwater, and as it lifts she sees a thin line below the base of his skull, where no new hair will grow: the site of his mesh implant.

She skims the wall with her fingers for propulsion, adjusting the force she exerts following her initial miscalculation. The shaft plunges several storeys beneath her unsupported feet at the perpendicular junction, a drop so dizzying as to make her eerily aware of what would happen should the magic spell wear off and gravity apply as it normally does.

There is another perpendicular turn, before they pass into what a sign above the larger bladed aperture denotes the Passenger Holding Area. It is a cylindrical chamber, with an airlocked doorway to the shuttle bay dominating one side. Along the other, a row of windows looks down into the cavernous interior of the space elevator's upper terminus, formally known as Heinlein Halfway Station.

There are seven people already inside the chamber. Instantly she recognises three of them as the other passengers who had travelled in her capsule. She hadn't spoken much to any of them, though they were all introduced when they boarded the elevator down on Earth. Their names are Kai Roganson, Davis Ikicha and Emmanuelle

Deveraux. The other four comprise the family she has been told about: a man, a woman, a girl and a younger boy. The children are spinning in the air, laughing fit to burst.

Their mother warns them to cool it down or they might be sick. A sign on the wall cautions passengers against unnecessary manoeuvres in micro-gravity. Alice is dismayed that neither entreaty appears to be having an impact.

They are small, however. Perhaps the sign is generally more concerned with the greater hazards deriving from the potential of adult collisions.

She has learned that many rules do not apply so rigidly to children, or at least that some discretion may be applied in their enforcement.

The children are wearing miniature versions of the same environment suit as was issued to everyone else. It is designed to create a perfect seal with a rebreather mask in the event of a pressure loss, but in practice it functions principally as a giant diaper, collecting and filtering secretions during what could be an eleven- or twelve-hour journey between gravity-dependent toilet facilities.

Astronaut training used to involve learning to pee through a suction tube (crucially disengaging without spillage). She learned its history by way of background prep for the mission. She thinks of the commitment and determination required simply to enter the selection process, the punishing multidisciplinary programmes and simulations that had to be mastered, the sacrifices and risks driven by an unquenchable desire to reach space.

This triggers a connection in her memory and belatedly, she gets the joke. The right stuff.

She's had plenty of preparation and been briefed exhaustively, but none of it was about making the journey. Like everybody else in this chamber, she got here by stepping into an elevator. None of them was trained for the ascent any more than a commercial airline passenger gets flying lessons.

"Everyone, this is Dr Alice Blake, as some of you already know. Alice is here with the Federation of National Governments."

He reprises introductions for the three she has already met, then indicates the four she has not.

"Dr Blake, this is Mr Sayid Uslam and his wife Arianne. And of course, taking advantage of the environmental conditions over there are their two children Karima and Zack. They are here on a sightseeing vacation."

Alice puts the name and the face together. Uslam is an energy magnate, a riches-to-ultra-riches entrepreneur whose family name has run through the infrastructure of Jadid Alearabia since the days of post-oil and post-war reconstruction.

Mr Uslam nods and offers the empty smile of someone who knows Alice is not important enough for him to care who she is or why she is here. His wife doesn't even look, instead floating closer to the children who are now bumping their heads against the glass despite signs specifically warning passengers not to touch the windows.

Alice does not believe this is one of those areas where discretion must be exercised.

"What ages are your children?" Alice asks their mother.

"Zack is six and Karima is almost eight."

"Then presumably at least one of them can read the notices regarding contact with the glass."

The woman's eyes flash with barely suppressed outrage. In Alice's experience this is often the emotional response when a person is confronted with dereliction of their responsibilities. In this instance it does not prevent her from making amends.

"Zack, Karima, don't bump the glass or this lady here will have us thrown off the space station," Mrs Uslam tells them.

This last seems an unnecessary level of threat, but children sometimes require exaggeration in order to make a point.

There ensues a silence in the chamber, an awkwardness that Alice has learned often follows when a person's behavioural shortcomings have been made explicit in the company of others.

The individual most uncomfortable in the aftermath appears to be the escort, which is when it occurs to her that the one person he has not introduced is himself. People are often welcoming of a distraction at such moments, so she decides to offer one.

"Forgive me, but I don't believe you told me your name."

"Oh, my apologies. I'm pretty sure I did, but I'm forgetting you were a little woozy."

He is mistaken. Her memory is functioning perfectly now, and she only ever has to be told someone's name once.

"Also, on CdC you get used to people's names showing up on your lens, so we can be a little lax about introductions. I'm Tony Chu. I am the Uslam family's official guide on their trip, but up here, we're all about efficiency so everybody doubles up on tasks to avoid any unnecessary redundancy. I'm to make sure you get to CdC and are met by your official liaison. There was a flight delay from New York, I believe?"

"Yes. I was supposed to be meeting up with a delegation before we took the hydrofoil, but I didn't make it. I believe they are already on CdC."

"As will you be, soon enough. You're halfway there, after all."

He smiles again, indicating a plaque above the shuttle bay door. This time she more quickly identifies the note of tour-guide insincerity.

The plaque reads:

Once you get to earth orbit, you're halfway to anywhere in the solar system.

— Robert A Heinlein

"What are they doing?" asks the little girl, staring down into the expansive vault that is the core of the facility.

"They are unloading the freight compartments of the elevator car that these other passengers just arrived on," Chu replies. "That's why you're having such fun floating around."

He turns to address the adults. "We don't have any centripetal gravity systems here on Heinlein because principally this place is about processing heavy cargo. We've got the strongest stevedores in human history: one person can move a forklift load with their pinkie."

Alice glances into the cargo bay. She counts six shuttle docks, three either side of an octagonal chamber.

"The freight is broken down into smaller loads and sent to different destinations around CdC."

"Are any of them androids?" asks the little boy.

"Remember, sweetie, we spoke about this already," his mother reminds him; not for the first time if the weariness in her tone is anything to go by.

"We have some of the most advanced automated systems known to man," Chu replies with professionally cheery indulgence. "But if you mean robots or cyborgs like in the simworlds you may have seen, then I'm afraid not."

The kid looks crestfallen, like he had been hoping his spoilsport mom was lying or misinformed.

Chu reads it and responds with cheerful mock-incredulity.

"You saying space isn't cool enough?"

The boy blushes, shaking his head bashfully.

Alice thinks of the stuttering history of AI, the intoxication of the early days when a few leaps in progress made people believe this was the beginning of an exponential acceleration. In fact, the sum of what those leaps achieved was merely to educate scientists as to the true complexity of what they were trying to comprehend.

Someone once described it as like building a tower to the moon. Every year they congratulated themselves on how much higher the tower was, but they weren't getting much closer to their target. In fact, the higher they built, the more they were able to appreciate its true distance. To Alice, the significance of this could not be underlined more firmly than by the fact that she has just ascended a tower to space, an engineering feat that proved considerably easier to achieve than the artificial replication of human intelligence.

"There are no androids here," the kid's mother affirms. "And when we get to CdC, there will be no androids there either."

Her tone is final, but her words remind Alice that she was assured there would be no children.

As the shuttle-bay lights come on, indicating the arrival of their transport, it is a timely reminder that she has no more first-hand knowledge than this child regarding what awaits her when she finally reaches Ciudad de Cielo, the City in the Sky.

AWAKENING (II)

Jesus.

A near-empty bottle of Scotch on the night stand, a faint tang of vomit from the fold-away john. A headache like artillery fire, pounding explosions of light and pain. Knuckles bloody on both hands, dried blacker than the skin beneath. A faint memory of punching somebody, no recollection of who. And, of course, a hooker passed out naked on the bed alongside her.

Yep, must be Tuesday. Or Thursday. Whatever.

Nikki fumbles for the button and turns on a light, confirming that she's in her own place, so at least she doesn't have a walk of shame to deal with. Less happily this means she's got to get rid of the hooker, which is complicated by the fact that this wasn't a paid gig.

"Hey, wakey-wakey," she says, giving the sleeping figure a shake. With her face turned away, Nikki can't see who it is. Probably Donna, going by the short crop. She remembers talking to Donna in Sin Garden.

"Come on, sleeping beauty. Time's up. Off you fuck."

The girl stirs and rolls around on to her side. It's not Donna. It's Candy, but with a new haircut. That's what she calls herself when she's dancing or turning tricks. Her real name is Candace. She's a sous-chef at one of the fancy restaurants over on Wheel Two. Everybody here's got two jobs, and those are just the official ones.

Nikki remembers now. She talked to Donna but it was about business. Donna owes her money. She wonders if Candy stepped in by way of distraction. No. She met Candy in the Vault. But who did she punch, and where? Shit, it's all so blurry.

She drank so much last night, except according to the clock, last

18

night is not last night. She's only been asleep a couple of hours. The hangover is kicking in but technically she's still drunk. Wouldn't take too much to get a buzz back on, except she has work to do.

She didn't really mean to sleep at all. As far as she can work out, the last time she woke up in this bed was only about eight hours ago, though she really, really can't remember shit beyond that.

She has to get dressed. She reaches for the floordrobe and grabs the garments she discarded in an eager hurry not so long ago.

"You gotta be someplace?" Candy asks blearily. "I thought you were on Pacific phase."

"Only for my day job."

"Shit. Well, I'm on Meridian and I've been working eighteen hours straight. Can't I crash here a while?"

Nikki thinks about it. Either way she's going to be rid of Candy in about five minutes, so she might as well bank a favour.

"Okay. But that don't include refrigerator privileges, all right?"

Candy sighs.

"You okay, Nikki?" she asks. There's concern in her voice, which makes Nikki's hackles rise.

"The fuck is it to you?"

"Just asking. You were in a weird mood before you fell asleep. You were crying. You want to talk about it?"

"I thought the reason people paid hookers was so they didn't have to talk to them after they fucked."

Candy sits up in bed, wide awake now. Pissed.

"Oh, you're gonna pay me for last night, is that what you're saying? Because I thought it was something else."

Nikki shrugs.

"Whatever it was, it don't make you my goddamn confidante, like I'm gonna share my emotional burdens with you."

"You were happy enough to share plenty of other things just a few hours ago," Candy replies, voice all coy and sing-song.

"Yeah, well, don't flatter yourself. Pussy is like fried chicken from Monty's Late-Nite Take-Out. I only feel like eating it when I'm drunk."

Candy looks pityingly at her. Candy. The hooker.

19

"That line would only work if you ever fucked somebody sober. I work the Vault, remember? I seen the number of guys you leave with. Seems to me when you're drunk you got just as much an appetite for cock as for chicken."

Nikki knows she's got no come-back for that.

"I guess we're all lonely up here," she offers, pulling a shirt over her head. "Even a cold-hearted bitch needs to feel somebody likes her now and again."

Candy shakes her head.

"They don't like you, Nikki. It just seems that way because they don't hate you as much as you do."

FUTURE INVESTMENT

After the g-forces and the sheer counter-intuitive strangeness of the elevator ascent, the shuttle flight is remarkable in presenting so little sense of movement. It is silent and smooth, the distances covered making progress almost impossible to register via visual cues. It is, consequently, a little boring. Alice has no idea what time it is in New York, the last place she started a day by waking up in bed, or in the Pacific archipelago where Ocean Terminal is situated; she only knows that it no longer matters. She is tired but not sleepy, unable to concentrate on her work for the squeals inside the passenger cabin and the constant threat of collision with a small human missile.

The cabin is kitted with sim-tech options for the amusement and distraction of those lacking the discipline to apply themselves more constructively throughout the journey, but nothing to compete with the novelty of microgravity. An overhead panel warns passengers that they should remain seated and secured at all times, and before launch the pilot made an announcement to similar effect. Nonetheless, as soon as Mr Uslam enquired as to whether his children might be permitted to regard this "more as advice than instruction", Tony Chu was quick to acquiesce.

It is a small form of corruption, unacknowledged by either party. Often the very wealthy do not even need to spend their money in order to purchase special treatment.

Each of the other passengers has been kicked or thumped at least once as the children swim and swoop back and forth between the facing rows of jump seats, yet Alice appears to be the only one prepared to register her displeasure.

"They're just kids," says Deveraux, in response to Alice's sigh of exasperation at the latest near-miss.

Alice does not understand the relevance of the point she is attempting to make. Children should not be exempt from safety considerations merely on the grounds of their age; indeed, the necessity of obeying such instructions should be driven home to them at every opportunity during these formative years.

Tony senses the rise in tension and intervenes by attempting to broker conversation between the adult passengers.

"I'm not sure how much you all got to talk before your ascent, but Dr Blake is with the FNG and will be working with the Security Oversight Executive, is that right?"

They had exchanged polite small-talk on the ocean platform but Alice had not volunteered any information regarding her new job. This was due to having been warned that CdC personnel could be prickly about the issue of federal oversight, or "undersight" as they preferred to call it, in reference to the FNG being based on Earth.

It would not have been top of her list for an ice-breaking gambit. She wonders if Tony chose it deliberately, what private resentments are concealed beneath his professional smile.

"It's really just a fact-finding and observation brief," she says, aware that nobody here has clearance to be told what her true role will be. They are unlikely to guess, either. People tend to under-estimate Alice's age by at least five years, and that is not the only reason they would be surprised by her seniority. She stopped being bothered by it long ago; these days she appreciates how she can make it work for her. Her remit will be to root out corruption, and in her experience people are far less circumspect about such things when they don't believe you have any power.

"You're here so the FNG can tell the Seguridad how to do their job," says Ikicha, his back stiffening. "Fact is, the governments down below should be learning from how security does things up here, not the other way around. This is as close to a city without crime as mankind has ever seen."

Davis Ikicha is a senior engineer working on the ramjet engine project. Seated next to him is Emmanuelle Deveraux, a physicist attached to the laser propulsion team. Professionally speaking, she is his rival, but it is clear that it is Alice who is perceived as their enemy.

"There is no such thing as a city without crime, Davis," she says, fixing Alice with an insincere smile. "Or, at least I'm sure the doctor will be able to find some so that the FNG has a pretext for sticking its nose in and replacing the Seguridad with its own law enforcement agency. They've been looking for a reason to do that since this place began."

With the Uslams conspicuously oblivious to their fellow passengers, Alice casts a glance opposite towards Kai Roganson, who said little on the ocean platform and volunteered nothing regarding his own position on CdC. He does not contribute to the discussion regarding Alice's perceived role, but it is clear he is paying attention and he wants her to know as much. His eyes glow pink as he stares directly at her.

The rec light in a lens originally functioned as an automatic notification to let people know they were being recorded, but it was quickly hacked and bypassed to the point of being redundant, particularly given how many people were recording close to permanently. These days, if somebody flashes the rec light, it is by way of reminding you that your actions are being committed to data. It is usually a polite warning, but in this case Alice interprets it as a gesture of passive-aggressive intimidation.

"Believe me, nobody is more enthusiastic than me about what we are doing on CdC," she insists brightly. "I am here as a wholehearted believer in the *Arca* project."

"Yeah," replies Ikicha coolly. "The FNG always say that. Right before they choke off funding to something."

She knows this is an argument she cannot win. A tense silence might ordinarily have ensued, but there is too much noise from the kids for this to be the case.

Alice detects an upwards shift in the pitch of their squeals as something new piques their excitement.

"Daddy, Daddy," the little girl shouts. "I think I see it."

Unfortunately, nobody else can while the kids are obstructing the windows, a state of affairs that finally prompts a command from their father.

It proves too much to hope that they will strap themselves into their seats, but at least they hover in one place for a few blessed moments, long enough for everyone to get a look at their destination.

It is still just a grey shape against the black, but it is large enough to be distinct from the white dots that are stars or other shuttles.

"We're going to a real spaceship," the little boy declares boastfully.

"We're not going to a spaceship," his sister corrects him. "The CdC is a space station."

"Daddy said it was a spaceship," he counters aggressively. He clearly doesn't like big sis having the upper hand.

"No, Zack, darling," says his mother, with the urgency of putting out a fire before it really gets blazing. "I'm sure Daddy said they are *building* a spaceship."

He still looks pissed, like he doesn't appreciate the suggestion he picked it up wrong. Mom shifts tactics and moves to distract.

"Why don't you ask these people who work there? I'm sure they could tell you everything about it."

The kid turns to look at them.

"Are they building a spaceship?" he asks everyone and nobody in particular.

"Yes," answers Deveraux. "The CdC is the space station where we are building *lots* of spaceships, testing out their designs and learning step by step. It is a very long process towards ultimately building a super-spaceship which will be called the *Arca Estrella*. It is going to take our explorers across the galaxy in search of new planets we might one day call home."

Deveraux's tone is assured, someone used to talking to young children. Perhaps she has had some herself, though they would have to be grown up by now; the CdC is not a place for home-makers but for people committed to their work.

"Why?" the boy asks.

Deveraux laughs, sharing a look with Ikicha.

"Good question," he says.

"We're building it because our Earth won't last for ever," Deveraux answers. "One day the sun will expand to a hundred times its size and gobble us up, so we need to be someplace else before that happens."

24

The boy looks appalled, genuinely afraid.

"When?"

"Not for a few hundred million years," she assures him, but it doesn't appear to offer the kid any comfort.

"The sun is going to explode? Our planet is going to be gobbled up?"

Tears form in his eyes. He looks to his parents like he's appealing for them to say it ain't so.

"Don't worry, Zack," his father tells him. "Listen to the lady. She is talking about hundreds of millions of years from now."

The boy's lip is quivering. Alice knows how he feels, having gone through the same thing when she was around that age. He is too young to grasp the distinction between the vast timescale Deveraux is talking about and his own lifespan. The only thing he is taking in is that the world he takes for granted will one day be gone. It is his first encounter with his own mortality, which is why it won't help to explain that he will not be around to worry about the death of his native solar system.

His sister's expression is more thoughtful. She has run the numbers and come up with a different query, one that a great many people have been asking throughout the decades since this undertaking began.

"If we will be safe on Earth for millions of years, why are we doing this now?"

"Another good question," Ikicha observes. "As the people Dr Blake works for might ask, why should we be spending colossal amounts of money, pouring so much of our time and resources into reaching another planet when we still have so many problems to solve on the world where we already live?"

Alice says nothing. She doesn't mind being misrepresented, for if this is all Ikicha sees, her true self will remain camouflaged.

The little girl gives her a thoughtful glance as though impressed by the point Ikicha is making on her behalf. A good straw man *should* seem impressive though, so that its creator looks all the stronger knocking it down, which he proceeds to do.

"But what if the first men had all said to themselves, if it's safe in here, why leave the cave? If it's safe on our little patch of land, why cross the river? If it's safe in our little country, why cross the sea?"

"Every time we explore further, we make a bigger world for ourselves. A better world," Deveraux says warmly.

Karima looks sold. The Ikicha-Deveraux double act works nicely, and Alice is content to have played her silent losing role if a valuable lesson has been learned.

"So where is this new world, this new planet?" asks Zack, an explorer's curiosity overcoming his first encounter with inevitable death. "When can we go there?"

"The *Arca Estrella* will take a very long time to build," Deveraux answers. "We don't even know what form it will eventually take: we are learning as we go. Merely building CdC to its current state has taken decades. But even once the *Arca* is finally launched, it will take many more decades, maybe centuries to find a new planet where humans can settle down. That is why it's such a vast project: people will live their whole lives on board without ever getting off. Some will be born there and die there. It will be their children or even great-great-grandchildren who reach the new world."

The boy frowns, sussing that this means it won't be his next vacation destination. His sister looks unsatisfied too.

"But if nobody alive now will be around when the ship reaches another planet, why are they doing it? I mean, what's in it for them?"

Deveraux looks to Mr and Mrs Uslam and wins a knowing smile for her efforts.

"Parents do these things for their children, and for the children of the future – even a thousand years in the future. You wouldn't be flying in space right now but for the efforts of all the people who worked on problems that they knew would never be solved in their lifetimes. Do you understand?"

She nods solemnly, the pleasure of microgravity suddenly taking on a greater significance than if Deveraux had put some dizzying dollar value on it.

Meantime, the CdC is close enough for Alice to make out its

shape. It looks a lot like a barbell: two great wheels either end, rotating around a long, narrow central structure known as the Axle. This part is mostly cylindrical, a labyrinthine zero-g complex the equivalent height to a five-storey building, and once comprised the entirety of CdC before the first wheel was constructed. From this distance she can't visually discern which is Wheel One and which is Wheel Two, but she knows the latter's construction benefited from decades' worth of experience (i.e. mistakes) accrued on its predecessor. Consequently Wheel Two is the more affluent habitat, where the rich and connected live and the Quadriga companies all have their HQs. Between them, they accommodate a hundred thousand people. Each of the wheels has four spokes connecting to a central hub that rotates around the Axle. On the outside, the wheels are flat, grey and uniform. On the inside, they look like somebody cut a long rectangular strip from a city and rolled it until the two ends met in the middle. This far out Alice can only see the indistinct twinkling of lights, but she knows that if you look directly up through the canopy, you will see the rooftops on the other side. The canopy itself is one of the engineering advances that made CdC possible, a super-strong transparent nanocarbon that lets through certain light frequencies but crucially blocks radiation.

Other shuttles appear like dots on a diagram, their flight lanes pointing to the destination. They fly back and forth twenty-four hours, the constant delivery of materials and supplies.

Parallel to the Axle, a pair of slim arms connect to a platform two-thirds the length of this central core, forming the "dry dock" jetty that tenders the many test vessels in various stages of construction. It looks so still, so peaceful, but Alice knows she wouldn't be bound for it if that were true.

"In the original plan," Chu informs them, "a construction platform was intended to move back and forth along the *Arca* as it was put together. This was back when they said the project was going to take twenty years. Now the CdC dwarfs the structures it was intended to build. Mothers do tend to swell when they are pregnant, after all, and it's not all the bump."

As they approach close enough for Alice to make out the skeletal forms of partially assembled craft, the sight triggers the memory of a dead lizard she saw when she was seven. It was alive when she first encountered it, being tortured by some older boys who had caught it by the edge of a pool. Alice had run away, disturbed by the eager pleasure of their cruelty, and it had gone from her mind until she happened upon its sad corpse near the same spot a couple of days later. It was part flesh, part skeleton, missing sections where the ants had stripped it. The test vessels are similarly incomplete, her mind having to fill in the blanks in order to imagine what they might eventually look like.

The flashback is unwelcome, almost obscenely inappropriate, and she wonders what perverse function of the subconscious vomited it forth at this time. As Deveraux just explained, the *Arca* represents the noblest of aspirations and the most selfless of endeavours: nothing less than the apex of human civilisation and the pinnacle of human achievement.

Perhaps this memory has surfaced now as a warning against complacency, reminding her that civilisation as a process is not irreversible. Even as we build the *Arca Estrella*, our primal state still lurks dormant beneath the surface, ready to rise if we are not vigilant.

CHAOS AND ETERNAL NIGHT

Nikki pulls on a jacket as she descends the cramped staircase, brushing her elbows against the walls. The air temperature seldom fluctuates between twenty-two and twenty-three degrees, but she's not wearing it to keep warm. It's to cover up what she's got strapped underneath.

She slips out the back entrance and stops to grab a shot from a vending panel. She knows it will chemically neutralise the effects of the alcohol on her system far more effectively, but if she had the choice she'd still sooner have a double espresso than this shit.

She throws it back and winces at the sickly flavour. Tastes like medicine and guilt.

Twenty seconds later she's turned the corner and is walking down Mullane. The streets and passageways around here are all narrow, the buildings crowding in on either side. If you look straight up you can just about glimpse the canopy, but you're only going to see a sliver of black.

The earliest parts of Seedee are all like this. The apartments are little more than pods, the ceilings eight feet high apart from inside some of the ground-floor public areas. The streets here on Wheel One are all named after early astronauts, indicating that this was one of the first phases of Seedee's construction. Before it was part of Wheel One, it was the first large-scale art-grav area ever built, whirling around the central trunk on the end of an arm to generate the centripetal forces that kept its inhabitants on the ground. Out here amidst such endless emptiness, ironically space remains a precious commodity.

The accommodation was state-of-the-art for the time, living spaces you could walk around in, eat and drink in, piss in. To the pioneers of those days seventy years ago – the scientists and engineers used to the zero-gravity space-station conditions that preceded it – this was luxury living.

As material fabrication and construction technology evolved, the spinning arm got a counter-balanced partner, then two more, then they filled in the blanks until there was a wheel. One wheel became two, and while space remained at a premium, the living habitats had long since stopped being built to reflect the common cause and comparatively equal status of the people living there. There's always more room for those with more money. It's no longer the scientists and engineers and architects who live in this neighbourhood, though they still come back here for their fun.

It's busy on Mullane right now, because it's night-time.

That's a joke. On Mullane, it's always night-time.

There are three time zones on Seedee, eight hours apart, but they're not separated by distance. Medical research proved that folks working shift systems were cutting a decade from their life expectancy, particularly where overnight work was part of the deal. When they said "these night shifts are killing me," they were speaking more literally than they knew. So on Seedee, you don't work a shift pattern, you live a phase: Atlantic, Meridian or Pacific. Your days and nights have a regular, normal rhythm of work, rest and play.

Leastways, that's how it goes for respectable folks. Nikki not so much.

Mullane Street's economy is based around a state of permanent night. When it rolls around two a.m. Pacific and it's time to hit the hay, the folks on Meridian phase are just getting ready for some R&R.

Ciudad del Cielo boasts some of the most advanced entertainment and leisure technology mankind has produced. As well as the full-immersion sim-tech chambers, you can play sports in motion pods that track your physical movement and map it perfectly to generated environments. You can play a round of golf at Augusta or go up against a friend on the Centre Court at Wimbledon. You can even free climb the Grand Canyon thanks to the fluid terrain-generation systems in the 360-degree spheres.

And that shit is always popular, sure, but up on Seedee they soon discovered that the more advanced the tech we surround ourselves with, the more the Caveman Principle kicks in. You can design a ship to take you to the stars, but you gotta feed the beast that's building it, and not just with the highest quality fabricated protein and the Quadriga's Officially Licensed Ale.

Hence it's always busy down on Mullane, people rolling in and out of the bars, the diners and the constantly changing roster of other establishments catering to every appetite. Night clubs, people still call them, though the night part seems kinda redundant under the circumstances, especially when there's so much variety that could be denoted by a wider range of prefix: dance clubs, strip clubs, fight clubs, sex clubs.

Used to be they stopped building past a certain height because the gravity gets less the higher you go. Then they realised there was no reason to stop. Over in W2 the rich keep high-rise cabins for when they want the benefits of sleeping in microgravity. Round here, they rent the upper levels of the highest structures by the hour for float-fucking.

The place looks like it's thriving but nothing's easy here. Margins are tight, business is competitive, so you always need an angle, a niche market to corner or a taste you can cater to better than the joint across the street. But most importantly, you need to stay on the right side of influential individuals. Or at least not on their wrong side.

That's why Nikki is here right now. Everybody's got at least two jobs and this is one of hers. Nikki Fixx, they call her.

She's a mediator.

She heads into Sin Garden, the thump of dance beats like a cardiac rhythm permanently pulsing to keep the drink and the money flowing. She was in here maybe seven or eight hours ago, but Lo-Jack wasn't around. One of the bar staff said he had switched phase because of a woman he was seeing, some straight-peg chemical engineer who lives on W2 and has no idea how he spends his hours while she works her Pacific-phase day job. It sounded just about plausible but Nikki had let it be known she would come back to make sure the guy wasn't ducking her.

She catches his eye as she moves through the crowd, his brow rising like he's the one who's been trying to reach her. Lo-Jack finishes making a mojito for the customer at the bar. He's not going to interrupt such an important process, one of the joint's biggest draws. Every bar owner on Mullane has a line on real booze, but Lo-Jack also has a line on real mint leaves, backhanding some botanist who has access to the biodomes along the outside of the Axle. They're growing all kinds of stuff there, experimenting with sustainable crops that remain unaffected by gravity.

The customer sips her mojito and grins approvingly. Nikki pegs her for an accountant or a bureaucrat with the Quadriga or the FNG, out taking a walk on the wild side. Her two friends are sticking to Qola, saving their money for other thrills. Lo-Jack's signature cocktail will be the best drink the girl has ever had. She'd get a better mojito at any decent joint down below, but this has a taste she's never tried before: something naughty.

Lo-Jack gives Nikki a nod and they talk at the end of the bar, a spot that's comparatively quiet because it's underneath a speaker rather than in front of one.

"I was hoping you would drop by," he says.

Sure you were, Nikki thinks.

He offers her a shot but she declines. She needs to be straight while she's working; today, at least. Not for this shit, but there's something happening later on that she'll need her reflexes sharp for.

"Had some flathead from the FNG in here, carrying out an official inspection. Said I need to submit a complete inventory with all receipts and permits. The prick is standing right there, eyeballing bottles of stuff for which he knows there is no fuckin' permits, and for which there sure as shit ain't ever gonna be any receipts, telling me if I don't file within seventy-two hours, they'll be back here to confiscate. The hell is that about, Nikki? This some kind of shake-down? Ain't this precisely the kind of shit I'm paying you for?"

"He leave a name?"

Lo-Jack taps two fingers against his palm and sends across the data-sig the guy left. It animates on Nikki's lens like a business card. Quadriga or FNG, the suits love that old-school shit.

Luis Gadro, it says. Federation of National Governments. Department of Franchise, Licensing and Trade. Like Lo-Jack said, flathead.

"I'll see that it's dealt with. But you musta known this was coming, soon as we heard there's been another FNG restructuring. We've been through it a dozen times before. They bring up some new blood from below, young hot-shots keen to make an impression. I see it as my duty as a citizen of some standing in the community to give such eager new arrivals an education regarding how things really work away from terra firma."

"Might not be that simple. Word is there's some new FNG undersight fuhrer coming in to replace Hoffman. Gonna be running a new broom through Seguridad. Could make things tricky, don't you think?"

Nikki has heard the same. It's not been giving her sleepless nights. It's just politics between the Quadriga and the FNG: nothing that will affect the lowly souls who operate down here in the gutter.

"A new sheriff in town?" she says. "Glad to hear it. That's what this place needs. Somebody who'll go through this rotten place like an enema and clear out all the corruption. So anyway, where's my fuckin' money?"

Lo-Jack gives her a look of outrage and surprise. He oversells it. Nikki doesn't like his chances of keeping many secrets from this chemical engineer he's banging.

"What, you want money when I got this threat hanging over me? When you ain't delivering on your end?"

"You think you're paying me to grease the wheels with the flat-heads, Lo-Jack? Keep your licence clean? Tell me, that psycho asshole Julio's people been in here lately, trashing the joint, starting fights? Making the paying customers think they'd be safer dancing someplace where they don't mop up the blood along with the spilt Qola at closing?"

"We never close," he replies wearily. "But no, Nikki, you know they ain't."

"Then you also know why that is. So pony up."

Lo-Jack sighs and reaches under the counter. He hands over the payment, prepaid chargeable tokens sealed in an opaque vacuum wrap: untraceable, Seedee's closest thing to used bills. It's the length and width of a pack of playing cards, though about a quarter the depth. Looks right but she'll count it later.

She's on her way towards the street again when she feels a tap on the shoulder. Her hand reaches instinctively inside her jacket as she turns, but she has already recognised the voice. It's Garret, a boyishly skinny hooker who trades off a cherubic face that looks at least a decade younger than the truth.

"Nikki," he says. "You got a sec?"

"For you, beautiful, usually. But not always. What's up?"

"Got stiffed last night, like night-time Atlantic. Guy got the sugar then refused to pay. Said he didn't realise it was a rental deal, and by that I mean he made out like he couldn't understand the concept because, shit, that would be illegal and he'd have to report me."

"You get a name?"

"No, it was protected. But I always lens my clients."

Garret transfers the image. A moment later Nikki is looking at a grab of some smug prick who's just oozing FNG entitlement.

"I asked around and it isn't the first time he's pulled this shit to get some free action."

"I'll find him," she says. "What you due?"

"Two hundred."

Nikki eyes him with open scorn.

"You're pretty, Garret, but nobody ever paid you two hundred. Come on, don't waste my time."

He shrugs.

"Okay, one twenty."

"You'll get it. Minus commission. Call it a hundred."

"Deal," he says.

They shake on it, the pressure of his grip enough to cause a twinge in her right hand.

She looks again at the marks on her knuckles. She definitely hit somebody but it still isn't coming back. She's pretty sure it didn't happen between her last waking up alone on Atlantic morning-time and passing out drunk with Candy a few hours ago. The marks and the ache suggest it's older than that, but what's really troubling her is she can't remember what happened before she last *went* to bed alone.

"Hey, I'm a little blurry about the past twenty-four hours," she says to Garret. "Been hammering it pretty hard, I guess. Did you see me in here recently? I hit anybody?"

"Not while I was around. I saw you talking to Donna. She told me you were looking for Giselle."

Unfortunately, this is from the part Nikki does remember. It's coming back clearer, too. It's Giselle who owes money. Okay, Donna owes too, but not as much. And Donna owes less now, because she gave Nikki some valuable info about Giselle.

"She's got a little secret," Donna said.

"A secret she told you?"

"No. A secret I sussed for myself. One that keeps getting harder to cover up."

She accompanied this with a subtle gesture, curving her open hand around her belly.

You don't get pregnant on Seedee. It's a working environment like no other and so the employment terms reflect that. You gotta have insurance: men and women. Paternity is easy to establish in the case of a dispute. If you want to keep the kid, you need to go home, and that's expensive, hence the insurance. The space elevator and the ion shuttles have colossally reduced the price per kilo of putting people into orbit, but it's still an exorbitantly expensive business. That's why the minimum stay is a year unless you've got the funds. Most people don't got the funds. Hence the insurance. And a lot of people don't got the funds for that either: people like cleaners and cooks and waitresses moonlighting as hookers because it pays three times their other jobs combined.

If you're pregnant without insurance, abortion is mandatory. They're nice about it, Nikki's heard, and the treatment is top notch. You just show up and they'll have you processed in a matter of hours, quality after-care too, but it's not an elective procedure.

"How'd that happen?"

35

"You want a diagram?" Donna replied.

"You know what I mean."

"No idea. Like it matters."

"So what's the problem?"

"Whisper I heard is she wants to keep it."

"Giselle is behind and ducking me because she's saving for a ticket?"

"I couldn't say," Donna told her, giving Nikki a butter-wouldn't-melt look, like she didn't just sell out a sister-in-trade for a hundred off her own arrears.

"Don't imagine she's planning to settle her tab before she boards that shuttle, neither," Nikki mused.

Donna's face had turned harsh.

"Yeah, and why should she? Selling her ass up here just to end up broke because it took all her money to get home again?"

"I don't make the rules, kid."

"No, Nikki, you don't. Because if you did, you'd need to care about something other than where your next pay-off is coming from."

THE SELF DELUSION

"Free will is an illusion, one created by our minds to make us feel better about how little control we truly have over our actions."

A wave passes through the audience, everybody sitting up a little straighter as the words hit home. Intellectual curiosity becomes spiked with a measure of fear as is always the case when something unpalatable issues from the mouth of an incontestable authority.

Alice is sitting near the front of the lecture theatre, within metres of where Professor Maria Gonçalves stands onstage. Her posture is surprisingly meek, like some comfortably obscure academic unused to addressing more than a handful of people at a time. This could not be further from the truth, though perhaps it is reflective of how Professor Gonçalves's lectures are usually conducted to camera rather than before a live audience. This would also explain why her gestures are modest and intimate, her head seldom rising to meet the gazes of all but the first few rows.

She looks older and tinier in the flesh than Alice was expecting, but then she reminds herself that the woman is pushing ninety years old, and many of the lectures she has seen were recorded as many as three decades ago. Her hair seems whiter than on-screen, her skin darker. Her voice is unmistakable though: quiet but authoritative, her accent an unusual blend of regional remnants smoothed away by decades off-planet.

Among the exclusive privileges afforded by being on CdC, the opportunity to see and hear this living legend of neuroscience in the flesh is up there with floating in microgravity. It is not merely a luxury of being in space, but of Alice's status amid the incoming FNG delegation, part of the Quadriga's efforts to roll out the red carpet.

It is also, she suspects, so that certain individuals know where she is, having been carefully chaperoned since she got here. She is currently flanked by Andros Boutsikari, the head of the Seguridad, and Wolfgang Hoffman, the man Alice is here to replace as Principal of the FNG's Security Oversight Executive.

"Back in the twentieth century, Dr Benjamin Libet conducted an experiment the consequence of which took us decades to comprehend. It could be argued that we are still digesting it even now. He wired volunteers to an EEG, placed them in front of a clock and asked them to record the precise time when they decided to move a finger. The EEG allowed him to record, to several decimal points of accuracy, when the brain made its decision. What the resulting scans showed was that the brain decided to act *three hundred milliseconds* before the subject became aware of it. He demonstrated that while the subjects *thought* they were making a conscious decision to lift a finger, in truth their brains had already ruled on the issue a third of a second ago.

"I want you all to let that sink in for a moment, to truly contemplate the implications. Such as the possibility that I could turn all of you here into my robot slaves. Damn, did I say that out aloud?"

There is a ripple of laughter throughout the auditorium. It punctures the tension, though Gonçalves completely fumbles the line. Alice thinks it sounded scripted, conspicuously for being out of cadence with the rest of her delivery. Some staffer with a grounding in PR perhaps wrote it for her. Not only is Gonçalves unaccustomed to speaking in front of a large live audience, she is also unused to tailoring her content for mass consumption. Just about everybody on the planet knows her name and is aware of the impact of her work, but most people who have heard her speak before will have done so in a purely academic context, watching playback of talks filmed in her lab here on CdC.

Alice has not only seen several volumes of such videos, but has read Gonçalves at length. She strongly doubts that the rest of today's audience fully appreciate what a privilege they are enjoying, though they will have gladly inferred that it is an honour, as that would be befitting their status. The room is full of senior FNG delegates and Quadriga execs, and though the latter might be only feigning interest in the scientific content of the lecture, Alice has little doubt they could tell her what Gonçalves's work at the Neurosophy Foundation is worth to them per quarter.

The Quadriga is the consortium of four mega-corporations, formed to pursue the *Arca* project. Its internal relationships are infinitely complex and sensitive, as is the consortium's relationship with the Federation of National Governments. Alice knows people who have literally written PhDs on both.

"Of course, I'm not really here to tell you that free will is an illusion," she goes on. "No. In fact, the truth is more disturbing. It is *consciousness itself* that is an illusion. When our brains make a decision, our minds create a narrative after the fact, but that process of retrospectively fabricating a continuous narrative is going on at every moment, fooling us into believing we are experiencing the world objectively through our own singular perspective.

"If I may draw upon a comparison that should make sense to most of you here today, people complain about the Quadriga having a Byzantine command structure where it's seldom apparent who is in charge of what."

There is another ripple of laughter, this time polite rather than genuine, though to Alice this line sounded more like Gonçalves's own thoughts.

"Believe me, it's a paradigm of unified purpose compared to the brain. Multiple competing systems are permanently striving for attention, each of them with its own command centre urgently processing information to offer up in support of its case. It's been described as a maelstrom, a raging chaos of simultaneous processes and events. As one such command centre temporarily attains primacy over all the rest, the brain retrospectively rationalises the outcome and constructs a narrative to give the impression that a solitary unified entity was at the helm the whole time. In short, consciousness is a lie your brain tells you to make you think you know what you're doing."

None of this is new to Alice. It's kind of a dumbed-down stump speech tailored to the corporate audience. She finds it disappointing to witness some people's surprise, evidently never having heard this stuff before. Nonetheless their response smacks of curious amusement rather than being intellectually engaged, as though the speaker is sharing mere colourful factoids for their entertainment.

What is truly incredible is that so many people here have willingly adopted Neurosophy's technology without grasping the first principles of what lies behind it, but she guesses it's the same as how so few automobile drivers throughout history could have told you about the workings of the internal combustion engine.

Gonçalves is already blowing a few minds but she is merely warming up. As anyone who knows the first thing about her would anticipate, she's not here to talk about the brain in general, but about memory.

Alice wishes the professor could give her some pointers regarding what is wrong with her own right now. Maybe it's to do with getting used to space, in combination with an extreme form of jet lag, but just like on the elevator, when she woke up a few hours ago in her room, it was as though her short-term memory needed a reboot. She could recall all the details about her trip, and even the meal she had upon arrival, but she had no recollection of getting undressed and going to bed. This bothers her as she likes to know how long she has slept, to ensure it is within recommended parameters.

"Memory is not a unified process of thought either," Gonçalves explains, calling up a holographic model of the brain. "There is no single location where the brain stores your memories. Instead, it works a little like the random-access model of computer memory, with the information broken down and distributed to different areas. Where it differs from the computer model, of course, is that word 'random'. The brain's sorting system is more specific. Visual information, for instance, is archived in the occipital lobe, while emotions go to the amygdala."

Alice is three rows from the front, from where she can see the backs of around thirty heads. The scars are only visible on the close-cropped, but it's a safe assumption most of them have had the mesh procedure. It is not compulsory for employment aboard CdC – that would be illegal – but if there are two candidates for a post and only one has had a mesh implanted, there's no contest as to who would get the job. However, it has to be stressed that people don't regard undergoing the procedure as a price for getting a job up here; rather, they see the opportunity to get it as one of the benefits. These days, just about everybody has a lens rig, but that's merely a wearable accessory, a data and comms device for rendering second-hand information like its i-ancestors. You can pop out the contacts (though these days you seldom need to for comfort), disconnect from the wrist disc and tap out the sub-vocal. Whether the format be text, pictures, audio or video, it's still a matter of passive consumption of the information on the part of the user, and what you retain is up to you.

The mesh, however, allows the uploading of information – effectively new memories – directly to the human brain. You don't need to read or experience new information, you simply *know* it, and you can't forget what you learned or choose to switch it off at the end of the day. It's a whole other level of tech, and if you want that, you need to go to Neurosophy on CdC, because that's the only place where the implant surgery is legally approved. Technically, those volunteering to undergo it are signing up to be part of a long-term medical trial. The trial itself was only given the go-ahead on the understanding that approval to offer the procedure on Earth would not even be applied for until a sufficient proportion of its first generation of subjects had died of old age without demonstrating side effects or exhibiting behaviour that might offer grounds for concern. And as each refinement or upgrade to the technology effectively resets the clock on that stipulation, the procedure looks like remaining an option exclusive to CdC for a long time yet.

"If you take a single experience, such as a day at the beach, vast quantities of information are processed and filed away in multiple locations."

As she speaks, different areas of the holographic brain light up, the words Sight, Motion, Smell, Language and others orbiting the organ briefly before pinging off to their respective destinations.

"What makes this such a remarkably efficient storage system is that reliving just one element, the smell of sun lotion for example, can cause the brain to rapidly retrieve all those other constituents to form what feels to us like a unified and vivid memory.

"Where it gets complicated is that all memories are highly subjective and individualised. Two people can have roughly the same experience, but the differing ways their brains categorise that information has consequences for how it is reassembled. That day at the beach, one person merely saw 'boats'. The other person is a yacht chandler and thus sub-categorised the information in a way the first couldn't: she saw skiffs, catamarans, ribs, rigid hull dinghies. And this, ladies and gentlemen, is what prevents me from creating my robot army. For those of us in the business of artificially inserting information, it puts intractable limits on what we can achieve."

Gonçalves smiles at the response. She still seems timid in the face of an auditorium full of people, but despite her shyness there is no mistaking the pleasure she takes in seeing that she is connecting.

It amuses Alice – and, she wonders, does it amuse the professor? – to see people touch the site of the procedure on the backs of their heads each time she mentions robots, or in any way alludes to the risks they don't like to think about. It's like involuntarily scratching when someone starts talking about fleas and head lice.

Developed in collaboration with her late colleague Dr Sandy Shelley, Gonçalves's revolutionary innovation involves the insertion of an optogenetic mesh between the brain and the meninges, carried out via surgical nanobots through a small incision near the base of the skull. The technology was first proven viable more than three decades ago, but came to a halt after a fire ripped through the Neurosophy Foundation's original site on Wheel One. It was a sobering demonstration of the limitations of the supposedly fool-proof safety systems that were designed to respond to the most feared danger of life in space. The automated response mechanisms contained the blaze and prevented it from spreading beyond the lab where it started, but not without trapping Dr Shelley inside, with fatal results.

Though Professor Gonçalves was mercifully spared when the tragedy struck, it nonetheless came close to destroying her too. She was devastated by the loss of her closest friend, the person she described as "the real genius in our partnership", and for a long time was unable to face the onerous task of rebuilding their work from the ashes, alone. Eventually, however, she drew upon the same strength that had seen her survive refugee camps in her childhood, and endeavoured to succeed in lasting tribute to Dr Shelley's memory.

"As you are all aware, many of you first-hand, we can now rapidly insert large quantities of new information into the human brain. However, it is this individualised natural storage system that makes it impossible for us to create false memories, or to implant someone else's memories in your head without you being aware of it. For instance, we can upload highly detailed information about a town so that you know your way around when you get there, but we can't give you the memory of having been there before."

That was what concerned everybody when the reconstructed technology was first unveiled: the fear of remembering something that never happened. At a legal level, people were worried about concepts such as falsely providing an alibi for someone or being implicated by their own memory in events they had nothing to do with. More viscerally they were simply squeamish about the possibility of remembering something that never happened – or that happened to somebody else. This had proven to be an unfounded concern, due to the "watermark effect" that people experienced when a non-native memory was accessed by their mesh: a conflict between this new data and what the rest of their brain – and body – was telling them.

Alice understands the principles and does not harbour any irrational fears regarding the implications. Nonetheless, even now that the option is open to her, she has no intention of having the procedure. She wouldn't let anyone mess with her brain, not even if the mesh was implanted by Professor Gonçalves herself.

In her case this is less a matter of squeamishness than snobbishness.

Since childhood Alice has enjoyed what have been described as prodigious powers of retention, though she would contend that discipline and endeavour have played a major part in this: the more she studies, the more she knows. Some might say her distaste for memory enhancement is like a naturally attractive person being scornful of someone undergoing cosmetic surgery. However, the phrase "easy come, easy go" seems apposite. Alice is a believer in hard work being its own reward, and that you place a greater value on what you know when it has taken genuine effort to learn it.

"Perhaps the best illustration is in the truth behind the mythologised notion – which I believe is widely held on Earth – that a mesh allows you to learn a new language overnight. This is no more true than the notion that you can similarly learn to play the piano overnight or instantly master a technical skill. In these cases, we encounter the issue of muscle memory. When we learn to play an instrument, through repetition and practice, the signals controlling our fingers no longer originate entirely in the hippocampus, but also in the motor cortex, the cerebellum and the basal ganglia."

Everyone is familiar with the disconnect. Many who had tried it said it was actually more frustrating trying to learn the piano after an upload than it was naturally, because your mind knew what it wanted to do but your fingers wouldn't cooperate. Thus the mesh works principally as an instant-access reference system for retrieving information, something that is highly desirable in an environment such as CdC, requiring such a volume and variety of technical knowledge.

"In the case of uploading a new language, you cannot speak it because your mouth and your tongue may not know where to begin. What we are uploading therefore is essentially a rapidly accessible translation dictionary, whereby you know what the words mean and can instantly deconstruct much of the syntax and grammar, but crucially what you infer and understand will be different from person to person. This is why, even if you upload the entire dictionary of your native language, the way your vocabulary developed individually means it won't necessarily occur to you to use these new words in everyday conversation.

"So to reassure you one last time regarding why I cannot create my robot army, the crucial thing about how our technology interacts with the human brain is that the information we insert cannot alter who you are. Rather, it is who you are, your very individuality, that uniquely alters the information."

IMPORT DUTY

Nikki instantly detects a rise in tension as they make their way out on to the floor of Dock Eleven. It's more than just the usual silent anxiety that attends an important pick-up. Her instincts tend to serve her well when it comes to these situations, and something feels off.

It's not coming from her people, though maybe she's picking up that they're feeling it. She's here with Felicia, who always carries the permits and paperwork (albeit there's no actual paper), as well as Tug and Kobra, two of Yoram's most dependable lieutenants. They've all done this twenty times at least: same routine, same schedule, same bay.

There's a shuttle coming up through the floor right now, rising diagonally from an escalator shaft, a haze around the wingtips where the moisture in the air meets the freezing cold of the metal. The one they're here to pick up from should have been fully unloaded by this point and being prepared for its run back to Heinlein.

The shuttles land on the outside of the wheel, after equalising their velocity and locking on to the auto-approach system. Once stationary, the craft are anchored to a platform which flips upside down then passes through the wheel to the surface. Nikki hates shuttle travel and has done it as few times as possible. She remembers the weird lurching sensation in her gut; not from the platform turning, which oddly exerts no sensation whatsoever, but from the moment when the spin of the wheel starts exerting its pseudo-gravitational force. It is merely one of a long list of things she detests about space flight.

Each of these cargo docks is like a horseshoe, overlooked by two levels of platforms along each of which are multiple delivery points. There's constant traffic in and out of these places, maintaining the flow of supplies and materials like CdC's vascular system.

Ground level is where the paperwork is cleared and the payloads distributed. A system of conveyor belts and elevators takes the crates and pallets from the shuttle to their allocated delivery bays, with the larger and heavier items sent higher up where the gravity is lighter, making handling and transfer easier. The bulkiest payloads flying into CdC tend to be hoppers of raw materials for the fabrication processors, but there are dedicated shuttle docks for handling that stuff. Dock Eleven is one of the many dispatch and distribution hubs handling a constant variety of freight, which is why Yoram chose it.

There is the usual hum and whir of machinery, but unfamiliar shouts are ringing around the dock. That's what's setting her off, Nikki realises. There are new personnel among the ground crew. Something has changed, and everybody senses that they might need to be a little sharper.

She doesn't recognise the manifest administrator who strides across to check Felicia's credentials and verify her order. There are other new faces hefting boxes on to the conveyor. She scans the admin's code-badge with her lens. Officials don't wear nametags: if your lens doesn't let you download their details, then you're not cleared to know their identity.

His name is Brock Lind. He seems officious but polite. Nikki doesn't need to read anything into the fact that he's new, but she can't ignore how that instinctive sense of unease is gnawing at her.

Felicia transfers her details, verifying who she is and what she is here to collect.

Lind has that frozen look people get when they're scrolling too much data on their lenses, or waiting for something to update.

"There should be five pallets," she states, verbal confirmation remaining an important failsafe against misunderstanding or misfiled details.

Lind frowns.

"There doesn't appear to be anything listed. The last shuttle has been processed and all payloads allocated."

Nikki fixes him with her gaze, letting him know he's under scrutiny.

"That can't be right," Felicia insists. "Despatch from Exo-Chem Industries for Agritek Laboratories, CdC Wheel One. Arriving on Shuttle *Hermia*, zero-five hundred hours."

Lind gives his head a subtle shake, his tone polite but certain.

"The last shuttle to offload was *Khlestakov*. I don't have a listing for your delivery on the manifest and I don't have *Hermia* scheduled to land here either."

"This is bullshit," Felicia insists.

"Calm down," Nikki warns her. She is suddenly aware that in her rising panic, Felicia might say something indiscreet, like asking the guy if this is a shakedown. It might well be, but if so he will make that known in time. Right now there is no reason to let him know there is anything illegal going on.

"I'm sure there's just a snafu someplace," Nikki continues, "and Mr Lind will be able to help us get to the bottom of it."

"I'm all over it," he agrees.

Nikki watches him gesture with his fingers, working an invisible display on his lens while speaking to someone over his sub-vocal.

"Yes, Angela, I'm sending the details through now. Exo-Chem, for Agritek. Shuttle *Hermia*. Ah. I see. Well, that would explain it."

"What?" Felicia asks impatiently.

He gives them an apologetic sigh, biting his bottom lip.

"I'm afraid it turns out there's been an incident on W2. An unscheduled all-stop. Nothing's been able to land there since it happened, so all shuttles are being diverted here to W1. They're pulling in the Meridian staff for overtime. It's about to get real busy in here."

Nikki looks up the local feeds on her lens. He's not lying. W2 has stopped rotating and is in a state of lockdown until they can get the problem fixed, after which everybody is going to be busy mopping when the gravity comes back on.

"So where the hell is our stuff?" Felicia demands.

Lind pauses, searching again.

"On auto-approach now. Dock Two."

"Dock Two? That's all the way over on fucking Sharman."

"Sorry. They've altered the landing priorities. Updated all our schedules."

"With the stuff bound for Wheel Two jumping the queues, no doubt," Kobra grumbles wearily.

"Looks like," Lind agrees with a shrug. "Tough break. What you gonna do?"

It's a rhetorical question, but Lind looks to Felicia and to Nikki as though they might answer.

"We'd better hustle," Felicia says, already starting to head out of the dock.

"I'll catch you up," Nikki replies.

She turns to Lind.

"Just want to apologise for my colleague there, Brock. She's under a lot of pressure to meet targets."

"Don't worry about it. Who isn't?"

"Still, you were just doing your job, and she shouldn't have spoken to you like that. So I'd like to make reparation by way of a little heads-up."

"About what?"

"You're new, aren't you?"

"Not to Seedee, but this is a new position, sure. I worked in cargo management before."

"You had a safety inspection lately, from the FNG Compliance people?"

"Not since I started here, no."

"Well, forewarned is forearmed. They can issue on-the-spot fines for code violations. There's a scam they run, a health-and-safety deal to do with pressure seals on the platform access hatch. Let me show you."

Nikki leads him around the side of the shuttle, out of sight of the freight handlers. She crouches down next to a maintenance channel leading down into the shaft through which the shuttle platforms pass. Upon her fingers brushing the interface panel, an LED sign illuminates, warning her that she must be wearing a safety harness and tethered to two anchor points before entering. She twists the hydraulic safety bolts and slides back the lid, a blast of cold escaping from the gap.

"You see this?" she asks Lind, pointing inside.

He crouches beside her and leans forward.

Nikki sweeps his legs and pitches him over, thrusting his head into the shaft until he is pivoting on his thighs, prevented from falling only by the grip she has around his ankles.

He looked just a moment too long, after he asked "What you gonna do?" That's all it took to give away that he was lying. He'd been covering it pretty good, but he was anxious and he wanted reassurance that they were buying it.

"Holy shit, what the fuck you doing?" he asks. His voice disappears into the vastness of the shaft.

"Where's our stuff? Who paid you off, you little prick?"

"I don't know what you're talking about. I swear. I just got transferred here. Jesus Christ."

She lets go for a fraction of a second. Enough for him to feel himself drop.

"I asked you a fucking question, Brock. What happened to our shipment?"

"Okay, I'll tell you," he whimpers. "Just pull me up."

"Wrong way round. Answer first."

"Dock Nine. The *Hermia* is landing at Dock Nine." He answers in an urgent squeal, breathless and desperate.

"Why did you tell us Dock Two? Who you got on Nine waiting to steal our shit?"

"I don't know, I don't know," he gibbers. "I got a pay-off to reroute *Hermia*. Guy in a bar last night. I don't know his name. Never saw him before. He wasn't the kind of guy you ask a lot of questions. Please pull me up, oh Jesus."

"What he look like? Send me his pic."

"I don't have it."

"Bullshit. You didn't record him? Weird stranger comes up in a bar and bribes you and you don't take the guy's fucking picture at least?"

"He made me delete."

"Describe him."

"It was dark. I only—"

She lets him slide another couple of inches.

"Okay, big, blond, tan jacket. Tattoo on his neck, some kind of Greek symbol."

Omega. One of Julio's people.

Fuck.

OPEN SPACE

"An interesting choice of example," Boutsikari observes. "Tailored to her audience, perhaps. I very much doubt the professor's thoughts ever turn to the beach."

They are standing on the terrace in front of the Ver Eterna hotel, where most of the audience has congregated after exiting the lecture theatre. There is a busy clamour to talk to the professor, who appears to be putting a brave face on confronting such an eager throng. She is standing close to the glass walls of the lobby, protected by an ever-vigilant entourage who are not only ensuring she is not overwhelmed, but also, Alice is sure, subtly vetting who does and doesn't get close enough for a one-on-one. Alice would love to talk to her but suspects there is little of substance she could discuss in the few moments she would be permitted.

The others seem content with merely being able to say they have met a remarkable individual in the flesh, but Alice does not understand what satisfaction people derive from this.

"Not one for vacations," Hoffman agrees. "She would regard a day away from her work as a day irretrievably wasted. I suspect she is counting the minutes right now. I wouldn't like to contemplate what has been traded behind the scenes to get her to do this."

"I wasn't merely alluding to her dedication to her job," Boutsikari says.

"You're talking about her personal experience," Alice suggests. "Raised amid civil war and spending years of her childhood in a refugee camp."

The Seguridad chief nods. "Yes. I doubt we would enjoy hearing the examples she *could* have chosen to illustrate her point."

"Is it true that she has never left CdC since arriving here?" Alice asks.

"I believe so," Hoffman replies. "It's not an uncommon phenomenon. People can begin to feel disconnected from Earth, particularly if there are memories they don't wish to be reconnected to."

The terrace fronts on to Central Plaza, the showpiece "open air" precinct that has been designed to be W2's social hub. It is the widest open space on CdC. Strictly speaking the biodomes along the Axle are larger, but as well as having no artificial gravity, they are dedicated to agricultural experimentation and only accessible to a small number of authorised personnel. Hence Central Plaza would still be a popular destination even if its sides were not lined with upscale bars and restaurants.

Alice was sceptical as to both the "open" and "air" parts of this, imagining from descriptions that it would feel much like simulated outdoor environments she has visited in Las Vegas and Jadid Alearabia. However, as she glances at the crowds passing through the square between the hotels and office complexes, she does genuinely feel like she is outside. Partly it is the movement of cool air in random eddies rather than a constant chilling blast. Partly it is the way the sound carries; or rather the way it does not. But mainly it is the sunlight shining down through the transparent canopy: the way it plays on the surfaces around her and the feeling of its warmth on her skin.

It is constantly jarring to feel so aware of strong sunlight and look up to see a black rather than blue sky, but the crucial thing is that it does feel like a sky rather than a ceiling.

"She has written that coming here made her feel hope again," Alice says, having been quite inspired by this notion. "She admitted that she had been close to suicide. She called it the hope that saved her life. After everything she witnessed and endured, relocating herself to CdC allowed her to believe we are capable of outgrowing our basest instincts."

"Well, hopefully not all of them," Hoffman says. "Otherwise Andros here would be out of business."

Alice spies a flash of annoyance in Boutsikari's face, which she infers is related to her own presence. Perhaps he is concerned that Hoffman's humour is inappropriately flippant. However, the German has a warm twinkle in his eye to which the Seguridad chief cannot help but respond with a smile.

Alice suspects he is merely trying to lighten the mood, as the conversation was threatening to take a gloomy turn. Back at the FNG building in New York she often heard it said of Hoffman that he is effective in his job because he is a people person. This was usually by way of implication that a contrasting lack of such qualities in Alice might prove problematic when she takes over from him.

Before being appointed as Principal of the Security Oversight Executive, Hoffman had been a high-ranking officer in the Frankfurt police. As well as boasting such extensive hands-on experience, there was the added consideration of his having worked in one of the world's major financial centres, giving him an appreciation of the subtleties required in balancing state and private interests.

Alice has studied law enforcement first-hand on three continents, but knows there is going to be resistance bordering on resentment towards anyone who has not walked the walk. The fact that her job is not law enforcement itself, but assessing its policies, procedures and effectiveness, is unlikely to temper this resistance; indeed, she anticipates it will probably make it worse.

So far Boutsikari hasn't shown her anything but courtesy, though how long that lasts will be the real question. As the chief executive of CdC's private police force, she is sure he will be trying hard to keep his FNG overseer sweet, but doubts he is happy about having someone as congenial – and compliant – as the incumbent being replaced.

Alice takes a sip from her iced water and subtly looks Hoffman up and down, assessing the shoes she is going to have to fill. The first thing to strike her is that they are exorbitantly expensive shoes.

Alice is in a smart enough suit; one she reserves for social duties rather than everyday office wear. On this terrace she feels, if not underdressed, then conspicuously like the government worker among so many high-level Quadriga management personnel and senior executives from major sub-contractors. As head of Seguridad, she knows Boutsikari is earning at least ten times her salary, his clothes looking commensurate with that. And yet technically he is answerable to her, which in time will present a great number of awkward issues to be negotiated. Right now, the most immediate of these is regarding how well her predecessor has scrubbed up.

As well as the suit and the shoes, Hoffman has had very pricey cosmetic work done too. For a man of his experience, he looks a lot younger than the file photos taken before he left for this post more than five years ago.

Part of her remit is to look into how some of the FNG overseers up here might be getting too cosy with the people they're supposed to be supervising. She had thought she would have to dig for evidence of this, but it appears to be staring her in the face. Unless, of course, Hoffman bought all this with an advance on his next salary. He is taking up a position on the board of a private law enforcement and security company back on Earth, one wholly owned by the same corporation as Seguridad.

It has often been proposed that FNG personnel who have held supervisory posts on CdC should be barred from accepting jobs inside Quadriga corporations within five years of leaving their current positions, but there has never been the political muscle to get it through. The contrary argument has always been that with the Quadriga comprising the four largest corporate entities on Earth, this would place an unfair restriction on future employment.

The counterargument is that there will always be plenty of opportunities for individuals of such valuable experience, to which the standard response is that individuals of such experience should be at the disposal of whoever is prepared to pay the market rate.

When it comes to such intractable disputes, the arguments matter less than practical political strategy. Alice is sure that her lack of interest in material wealth is one of the principal reasons the Oversight Committee chose her for this job – and one of the reasons she will not be a popular appointee.

Alice has another look towards the professor, who is now signing a book and thus instantly multiplying its value by a dizzying factor, should the copy make it back to Earth.

"You sure we can't get you something a little stronger than that?" Boutsikari asks, indicating her glass of water.

She had a look at the price list when she first got to the hotel.

Alcoholic drinks and even coffee are expensive on CdC, as she was warned, but eye-wateringly so in a place such as the Ver Eterna. Boutsikari has repeatedly made it clear he is picking up the tab, but while this does not exactly constitute taking a bribe, there are still ethical implications, and accepting such gratuities is explicitly prohibited by FNG directives.

"No, I'm sticking to this, at least while I acclimatise. I have barely been here twenty-four hours."

Everything here is expensive, partly because most things have to be imported, but also as an inevitable inflationary consequence of wages being high compared to Earth. This has led to accusations of what Marxists used to call the Great Money Trick, whereby an employer controls the sale of essentials to his workers and thus ends up recouping all their wages. However, the Quadriga was devised to create a permanently evolving internal market on CdC, with the added safeguard of price controls on basics.

Alcohol is categorised as a luxury, so Alice derives some satisfaction from seeing just how pricey it is. There were those who argued that CdC should have been a dry zone from the beginning, but Alice had a PhD in why that was never a viable option.

Drug prohibition had been among the most catastrophic governmental policies of all time, wreaking havoc for over a century until the mass scandals of the 2020s. Leaked information revealed the extent to which lawmakers across the globe were in the pockets of those who stood to lose the most if the war on drugs ever ended. Retrospectively it made perfect sense of their otherwise inexplicable intransigence, which is why the scandal was referred to thereafter as "2020 vision".

Their very illegality had made some drugs more desirable. Once that had been removed, people's choices and decisions were based on different considerations. But while the appeal of other drugs had proven fickle and transient, the popularity of alcohol remained stubbornly enduring. It had been part of human culture for thousands of years, and implicated in the worst of human behaviour for just as long. As someone with an interest in criminology and law enforcement, Alice wishes it could be simply disinvented.

As she takes another sip of water she feels an uncomfortable sense of scrutiny, but not from her two wine-quaffing chaperones. A moment ago she had another glance across the plaza, and something must have caught her eye. In Professor Gonçalves's terms, her conscious mind was belatedly adding it to the narrative.

She looks again and this time she sees it. About thirty metres away she catches a glimpse of a man standing still among the throng crisscrossing the plaza. She only sees him for a second before she loses him in the moving crowd, but he is looking in her direction, an intent expression in his fixed gaze.

She thinks of the most taciturn of her travelling companions on the journey from Earth, the glow in his lens letting her know he was recording her. With a shiver she wonders with whom Kai Roganson has shared his grabación, and to what end.

A more rational thought counsels against such paranoia and its roots in egotism. Alice is surrounded by wealthy and influential people, any one of whom would be a more plausible subject of an angry glare from a passer-by.

She looks again but can't find him. Indeed, her view of the plaza is blocked by the approach of someone who most definitely has her eye on Alice.

"Dr Blake? I would appreciate an opportunity to speak with you."

The woman addressing her has a severity about her attire, matched by a facial expression that is pointedly unsmiling. This is in contrast to everyone else who has been presented to Alice since she got here. Whatever the newcomer wants to talk about, Alice doubts it will feature recreational recommendations.

Alice recalls catching her eye as they filed out of the lecture. The woman was up near the back, trapped by the exiting crowd as Alice was escorted towards the door by Boutsikari and Hoffman. Significantly, both of them take a step to block off her access again now. It is an unmistakably defensive gesture, but Alice is not sure whether it is she who is being protected, or her two male companions.

"Helen, why don't you let Alice's feet touch the floor a while before you start dictating your to-do list?"

It is Hoffman who makes the suggestion, his tone genial. He

leads the new arrival away by the arm while Boutsikari similarly guides Alice in the opposite direction. Evidently it is not only Professor Gonçalves whose interactions are being carefully vetted.

"What the hell just happened?" Alice demands, barely managing to contain her anger. "That was staggeringly rude. Who was that woman, and what makes you think I can't decide for myself who to have a conversation with?"

Boutsikari lets out a sigh.

"I apologise, but please believe me when I say that we are merely trying to ease you into things and avoid uncomfortable confrontations until you at least have your foot in the door."

"Who was that woman?"

"I'm sure you'll find out soon enough, and you will be retrospectively grateful for the postponement. Let's just say that in your new position you're going to meet a lot of people who believe your agenda should be their agenda."

"And your protecting me from her wouldn't be because my agenda will have implications for *your* agenda, would it?"

Boutsikari gives her a practised diplomatic smile.

"City-wide or in a crowded room, I do what it takes to keep the peace."

Alice feels a stinging pain in her forearm and the glass leaps from her hand in a reflexive twitch of her fingers, smashing to the ground at her feet.

A number of things happen during the same microsecond. Alice hears someone shout "Gun!", and as her eyes sweep around in search of the threat, she sees a figure in a mask on the far side of the plaza. He fires off another shot in her direction as Boutsikari hauls her out of the way, then he is gone, disappeared into the oblivious crowd.

Back on Earth, this would have been the cue for anonymous guests to reveal themselves as bodyguards, flocking to their charges like a Roman legion into formation. Here, only the professor's entourage respond, huddling about her with the speed of instinct while screams ring out and people wheel around in startled panic.

And that's *before* the gravity goes off.

MARKET FORCES

They take a static over to Resnik Street. Nikki and Felicia are sitting opposite Tug and Kobra in a car full of construction workers, the smell of sweat and plaster dust filling the air. Resnik is a quarter turn away but not as far as Dock Two. Lind intended to send them halfway around the ring to get them as far out of the picture as possible while Julio's people made off with Yoram's shipment.

The statics are CdC's high-speed transport facility, a system of parallel underground channels close to the outer wall. Most of the channels are reserved for moving materials but there are passenger routes circumnavigating the wheels too. The cars are known as statics as a joke, suggesting that they don't move around the wheel – the wheel moves around them. This isn't true, of course, otherwise you'd have to go most of the way around the wheel if you wanted to travel one stop anti-spin, but like many terms on Seedee, once it stuck, it stuck.

It's the fastest way to get around, but Nikki knows they might still be too late. If the *Hermia* landed at Dock Nine around when it was scheduled to arrive at Dock Eleven, then they're screwed. Just need to hope the rerouting and the congestion due to the all-stop on W2 has bought them some time. Even then, the best-case scenario is going to involve a fight.

She discreetly checks her kit. Tug and Kobra notice and reflexively check theirs too, stone faces hiding anxiety.

Yoram has someone on the payroll at Agritek. That gets them the cargo manifest entries they need and the clearance to be able to turn up to the dock and take delivery. It's merely one end of a chain stretching all the way back to Earth, and there are people taking coin at every link: at Heinlein, at Ocean Terminal, at the maritime shipping lines, right back to Exo-Chem in San Francisco, where the exports originate. The payloads are sealed under official witness, to prevent precisely this kind of abuse, which means that guy needs paying off too.

It is a phenomenally complex and delicate operation, employing the world's most advanced transport technology and spanning literally astronomical distances. Yet sometimes its success and survival still comes down to knocking somebody on his ass.

That's the nature of the business, though. The end-point consumer might be in space, but bootlegging works on the same principles it always did since the Industrial Revolution. And even after factoring in such a mess of overheads and logistics, not to mention Yoram's profit margins, it's still cheaper for the bar owners than going through official channels.

The Quadriga's official line is that it wouldn't waste valuable freight space on something as frivolous and enduringly disapproved-of as booze. Not when it has the technology to brew its own shitty beer on-site. It is named Estrella, after the *Arca Estrella*, but on Seedee they call it Qola: Quadriga's Officially Licensed Ale. It sells well on Earth, where it is an expensive aspirational brand – the beer they drink in space. Which they do, but only if they can't get hold of anything better.

The Quadriga does import a certain quantity of luxury lines for the high-end hotels and restaurants, but they're way out of the ordinary workforce's price range, even on Seedee where wages are famously far higher than down below.

In other words, they were pretty much asking for this shit to happen. It's not only alcohol, either. The shipment they're chasing right now also contains a pallet packed with spices like they used to pack heroin and cocaine in centuries gone by. In a world of largely synthesised and fabricated foodstuffs, you'd be amazed what a packet of genuine chilli powder changes hands for.

There's a whole alternative economy on Seedee, and the received wisdom is that if it wasn't the Quadriga's intention, then they probably wish it was, because it's a raging success story. The only real opposition comes from moral zealots in both the FNG and within the four-headed consortium. True-believer types who keep going on about how CdC should be clean and pure because it's the birthplace of mankind's future.

The Quadriga wins both ways out of this, though. They get to placate the crusaders with a bit of posturing, meanwhile they're jacking up the rent and franchise prices for the bars on Mullane. And it *is* merely posturing. That's why they're happy to turn a blind eye, or more accurately are happy for officials to take a *cut* to turn a blind eye, when there's bottles on open display that they know nobody ever sanctioned for import.

Damn straight they're aware this stuff goes on. They always knew it would happen once the *Arca* project advanced from being the preserve of an elite crew of pioneering experts working in conditions that hadn't changed since the era of Skylab and the International Space Station. You got a massive construction site and a resident population, people living here for a year at a time minimum.

The noble theory is that folks should come here to knuckle down and think about the future: play their part then come home with a great résumé, stories to tell and a big wedge saved to build a better life down below. Problem is, though the money is good, the trick is not spending it all in the time between your shifts: another thing that ain't changed since the Industrial Revolution. Besides, after a few years it became clear that a certain type of person comes to Seedee because they don't *want* to go home. They don't want the life they had down below, they ain't saving up for anything and they sure as shit ain't thinking about the future.

Bottom line is that on Seedee, somebody's always looking for a good time, and there is a lot of competition to meet those needs.

It's clear something is going down as soon as they turn the corner out of Resnik. On the concourse in front of the main entrance to Dock Nine, there are dozens of people milling around, not only couriers and logistics managers there to collect materials, but the dock's freight handlers too. Moving close, Nikki can see that the doors are closed, a guard standing in front. She's never seen that at a dock before, didn't know there even *were* doors.

"The place is in lockdown," someone says. "Seguridad showed up and cleared everybody out."

"Why?"

"Heard it's some biohazard threat they need to contain before they can open things up again. Total clusterfuck. My consignment is already delayed because of the all-stop on W2."

Some people are looking pissed, but nonetheless resigned to waiting it out. People are like that here. They do as they're told.

"Let's try another way inside," Felicia suggests.

She leads the group away from the main entrance and around the side, where a ramp climbs towards the lower-gravity receiving points on the platforms overlooking the shuttle dock.

As the ramp flattens out approaching the entrance to the lower platform, they are met by a uniformed Seguridad officer barring their progress.

"Sorry, the receiving decks are closed right now. I need to ask you all to return to the concourse until the situation is contained and we have the all-clear."

They stop in their tracks a few yards from the guard. Kobra sighs with exasperation.

"The shuttle we're waiting for gets diverted, and when we get here the doors are barred and the place is in lockdown? This is bullshit. We're being jacked, man. I ain't having it."

Sensing the aggression, the guard draws his sidearm, a resin gun.

"Do not approach any closer. Once again, I need you all to return to the concourse and wait. I realise it's inconvenient but the sooner everybody cooperates, the sooner we can get operations back to normal."

His voice remains calm but Nikki can see that he has engaged the target-finder. She sees the sensor dance back and forth, reading and logging their shapes and positions. It's a defensive weapon, designed to immobilise rather than injure. It fires a splatter-charge of liquid plastic that dries hard in less than a second, freezing you in its grip. It's a bitch to get off. They need to take you to a special-ised facility and bathe you for hours in a chemical solution.

There's a comparatively slow reload mechanism when you're firing cartridges of that stuff, but the flatfoot would be able to tag at least two, maybe even three of them at this distance, even if they were all to rush him at once. Which they are not going to do.

"We're just leaving, officer," she says.

He watches them back away, lowering the barrel as they retreat.

"What, we're giving up?" Kobra asks.

"We're not going to be much use if we all get tagged with cum-shots," Nikki replies as they descend the ramp.

"That's a month's supply we're walking away from."

"We're not walking away. We're just taking the scenic route."

Nikki takes them back out past the still-busy concourse and down a fire-sheet. It's a narrow lane between buildings barely wide enough for people to pass, as that isn't its purpose. There isn't the space on Seedee to have fire gaps wide enough to be worth the name, so instead there are these channels that can be filled with rapidly expanding flame-retardant foam to prevent a blaze spreading.

She takes an auto-adjusting ratchet from her kit-belt and unscrews a panel in the floor.

"Where's this taking us?" Tug asks, looking in particular need of convincing as his frame is going to be the hardest one to squeeze down the resulting hole.

"Mag-line. There's a dedicated conveyor channel that takes smaller packages to the despatch centre about a block that way. We can crawl along it to the rear of the sorting depot."

The mag-line is a low-energy electro-magnetic repulsion hover system for moving supplies around a vast network of sub-surface conduits. It's fully automated and computer controlled, crates having their details scanned and analysed at every junction and exchange so that traffic can be managed and in some cases prioritised. The network is so extensive that if you know how to hack a crate and programme the code for your destination, you can in theory post yourself anywhere on the wheel. In fact, she is aware that that certain establishments on Mullane have been known to use it as a high-tech version of the bum's rush if a drunk client gets out of line.

"How's that gonna work? We'll all get squashed flat by a moving crate."

"Everything's on lockdown, genius. Nothing is moving."

"So what happens if it starts up again?"

"Then you get a free ride to the despatch centre where they slap an 'oversize goods' label on your fat ass."

The overhead clearance is only about three feet. It's slow going, interrupted by having to push cargo out of the way or, when it proves too heavy, squeeze themselves past it. Eventually they reach the rear of the sorting depot, the side even the freight-handlers never see unless something gets stuck. With the elevators offline, they need to climb maintenance ladders to reach the back of the lower-gravity platforms, though it's only the first twenty feet or so that's taxing. After that it just keeps getting easier.

Nikki emerges on to the lower of the platforms, where the receiving areas have transparent safety barriers keeping people back from the drop. The four of them peer cautiously down into the dock. Nikki has never seen or heard one so quiet.

There are only four people there, all male. They are standing around a large plastic slab that is sitting on a hydraulic trolley, waiting to be rolled out.

"Doesn't look like Julio's people," Felicia whispers.

"I don't care who they are," Kobra replies. "That's our fucking stuff."

They don't look like dock management. They aren't Seguridad either: no uniforms and no badges. Nikki doesn't know who these people are, but they've got the place in lockdown and are calling the shots.

"I don't like it," Nikki cautions.

"What's to like? We've got the drop on them and they're about to walk out of here with our shit."

Kobra draws a weapon and raises himself into a kneeling position. The shift of his bulk causes the slightest creak to issue from the platform's support stanchions.

It's enough.

A fraction of a second later the air fills with plastic flechettes, fired in controlled volleys from each of the figures below. Their responses were instantaneous, a drilled combination of reflex and discipline.

Nikki's reactions aren't what they once were, but the height and the distance give her enough time to drag Felicia down with her, behind the glass barrier. Tug takes two in his upper arm, turning quick enough to protect his head, while Kobra's tessellar shirt, which the darts can't penetrate, does nothing to prevent four of the plastic missiles tearing into his face and neck.

Kobra collapses painfully to the floor a few metres ahead, like a puppet whose strings have been cut, arms and legs alike suddenly useless. Nikki hears a horrible crunch and sees broken teeth scatter on the ground amidst a spray of blood, Kobra taking no measures to cushion his fall.

The last time Nikki saw someone go down like that, it was in LA more than twenty years ago, and the victim was dead before he hit the floor.

WARNINGS FROM ON HIGH

Alice is still spinning from Boutsikari's intervention when she feels as much as hears this deep, grinding crunch. It is like that moment just before a train or a bus comes to a stop, when she can still sense the forward momentum. Except that when the wheel stops, that momentum is multiplied by a hundred, and there's no gravity to stop her after the jolt.

The ground stops and Alice simply doesn't. She is pitched forward, pinballing off other bodies, but slowing enough that she thinks she can grab a railing coming up ahead. As she reaches for it, someone else barrels helplessly into her, and a moment later she is shooting up towards the canopy with disproportionate velocity.

It wasn't the collision, she realises, but a vent. The bump knocked her into its path, only for a moment, but without gravity to retard her progress, the air resistance is no match for a fan-driven current. It sends her rising at speed, like a leaf on the wind.

She braces for contact with the canopy, reassuring herself it only *looks* like glass, and somehow manages to flip herself so that it is her feet that hit the transparent barrier between the wheel and open space. The impact is felt mostly in her knees, and once again seems disproportionate, this time in a kinder way, reminding her that her legs are only absorbing the force of an air vent, after all.

She rebounds with considerably reduced energy, floating very slowly downwards into open space above the plaza. Below her she can see dozens of people, all still somehow on the ground. Looking closer she observes that they are now tethered to fixed objects or to each other, from lines clipped to their waists or wrists. Among the crowds, if they even noticed the shooter, he will have been forgotten in what happened next.

Not so hard to spot the new girl, she thinks, which is when she realises that if she was the shooter's intended victim, then she is now presenting a very easy target. She thinks of the man who was staring at her. The shooter was wearing a mask but it had to be him. He was standing in roughly the same spot.

She looks at her arm and sees blood drift from it in tiny red balls.

The wound is not what she was expecting. There is a plastic dart sticking from her forearm. It is about half the length of her thumb, and only embedded in the top half-centimetre of skin. Best not pull it out though, she reasons, but she knows nobody is going to kill her with one of these. Down on the terrace, she can see that the people around Gonçalves have relaxed their state of alertness, some even laughing with relief. With the gravity off, there is no option for anybody to go chasing down the gunman, even if they had noted what he looked like, but from their subsequent reactions she discerns that whatever just happened, it wasn't an assassination attempt.

Then as she reaches a height of around fifty or sixty feet, she hears another shudder that confirms how being shot again with a dart gun is not the biggest danger facing her right now. If the wheel could stop without notice, then it could restart at any second too.

Her heart is racing but she is resistant to the idea of calling for help. She doesn't want the first thing anybody knows about her to be the fact that she had to be rescued while everybody who was used to the place dealt calmly with the emergency. She was totally unprepared, however. Not only did they equip themselves with retractable tethers, but as she looks down she can see several people using compressed air canisters as propulsion devices. A handful are employing them to guide themselves back to ground where they can find anchor, but the majority are engaged in a pre-emptive clean-up operation. Hotel and restaurant staff are expertly directing themselves into position to retrieve glasses and crockery, while using suction devices to trap balls of fluid.

"It's so they don't short anything," says a woman's voice. It comes from behind Alice, but she can't immediately see where.

"When the wheel turns again and it all goes splat," she continues, "you'd be amazed where fluids can end up."

Alice gets a fix on the source. She is rising gently from beneath and to her right, expertly discharging blasts of air from a cylinder the size of a marker pen. It is the woman Hoffman led away. Her expression doesn't look quite so severe now, but perhaps this is merely because Alice is grateful for her approach.

Upon the woman's invitation, Alice offers a hand, expecting it to be gripped. Instead she extends a tether from a wristband and attaches it to a belt-loop on Alice's waist.

"Thank you," Alice says meekly.

"Didn't they give you one of these?" the woman asks.

Alice is not sure whether she means the wrist utility or the air cylinder. She is about to say no when she flashes back to a welcome pack that was waiting for her on the bed in her hotel room. She must have flaked out last night, meaning to open it in the morning, but she hurried out without doing so.

"I'm Helen, by the way," she says in an accent suggesting she just got here from the Deep South. "Helen Petitjean."

Alice is about to introduce herself but remembers it would be redundant. She decides to do so anyway. Some archive inside her head just relayed the notion that Southerners traditionally place a premium on politeness, so she opts to go with it.

"Alice Blake. Pleased to meet you, and many thanks for going to this trouble."

"My pleasure."

And your opportunity, Alice thinks.

Happy that the tether is secure, Helen fires a few bursts of air and gently directs them not down, but towards the roof of a nearby building.

A plate spins through the air and Helen minutely corrects her course to avoid it.

"I don't have a free hand," she explains. "And I see you've injured yours."

"It's not serious."

"Best not take the dart out for now," Helen counsels.

Alice sees the plate clip the edge of the building. It drifts there gently, but the momentum is enough for the impact to fragment it into several shards.

"Shouldn't they be unbreakable?" Alice suggests. "Plastic, maybe?"

"It's remarkable what you come to consider an exquisite luxury," Helen replies. "But eating off china is definitely one of mine. The more advanced our technology, the more we appreciate basic tactile things."

"Such as my feet touching the ground," Alice agrees, as they skate between rows of rooftop vegetation, coming in fast. They skim off the surface of the topsoil and Helen skilfully uses the cylinder to brake so that she can grip a handrail before they float off again. Alice notices a tiny scar in the surface where her heel clipped what turns out to be a transparent membrane keeping the soil in place.

"You're going to encounter that a lot here: the constant struggle between the future and the past. Everything is really new and really old at the same time. Here on CdC we're relying on infrastructure technology that was put in decades ago. It's ancient compared to what people are used to on Earth. And yet other things are cutting edge because they are developed here.

"My background is architecture and city planning. I consult on designing habitat and social environment, both for CdC and for the *Arca*. The whole thing is an exercise in never knowing what you need until after you need it, discovering how every one of your contingencies creates new problems. One of the biggest dangers is thinking the tech you are developing will save you from more basic concerns. Future versus past."

"You mean like how by creating artificial gravity, we no longer need to worry about stray fluids ending up where nobody antici-pated?" Alice asks, as a volume of what she takes to be hot coffee floats past and just misses their heads.

"Well, precisely."

Helen attaches a tether from her waist to a railing and begins to pull them both around the edge of the roof towards the entrance to a staircase.

"Is it about to start up again?" Alice asks, failing to keep a hint of concern from her voice.

"Oh, no. They'll sound an alarm before they do that, give every-body time to get someplace secure."

"How long is it likely to take?"

Helen shrugs.

"Could be twenty minutes, could be ten times that. The knock-on disruption will be longer, though. Won't be any shuttles landing on this wheel until they're sure all the systems are responding properly."

Helen opens a roof-access door and tugs them both gently down the stairs into the uppermost storey of the building.

"We'll be safe waiting it out in here," she explains. "There are plenty of anchor points inside."

They bob their way into a room where Helen detaches Alice's tether and reattaches it to a shelving unit that proves bolted into the floor. It appears to be a storage room for materials used in cultivating the vegetation above, rooftops being used for agriculture on CdC like they might host solar panels on Earth.

"So what is it that you wanted to talk to me about?" Alice asks. "Or more pertinently, what is it that Hoffman and Boutsikari *didn't* want you talking to me about?"

Helen seems momentarily surprised then acknowledges Alice's candour with a knowing smile.

"Oh, they just don't want anybody messing with the airbrushed brochure version of this place."

"And what's the non-airbrushed version?"

"Like I already told you: future versus past. The tension between the old and the new. This is the most advanced place in the history of human civilisation, and yet some people seem intent on recreating a mid-nineteenth-century frontier town, or maybe Chicago circa the 1920s."

"I've heard there is an illegal alcohol trade," Alice says. She thinks of the bar prices on the terrace. "I suppose that was inevitable."

"That's just the tip of the iceberg, honey. And it's an iceberg on a collision course with the *Titanic*. You know, once upon a time, bloated executives went to South-East Asia on corporate junkets so they could screw prostitutes half their age, a hedonistic playground far away from prying eyes, husbands, wives and consequences. Now they're getting that in space."

"Prostitution?"

"Any fleshly indulgence you can think of, it's on sale up here. And where there's criminality and exploitation, there's also violence, but you aren't gonna hear about that from Boutsikari and Hoffman. With you coming in, I'm hoping things can change. See, they could clean it all up if there was a genuine will to do so."

"So why wouldn't they?"

Helen gives her a look that is pitying of Alice's apparent naïveté. It's a manner Alice has always found useful in encouraging people's candour.

"What you see here, CdC, the *Arca*, this whole glorious undertaking has been a product of people sacrificing the short-term view for the greater good. Thinking about what is going to benefit us all in five hundred years and not what is gonna benefit yourself individually in the next ten minutes or the next financial quarter. Not everybody sees it like that, though. It's human nature. Some folks are always gonna be looking to make hay and to build their little fiefdoms."

"You're saying one of those people is Boutsikari and one of those fiefdoms is the Seguridad?"

"If only it were that simple. There are fiefdoms within fiefdoms, powerbases within powerbases. The Seguridad is riven with corruption but Boutsikari is a political animal and a pragmatist. He subscribes to the argument that the illicit trades here aren't doing any real harm, that they keep everything ticking over, but he is being dangerously negligent. There is tension in this place. You can feel it. And it's building up to something bad, something explosive."

"This is what you were going to talk to me about down on the terrace, in front of Hoffman and Boutsikari?"

Helen fixes her with a fiery stare.

"I most certainly was, and don't you for one minute imagine otherwise. This whole mess is the result of keeping things under wraps that should be out in the open. I'd have let Boutsikari know that once you take over from Hoffman, I don't expect things to simply keep ticking over."

"And what is it you think I can do?"

"It's what Boutsikari thinks you can do that matters. His great fear, one that is widely shared around the Quadriga, is that if they aren't running a tight ship, you will report back with the recommendation that FNG takes over the policing of this place. If you let it be known you'd rather merely bring the Seguridad to heel, you'll get the support and protection you'll need."

"Protection? So you're anticipating that the people running these illegal operations will make me a target?"

"Naturally. If you can't be bought – and I'm betting you can't – then they'll have to solve the problem some other way. But trust me, honey, the gangsters are not the people you need to worry about. The biggest threat is gonna come from the cops. So I'm about to do you a favour here and now by warning you who's the most dangerous one . . ."

MOONLIGHTING

Nikki crouches over Kobra, feeling for a pulse. It's there, strong as ever, but he's out cold and she doesn't understand why he went down the way he did.

There are no firearms on Seedee. Put a hole in the canopy and you could kill yourself and everybody in the immediate vicinity before the emergency seals contained the damage. That's why people print their own flechette pistols. If you want to hurt somebody, to literally make your mark on them, these little plastic darts will do the job. They are messy, bloody and painful, which is why Nikki carries one primarily as a deterrent. They will do some nasty damage, so you don't want to be shot, but they're not intended to kill. You could theoretically die from blood loss if you were real unlucky, but Kobra hasn't sustained that kind of damage, and besides, he dropped right away.

Kobra moves, suddenly lurching as though in shock. He puts a hand to his injured mouth.

"Fuck. What the hell?"

"You okay? You went down with a thump."

"Something turned the lights out, just for a second. Don't know what."

"One of those darts was tipped, maybe," Nikki suggests.

They scramble back the way they came in, down the maintenance ladders, figuring that if they were seen, their pursuers will be searching the publicly accessible areas. They are breathless and numb in their egress, Felicia finally breaking the silence as they crawl along the conveyor belt.

"Who the hell were those bastards? They weren't Julio's people, but we're definitely getting jacked."

"That was private security."

72

"Private security? Ain't that we're paying *you* for, Nikki Fixx?"

"Did you see how they responded? To a threat enjoying an elevated angle of fire? They didn't blink, they didn't flinch and they didn't miss. That's serious training. I'm talking a whole other order of magnitude. Answerable to and protected by the highest high."

"Then what are they doing stealing our contraband? Our money's a speck in the sky to those assholes."

"You don't understand, Felicia. You ain't getting jacked. It's worse. You're getting shut down."

Nikki sees a message appear on her lens, tagged high priority. She reads the details, acknowledges.

"Fuck," says Felicia. "What the hell am I supposed to tell Yoram?"

"Not my problem."

"The hell it ain't. You were there. This is your mess too."

"Maybe, but you're out of time. Right now I gotta go do my day job."

CONTAINMENT

Alice stands upon grateful feet in a private room off the lobby of the Ver Eterna hotel, enjoying the certainty of her own weight.

After the wheel resumed spinning and the gravity came back on, a paramedic located her as she emerged from the building where she and Helen had waited out the all-stop. He removed the dart with a specialised sterile device and treated the superficial wound with a speed and expertise that all combined to indicate this type of injury was far from a rarity. The paramedic then asked her to come with him, she assumed to the infirmary or a first aid station for further checks. Instead he escorted her here and asked her to wait.

Boutsikari enters a few minutes later, his expression a dark contrast to the relaxed geniality of the terrace. He is accompanied this time not by Hoffman but by a senior Seguridad officer, his face so stony-set that for a split second Alice wonders if she is about to be arrested. He doesn't introduce himself, but her lens tells her who he is: Captain Rapresh Jaganathan.

"Dr Blake, we have just learned of a very serious situation," he says.

"Is it Professor Gonçalves?" she asks, fearing what tragic development she might have missed. "Is she all right?"

"She was unharmed in the incident. And my apologies for your injury. We are making rigorous efforts to apprehend whoever fired the flechette, and ordinarily it would be our number one priority."

"What knocked it off the top spot?"

Boutsikari trades glances with the officer accompanying him, still as yet not formally identified. Whatever this is, they need time to build up to it.

"We believe we may be dealing with a murder. A body has been found down in the Axle."

He leaves it at that for a few moments, giving her time to catch up on the implications. There has never been a homicide on CdC.

"You *may* be dealing with a murder. You mean you're not sure?"

"Actually, we're damn sure," Boutsikari replies gravely. "I'm heading there in person right after this to assess for myself, but going by the images that have just been sent by the officers on-scene, there's not much room for doubt."

"Can you flash them to my lens?"

"If you insist, but with the caveat that they are extremely disturbing."

"I insist," Alice says.

Two seconds later she is regretting it.

"That's . . . definitely not a suicide," she responds, fighting hard against the queasy feeling in a stomach that is still recovering from the effects of the all-stop.

Boutsikari stiffens, seeming to stand a little taller even as she reels from the images overlaid in her lens.

"Captain Jaganathan here will be in charge of the investigation," he states. "He is one of my most experienced and trusted officers."

The stony-faced Jaganathan gives her the curtest of nods, as though concerned that no informality should contaminate the seriousness of the situation.

"You will, of course, have full access to all reports and communication," Boutsikari goes on. "But it is imperative that what we are dealing with remains strictly confidential. As you will have ascertained from these images, there is an extremely dangerous and highly disturbed individual at large on CdC, and in such a contained environment, the potential for panic is something of which we have to be acutely conscious. That is why I am recommending – and indeed humbly requesting – that no details regarding this incident reach Earth until we have a firmer command of what we are dealing with."

Jaganathan takes a step forward to stand alongside Boutsikari, both of them towering over Alice in the tight little room.

"I would just like to concur with Mr Boutsikari," he says. "This is already a volatile and delicate situation, but for the moment we have the option to contain it. If it leaks down below, whether the conduit be FNG or Quadriga, we will find ourselves at the eye of an almighty storm. I for one always find it easier to do my job when the weather is calm and clear."

Alice takes half a step back in response, both of their gazes locked on her in a manner that takes her very little time to decode. They look determined, resolute, calm and in control.

They are crapping themselves.

She wonders how long Boutsikari deliberated keeping the whole thing secret from her, hoping the Seguridad could solve the case and present it as a fait accompli before she found out. It must have been tempting, but ultimately not worth the risk. Instead he had opted to bluff by playing Mr Take-Charge, figuring Alice wouldn't want to be making a major call on something as massive as CdC's first ever homicide before she had even officially taken up her post.

He is right, too. She hasn't had time to assess the landscape, so she isn't about to make a move when she has no reckoner for calculating the consequences. There is no question but that this is a crisis, and that is the worst time to be doing anything rash. But equally, she understands that in every crisis there is an opportunity. She is here to stare down all that Hoffman turned a blind eye to, and she knows Boutsikari is not going to make that easy for her.

She recalls what Helen Petitjean just told her, regarding the Seguridad chief's greatest fear.

If you let it be known you'd rather merely bring the Seguridad to heel, you'll get the support and protection you'll need.

"I completely agree," she tells them. "We all understand the consequences of this reaching Earth. And that's why I want a homicide detective leading the investigation. With respect, Captain Jaganathan, I don't believe that's your principal area of experience."

The two men look at each other, wrong-footed and wary. Nor will what she is about to say next put them at ease.

"Who do you have in mind?"

"There's an officer whose methods I've been hearing very interesting things about," she says, fixing Boutsikari with a look that confirms they both know what she means. "Very interesting things indeed. Her name is Nicola Freeman, and according to her record she is the person most qualified to handle a case such as this. I think I could learn a great deal about policing here on CdC from observation of how she operates."

"Fuck me," says Jaganathan. "Nikki Fixx? Are you serious?"

"She's serious," Boutsikari replies gravely, already reading the game.

MURDER ONE

Nikki propels herself up the last hundred metres of the shaft, a strong tug on a handle enough to send her hurtling like a bullet along a barrel. As her body is rapidly reacquainted with the sensation of zero-g motion, it occurs to her that she should have hit the head before she left. It's been a while since she's been to the Axle, which is why she forgot that it's wisest to go on an empty bladder, because you don't want to be taking a piss there if you're not used to it. With any luck she won't be kept too long. She doesn't even know why they need her up here. Down here. Whatever.

People always talk about going *up* the spoke away from the wheel, but when they get there they refer to being *down* in the Axle. That's Seedee for you. Up becomes down, and what's really messed up is the old and the new. A lot of advanced science stuff goes on down here because of the zero-g environment, and yet it's the oldest, clunkiest part of CdC. In fact, the Axle is what was here before anyone really thought there was going to *be* a CdC. Parts of it are more than seventy years old, and it never fails to creep Nikki out.

Anyplace else on Seedee, you can forget where you really are. Even up on high levels where the gravity is weak, you're still in what is recognisably a living space or a work environment. But here, you might as well be on the ISS. Every second Nikki spends here she is unnervingly conscious of being in a decades-old tin can floating in space, the barrier between life and instant freezing death mere millimetres thick. It is a thought Nikki prefers to be in chronic denial about.

Security is tight here at the best of times, not only because of the science labs, but because you have to pass through the Axle to get to the dry dock. Access to the test vessels themselves requires ultra-high-level clearance, but you ain't even getting near the gantries unless you're absolutely supposed to be there.

Everything appears to be locked up extra tight today.

As she nears the end of the shaft she can see a Seguridad officer watching her approach through a Plexiglass window above the ingress hatch. He has had plenty of time to lens her so he knows who she is and why she's visiting.

The suits love that shit. The lens ID database means that they don't have to talk to the little people even to state their name and business. It underlines their importance, and the fact that they don't need to speak to you reinforces the understanding that you don't have any reason to bother them. They can set their own ID parameters so that their name won't even be displayed to anyone of insufficient status, only their clearance level. Far as Nikki's concerned, that's just fucking rude. What's it gonna cost you to say hi?

Nikki always finds it's useful to talk to people, even for a moment. You never know what little nuggets you're gonna pick up just shooting the shit.

"Howdy, Officer Lopez," she greets him.

"Detective Freeman. They're expecting you."

Detective isn't a recognised rank in the Seguridad. It's a courtesy title reflecting the status she attained back on Earth, in the LAPD. Here in Seedee's private police force, there is only officer, sergeant (Nikki's actual rank) and captain. Beyond that it's all corporate bullshit: vice president in charge of whatever. They got a dozen of them. And then at the top is Boutsikari, who is chief executive officer, as opposed to chief of police. Like all the other suits, he was never a cop, and the prick is open about how he regards that as an asset in carrying out his job. Seguridad is a business, not an authority, not a service, and it sure as shit isn't a force.

But maybe Boutsikari's right. Nikki doesn't like to think of how much worse it might be if the man in charge didn't know how to piss with the Quadriga, and to do that, you need to speak their language and understand their rules.

"Heard we caught a body," Nikki says, fishing to find out as much as she can before she finds herself on the spot. She's still feeling shaken up by what happened earlier, and was hoping to spend some time today getting to the bottom of it. Instead she gets despatched to the Axle, and is wary of having no idea why she in particular got the call.

"That's one way of putting it," Lopez replies.

"They ruled out foul play yet?"

The officer gives her an odd look. Dumb question.

There's never been murder on Seedee. They love boasting about that. The only city with a flatline zero homicide rate. Course, it's bullshit, but it's an official matter of record, and when did the truth figure when it comes to corporate image? Never a murder, and a one hundred per cent record of suspicious deaths being ruled as the result of accidents.

Negligence invariably proves to have been a factor when the official report gets filed; trespass too. Every effort is made to ensure that workers' safety is assured, and CdC's record surpasses that of any major industrial facility on Earth, but space is still a dangerous environment to work in, especially if people don't observe protocols, blah blah blah.

Course, that doesn't mean they don't investigate. There's been a few assholes riding a jump seat straight to a private prison owned by the same firm as the Seguridad, where they serve a life sentence for offences that can never officially be disclosed.

Bottom line is it's never ruled foul play. That's the joke, even if Lopez didn't get it. Maybe he's new.

Nikki pushes off against the wall and glides at an easy pace so that she can stop without a thump when she reaches the first six-way conduit up ahead. The Axle looks like a giant tube from the outside, but inside it's a nightmarishly complex 3D maze. The conduits are bad enough but what she particularly hates are all the spherical and cylindrical chambers. Unless you remember to take note of the code above the hatch or aperture you entered through, if you spend any time inside you can become disoriented and forget which is the way out. Given how many of the link passages look identical, you can get lost real fast, even with an overlay map on your lens. The problem is like any map: you're screwed if you don't know which way up you're looking at it.

Nikki knows she's in the right place as she approaches the third six-way, because she can see police tape blocking one of the exits. It's an overlay on her lens, a universal one so that anybody happening by will see the area is out of bounds. There is no actual tape. Don't want to be messing around trying to unroll shit like that around here. She doubts Inventory would even have it. When is there ever a genuine bona fide crime scene in this place?

She grabs a handle at the six-way and very gently tugs herself through the non-existent barrier.

The first thing she notices is that Boutsikari is here, floating in the passage alongside two of his corporate underlings. Nikki allows herself a smile at the unintentional symbolism in front of her. Useless assholes literally hovering around doing nothing. She should get a picture, hang it in that art gallery on W2.

Boutsikari is talking to Captain Jaganathan, the only cop of any rank that she's seen here so far. The precincts are divided into wheel quadrants, and until now she never knew who technically had jurisdiction over the Axle. She should have sussed it would be Jag. He's captain of the precinct on W2 containing Central Plaza and all those Quadriga HQs, which is why he's the officer tightest with Boutsikari. Seeing him in charge of the scene, she is even less clear on why she has been summoned here. This is way off her turf.

She has considerably less confusion over why Boutsikari is here. His number one priority will be to ensure that whatever this is, it stays quiet. Since it became apparent that the off-planet site constructing the *Arca Estrella* was growing into a sizeable human settlement, the Federation of National Governments has always been – warily – accepting of a private security force keeping the peace. This is partly because it gets around the thorny issue of which government would have the right to enforce the law on an off-planet facility, and more problematically of which nation's law they would be enforcing.

The Quadriga understandably prefers not to have a governmental authority exercising that kind of power aboard its facility, and therefore has always – warily – accepted the FNG holding super-visory powers over its private security force instead. It is one of those messily pragmatic arrangements whereby both sides understand that isn't a problem until it's a problem. Hence the need to maintain the impression that Seedee is a harmonious model society offering few challenges to an anyway highly professional police service.

The idea of the Seguridad investigating a homicide triggers all of the political implications everybody has been trying to avoid for decades. Boutsikari will be under pressure from the Quadriga higher-ups to maintain the status quo, conscious that a murder could be just the excuse the FNG needs to insist on bringing in its own people: the thin end of a highly undesirable wedge.

Given what went down today, Boutsikari and his politicos taking over a scene like this would ordinarily please Nikki. The sooner they officially ruled "nothing to see here", the sooner she could get back to cleaning up her own mess. But what's got her alarms ringing is the possibility that this scene might *be* her mess.

She thinks back to the special-forces-looking psychos who had complete control of Dock Nine, people who had the look of high-level private security. That gave the whole thing a strong scent of Quadriga. And yet Brock Lind, that admin douche on Dock Eleven, told her he had rerouted their delivery after being paid off by Omega, which means Julio's people. Somebody is making a move, but she's not sure who and that means she doesn't know where the next threat is coming from.

Jag notices her approach and signals to Boutsikari by means of a tap on the shoulder. The Seguridad chief gives her a beckoning wave, which makes her all the more uneasy. For one thing, it is utterly redundant, but more significantly he looks keen to speak to her.

As he drifts slightly away from his entourage, Boutsikari reveals another member of the group who had been shielded from Nikki's view: a girl, maybe early twenties, though she is getting worse and worse at gauging anybody under forty. It's a result both of aging and of living here, where you don't exactly see a lot of teens and adolescents.

Too young to be one of the suits anyway. Probably some corporate VP's daughter on the fast track, getting an exec-level ride-along and a chance to see the workers tend the field. She's slappably fresh-faced and eager. Never worked for a living, Nikki is sure: certainly not as a cop or even a security guard, but in about a year's time she'll be getting paid five times Nikki's salary to tell her how to do her job.

Nikki's not close enough yet to get a lens ID. Either that or it's confirmation that she's a corporate blueblood and her details are not accessible at Nikki's paygrade, unless she commits a crime. But then a moment later, there it is: Jessica Cho. She's on a temporary Seguridad corporate clearance. Looks half Chinese, half something else, but Nikki couldn't guess what. The name Jessica sure isn't giving much away.

Boutsikari drifts into Nikki's path, his dressy suit and shoes indicating that he wasn't anticipating a trip to the Axle when he put them on today.

"Thought you would be at the Gonçalves lecture," Nikki says.

"I was," he replies darkly. "Supposed to still be drinking champagne and eating canapés, but somebody had other ideas."

Nikki decides to come straight to the point.

"The fuck am I doing down here in the vomit zone, Boots?"

She sees Jaganathan wince at this gratuitous display of disrespect in hailing the CEO. Jag doesn't get it, though. Nikki isn't doing it to piss Boutsikari off. She calls him Boots because she knows he responds well to it. He thinks it indicates that he is accepted by the cops on street level, or at least by *a* cop on street level. But mainly she's doing it to piss Jaganathan off. She's sure that from the moment he saw her arrive, he's been worried she'll do something he'll have to apologise for. The captain is very career-conscious. He's got his eye on a corporate gig, probably with Seguridad up here initially, then ultimately something sweet down below.

"Nice to see you too, Detective," the CEO replies drily. "You worked murder cases back in LA, didn't you?"

"About a thousand years ago. Why? You ain't telling me you're thinking of ruling this a homicide?"

"Up here, you're the officer with the most experience of this sort of thing, so why don't you make that call. Take a look for yourself. We're all keen for you to give us the benefit of your judgement."

She looks at him with an incredulity she can't disguise. He's being weird. Something is definitely off here, and it smells like a set-up.

She's worried she's about to be presented with the corpse of somebody connected to her, so they can watch her carefully, see if she cracks under the pressure of worrying about how much they already know. Back in her Homicide days, that's how she would have played it.

"We want your first-hand impression. Given your expertise, you may see things we didn't."

Jag hands her a paper suit and gloves as Boutsikari directs her towards the hatch at the end of the passage.

"You can't go in there without wearing these," Jag says. "Risk of contamination."

"Me or the scene?" she asks.

Jag doesn't answer.

Nikki grips an overhead spar and tugs herself gently forward. The officer in front of the hatch shifts aside. He gives her an anxious look, as if to say "rather you than me", which doesn't augur well for what is awaiting her.

The bladed aperture opens like a puckered asshole and looks just as welcoming under the circumstances.

"Take it slow," Jag says. "You don't want to touch anything."

Nikki drifts inside in a cautious, controlled motion, finding herself in one of those cylindrical chambers where it's easy to forget which way she came in. The asshole swishes closed behind her, Nikki looking back to make sure her trailing leg is clear. She never trusts those things. Then she looks ahead, into the chamber.

Heard we caught a body.

That's one way of putting it.

She understands now. What she is looking at is human remains, but this is not a body. This is a human being broken down into its constituent parts, floating independently, a collection of objects that it seems impossible to believe once constituted a living whole.

It takes her a moment to realise she isn't breathing. For a microsecond she entertains the paranoid idea that she has been shut in here and the air turned off. It hasn't, though. She just forgot to inhale.

The part of her that remembers being a real cop kicks in and helps her get it together. Seen worse in Venice Beach, she thinks. And at least this doesn't smell so bad, yet.

An on-site ID isn't going to be likely. On the upside, that means the game can't be to confront her with someone she knows. At this point she can't even determine the gender.

Darkly fascinated by what is drifting in the chamber in front of her, she is nonetheless aware of what isn't. There is hardly any blood, and there is no skin.

She nudges herself clockwise away from the hatch, concerned that a lung is drifting in her direction. The movement is enough for her to notice an object that was previously obscured by a bulkhead three metres above. It is a vacuum-packed bag that she recognises as a standard container for an emergency survival suit. These are the indoor equivalent of an EVA suit, designed for use in conjunction with a rebreather in the case of a major failure of the environment systems. Like life-jackets on an airplane, everybody knows where they're stashed and has seen them demonstrated, but very few people have ever had cause to wear one.

In a chamber such as this, the suits are stored behind wall panels. This one is floating free.

Nikki very carefully manoeuvres herself around the chamber and up, timing her movements to avoid collision. The body parts are gliding slowly enough for this to be just about possible, but as they occasionally collide with each other and change course, she does get brushed a few times.

There is a smell like fresh offal, nothing worse than at the meat counter as long as you don't think about what kind of meat it is. They've turned down the heat, she notices, the standard twenty-two degrees not being ideal for preserving the scene. Leastways, she assumes it's the cops who have turned it down. It could have been the perp.

She snags the vacuum pack by the instruction label and pulls it clear of the bulkhead where it had become trapped, handling it carefully. It is the standard opaque white plastic, but it isn't pulled tight against the contents like it ought to be. The seal has been broken. It's been opened and resealed with the zipper. Probably nothing, but it's against protocols. If you use one, it has to be safety checked and certified before being vacuum-packed again with a fresh sealing label detailing the date of previous use.

Nikki pulls the zipper open and has a look inside.

Fucking comedian.

There's an environment suit in there, of sorts. It's human skin.

At least this means she can state that the victim is white. Back in the LAPD, time was that was the first thing they wanted to know. Beyond that the ethnicity is anybody's guess. It's hard to tell when she can't even be sure whether she's looking at the inside or the outside.

Nikki is in the process of zipping the bag closed again when it hits her that there may well be a face in there. She's not sure how easy it would be to identify without it being stretched over a skull, but it's worth a shot. When she comes out of this chamber, she wants to be ahead of this in any way she can. She needs to know at least one thing they don't.

She pulls the zip open further and tugs back the flap, reaching her fingers reluctantly inside to pull at the folds contained therein. She has seldom been so grateful for gloves. A section comes loose and drifts away. She couldn't even say what it used to cover. She is about to retrieve it when her eye is drawn to what has been revealed inside the bag.

It's better than a face. It's a tattoo, of a Greek symbol. She'd recognise this piece of shit in any condition.

Omega.

THE HUMAN SHIELD

Boutsikari is waiting expectantly for Nikki outside the chamber. If he's wanting a full report, he's out of luck. She'll give him her overview, but she's keeping the name of the victim to herself, for now.

"This come with assembly instructions?" she asks.

"The two lab geeks who discovered it are in hospital, on meds for shock," Boutsikari replies.

And to keep them from talking, Nikki surmises. Even the Seguridad can't rule this one an accident.

"Who else knows about this? FNG aware yet?"

Boutsikari nods. He glances briefly towards the entourage. Nikki can't work out who specifically he's looking at, but one of them must be a fed.

"They're aware, but they're giving us a shot at dealing with it ourselves."

Boutsikari hits her with a look, making sure she understands the stakes. On the surface it sounds like a chance for Seguridad to demonstrate its fitness for purpose. But if it isn't dealt with to the FNG's satisfaction, it's the beginning of the end.

This case is a live grenade.

"I'm putting you in charge of the investigation," Boutsikari states.

Nikki looks towards Jaganathan. She can't help it, it's pure reflex. His expression is implacable, giving nothing away.

"Me?" she asks, as neutrally as she can manage. She doesn't want to make out she thinks he's nuts, but she doesn't want to give the impression that she's delighted either.

"I pulled your file. I pulled everybody's file. You know how to run a homicide investigation. You've a proven track record. None of the captains come close. I need a result on this, and you're my best shot."

Bullshit, she thinks. If he's laying on the compliments, it's to take her eye off something else.

She says nothing, letting him do the talking. Boutsikari is always playing an angle. The details and methodology are seldom obvious, but the one constant is the intended outcome, which is whatever best preserves or most benefits his expensively tailored ass.

"The Quadriga has always been terrified of something like this happening," he says, "but I think we should view it as an opportunity. Prove we can deal effectively with a homicide, and the FNG has less of a case for intervention."

"And what, the FNG is just gonna take our word that we dealt with it all proficiently, solved the case and got our man?"

Boutsikari swallows. If he wasn't floating right now, he'd be shifting uncomfortably on his feet.

"Well, not exactly. I've agreed to have an FNG observer assigned to the investigation. Full access, so that the feds can have no doubts as to how we operate."

He is poker-faced as he says this, but Nikki doesn't miss the warning, which is that under no circumstances should she let the feds know how she operates.

"Absolutely," she replies. "I'm sure that being accompanied by an FNG observer could only assist me in carrying out my duties efficiently and to the letter. So who's my designated stoolpigeon?"

Boutsikari glances back again.

"Jessica," he calls out. "You're up."

Nikki glances at her in disbelief, then looks back at Boutsikari.

"You're kidding me, right? 'Bring Your Daughter To Work Day' is my observer?"

Boutsikari allows himself a tiny smile, saying nothing.

Nikki lenses the spare wheel again. There's been an update on the girl's details, or rather to Nikki's access status now that Boots has given her this field promotion. The girl is nobody: FNG rather than Quadriga, and barely above the level of an intern. Nikki is sure she got the blueblood part right, though: young Jessica will be on the FNG fast track, and this ride-along is going to look good on her résumé.

She wonders what deals were done in order for the FNG to assign an observer whose word won't carry any weight in a he-said, she-said. That's when she detects Hoffman's hand in this: one last act of mutual back-scratching between him and Boots before he heads back to Earth. Once Hoffman's successor arrives – whoever he is – the days of rosy reports going back to FNG could be over. But giving a role to an inexperienced and manipulable pawn would sure make it easier for Boutsikari to give the FNG whatever impression he wants.

With this thought, the scales fall and Nikki finally sees the real reason she has been thrown into this. She's his best shot at a result, Boots said, which is probably true, and if she delivers, great. But if she doesn't, she is certain the observer's report will demonstrate that it wasn't the Seguridad's procedures and policies that were at fault, but the lead investigator's failure to follow them.

She's his fail-safe and insurance policy. As she previously observed, the case is a live grenade, and Nikki's job is to fall on it in order to protect everybody else from the explosion.

PART TWO

PART TWO

UNDER SURVEILLANCE

Nikki and her unwanted attachment walk through the doors of the NutriGen facility on Hadfield and are immediately confronted with a maze of a place: vats, pipes, machinery and displays floor-to-ceiling, forming an intimidating labyrinth of channels and corridors. Back on Earth, there would be a reception area and someone behind a desk to take their enquiry and point them in the right direction. Up here, there are no such luxuries of space or personnel.

Plus, if you have business here, it is expected that you should know where you're going. Company premises on Seedee get very few surprise visitors. Nikki definitely falls into that category.

She calls out to attract the attention of a woman shoving a heavy-looking pallet, its towering pile of plastic-wrapped cubes glistening with condensation. As soon as she looks up, Nikki recognises her, even without the info now appearing on her lens. Her name is Vera Polietsky, and Nikki's knowledge of her stems from her two other jobs. One is as a bouncer at a bar named Klaws, while the more lucrative involves the same establishment's more clandestine attractions.

As she approaches she eyes Nikki with conspicuous wariness, which is now mutual, as Nikki is concerned about what Vera might let slip merely from the briefest conversation.

Nikki shows her ID. It should already be appearing on Vera's lens, but it's an old habit that hasn't died after all these years on Seedee.

"Hey there. I'm Sergeant Nikki Freeman of the Seguridad, and this is Jessica Cho, official observer from the Federation of National Governments. Can you tell us where Dev Korlakian usually works? Big guy, sometimes known as Omega?"

The relief in the woman's face is unmissable. Whatever they want, it's nothing to do with her.

Chris Brookmyre

"He works upstairs in Processing, but I'm pretty sure I heard he didn't show up today."

Nikki gets directions from her and leaves it at that, saying nothing further about why they are here. It is imperative that the general population remains oblivious that there is a murder investigation under way.

The FNG is happy for Seguridad to have a crack at this mess as long as it stays contained. If reports of a murder on CdC get back to Earth, then it will be on every news bulletin on the planet within the hour. Every politician with an agenda regarding the FNG, the Quadriga and indeed the whole *Arca* project will be saddling up, turning the murder of one worthless asshole into the biggest clusterfuck in the solar system.

For that reason, it's not just the gen-pop that Nikki has to be circumspect with. There's barely a handful of Seguridad officers she can trust not to blab, intentionally or otherwise, so she has a limited task force who are in the know. The rest are out canvassing under very carefully worded instructions, to keep them from realising what they are really asking about. (There's always the risk that they might put it together by themselves, but from experience Nikki knows most of them are way too dumb, way too lazy, and often both.)

Jessica reaches to grab the handrail as they climb the stairs, the action pulling back her sleeve to reveal the edge of a bandage.

"You sprain your wrist?" she enquires.

Jessica pulls her sleeve back down.

"No. Burned it on the stove."

A mixture of smells hit them as they crest the second floor landing. It reminds Nikki quite pleasantly of the sea at first – briny with a hint of fish – but there is something else wafting in behind it that speaks more of the docks than the beach.

"What is that smell?" Jessica asks, her button nose turned up in distaste.

"They're making a new cologne," Nikki answers. "It's called Eau d'FNG."

Nikki throws out the insult to see how the girl takes it. She gets no response, not so much like she's ignoring it as that she doesn't even realise it applies to her. Definitely new to the job.

The second floor is more of a grid than a maze, rows and columns of tanks stretching half the depth of the chamber. These are where the beach part of the smell is coming from.

Behind the grid is a black wall, pipes running in and out of it at all levels and angles. This is the source of the less welcoming odour. A sign above the double doors says Processing.

Again, here on Seedee, up is down, down is up. On Earth, anything really heavy with structural implications for a building would be installed on the ground floor or in the basement. Here the giant tanks are up high for ease of moving things around in lower gravity. The weight is not in the tanks themselves, of course, but the thousands of gallons of seawater in each.

"It's fish," Jessica answers for herself as she crests the stairs and gets her first view through the rows of thick glass.

"Spot on. That'll be why you got the gig as an official observer."

Jessica stops in front of a tank and stares inside, ignoring Nikki's remark. There are hundreds of the fuckers in there, swirling around each other.

"So CdC does its own fish farming? It must be a big part of your diet," she adds, taking in the scale of the operation.

"Oh, it's even bigger than you think. But we ain't usually eating it pan-fried with lemon and butter."

"What do you mean?"

"Oh, they got the good stuff here too, Alaskan salmon and the like, that they serve up in the restaurants over in Central Plaza where I'm betting you ate so far. But most of this is for protein generation. S'why the company is called NutriGen: generating nutrition. Turns out farming fish is a quick and economical way to grow organic material for food fabrication."

Jessica looks towards the black wall and takes in the implications of the Processing sign.

"And is that . . ."

"Where the magic happens, yeah."

She looks a little sick.

"Hey, don't diss it. We live on that shit up here."

"What does it taste like?" she asks, distaste all over her cute-little-rich-girl dial.

"Like a thousand different things, that's the point. It's used as a base material in the process of fabricating different foodstuffs. It's not haute cuisine, but it's a decent approximation, kind of in the same way McDonald's is a decent approximation of a hamburger. Though I'm guessing you never ate much at Mickey Dee's."

Jessica doesn't respond to this either. She moves on, past an empty slot where they're swapping out a tank, then stops in front of another, staring at the fish like she's hypnotised.

"Man, you don't like to give much away, do you? Long as we're stuck with each other, why don't you tell me a little about yourself? Where you from?"

Jessica frowns, not taking her eyes from the tank.

"I grew up in lots of different places," she replies.

"Mom and Pop had FNG postings, huh? Okay, but everybody's *from* someplace, in their heart. I mean, like, where did you go to college? Where do you hang your hat these days back down below?"

Jessica doesn't reply. She looks at the blank slot along the row.

"Why is there no tank in that one?"

Nikki sighs. This one's all about reaching out and connecting with people. Fucking FNG.

"They bring in new tanks pretty regular. Replenish the stocks."

"Why do they need to replenish the stocks? I would have assumed the whole point of this is that the stock is self-replenishing?"

"Far as I understand it, it's to widen the gene pool, dilute the effects of inbreeding."

"I see," Jessica replies.

She doesn't seem satisfied by the answer. Or maybe it's something else she's not satisfied by. She's still staring into the tank, like something in there doesn't meet regulations on an FNG form she needs to fill out.

"What?" Nikki asks, impatient to get them moving again, though not looking forward to what awaits them in Processing.

"Why are the fish all avoiding that one corner? Do you see that?"

"You asking me to be a fish psychologist now? How the hell would I know? Don't look like anything to me."

It does, though. Nikki didn't notice it at first, but if she stares for a few seconds it's clear none of the fish are swimming into that area of the tank, like there's an invisible force-field in place.

It's hardly a priority right now, though.

"Come on," Nikki orders.

The smell hits them hard when they step through the automatic door. Nikki notices that the people working here have masks over their mouths and noses, but she figures she would still be smelling this through her ears. They're wearing plastic caps too, so that their hair doesn't reek of it when they clock off.

"Smells like an anchovy's asshole," Nikki observes.

Jessica looks like she's fit to choke.

"Aren't all these processes automated?" she asks, sounding pissed. "Why does anyone even have to be in here?"

Nikki laughs.

"It is automated, but somebody's gotta keep an eye on the systems. Oh, what, you imagined we'd have robots up here in Seedee, for doing all the nasty and dangerous jobs?"

She looks kind of sheepish.

"No, but I'd have thought a system like this would be self-monitoring."

"Yeah, I guess there's a lot of myths about Seedee down below. There's some of mankind's most cutting-edge shit in development up in here but we're no further forward than the scientists on Earth when it comes to the artificial intelligence problem. We can build the most sophisticated computer to monitor a system like this, but we still need a person on the spot to intervene if a gasket needs replaced."

"And we can't build a robot that can do that?"

"Maybe, as long as every gasket replacement operation was gonna be identical, which it ain't. They say you can make a computer recognise a chair, but it still doesn't understand what a chair *is*. If every tool or component is slightly varied, then you need a person and not a robot to fix stuff. And given every piece of trash is slightly different, then you even need a person and not a robot to deal with trash. Hence the shittiest jobs still need people to do them. That's why Maria G is such a big deal."

Jessica looks quizzically at her.

"You know, Professor Gonçalves? The lady somebody just took a shot at in Central Plaza?"

"I hadn't heard about that but I know who you're talking about."

Nikki takes careful note of this response, then continues.

"She was the one who realised we were on a fool's errand trying to simulate the most complex thing in the entire universe, and so put all her efforts into understanding and enhancing the real thing."

"The human brain, you mean," Jessica confirms. "Implantable memory technology."

"Course, there's always rumours that they *have* invented super-intelligent androids that pass for human, except they never told nobody, and they're keeping people doing shitty jobs as part of the cover."

"I can imagine how people would get paranoid up here in this environment," Jessica observes. "And you're right about the myths people have down on Earth regarding CdC. It's irrational, but it's still a scary idea that what you think is a person could actually be a machine."

"No," Nikki tells her. "That's only a little bit scary. What's terrifying, once you let that idea loose in your head, is the thought that you could be an android yourself and not even know."

There is a control booth up ahead, from which a woman in grey overalls is reluctantly emerging to investigate their unexpected presence. Nikki is guessing the ventilation system is pretty good inside there, as she isn't wearing a mask.

As she draws near, Nikki gets an ID on her lens: Angela Gloustein, Assistant Manager, Processing.

"Can I help you?" she asks.

Nikki straightens to attention, holds up her badge.

"I'm Sergeant Nikki Freeman of the Seguridad, and this is Jessica Cho, official observer from the Federation of National Governments. We're making inquiries about Dev Korlakian. We believe he didn't turn up for his shift today. We'd like to talk to anyone who works with him or who knows him personally."

"He's not on my phase but I know who you mean. I think he's buddies with Sol Freitas and Alex Dade. They're not here right now, though. They're all on Atlantic time."

Nikki is familiar with both names. Freitas and Dade are part of Julio's crew, bag men and muscle just like the late Mr Korlakian. She knows where she might find them but she can't go talking to these guys while Jessica is hanging around, because the only incriminating information they are likely to disclose will be on Nikki. She'll catch up with them later, when her spare wheel is safely tucked up in her FNG-approved bed for a regulation quantity of shut-eye.

"Oh, and there's also their shift supervisor, Frank Jacobs. He left a couple of hours ago, though."

"You know where he lives?" Nikki asks. Jacobs sounds like just the sort of guy she wants to talk to in front of Jessica: Omega's day-job line manager, who will know precisely jack shit about the activities that got him killed. A quiet little chat in the guy's apartment, all protocols strictly followed, line of questioning carefully controlled. She will learn nothing, but more importantly, so will the FNG.

"I can look it up for you. I think he's somewhere over in W2, though."

Even better.

"No need," says Jessica, fingers working her lens via an invisible interface. "According to his tracker, he's in a bar called Radiation, on Mullane. That's only twenty minutes from here," she adds chirpily.

Shit.

Jacobs is a typical corporate get-along. Theoretically, everybody on Seedee can be located at any time "for safety purposes", subject to the usual clearance hierarchy, unless they choose to disable the setting. It's entirely up to the individual: the Quadriga is very forthright about that freedom, and it states that nobody should ever feel they will be judged for choosing to go dark, especially on their own time. But ain't it funny how so many people in management positions never go dark?

Is it the case that ambitious people tend to be less protective of their privacy, or is it that the Quadriga tends to promote people who are willingly compliant?

Hmmm. Tricky one.

"Let me get that home address from you, Angela," Nikki says. It's desperate, but if she can drag her feet, then there's a chance Jacobs might finish up his after-work Qola and head for home before she and girl-scout reach Mullane.

"I've got that information too," Jessica announces. "Sending it to you now."

"Well ain't you just indispensable."

OPPOSITION RESEARCH

It is Alice's first time on a static. The motion is smooth and frictionless due to the magnetic repulsion system, making the sense of acceleration unnerving. It feels like falling sideways, totally unlike any motion she has experienced before. She can't help eating it up, eagerly taking in every detail of her surroundings, which makes her grateful that being a wide-eyed newbie is part of her cover.

The carriage is busy, she and Nikki having to stand opposite each other across the narrow aisle. It gives her an unaccustomed sense of power to be carrying out this deceit, even though she is sure Freeman is concealing considerably more truths from her.

Their visit to NutriGen told Alice nothing, and she has no doubt that Nikki is most satisfied with this state of affairs. By playing the part of Jessica, Alice hoped that Nikki might drop her guard: let something slip or conduct some of her normal business thinking that the FNG observer was too inexperienced to understand what was really going on. But so far she's playing it very cagey and thus exposing the flaw in Alice's strategy, which is that if Nikki really is as dirty as Helen Petitjean says, then she's not going to talk to any of the people she's got criminal connections with in front of Jessica.

There are a dozen conversations going on around her, conducted in myriad different languages. People come here from all over the world, though the American influence is manifest in the number of Spanish words that have gained official currency, from the name Ciudad de Cielo itself down to how video clips recorded on lenses are referred to as grabacións, or grabs for short. Spanish has been the most commonly spoken language in the US for more than a hundred years, but despite this ever-expanding majority, English remains the language of America's corporate face, and consequently the one with which it presents itself internationally.

Alice picks up enough from the chat to discern that some people are on their way to work, some are coming home and still others heading for Mullane in pursuit of a good night out. The clock on her lens reads 14:48 but it is meaningless. Alice is still getting her head around the phase system: it makes perfect sense to her in terms of time management in a world without day and night, but she isn't sure which phase she is technically on right now, or how you go about formally choosing. She has kind of just fallen into one by dint of when she woke up.

She thought somebody would come and talk her through it, but that hasn't happened. There were so many things the FNG officially prepared her for before leaving Earth, but official preparation and actual preparation are seldom the same thing. The practicalities of day-to-day living were something she knew she would have to develop a feel for first-hand, and there was a great deal about life on CdC that nobody could satisfactorily brief her on. That was partly why she was here, after all. FNG intel on CdC was limited by the veracity of its own people's accounts when they got back to Earth. Her reading of the existing material suggested a strong tendency for people to go native, or at least a reluctance to be entirely truthful about how they lived their lives while they were up here.

Alice grips the handrail as the car decelerates upon approach to the next station. She steals a glance across at Nikki, who is not holding on to anything but seems to be languidly reading the motion of the vehicle by intuition. There is almost an arrogance about her posture, an assuredness which Alice realises she envies. Alice always feels like she's physically apologising for the space she's taking up, while by contrast Nikki's body language is both a statement of belonging and a claim on her territory.

According to her file, Nikki is forty-five years old. Her face looks entirely less lived-in than her reputation would suggest, though Alice gets the impression of her being someone who was previously athletic but has latterly let things slide. She is tall and wiry, but with some extra weight around the middle, a hint of a paunch. Nonetheless, there is something lithe and solid about her, someone you wouldn't want to clatter into.

Alice's eyes are drawn to the barked knuckles of Nikki's hands. She understands that this is a woman who knows what it is to punch somebody in the face. Nikki is not in uniform, but Alice can discern that certain people in the car know what she is, still others precisely *who* she is. She notes also the occasional subtle nod and brief meeting of Nikki's gaze. Information is being passed between people silently, invisibly, by means far older than any lens system.

Overall, Alice's impression is of a highly dangerous opponent: one she will have to tackle while conceding a considerable home-court advantage.

SEEDEE CONFIDENTIAL

They are lucky with the static, or maybe that should be unlucky: one shows up right away, meaning Nikki and Jessica are on Mullane inside a quarter of an hour.

"He hasn't moved," Jessica assures her. "Jacobs is still inside Radiation."

"You know, I'm wondering whether we shouldn't wait and catch him at home a little later."

"Why would we do that? We're right here."

"Yeah, but the guy just worked his shift. Maybe he deserves some time to wind down before we hit him with the information that his work colleague is dead. A bar isn't the most appropriate place to break that kind of news."

"Yes, but breaking news is the reason time is of the essence," Jessica reminds her. "You heard Boutsikari: the clock is running on when word of this situation leaks down below."

"I guess you're right," Nikki concedes, figuring it was worth a try.

They walk into Radiation, Nikki sizing up the situation and quickly figuring that with a bit of luck she can get in and out without attracting much attention.

It's quiet. The Atlantic shift hasn't long finished, and the Meridian revellers would have moved on to other places. Radiation is the sort of joint where you start your evening rather than being the main event, though it's also popular with those planning to end their night early in the arms of an obliging partner-for-hire.

She clocks Jacobs right away, still in his work clothes, though not the overalls or they would smell him from here. The guy is sitting on his own. He is actually drinking a Qola, like Nikki had joked, though he's got a whisky chaser that definitely isn't corporate-approved. Saving money on the cheap beer so that he can spend the difference on decent liquor. He's got a CdC lone-drinker look that Nikki recognises, which is not to say he is hitting it hard. It's more about the fact that he's lost in his own little world right now, thinking about whatever it was he came to space not to think about.

She begins making her way over but is intercepted by a waiter who appears from one of the booths. His name is Ernesto when he's working here, but he's known as Rod if you're hiring him for his other talents; or talent singular, as indicated by the name.

"Hey, Nikki Fixx. Shit, are we due already? That sure came around fast. I'll go get the boss, but I don't know if he's gonna have everything ready for you."

"No, no, Ernesto, that's not why we're here," she corrects him swiftly. At least he said "everything" and never mentioned money outright.

"Okay, so can I get you a cold one? On the house, of course. Or are you ladies maybe interested in something else tonight?"

Ernesto does the Mullane micro-shimmy, a movement that's over in a blink, thus offering full deniability, but which to the trained eye advertises that everything's for sale. In an act of solidarity, or perhaps in appreciation of the principles of the conglomerate economy, he rounds it off with a glance towards the other goods currently on offer: two girls seated at the bar who Nikki recognises as Desi and Cooper. They don't pay her protection but nor did either of them charge on the nights they ended up back at her place. They could all interpret that many ways. Mostly Nikki prefers not to think about it.

"I'm on duty right now," she replies stiffly. "As is my associate here, Jessica Cho, official observer from the Federation of National Governments."

"The Fed . . ."

Ernesto freeze-frames, panics just a moment, looks Nikki in the eye to confirm this isn't a joke. Looks at Jessica, belatedly takes in what he should have seen straight out, that she looks buttoned-up so tight her head might pop.

"Yeah, I think I might just go check if they need any help in the kitchen. I'll let everybody know you guys are here, in case they can be of assistance."

He gives Nikki a parting look as he says this, his intentions mutually understood.

Attaboy.

"Due what?" Jessica asks.

"Oh, an inspection."

"Isn't that the remit of the FLAT?"

Nikki ignores this and proceeds towards Jacobs. He still looks miles away, oblivious to the brief conversation they just had with the waiter. Nikki puts down her ID on the table next to his whisky, loudly repeating the credentials she just told Ernesto for the benefit of anybody nearby.

"You're Frank Jacobs, right?"

"Yes, officer. How can I help?"

"I believe you're Dev Korlakian's supervisor."

"That's right. What's he done this time? He get in a fight again? He didn't show up today, so I figured the enfermería if he lost and the cooler if he won. You guys being here tells me it's the cooler."

"No, sir. We are actually keen to speak to Mr Korlakian about a matter but we're having difficulty locating him. We were wondering whether you could answer a few questions."

"Sure thing, for what it's worth. I can tell you where he lives and who his shift mates are, but beyond the sphere of the workplace, there's not a lot of overlap."

"When did you last see him?"

"Yesterday. Clocked on, clocked off."

"Anything strike you as out of the ordinary about him?"

"Yesterday in particular or in general?"

"Either."

"Apart from him looking like one big, scary motherfucker, no. Nothing unusual yesterday. I mean, he was in a hurry to finish up, but that isn't exactly a rarity. Up in Processing, folks don't exactly live for their job, you know?"

"But you indicated it's not unusual for him to get in fights," Jessica states.

Nikki shoots her a look, by way of reminding her that she is here to observe.

"Sure, but he never gave me any grief. Apart from covering his shifts when he didn't show because he was getting stitches or cooling off at the Seguridad."

"Did he seem anxious, troubled?" Nikki asks.

"We don't really sit down and pour out our feelings during coffee breaks. But if you're asking if I been worried he might be thinking of taking a shortcut, then not hardly. He doesn't talk much, doesn't complain much either."

"Aren't there disciplinary consequences for these no-shows?" Jessica asks, acting like she never noticed Nikki's previous glare.

Jacobs gives Nikki an incredulous look. She rolls her eyes, telling him "welcome to my world".

"I'm guessing you're new here? I don't know how it works in the FNG, but at a place like NutriGen, firing somebody is an expensive business. Or more accurately, replacing them is. You know what it costs to fill a seat on the elevator, right? There is close to zero unemployment on CdC and NutriGen isn't high on anybody's recruitment priorities. Who wants to come to space to liquidise fish?"

"Are you saying people at your facility are effectively unsackable?"

"No, but it's mostly moot. Everybody came here to work, and work hard: CdC attracts dedicated and diligent people. People know that if they don't make the grade, their contract doesn't get renewed at the end of their twelve months. But if there's a serious problem in the meantime, we have to work it out, with firing as a very distant last resort."

"And was Korlakian becoming a serious problem? Getting into trouble, not showing up?"

"It's not like it's happening once a week. But no, he isn't a problem. He misses a shift, he always makes it up. He's a good worker, Johnny-on-the-spot. Kind of guy who always seems to be in five places at once."

And now he can be in about thirty, Nikki thinks.

"Thank you for your help, sir," she says, wrapping it up, keen to get out of Radiation now that she's gone through the motions for Jessica's benefit.

They begin heading for the door.

"I thought you were going to tell him Korlakian was dead," Jessica says, reminding her of her bullshit.

"Yeah, I thought better of it after you reminded me we need to keep it under wraps. I just hope he didn't pick up on how you kept talking about the guy in the past tense."

"I was talking about events in the past tense, not Korlakian as a person."

Nikki sighs. She was hoping Jessica would be on the back foot over that. She's not shy of standing her ground. Must be an FNG thing, or a rich-kid thing. Either way, it comes down to an instilled sense of entitlement.

"What's a shortcut?" the girl asks as they reach the door. They have to wait as a group of about a dozen come streaming through. Office and admin types, ties loosened, kidding themselves like they're in Tijuana.

"Suicide. You get a lot of solitary types up here. Emotionally isolated. Came because of something they couldn't handle about their lives down below, only to find the thing they can't handle came with them."

"Yeah, but why 'shortcut'?"

"It means a shortcut home in a returning freight container."

The doorway is finally clear and Nikki is about to exit when she gets an alert on her lens: a facial match on one of the people who just walked into the bar. It takes her a moment to call up why she put it on her lookout list, by which time he is heading for the john. He's leaving someone else to get the drinks in, which tracks with what else she knows about him.

"You head for the static and I'll catch you up," she says. "Just gotta go to the bathroom."

"I'll wait," Jessica replies, staying next to the doorway.

"Whatever."

Nikki follows the guy into the Gents. Her lens tells her his name is Venkat Gopta, information she can only access due to her Seguridad privileges. He's a middle-ranking FNG pen-pusher, his status just high enough to block his identity from a rent boy like Garret.

"I think you're in the wrong place," he says with an awkward grin as Nikki barrels through the door.

She doesn't show her badge, instead waiting for him to read her ID on his lens. She figures he's the kind of prick who places way too much stock in rank and status.

"No, I'm right where I need to be, Mr Gopta. I heard that you might have information about some soliciting activity that's been taking place down the street at a place called Sin Garden."

He looks rattled: surprised and confused. He knows the cops seldom bother about this shit unless a specific complaint has been raised, which is the threat he's been using to get out of paying for services rendered.

"No, I think you've been misinformed. I mean, I've been in Sin Garden, sure, but I wouldn't know about any soliciting."

"I heard you may have engaged the services of a prostitute without realising the nature of the arrangement. Would that be about right?"

"No, officer. I mean, this would be the first I'm learning about it if that were the case."

"You're aware that the paid procurement of sexual activity is illegal on CdC under anti-exploitation ordinance?"

"Of course. But if I had dealings with a prostitute, it would be, as you say, without realising the nature of the arrangement."

"See, that's my problem here. Because I've got a grab of you doing business with a gentleman name of Garret, and it looks like you understood the nature of the arrangement pretty good, least until you reached the part where you're supposed to open your wallet."

This last part is bullshit. The grabación only shows Gopta for a brief few seconds, but he doesn't know that.

"Well, if opening my wallet is the issue, maybe we could come to some arrangement?"

He takes out a thick stack of tokens and patronisingly holds one up.

Nikki keeps her stare fixed in his face, not looking at the money.

"What does it take to make this go away?" he asks with a sigh, like this is just a drag to him.

"It takes you paying what you owe," she says, snatching the wad and walking away.

"Hey, I didn't hire every hooker on Mullane for a gang bang. That's over six hundred," he protests, grabbing Nikki by the shoulder.

She pivots and drives a fist into his stomach, sweeps his legs and stomps him in the nuts as he hits the floor. Nothing that will leave a mark.

"Not for a gang bang, but the way I heard it, you hired a lot of hookers and welched on the deal with your little threat. The all-you-can-fuck free buffet is closed. From now on you pay your way."

She pockets the wad and leans over him.

"Just out of interest, what was the price you agreed with Garret?"

Gopta moans and splutters.

"Two hundred."

"No shit? I'll be damned."

INFORMED CONSENT

Nikki can't see Jessica when she emerges from the bathroom, then she spots her through the window, waiting outside on Mullane. She's like an eager little puppy, keen to get going, except that with man's best friend you can rely on a degree of loyalty.

She is passing the gantry on her way out when she notices that Stan, the manager, is pouring somebody a shot of Glenfarclas twenty-one-year-old from its uniquely shaped bottle. Malts have an inflated cachet up here, anything representing variety and authenticity proving all the more desirable when the alternative is to drink the Quadriga's house beer. Somebody is splashing the cash, but that's not what grabbed her attention. The bottle looks close to full, just opened.

"Hey, that the real McCoy, or some other rot-gut decanted into an old Glenfarclas bottle?"

Stan pours her a shot to test.

"Hell of a way to shake down a freebie," he complains.

"I'm not," she insists, giving it a sniff.

It's Glenfarclas, sure enough.

"When did you get this?"

"Today. Ain't had this stuff in weeks."

"I know. Who did you get it from?"

He gives her a butter-wouldn't-melt look.

"A new supplier. Look, hey, I'd have bought from Yoram if he was offering, but he didn't have squat. Word is he never got his delivery."

"That's because his delivery got jacked. This Glenfarclas is *from* his delivery. Who sold this to you?"

"Come on, Nikki, you know I can't answer that. You and Yoram are not the only people who can flex some muscle and make threats."

"Maybe you'd like to talk about who you bought it from downtown at the cooler."

Stan's expression hardens.

"Yeah, maybe I would. About as much as you'd like me talking about who I usually buy from in front of your little FNG friend out there."

Nikki has no play here. She necks the whisky and heads for the door.

"Where to now?" Jessica asks, as Nikki leads her back towards the static station. She wants out of Mullane before they have any more compromising encounters.

"I figure we'll go to Korlakian's apartment, speak to his neighbours."

"Understood. But when we do, don't you think it would make them more cooperative if you didn't tell them straight out that I'm an FNG observer? So far none of them have had the clearance to have it automatically displayed on their lens."

"They have the right to know who they're talking to. I am only following Seguridad procedures regarding full disclosure. I wouldn't want my official observer to report that I wasn't keeping to the official protocols in interviewing witnesses."

"Yeah, but can we take that part as read? I can't help but think it's proving counterproductive. I'm not naïve about people's attitudes towards FNG 'undersight', as I believe they call it. You keep telling people that and they're just going to clam up."

That's the idea, Nikki thinks.

"I don't want to mislead anybody and I never like to burn any bridges. There are people who feel okay talking to the Seguridad but who would never talk to the FNG. If they find out later that I kept that from them, then they're not gonna trust me the next time."

"If you don't get a result on this case, there may not be a next time."

"Wait a sec: are you observing me doing my job, or telling me *how* to do my job?"

Jessica ignores this and casts an eye back towards Radiation.

"What were you talking to the barman about?"

"Whisky."

"What was his name?"

"What does it matter?" Nikki replies, before realising the real reason Jessica is asking.

"His data was not presenting. Absolutely nothing came up on my lens."

"Maybe it's a malfunction."

"No. I reset my system and my connection and ran diagnostics while you were in the bathroom. He's running some kind of hack or deploying a scrambling device. Shouldn't we investigate?"

"No."

"Well, I'm going to have to report it."

"I can't stop you, but I'd advise you to very quickly start adopting a 'no harm no foul' policy on shit like this."

"Why? Attempting to disrupt monitoring and information systems strikes me as a plausible indicator of illegal activity."

"It does, huh? So if you ain't doing nothing wrong, you ain't got nothing to hide, is that what you're saying?"

"No, but your double negatives aside, this is hardly invasive. It's merely a big database, one he consented to when he came here."

"Everybody's got a different threshold for what's invasive. I for one can't say I'm much enjoying being subject to one-on-one FNG scrutiny. And just because you take a job up here and sign a contract doesn't mean you truly consent. Corporations and governments don't get to dictate shit like that. That's why we don't have surveillance cameras mounted everywhere."

"I've seen plenty of cameras," Jessica argues, almost walking into an oncoming pedestrian as her eye is drawn by something she sees through the window of another bar.

"Sure, there are some in the big open public spaces, but not in every passageway and corridor. When Wheel One was first constructed, the Quadriga put cameras in way too many places, so they all got smashed. And I mean all of them: it was done on a point of principle. By way of response the Quadriga put in hidden cameras instead, the size of a pinhead. So people developed sensors to scan for them, and rooted them all out again. They tried developing new cameras that would be immune to the sensors, and the arms race went on for a while, until eventually saner voices prevailed. The consortium finally grasped that people didn't come here to be under surveillance. People feel cooped up enough in a contained environment like this, so the sense of scrutiny feels all the more intrusive."

"The people who vandalised these cameras," Jessica says. "Why weren't they fired from their contracts, kicked off CdC?"

"They weren't stupid. The operations were orchestrated, all done at the same time, and the people doing it wore masks, to make the point about anonymity and their right to it. It was civil disobedience."

"Not if property was damaged. That's criminal."

"When the property is perceived to be an instrument used in the violation of your rights, then that becomes a complex issue."

"The Quadriga could have written it into everyone's contract: take it or leave it."

"Which brings me back to my original point. They could have, but we're not building a prison or a police state up here. The whole idea is supposed to be that we're constructing a better version of humanity, aren't we? And that shouldn't start with the default assumption that people are always up to no good and need spying on."

"Seems moot to me when everybody's got a recording function in their lenses," Jessica says. She looks huffy, her short legs working hard to keep up with Nikki's stride.

"Except the crucial difference is the recordings are made and controlled by individuals, not the Seguridad, the Quadriga or the FNG. The grabs belong to whoever recorded them, which is why people have to state in a will that they surrender their recordings for police scrutiny in the event of a suspicious death."

"I assume our Mr Korlakian didn't make such a stipulation?"

"Apparently not," Nikki replies, leaving it at that. She would rather stay away from the fact that Omega moved in circles where it was mutually understood that you didn't want posthumously accessed recordings incriminating the people around you.

"But the point is that it's one thing for a private individual to be recording people, still another when it's a corporate or government entity. That's why etiquette states that I have to display a rec light if I'm recording as a cop, but not when I'm off-duty. Doesn't that etiquette extend to the FNG? I mean, I'm guessing you're recording right now, but your lens ain't glowing. Your cheeks are though."

Jessica looks flushed, and not from the effort of hustling through the gathering numbers on Mullane. Busted.

"Hey, don't get self-conscious about it. I mean, why should you FNG guys play by the rules when everybody else don't?"

"At least I'm trying to do some investigating," Jessica protests, stopping on the spot and folding her arms like she ain't playing the game no more.

"What do you think I've been doing this whole time?"

"Treading water. You barely scratched the surface with Jacobs back there."

"He didn't know anything. I could tell that straight off."

"He gave us some pointers though. If Korlakian got into fights, shouldn't we be finding out with whom and about what? It strikes me as unlikely this will all turn out to be about his day job. He had to have been dabbling in other things."

Nikki thinks about that Glenfarclas bottle, the special forces types who took control of Dock Nine, Brock Lind telling her how Omega paid him to divert their shipment. Damn straight he was dabbling in other things, but she can't investigate any of that stuff with this stoolpigeon observing, recording and reporting back.

Boutsikari has thus far been happy to turn a blind eye and feign ignorance regarding the likes of Nikki's unofficial practices. It keeps everybody content and onside while giving himself deniability. But now that he's being squeezed by the FNG, ignorance is no longer bliss. He'll be only too happy to receive whatever hard proof Jessica can supply, giving him the leverage he needs to manipulate Nikki, to discredit her or to flat-out fire her.

He told her he needs results and that he thinks she's the best chance of getting them, but if he really believed that, he wouldn't have saddled her with an FNG spy. From where Nikki's standing, it looks like she's got two options. She can do this with one hand tied behind her back and one eye closed, knowing she's being set up to take the fall when she inevitably fails; or she can pursue the truth where she knows it is likely to lie, and in doing so lay herself open in a dozen different ways.

Two options, but ultimately they're just different flightpaths to Planet Fucked. Which means she's gonna have to find herself a Plan C.

WHAT LIES BENEATH

It's the smell of food that tips the balance.

Alice is standing with her arms folded, facing down Nikki and creating a stand-off via the simple expedient of refusing to keep walking down Mullane. The weakness in this strategy is that Freeman could decide to resume her hurried stomp towards the static station, which would require Alice to follow in the service of her role as official observer Jessica Cho. If Nikki calls her bluff, she doesn't have a play, so she needs to come up with a move before that happens, or accept the consolation prize of merely staying close to her subject.

She wants to observe Freeman here, in her natural habitat. That, after all, is the point of the exercise.

Mullane is a narrow channel compared to what she's seen on W2, but broad for an older district. It looks wider the busier it gets, the bustle of human traffic emphasising the distance between facing shop fronts by filling it with colour and movement. The air here feels warmer than over on Central Plaza, even though the thermometer is stating that it's within the same range as everywhere else. It must be the cooking odours, the thump of music and the sense of a throng. It makes her feel outdoors, but in a different way from how Central Plaza feels like outdoors. Over there it's like it's always daytime, always morning, even: breezy and fresh. Here, in keeping with what she has been told, it always feels like night, and a muggy summer night at that.

"He gave us some pointers though. If Korlakian got into fights, shouldn't we be finding out with whom and about what? It strikes me as unlikely this will all turn out to be about his day job. He had to have been dabbling in other things."

She's still waiting for a response. Freeman is weighing things up, but it's only a matter of time before she starts asking herself who this little girl thinks she is, to be criticising her investigation like this.

"Why do you want me out of Mullane so fast?" Alice asks, deciding to stay on the front foot.

"I don't want you out of here. We've got to go talk to Korlakian's neighbours, and his place is over on—"

"Yes you do. You were looking for a reason to speak to Jacobs someplace else and now you're acting like Korlakian's neighbours are about to ship out for good."

"As you just reminded me, we're up against a clock here. So unless your lens got a location fix on Freitas and Dade, then I don't think there's anybody else around here that we ought to be talking to."

It sounds like a clincher for shipping out again, which is when the aromas elicit a hormone response that helps Alice dig her heels in. It's like barbecue: frying meats and spices. The memory of her visit to NutriGen and what the "meat" might truly consist of does little to alleviate the effect. In the best tradition of peasant cuisine turning scant resources into the tastiest of dishes, she's been told that the bars and diners on W1 have been perfecting their fare for decades. She was sceptical about this until her nose caught the first whiff.

"I'm hungry," she says. "This is the first time I've had the chance to visit Mullane and I've heard the food's great here. Or at least affordable. I'm on government wages, remember. Not supplemented by, you know, a second income," she adds, leaving it hanging.

Nikki nails her with a penetrating stare, like she's trying to look inside and see how much "Jessica" truly knows.

Her expression relaxes but doesn't soften. It goes from intense scrutiny to a smile Alice finds just the wrong side of cruel.

"Know what? Fuck it. I could use a bite and a drink myself."

Nikki leads Alice back along Mullane, making her way purposefully towards a place called Sin Garden. The music sounds like an assault from the second the doors open, thumping around a labyrinthine interior that seems designed to maximise the number of dark corners. Alice catches a glimpse of a dance floor somewhere beyond the maze of booths and tables, waiting staff slaloming a sweaty throng. She is instantly certain the place is in violation of its capacity restrictions, and the ambient temperature is noticeably in excess of recommended norms, with implications for both comfort and hygiene.

The smell of food is strong enough to indicate inadequate ventilation systems in the kitchen and very probably in the customer areas too. However, the principal effect of this is to precipitate a rumbling sensation in her gut, one that feels all the more pronounced as she takes note of the long queue before the hostess station. There has to be thirty people waiting for a table in the cramped and busy restaurant section.

Nikki waves towards the main bar and a man emerges from behind the gantry, bounding towards them with exaggerated geniality. He is thin but wiry, light on his feet but something dynamic in his gait. To Alice's eyes, he could equally have been a dancer or a boxer before he ended up here, where she reckons he could probably make use of either talent. His hair is close-cropped and silver-grey, a scar down his right cheek from the temple to the jawline.

"Nikki Fixx," he hails, holding up a hand for her to slap.

"Lo-Jack," Nikki responds.

They are friendly but not warm, familiar but not close.

"So what kinda trouble do you ladies feel like getting into this evening?" he asks.

"Allow me to introduce Jessica Cho of the . . ." she begins, then lets it tail off. "Know what? Fuck it. Lo-Jack, this is Jessica. She's my guest. I'm showing her around town, and she's hungry."

Lo-Jack glances momentarily into the restaurant section and gestures two waitresses towards a table whose occupants are in the process of leaving.

"No problem. Step right this way."

He leads them past the line towards the now free table, which is already in the process of being reset. There are loud sighs and angry exclamations from people in the queue. Alice feels her cheeks burning, but Nikki doesn't even give the impression of having heard.

One of the waitresses hands each of them a menu. Nikki gives it straight back without looking at the card or the woman proffering it, addressing the words "the usual" to Lo-Jack in a barely audible grunt.

Lo-Jack responds with a dismissive phony salute.

"I'll just be a mo," Nikki tells Alice. "Gotta go to the bathroom. You guys get her whatever she wants to eat and make sure she gets a mojito."

Alice has glimpsed enough of the menu to see this cited at the top of the drinks list as the house specialty. Apart from a selection of rare malts, it is the most expensive item there, costing more than twice the priciest meal.

Lo-Jack twigs her reaction.

"Don't sweat the prices, honey. If you're with Nikki, it's all on the house. Now what can I get you?"

The food reaches the table long before Nikki returns. The waitress also places down a mojito in front of Alice despite her having said she didn't want it.

Alice sits for a few minutes staring at both meals, mindful of how she was brought up not to eat until everyone has been served, but eventually the smell, her appetite and her suspicion that Nikki is on more than a bathroom break prompts her to tuck in. She wolfs down several eager mouthfuls of what is, as Nikki described, a decent approximation of a burger. She's certainly had worse on Earth, though she has to bear in mind that they do say hunger is the best sauce.

Meantime Nikki's burrito lies there going cold. Alice wonders what other business she might be conducting right now, and whether it is the real reason she changed her mind in suddenly deciding to come here. Helen Petitjean had left little doubt why her nickname is Nikki Fixx, and her unsubtle efforts to forewarn everyone they had spoken to today alluded unmistakably to whatever it was she didn't want them talking about.

Yet suddenly she had opted to bring Alice here, where she had dispensed with the warning and was flagrantly accepting gratuities from the management. What was that about? Did she think that "Jessica" accepting a free meal and a mojito was going to compromise her enough to provide some kind of leverage? If so she was very much mistaken. Alice intends to pick up the tab, laying down a marker to Nikki and to Lo-Jack.

Nikki saunters back at last, conspicuously unhurried, swaggering her way past the people in the line like she's basking in their resentment. It's reprehensible, and yet there is a secret part of Alice that is thrilled to witness it. She finds herself wishing she could have just a little of Nikki's essence running through her. Alice expends so much energy worrying about staying in line, following protocols and avoiding giving offence. Wouldn't it be cool to care just a little less? To be able to upset a bunch of strangers and not force yourself to do some kind of penance for it later?

Nikki slides into her seat and grabs the burrito with one hand, tearing at it messily with her teeth. Rice and sauce spill from her lips, trickling down her face and onto the table. She wipes her mouth with her sleeve and washes down the food with a gulp of an amber liquid Alice has not been able to identify. It smells like it could be whisky, but the volume is too large for it to be a spirit, surely. Surely.

"That hit the spot?" Nikki asks, as Alice gulps down the last of her burger. "You feeling better? Less cranky maybe?"

"Better, yes."

"You ain't touched your mojito. Get it down you," she says, through a mouthful of food, more of which tumbles down her chin. "Best mojitos in Seedee, this place."

Alice makes a play of nudging the mojito away from herself, towards the centre of the table. She says nothing but looks Nikki in the eye.

"What? You're gonna tell me you don't drink? Yeah, that's the kinda *joie de vivre* that should see you fit right in at FNG."

"Why did you bring me here?" Alice asks.

"You said you were hungry."

"No, I mean why did you bring me here specifically? Why are you showing me all this? The bar has a quite vast variety of what

I assume to be contraband alcohol openly on display, being merely the largest of about a dozen code violations I could list within thirty seconds of walking in the door. Code violations for which the proprietor has no expectation of being cited, for reasons directly related to the fact that he has no expectation of you paying for anything that is on this table."

"I like to think of it as community spirit," Nikki replies, washing down another bite of burrito with what, on balance, Alice decides is indeed probably Scotch.

"It looks a lot like bribery and corruption to me. So why would you show this to an official FNG observer?"

"I told you, I believe in full disclosure. I'm trying to help you understand the context against which this investigation is going to be conducted, which is a lot more grey and grimy and a lot less morally binary than you're used to."

"How would you know what I am used to?"

"I know how the FNG views things. They're all hung up on the ideals of this society we're building, and by that I mean the society that will be on the *Arca*, surviving in space for generations. Except they forget that we already got a society here, trying to survive in space. It ain't as slick and pretty as the academics and politicians would like it. But it ain't as ugly as they believe it is either. Point being, it is what it is, and we all do what we have to so we can all get along. Ain't no need to go getting our panties in a bunch over smuggled booze or whatever else gets you through the night."

"And what about the very people who are supposed to uphold the law and enforce the rules taking bribes and kickbacks? Is their corruption necessary for your society to get along?"

Nikki seems amused at Alice's indignation.

"You're making it sound a lot grander than it really is," she says, shaking her head. She wipes some sauce from her plate with her finger, holding it up so that it glistens for a moment before she pops it into her mouth.

"The black economy is the lubricant that keeps the whole engine running smoothly up here. That's the thing I need you to get your head around."

It strikes Alice that all of this is bordering on a confession. She isn't making specific actionable admissions, but it would be enough to put a spoke in her wheels by getting her suspended pending an investigation. However, Alice is not sure how much of what is being said will prove audible against the sound of the music. Which would be another reason Nikki brought her here.

"You're kidding yourself if you think you can stay squeaky clean on Seedee and still hope to get anything done, so why don't you drink your mojito. Make that your symbolic acceptance that you're gonna get your hands dirty. You won't get in trouble," she adds mockingly.

Alice pauses then reaches for the glass, but only so that she can push it a few inches further away.

"I know I'm new here, but I'm not ready to accept your jaded model of CdC after two hours on Mullane. I don't see the point of being a police officer if you have no respect for the law and just some self-serving arbitrary notion of right and wrong."

Nikki pauses mid sip of her whisky. The amused look is gone, something altogether more serious in her eyes.

"That's exactly what I'm trying to tell you here: something you won't have learned at your Ivy League school or at any FNG induction bullshit. When you're a cop, right and wrong ain't about hard and fast rules, and sometimes it ain't even about laws either. Forget the brochure version of CdC because you won't find any answers in there. If we want to make headway in this investigation, we're gonna have to deal with people and move in places that represent the harsher realities of life here. That means you gotta be prepared to turn a blind eye to lesser crimes."

"And who decides which are the lesser crimes, Detective Freeman?"

"In my experience, bootlegging and payola are less of a threat to society than flaying a human being and turning the body into a real-life exploded anatomy diagram."

"And in my experience, laws aren't worth anything to a society unless the people enforcing them respect what they mean."

From Nikki's sour look and her silence, Alice knows she laid a glove on her with that.

Freeman is only on the ropes for a moment, though. Her crooked smile returns and she directs her gaze towards the contentious mojito.

"Can't believe you're gonna to let that go to waste."

Alice interprets it as a concession of defeat, though if so it is a pitiably small victory.

As Nikki reaches across to grasp the glass, a man dressed in overalls appears at the edge of their table, red-faced and breathless.

"Nikki," he gasps, causing her to turn.

She looks at him, calm and curious. She gives no indication whether she recognises him, but clearly he knows who she is.

Alice didn't see where he arrived from. This would be difficult to discern, given the confusing layout, but she's pretty sure he can't have come from outside, or she'd have noticed his approach. He looks like he's been running, which makes her wonder how far this place goes on for. Maybe he has come from the dance floor, but he doesn't look dressed for it.

He leans over, cupping a hand to Nikki's ear to make himself heard over the music. Alice doesn't catch a word of it, but she can tell from his expression that it is as serious as it is urgent.

Nikki looks up at him, suddenly alert.

"Downstairs?" she says. "Right now?"

He nods gravely.

"Shit."

She gets up from the table, the man already striding ahead to lead her.

Nikki turns to Alice.

"You stay here, understand? Don't move. Let me handle this."

Alice watches her hurry out of the restaurant area. She deliberates for precisely as long as it takes to realise that if she doesn't follow immediately, she will lose Nikki in the labyrinth, then gets to her feet and starts running.

Nikki disappears from view as soon as Alice rounds the first corner, but she remains traceable from the sight of people moving sharply to let her through. Alice has to give her this much: for all her faults, when somebody needed her urgently, she dropped everything and went flat-out to assist.

Alice hurries along in her wake, racing to pass the people Nikki just scattered before they merge back into her path again. Veering right beyond the edge of the dance floor, she turns into a short corridor just in time to see a bouncer step aside, holding open the door he is guarding in order to let Nikki pass through without breaking stride.

Alice is extended no such courtesy. He lets the door swing shut and steps in front of it, blocking her path.

"I'm with her," she calls out over the ubiquitous thump of the music. "Sergeant Freeman."

The bouncer looks sceptical, saying nothing, not flinching in his stance.

Alice gestures a command so that her ID – or rather, Jessica's ID – flashes up in his lens.

"I'm on FNG business. Official observer. Let me through."

The bouncer steps aside with a reluctant expression, muttering "It's your funeral," as he holds open the door.

She heard Nikki say "Downstairs" but it's still a surprise to see a staircase descending ahead of her. In her perception of CdC, everything is built upwards from the curving surface of the wheels' interiors, with nothing beneath except for the utilities infrastructure: vents, ducts and crawlspaces. Clearly, she's going to have to revise that quickly.

Alice almost trips in her haste, shooting her hands out against the encroaching walls to steady herself. They are rough, grazing her palms on a crude plaster skim indicating that it is an ad-hoc amendment to the structure, rather than part of the original design. Hitting the bottom, she finds herself in a dimly lit passageway, several doors on either side. Neither Nikki nor the man who came to fetch her are anywhere to be seen.

She can still feel the thump of the beat from upstairs disturbing the very air. The music itself is comparatively muted and indistinct, making the space seem all the more isolated and claustrophobic.

She hears a sharp crack, the unmistakable sound of an impact on human flesh from behind the door to her right. It is followed by a gasp of pain, then a muffled moan.

Alice tries the door but the handle turns uselessly. It is maglocked, the interface showing up on her lens as inaccessible. She doesn't have the clearance level or the local override code.

She hears more noises from the other side of the passage: a strained grunt of effort, a spluttering cry of agony. Her lens indicates that this interface is active but not locked.

She turns the handle cautiously. Music hits her first, different from upstairs, before she opens the door wide enough to reveal something she's going to have a hard time unseeing.

The room is done out like something from an eighteenth-century French chateau; or at least the set from a cheap sim trying to evoke the period. There are couches and chaises longues, as well as some kind of swing contraption suspended from the low ceiling. There are ten, maybe a dozen people in there: she can't be sure. It's diffi- cult to tell given their interlocking positions. There are heads here, bottoms there, a churning blur of writhing nakedness.

Her intrusion is largely ignored, but for one guy looking up and saying: "Hey, you wanna jump in?"

A galaxy of no, she thinks, closing the door again, wishing she could thus undo opening it.

Belatedly it hits her, the name of the place: Sin Garden. As well as a bar, it's some kind of sex club – literally an underground sex club.

She looks back towards the stairs and then to the other doors on either side of the passage, wincing to think what might be behind them, and how bad it must be if Nikki had to come running. Then she looks closer into the gloom and observes that where she thought there was a dead end, the corridor actually continues after a ninety- degree turn.

The turn reveals itself to be an s-bend, leading to a longer straight, this time without rooms leading off it. The walls are solid, lined with ducts and conduits, thick lines of cable and piping. She real- ises that though she has not passed through a door per se, she is no longer within the Sin Garden premises, but in a passageway somewhere beneath Mullane.

The music is all but gone, only a hint of the beat detectable. She can still make out a hubbub of voices and wonders why that would be carrying where the music did not.

She starts as she senses movement around her, her reflexes responding as though she is being snuck up on or ambushed. There is nothing to be seen, only a rumbling vibration from the floor indicating that something just went shuttling past beneath her. A few paces further on, she sees a warning sign on the wall, above an access panel inset into the floor. It features a stick-figure image of a body falling away from a ladder.

DANGER OF DEATH:
MAINTENANCE SHAFT DESCENDS TEN METRES.
HATCH WILL NOT OPEN UNLESS HARNESS
CONNECTION IS DETECTED AT TETHER POINT.

There is a steel loop anchored to the floor next to the panel, a run-stop pulley system monitored by a sensor. The sight of it makes her queasy, as does anything that reminds her that for all it looks like a thriving city, CdC is still clinging permanently to the edge of oblivion. Ten metres, the sign says. She wonders what is beneath the bottom of the shaft: how thick and robust is the final barrier between life and airless freezing death. She wonders also what just rumbled beneath her feet, because that didn't come from ten metres below.

She is sure the hubbub is getting louder. Maybe she is underneath the dance floor, or maybe she is nearing a route back up.

As she approaches another bend, the sound gets louder still. She turns the corner into a longer stretch, still flanked by pipes and cabling, but at the end, about fifty metres away, is an open doorway. Through it she can see that the space widens out into a concourse.

She is disorientated by the layout but she is pretty sure this is a second thoroughfare vertically parallel with Mullane. It is low-ceilinged and not as broad, but there are hordes of people traversing it, almost as many as she saw on the street above.

Jeez, she wonders, not everybody's down here having sex, are they?

Then she catches a glimpse. Like upstairs, again it's the sight of people getting out of the way that she is able to track, though this time it's more sudden, more violent. People scatter, briefly clearing the view from the doorway to Nikki, who is wrestling someone to the ground.

Alice sees a woman rush to intervene, crouching down and attempting to haul Nikki off whoever she is trying to restrain.

"Hey!" Alice calls out, breaking into a sprint.

The woman looks up to see where the cry came from, then turns her head to look down the passage. She climbs to her feet as Alice reaches the last few metres, balling her fists and readying herself in a stance.

Alice steels herself and accelerates, building up momentum for the moment of impact. Then a door swings shut at the end of the passage, and a fraction of a second later the floor disappears from beneath her feet, swinging away from her in two separating halves.

Alice tumbles into blackness, hitting cold metal a few feet below with a flailing thump, before something solid slides into place above her and seals with a hiss.

She rolls on to her back and hammers at the panel that has just closed above her head. It makes a loud and tinny bang, like she's inside a drum. It's not heavy but it is metal, so she isn't going to be able to punch through it or even buckle it out of its frame. She tests the sides, thumping them with the edges of her balled fists. They are less giving, more substantial. What is above is a lid. This is a crate. She's trying not to panic, but she can't help thinking about that hiss, the implications for whether this box she's just become trapped in is airtight.

There is a shudder, the smallest sense of vertical movement, as though the crate has been raised up and is no longer resting on the floor of the tunnel. At the same time, she feels all her hair stand on end, a response to something electrical, magnetic. The box begins to move, accelerating along the axis she is lying. She puts her hands to the sides, anchoring herself so that she isn't bashed around. She recalls a moment from childhood: a spider climbing into an open matchbox, a boy sliding it closed and shaking it. His gleeful hand sliding it open again, shaking out the broken pieces.

Alice feels a pull towards the bottom as the crate rapidly decelerates. Then it shunts sideways, smoothly but swiftly, like it's being moved to a new channel, and a moment later it is accelerating again.

She smells something, sweet but sickly. Cloying.

Alice feels woozy. She knows seasickness is worst when you can't see the horizon, your eyes unable to track the movement your body is feeling. Her eyes can see nothing at all, but she doesn't think that's the source of the weakness creeping over her.

She feels her arms become limp, her eyes begin to close.

THE DEPARTED

People are scattering all around her as Nikki tumbles across the floor, trying to maintain her grip on the guy she's just tackled. She's grateful it's all coated in that rubberlike stuff they're so fond of in the reclaimed sub-surface. Everything is covered in it here beneath Mullane.

Before it became a neighbourhood of any description, the area was primarily used for construction and fabrication works, back when they were building this section of what became the first wheel. Mag-line conveyor channels were laid beneath sub-surface storage vaults, distributing materials to manufacturing facilities as the section gradually grew its way around into a ninety-degree arc. So much had to be done beneath the surface of each extension before the canopy caught up and allowed people to work above without EVA suits.

Later, once Mullane got repurposed as a residential area, the mag-line channels remained functional but these days they are primarily used by through traffic, passing underneath the neighbourhood. However, the vast network of suddenly redundant sub-surface storage vaults offered all kinds of potential in a burgeoning entertainment district.

Nikki and her fugitive are rolling over and over, trying to be the one who finishes on top. According to her lens his name is Anders, but that's merely the hacked alias he's currently rocking. His real name is Fernando.

Folks are getting out of the way so they don't get bowled over but they're not panicking. Two assholes rolling on the floor trying to throttle each other is not exactly an exotic sight around these parts.

She doesn't identify herself as Seguridad. It's not like anybody would rush to her aid out of a sense of civic duty if she did. They'd just look the other way a little harder.

She's almost managed to pin him when Nikki feels two hands around her shoulders, trying to pull her off. Fernando's girlfriend Julia just came up on the flank. She must weigh forty kilograms soaking wet, so she's not the strongest, but her intervention is enough to loosen Nikki's hold, allowing Fernando to change grip and shift his weight. The world turns upside down again and suddenly he's on top of her.

Lying flat on the floor, Nikki looks up in time to see Julia staring intently towards the corridor leading back to Sin Garden, where a door has just closed. She signals to her partner and he lets go, rolling off and scrambling to his feet. The two of them book, zigzagging among the oncoming bodies. They're out of sight before Nikki is even upright, impossible to track in the crowd. Nikki knows there's got to be eight or nine doorways out of here. They're gone.

A young male Seguridad officer in uniform hurries over to where she is crouching, breathless. She doesn't know how much he's seen, but he came to check on her rather than chase after fugitives, so at least she knows he's got his priorities straight. She thinks of some of the overeager Nazi whackjob rookies she worked with in LA. They'd leave the victim bleeding out while they chased after the perp, thinking only of the take-down.

"You call this in?" he enquires.

He knows to ask, understands that it's her decision. Attaboy.

"Carlos, right?" she asks, though her lens already tells her this.

"Yes, ma'am."

"Forget it. I know who they are and what it was about. I'll be catching up to them soon enough."

"Understood."

Nikki makes her way back upstairs to Sin Garden, where it's really filling up.

When she gets back to the dining area, there is no sign of Alice. Given the growing line waiting for a table, she is surprised to find that their plates are still there, the remnants of their food not enough to look unfinished. Maybe it's the untouched mojito that swung it, sitting in no man's land between the two plates.

"You see where she went?" Nikki asks their waitress.

"She took off after you."

"Just like I told her not to."

Oh well, Nikki thinks. The girl didn't follow an explicit instruction, so it's her own lookout where she ended up. Nikki can't be responsible for her, and she can't waste time searching either. She's got pressing inquiries to make: an urgent investigation to pursue.

DAMAGED GOODS

Alice opens her eyes and lets out an involuntary gasp. It takes her mind a while to remember why but her body recalls instantly, reacting with shock. Her memories fall into place quicker than in recent awakenings, but there's still something sluggish about the time her brain takes to come online.

There is light: that is the first improvement upon her previous situation. And she is stationary, which is the second. This proves less clement when she discovers that it extends to her own ability to move.

"Hey there," says a friendly male voice, noticing that she is back among the living. "You're okay. Don't try to move just yet, though. There's a scan running to check you haven't damaged anything. And the restraints are to make sure you don't hurt yourself until we're sure whatever you got drugged with has worn off."

She is lying on a table, her hands, ankles and neck secured by insulated loops, reminding her of her journey to Heinlein Station. Unlike on the elevator, there is no emergency override option visible in her lens. In fact, there is no information appearing there whatsoever.

She turns her head and takes in her surroundings. It doesn't look like any kind of infirmary or first-aid station. She is in a cluttered, low-ceilinged room strewn with tech in various states of disrepair. If this is any kind of hospital, it's one for machinery.

There is a man seated at a workbench, looking back at her. She had a momentary fear that it would turn out to be the man she saw in the crowd on Central Plaza, but he was white. This guy has dark skin and grey dreadlocks running half the way down his back, tied in a band presumably to keep them from getting in the way. She can vividly imagine them dragging circuitry and components

133

off the edge of a workbench. His expression is relaxed, which seems at odds with the chaos of the room, and with the fact that he has a prisoner strapped to a table.

Alice can feel her heart thump as she becomes conscious enough to appreciate the gravity of her situation.

"Where am I?" she asks anxiously. "Who are you?"

Once again, there is no information appearing on her lens. She goes to reach for her wrist disc to run a systems check, but not only are both her arms locked in place, a glance reveals that the disc itself is missing.

"The far more interesting question here would appear to be: Who are *you*?"

He spins around on a revolving stool, enough to reveal that he has her wrist disc clamped in a brace attached to several devices, one of which is a micro-projector making a screen of the wall in front of him.

Alice's familiar lens overlay readout is scrolling in front of him, displaying information that is supposed to have a biometric lock, visible literally to her eyes only. He has hacked into it to a degree that she has been explicitly assured is impossible.

"What are you doing?" she asks, her voice catching in her throat.

"I'm erasing your memory."

He speaks with a calm that unnerves her.

She looks around at all the disassembled tech, her mind dredging up the worst crazy rumours she grew up hearing about CdC. Her wrists strain almost involuntarily against the loops as she wonders what kind of a nightmarish cyber chop-shop this might be.

He reads it, lets out a quiet laugh.

"No, don't panic. I don't mean your actual memory. Not even Prof G has designs on that shit. I'm talking about your grabs, your lens uploads. There are some people who are concerned that you were backstage without a pass, so to speak, snooping where you weren't welcome and witness to what you had no right to see."

"If you mean the orgy, please, I swear, I was only in there a second and I have no intention—"

"They didn't tell me what specific content the problem was, and

I didn't ask. Best for my own protection and peace of mind. I was asked to wipe everything from today, so that's what's happening."

"But you can only wipe what's local," she states, hoping to warn him that his actions here will have an indelible record. "You're going to get in real trouble for this. My grabs are automatically uploaded to FNG."

"Yeah, they were," he says, hovering a finger over her wrist unit. He makes a gesture to execute a command. "And now they're gone."

She glances at the wall and sees what he was accessing suddenly vanish.

He seems very calm, but perhaps this is because he doesn't know who he is really dealing with and how dire the consequences of abducting her. She doesn't want to break cover, but she's scared of where this might be going. To keep playing Jessica is looking like a risk she can't afford to take.

"Whatever it is, I saw what I saw," she insists. "As you said, you can't wipe my *real* memories."

"Nope. But witness testimony doesn't have the same traction without grabaciónes backing it up. Things tend to be a lot less binding when it comes down to 'he said, she said'."

"The 'she said' may have a little more traction than you're anticipating when 'she' happens to be the incoming Principal of the FNG Security Oversight Executive."

He pauses a moment, fixing her with a stare. It's long enough for her to think she has thrown a clog in his gears. Then he points a finger towards the projection of her lens readout.

"Yeah, um, I caught that pretty early. But too late for it to make a difference. See, 'she' was concealing that rather salient fact, otherwise I wouldn't have taken this gig."

"Let me out of here, right now," Alice says. She tries to make it sound like a command, but she doesn't pull it off, her pitch at outraged coming off more as desperate.

"Just as soon as I'm done here. And I wasn't kidding about the lingering effects of the drug. You stand up now, you're liable to fall right down again, and I don't want you any more pissed at me than you already are."

"There are ways to mitigate that. Who are you?"

"Way I see it, the fact you don't *know* that is among the things I got going for me, and I'm not about to give it up."

"Who are you working for? Who gave you this gig?"

"And I'm afraid that's another question you can't compel me to answer."

"You'd be surprised. I could compel you on to the next free shuttle bound for Heinlein. It would be in your long-term interest to cooperate. Who are you working for? How did I get here?"

"Even if I was minded to, I could only answer one of those questions. You were sent here in a mag-line crate, but I don't know how you ended up inside it. I was given payment and instructions separately."

"Payment in advance? No proof required that you're delivering on your end?"

"It's a matter of trust. Mainly of me trusting them – whoever they might be – to wrap my legs around my neck and use my ass for flechette practice if I fail to deliver."

"You're really claiming you don't know who they are?"

"That's right. And it didn't appear they knew who you really are, either. That particular revelation was my own special surprise to unwrap."

"Have you heard of a man named Dev Korlakian? AKA Omega?"

He looks at her blankly, but she can tell it's not a no. He's stonewalling again.

"Remember what I said before, about mitigation? Toss me something here."

He shrugs.

"Okay. Yes, I have heard of him."

"Do you know who he was working for?"

"NutriGen," he replies.

"I thought you were trying *not* to annoy me. Who else was he working for?"

"I'm not sure I'm minded to answer that, Alice. But I have to say I'm mighty curious that you've used the past tense twice when asking about him. Are you saying Omega reached the end of his alphabet?"

Alice realises she's just screwed up. She doesn't know who this guy is or who he's connected to, and she's just told him Korlakian is dead. From the current context, it's unlikely he will assume that it was from a sudden illness or an accident at work.

"I'm merely trying to locate Mr Korlakian and his known associates," she says, closing the stable door as this horse gallops off towards the horizon. "And it's 'Dr Blake'."

"Oh, don't I know it," he replies, indicating the readout. "And most definitely not Jessica Cho."

"Wait, can you just edit that stuff?" Alice asks.

FNG identity protocols prevent her from falsifying her ID information. She was able to get her tags amended to pretend she was a junior FNG staffer, but even that had to be carried out under official endorsement. Her problem here is that, as Nikki was so aware, nobody is going to talk to her while they know what she represents.

He holds up his hands, wiggling his fingers eagerly, like a magician onstage or a surgeon about to cut.

"That would be illegal," he answers, smiling.

She knows that on Earth it's the wrist unit that broadcasts whatever identifying information you wish to share, meaning that what appears on the viewer's lens is no more reliable than asking someone their name. Government and corporate premises usually run a localised identity-verification database, tracking everyone who is on-site, but outside there are just too many people. Up here, however, it's a closed and limited environment: like a single giant building.

"How is it done?" she asks.

"Your lens runs facial-recognition scans on everybody you look at. It then refers to the central database for the corresponding data. That's when permissions come into play: who's allowed to know what about whom."

"I would refer you to my previous remarks about annoying me. I wasn't asking how the system works. I'm asking how you can be editing it."

He gives a knowing chuckle.

"My God. You can't be telling me you've hacked the central database."

The very notion makes her even more woozy than she already was, as this would mean CdC's entire identity system is fatally compromised. If this joker could hack into it, then presumably the Quadriga could manipulate it too, meaning nothing on it is truly reliable.

He shakes his head, amused by the appalled expression on her face.

"What do you think I am, some kind of a god? Nobody can hack the central database."

Alice breathes out again.

"What I *can* do is run a hack that fools the receiver into thinking it has got its information from the CDB, when actually it's coming straight from your local device."

"Could you do that for my wrist unit?"

"Sure. And I could trick it out so that you can edit that information yourself. But this would be a special service I only extend to those in a position to offer *mitigation*," he adds.

"You got yourself a deal," Alice tells him.

"Can I have that in writing?"

"I'm assuming you've already got my verbal agreement on a grab."

"How do I know you'll honour it?"

"This would have to be another matter of trust."

He gives her a look acknowledging that granting her this is his only play.

A few seconds later he is calling up some arcane-looking code screen on her wrist unit, making changes too fast for her eyes to track.

"Out of interest," she says, "what else can you unlock on this thing?"

As he turns to answer, his attention is rapidly diverted by the sound of someone smashing his door down.

HOSTILE TERRITORY

Nikki takes a static over to Scobee, which is deep in the heart of Julio's turf. It's as she walks past one of the bars he runs that she realises there was an upside to having Jessica hanging around her like a fart in zero-g, which is that the girl was effectively a human shield. Long as Nikki showed up somewhere with a conspicuous FNG dork by her side, it immediately let people know she was here on some kind of official business, and not anything they needed to draw their weapons for.

Julio Martinez and his crew started off running protection in Scobee's entertainment district, which was a burgeoning competitor to Mullane at the time. They had a limited line on a supply of rum and tequila which they marketed via a strategy patented in Chicago circa 1929, in that Julio's thugs broke your place up if you didn't stock his booze.

Julio tried expanding into Mullane a few years back, sending his boys in to start fights. Sometimes they escalated into wreckage, but even when they didn't, they succeeded in his intention of damaging a place's reputation. People wanted to unwind and have a good time, and if they couldn't do that safely without worrying that they might end up collateral damage in a brawl, or busted up by some psycho for looking at him wrong, they would stay away.

That was when Nikki stepped in. Essentially she undercut Julio's protection rates, and thus nurtured a mutually beneficial partnership with Yoram Ben Haim. Nikki, with a badge and Seguridad backup on her side, ran Julio's assholes out of town, leaving Yoram with a near monopoly of supplying contraband drink and other illicit commodities.

Mullane thrived due to the security and stability it enjoyed, rapidly outgrowing Scobee, which became synonymous with lone-drinker dive bars and home-stilled gut-rot. The price of this success was that Yoram couldn't keep up with demand, leaving the door open for other suppliers to make inroads into the market. Guys like Lo-Jack can't afford to run low, so they buy from whoever is selling, and it's something of a sacred code among Seedee's bar owners that they don't tell suppliers who else they're buying from. If you want them to take your goods, you have to give them something worth buying and you need to give them it on better terms than your competitors.

These days, one of those competitors is Julio. He retreated to lick his wounds but he never went away. Julio got himself into the import business somehow, with a line on primo tequila. At first people were suspicious, reckoning he was distilling his own stuff and decanting it into old bottles. With the ability to easily fabricate the kit, and a million hidden nooks to set up in, lots of people up here have a crack at brewing their own liquor, but it generally tastes like shit. Even the more accomplished and official attempts at vodkas, gins and tequila taste rough or artificial, which adds to the desirability – and consequent dollar value – attached to genuine imports.

But though Julio's people are known to recycle the bottles – indeed are protective and fastidious about it – what is inside them has been repeatedly proven to be exactly what it says on the label: the real McCoy, one might even describe it. Not just Jose Cuervo either: AsomBroso, Milagro Unico, Casa Dragones and of course, Don Julio Real. Julio is supplying them all, and for the life of them neither Nikki, Yoram, nor anybody else has been able to work out how he is bringing it in.

Julio was never going to settle for just one slice of the market though, which is why Yoram was already getting edgy even before that major shipment went missing. Tension has been rising steeply between the two factions, so the business that went down at Dock Nine is likely to have both sides on a war footing.

Nikki checks her arsenal as she comes up the stairs on to Seddon Street. She's got her standard-issue Seguridad "stopper and sticker" load-out: an electro-pulse blackjack and a resin gun. She's also packing a flechette pistol, which is definitely not standard issue, but nor is it going to do her any good down here, where trouble is most likely to be at close quarters. Those things can cut you up, but they're never going to stop anybody. Well, apart from Kobra, but that was out of the ordinary. Dart had to have been tipped with a rapid-action sedative, like in the micro-capsules fired by 'goodnight guns', the suppression rifles the Seguridad keep in case of riot.

Nikki heads for Ludus, a boxing gym that she's heard Omega liked to frequent. She wants to get the view from Julio's camp while she doesn't have Jessica present to hear the wider context. Nikki doesn't know whether any of Omega's circle will be here, but she's confident she'll be able to threaten or bribe someone who can tell her where to find them.

The place is ringing with thumps and clangs and echoes, a low-ceilinged chamber that looks larger because of the mirrors along two walls. There are two guys sparring in the ring, stop-start stuff, a trainer coaching specific moves. Close by she sees a woman hitting combinations, one-two, one-one-two, sweat flying off taut muscles as she pounds the pads being held up by a dude twice her weight. People are working speedballs and heavy bags, so intent upon what they're doing that Nikki's entrance barely merits the briefest glance.

She feels a pang of guilt, thinking of how long it's been since she worked up a sweat with her clothes on. Then she realises it's only a dormant reflex. She used to feel bad any time she saw someone working on their fitness, but eventually it wore off. She's past the stage of worrying she ought to be in better shape. Now it's more like she's feeling bad about how long it's been since she even felt bad about it. Meta-guilt.

She's got the build of a skinny drinker these days: someone who doesn't mind missing a meal if there's good liquor to be had instead. Or even not-so-good liquor. Fuck it, Qola too if it's all that's on offer. When it comes to getting down and dirty, she's still got the moves when she needs them, but she's not as strong or as fast as she used to be.

She flashes on a time when she *was* strong and fast, the tired-limb feeling she used to luxuriate in when she had pushed herself to the limit. The memory instantly makes her feel blue. Where did that come from?

Had to be the smells in here: a warm fug of sweat, leather and muscle rub, taking her back to a place where she used to lose herself in pumping the weights and pummelling the bags until the salt sweat was stinging her eyes. Back in Venice. Back in LA. Back when she was a real cop.

She hates the way that shit can simply pop into her head, unbidden. She wishes she could stop it, put a seal on it.

She knows there are options. She had the mesh implant way back, and though they don't publicise it, the technology doesn't only allow them to add memory data, but to take it away also. The latter is in the pilot stage, far less advanced and far less sought-after, but she knows people who have had it done, such as Liberty, one of the hookers she looks after.

Like many workers on Seedee, Liberty came up here to get away from something terrible, only to realise she had brought it with her in her head. In desperation, she signed up for the pioneering procedure of having a specific memory erased. It worked, but Nikki isn't sold on it.

"I don't get the nightmares any more," Liberty told her. "I'm not scared all the time. But I have this emptiness, this hole in my mind that I can almost touch. I still feel the same sadness but I can't remember why."

Nikki's not sure whether that might be worse. Her memories eat away at her, attacking without warning and laying a siege that only an oblivion of drink, sex and sometimes violence can lift. But she also knows there's a part of her that needs her pain.

Nikki casts an eye around the machinery, the glistening limbs and straining faces. She's got lucky. Sol Freitas is locked into a gyroscopic weight-resistance machine, knocking out reps with those powerful arms of his. He's in the moment, totally focused, mind elsewhere.

She approaches from the side so that he doesn't see her until it's too late. He can't even begin to disengage from the locking mechanism before she has placed one hand on the modulator, the other guarding the safety override.

His eyes bulge upon recognising her, a shake of the head from Nikki warning him not to move. He knows that if she ratchets up the frequency on this thing, it could rip even *his* arms out of their sockets.

She senses movement from behind and in a twinkling drops her hand from the safety and seizes the jizz cannon, pointing it into the face of the guy who was planning to intervene.

"Seguridad," she warns, but it's the resin gun that really makes him back off. Nobody wants to be dealing with the aftermath of a cum shot.

What the guy doesn't realise is that the paperwork she'd have to fill in to officially report discharging her weapon is just as messy and takes even longer to be fully free of.

Freitas stares at her wordlessly. It's more than the usual code of silence – more like he's trying to contain his rage.

She stares back for a few seconds, seeing if frustration and curiosity cause him to break first.

"What?" he grunts aggressively.

"I'm looking for your buddy, Omega. Hear he didn't show up for work and everybody's just worried sick about him."

She says this so she can monitor his reaction, see if he knows.

He rattles the gyro-grips like he might burst free, enough to rattle the whole frame of the machine. It's not a show of defiance. He's angry and he's hurting. Probably down here working out because he doesn't like where his head would be otherwise.

Oh, he knows.

"Yoram didn't need to send his pet rentacop around. We already got his message."

"I'm here on official Seguridad business. Yoram didn't send me. What message are you talking about?"

"For all the practice they get, you'd think cops wouldn't be such shitty liars. You know what I'm talking about. That fucking slaughterhouse. We saw pictures."

"Yoram sent you pictures?"

"Well he didn't put his signature on them but like I said, we got the message. I take it the Seguridad already ruled it an accident?"

"Well, we like to be thorough, so we're not ruling anything out and we're not ruling anything in. That's why I'm here asking questions."

"Yeah, so I heard. You and your sidekick. FNG got you on their leash pretty good," he adds with bitter derision.

"Don't kid yourself. She's nobody."

Something about this pleases Freitas. Something Nikki doesn't like.

"Used to be Nikki Fixx was the one with eyes everywhere. These days looks like you're gonna be the last to know."

Nikki ignores this. These assholes love making out they've got the skinny on something to try and take your eye off the ball. She isn't falling for it. Something is bothering her, though: a niggling thought in the back of her mind that she can't quite pin down. It's that feeling like she missed something that was right in front of her, but when she tries to concentrate on it, it only seems to get more clouded. It is something to do with Omega, Freitas and Dade, beyond their link to Julio and yet central to it too.

"What time did you last see Omega?"

"Fuck you, Freeman. I ain't telling you shit."

"I'm just trying to find out what happened here. Could be there's someone very dangerous on the loose."

"You know what happened. Omega jacked your shipment and this is Yoram getting payback."

She scoffs.

"You seriously think Yoram would cross that line over missing whisky?"

"Six months ago, probably not. But now he's overreacting because he's seeing the straws in the wind."

"Don't flatter yourself, Sol. I ran Julio and his chimps out of town once before. Yoram knows I could do it again if it came to it. He wouldn't need to do this."

She's trying to provoke him, but instead he looks kind of smug behind the anger, like this is the one thought giving him comfort.

"You look kinda tired, Nikki. Old. Like you been up all night and you can't take the pace no more, you scope me? Gotta be tough work, cutting a man up like butcher meat. Need a strong stomach for that shit. But we'll see how strong your stomach really is when we come back at you, because you're right: someone dangerous *is* on the loose, and his name's Julio fucking Martinez. Julio got a play he ain't made yet, and when that comes through, Yoram's gonna need more than some ageing rentacop bitch to protect him."

A FEARSOME PROSPECT

Alice shudders with fright as the door flies open, trailing sparks from whatever has shattered the lock. It pivots violently on its hinge, catching the edge of a table hard enough to scatter the contents of the half-empty takeout cartons that were resting on it.

The first person through it moves like he was propelled forward by the blast. Even as Dreads lunges towards a workbench, perhaps to retrieve a weapon, this guy is already upon him, unleashing some kind of telescopic cosh that extends and whiplashes in a single movement, catching Dreads on the temple with a horrible sound. It spins him into a second, even more sickening impact with the wall, from which he rebounds and tumbles to the floor like a dead weight.

By this time the second man through the door is on top of him, raining down four or five sharp blows to his back that knock the wind and any residual fight out of him.

They are followed by a woman dressed in a flight suit, like the one Alice was given for her journey here from Earth, except this one looks like it's clocked up a lot more miles. Better fitting, too. She looks Indian or Middle Eastern, mounds of thick black hair tied up in a bun.

Dreads raises his head to look up at her, like he's having to peel it from the floor. From this angle, Alice can't see his expression.

"What the fuck?" he splutters, breathless and shaky. "What is this about?"

"We need your toys and your services, Trick. Urgently and exclusively."

Trick, Alice thinks. It's a nickname, but it's a start.

The guy with the cosh prods it into Trick's back by way of warning, while the other one carelessly disconnects Alice's wrist sensor and tosses it aside. It's the tech it's connected to that they are interested in – and its designer, apparently.

"Come on, you can't take my stuff. I make my living from that shit. I'm always for hire, everybody knows that. You want me to do something for you, you just need to cross my palm."

"No, Trick, you don't work for yourself. Not any more. You work for us now. Starting right away."

She gives a nod and the guy with the cosh lashes him once on the back of each leg. He screams with pain and tries to curl up, but his assailant has a foot pressed to the base of his spine, pinning him in place.

"What the fuck is in your heads?" he yells. "You want me to help you, why you got him beating on me? You think physical pain is conducive to my ability to carry out complex calculations? You think this is gonna encourage my cooperation?"

"I've got him beating on you so you understand that this isn't a negotiation. You're not *helping* us. You're doing what you're told. Starting with getting to your feet, right now. We're shipping out."

The man with the cosh steps aside, allowing Trick to climb up on shaky legs. He casts a glance towards Alice, and it's like she has been suddenly noticed, or belatedly considered relevant.

"Who's this?" asks the other man, bundling Trick's kit into a shockproof case.

"She's nobody. I gave her a sedative. Her eyes are open but she isn't gonna remember shit. Her unit is detached too, so no grabs. Leave her alone."

"Wendy Goodfellow," Cosh Man states. He's getting this from his lens, Alice deduces. Her detached wrist unit is already spoofing her ID, and Trick must have given her an off-the-peg alias. "She's a vital-systems officer on test-flight vehicles. Sounds like the kind of person who would remember details."

"That isn't her name, you asshole," says the other one, walking over to the table where Alice is restrained. "Why do you think she's in this chop-shop? That's hacked information."

"Well, either way, I reckon we better check how responsive she is." A horribly lascivious grin plays threateningly across Cosh Man's face as he speaks. "Long as you're saying she isn't going to remember anything."

Alice feels her pulse race, her wrists and ankles straining against their bonds. She looks towards the woman, who is staring back intently, scrutinising her. Her fingers are tapping commands, her expression one of growing disquiet.

"Walk away now," she states firmly. Gravely.

"Why?" Cosh Man asks.

"Because I don't care what anybody else's lens is telling them." The woman's voice is calm, but in a manner that indicates she's trying hard to contain her true emotion. "I'm running off primary and I know what I'm looking at."

"Which would be what?"

"Project Sentinel."

Both react instantly to these words. They don't ask: "Are you serious?" They don't ask: "Are you sure?" They know she is serious. They know she is sure.

"Holy fuck."

"Well, shit, why you saying walk?" asks Cosh. "Can't we solve ourselves a serious problem while she's restrained like that?"

Alice looks to Trick in desperation. He is in no state to stage any kind of rescue. His fingers are moving though, like he is working something via his lens.

"Did you hear what I just said?" the woman demands, her voice rising. "Don't you understand what she is?"

There is a moment of silence in response, punctured by the smooth whir and clunk of Alice's restraints being unlocked and withdrawing into their housing.

The three intruders trade looks, the two males looking to the woman for their cue.

Alice pulls herself slowly into a sitting position, causing both of the men to start.

Their boss finds her voice once more: resolute, controlled and unmistakably fearful.

"Let's grab what we came for and get the hell out of here."

FROM THE VINE TO THE BOTTLE

It feels hot up here on Yoram's rooftop. It always does. Nikki wonders whether he bribed somebody to adjust the localised temperature settings so that it's more like his native Beirut, or maybe the temperature up here is supposed to be warmer for the benefit of the crops. Almost all of the roofspace on Seedee is used for growing, as these are the only areas that are sufficiently expansive and exposed enough to catch much sunlight. There is a soil bed a metre deep, lined with irrigation channels and programmed sprinklers. Yoram's rooftop is at such a height that there is just about enough gravity to hold the soil in place, but there is the standard breathable membrane on top anyway, to prevent it all floating away if there's an all-stop. On Seedee, every square metre of soil is accounted for and its yield carefully audited: botanists monitoring conditions, rotating crops and adjusting what gets planted according to constantly shifting supply and consumption data.

Nonetheless, cross the right palm with a lot of silver and you can carve a little slice for yourself. Yoram treats this place as his personal oasis, though there's only one small corner that he actually tends. He's got a decent-sized pad by Seedee standards, but when he's home he's usually to be found up here, tending his vines or just sitting out feeling the sun through the canopy.

Nikki is reminded of jetlag any time she's up here. It's that sensation of being out in daylight when your brain is telling you it's night. It's a result of her usually having come from Mullane, where it always seems dark, even outside on the street. The buildings are close together, keeping the ground level permanently in shade, whereas if she's up here with Yoram, it's always daytime.

Back in Lebanon, Yoram ran a wine export business. He wasn't a crook, but he was, by his own description, a slippery operator who played every angle to get the best deal. He was a family man too: a wife and two daughters.

Then he lost all of them in a heartbeat when a truck driver had a seizure and crashed into the café where they were eating.

He came to Seedee because there was nothing left below. His business collapsed after he couldn't bring himself to work there any more, couldn't live in the wreckage of the life he had built. He got a job here on Wheel One in import logistics. Officially he still has it, but he needed other ways to occupy himself. He needed something new to build.

Nikki slept with him once. They don't talk about it. He cried, showed her a ruined side of himself he didn't intend her to see and that Nikki didn't have it in her to deal with. She just had too much wreckage of her own to shore up.

Yoram is crouched at the trellis, secateurs in his hand, a safety line clipped to his belt. The gravity is light up here, and it's easy to forget, especially if you just came from below. Move too fast or trip over your own feet and you could accidentally hurl yourself over the barrier.

He normally seems more relaxed when she visits him in this, his sanctuary. Instead he is agitated and irritable.

"I don't get what is going on, Nikki. It's a mess, but I thought there was a sense to it, you know?"

Nikki doesn't follow, but she knows better than to say as much. She lets him talk. It's better that way.

"These people on the dock. Felicia told me. I get it. High-level operatives, confiscating our stuff. They're shutting us down, I figure. Shutting everybody down. There's a load of new-broom bullshit coming down from FNG. New people in oversight positions, trying to make a name for themselves. We've all seen this before. I can ride it out, I figure. Everybody's in the same boat."

He turns and looks up at her, restless frustration in his expression.

"But now I'm seeing my goods showing up all over Seedee. And I've no doubt it's my goods, because you could walk down Mullane and play bingo with the manifest. Talisker, check. Craigellachie, check. Glenfarclas, check. What the fuck, Nikki? What the fuck?"

She stands there and takes it, being scolded like a schoolgirl. She doesn't have a comeback anyway, but she's primarily interested in watching Yoram, listening to him vent, so she can sniff out what he knows. He hasn't mentioned Omega, or even asked why she's here, and that's worrying her.

She knows she shouldn't let Sol's smack-talking get into her head, but there is a part of her that still can't help thinking like a cop, and that part knows Yoram is the obvious first suspect. Whatever other bullshit Sol threw into their conversation, he clearly believed Yoram was responsible. What she's having to ponder is whether *she* believes Yoram would do something as crazy and reckless as this, never mind as brutal. Surely he'd know the firestorm it would bring down?

But what if Sol wasn't talking smack about this play Julio hasn't made yet? Yoram's just lost a major shipment, leaving him without product and therefore without presence. What is he capable of if he's pushed into a corner?

"Used to be nothing happened around here without you had the skinny. That's what I paid you for. Now I'm starting to wonder whether your eye is still on the ball."

This last bothers her, recalling what Sol said about her being the last to know. Is it possible he wasn't just yanking her chain? The last to know what?

"I mean, what do *you* think is going on, Nikki? Felicia says Omega paid off this pen-pusher to divert our shipment. So these new guys who took our stuff: are they in with Julio? Because the word I'm hearing is that Julio's up to something and he thinks it's going to make him cock of the walk."

"I'm hearing something similar, but no details."

"Sounds like I'm getting caught in a pincer movement. Who are his new friends? Somebody high up in the Quadriga? I want to know what connections he has, because this thing at the dock happened as a knock-on effect of the all-stop on Wheel Two, and it wasn't the only thing that went down around that time."

"Yeah, I heard somebody took a shot at Maria Gonçalves. Who the hell would do that?" she asks idly.

"Oh, that's what you heard?"

His tone is oddly aggressive, challenging. She doesn't get why, but she knows she has annoyed him in a way that has exacerbated how pissed at her he was already.

"What?"

"So you haven't seen the playback?"

"I've been kinda busy," she replies, then hopes the sarcasm in her tone doesn't tip him off that she's dealing with something major.

"Take a moment," he says. "Have a look."

He sends her a list of time-stamped grabs, the top of which she begins to play in her lens. She never likes doing this, as it always makes her feel vulnerable. It's not like she's worried Yoram is going to cold-cock her while she's distracted, but it's too instinctive for reason to override it. The only time she would be comfortable standing up and surrendering that much of her field of view to a recording is alone in her apartment, but then if she were there she wouldn't need to be watching it on her lens.

The grab shows the terrace in front of the Ver Eterna hotel, taken from somewhere up high on the opposite side of Central Plaza. The terrace looks crowded, another of those corporate receptions with waiting staff carrying champagne and canapés, each tray worth more than they earn in a month. At this distance and running as much lens opacity as she dares, she can't make out anybody's face clear enough to ID them. She's pretty sure one tubby bitch close to the front is Hoffman, and because she knows what's about to happen, she figures the bird-like woman near the wall at the back for Gonçalves.

They're all standing around, chatting, being rich and important. Suddenly everybody moves, as though the music just started at a dance. Prof G's entourage go into action, surrounding their boss, getting her down out of sight. Then the all-stop happens. This throws Nikki because she had assumed it happened first, that the all-stop was part of the plan to take a shot at the prof: people floating in zero-g make easier targets, though it was never likely the professor or her people would fail to get her anchored quick-style.

There were some very high-level people on that terrace, one of whom presumably had the authority to call an all-stop in response to what he or she perceived as an attempt on the professor's life. It was a panicky response though, because if the prof was injured, it wasn't going to help anybody's med-evac and first-aid efforts if there was no gravity.

She watches the ensuing familiar ballet: items gracefully floating away while people drift horizontally for a few moments before finding something to clip on to.

She has learned pretty much nothing. She looks at another feed, one showing the same thing from an angle roughly opposite. It shows the view over the heads of the people on the terrace, probably a camera sited on the Ver Eterna surveilling the plaza. It's as busy as always, people traversing the square in all directions. Nikki sees someone in a mask. She has to play it twice to pick out the figure in the crowd, to know whereabouts in the square she should be looking.

The assailant raises a weapon, fires silently, turns away and blends in again. There's maybe two people even notice the incident, and they're not about to give chase. Most of the folks walking Central Plaza are good, respectable and well-paid W2 residents, who have only heard of flechette-toting bad guys in news reports and tales about the older wheel's underworld.

"Okay," she says to Yoram. "Here's my professional analysis. Some asshole lets loose a flechette at Prof G, it hits a bystander instead and there's an all-stop. It's not a serious attempt on the prof's life. Nobody expects a kill shot from a single plastic dart, especially from distance, so it's gotta be some kind of statement. What am I missing?"

Yoram frowns, like he can't believe she's not getting whatever it is.

"What you're *missing* is that the shooter did not. The target was not Gonçalves. It was Alice Blake."

"Who's that?" she asks, damn sure the answer is not going to make her look good.

"She's the incoming Principal of the Security Oversight Executive. Whatever the intention, both dart and statement were aimed at her."

Nikki is reeling.

"How come you know this?" she asks.

"How come you don't?"

"We hadn't been told the identity of Hoffman's successor. Only that they would be taking over soon."

This sounds pitiful as it tumbles from her lips.

Freitas and Yoram are both right. She used to be the first to know, and now she's the last. Paying attention to the wrong things, taking her eye off the ball, letting contacts slide. Getting sloppy. Getting old.

"Someone lensed her on the way here. Shared a capsule and a shuttle with her, put two and two together."

Yoram delicately handles some of his so caringly cultivated fruit.

"The picture was on certain grapevines," he adds damningly. "But there's better footage of her taken during the all-stop."

Nikki starts the first grabación again. The victim is too far away to get a decent look at.

"Not from what I've seen so far," she observes.

"Have patience. Keep watching. She becomes quite conspicuous."

Nikki lets it run past the point where she previously switched feeds. The ballet begins, the crowd on the terrace reacting to the loss of gravity with practised calm. Then she sees a female figure, the one who was shot, drift helplessly into the air, her back to the camera. It figures that it would be a recent arrival. There's always a noob left floating after an all-stop.

The figure slowly turns to face the camera. With a jolt Nikki recognises that it's Jessica.

She experiences a moment of glorious relief at Yoram's misapprehension, and is about to tell him he's got his wires crossed because this is nobody. But the feeling evaporates as she realises she's been played.

How can a kid like that be in charge of the SOE, she asks herself, then realises that her stoolpigeon could be ten years older than she estimated.

Jesus, can this get any worse?

Nikki flashes on "Jessica" tugging her sleeve back down over the bandage she asked about.

Burned it on the stove.

Fuck.

She remembers noting that when she told Jessica about Gonçalves getting shot at, she didn't ask if the professor was okay. At the time, Nikki simply thought this was indicative of a typical bloodless FNG autocrat. But now she can see that the reason Jessica didn't ask was because she already knew. She was right there. She was the one who got hit.

And then, in answer to her question, it does get worse.

The grab shows Blake being rescued by none other than Helen fucking Petitjean, one of the most hawkish moral crusaders on Seedee. If she and her fellow zealots had their way, the Seguridad would become a latter-day equivalent to the religious police that cracked the whip in Arabia before the oil ran out and civil war engulfed the region.

"You got one thing right," Yoram states wearily. "It wasn't a serious attempt on her life. She is yet to put her feet under her new desk and somebody's taking a shot at her. Why would anyone do that when she hasn't even had time to make any enemies? I mean, in Central Plaza, broad daylight, with a non-lethal weapon? It's pure theatre."

Yoram's been thinking about this, she can tell. He looks like he hasn't slept in a while.

"You reckon it was staged?"

"I don't know, but I think its purpose was to create a ready-made excuse to heighten security and close down activities such as ours. 'Look at these people, they're out of control. We need to clean up this town.' That's what they'll be saying."

"Nobody's made a huge deal of it so far," Nikki counters.

The authorities have a bigger matter to deal with right now, but she isn't going to bring that up. She's still waiting for Yoram to mention it, and it's getting suspicious that he hasn't. He knows Alice Blake is the new SOE chief but he doesn't know about Omega?

"It's early," Yoram responds. "Think about these private security types at the dock. They steal our shipment and it ends up in Julio's hands. This must be the secret weapon he's been dropping hints about."

Nikki recalls Sol Freitas and his smug threat, talking about straws in the wind.

Julio got a play he ain't made yet.

"Don't you see? A crackdown would be the perfect cover for some secret Quadriga outfit to take over our operations. It would make sense for them to team up with a useful idiot like Julio, initially at least. Then they'll quietly get rid of him too once he's fulfilled his function. Julio's dumb and egotistical enough not to see that."

Nikki has to concede it wouldn't be the first time the authorities effectively licensed a gangster to practise as a means of getting a handle on the whole trade. However, down in the mortuary right now there are about forty different pieces that don't fit the picture Yoram is putting together.

Unless killing Omega was Yoram's idea of a pre-emptive strike.

There is an intensity about his face as he finally stands up, a stolid determination in his stance as he steps away from his cherished grapes. He gazes out across the rooftops, through the canopy at the Earth, which is a blue globe in the distance.

"You know, it was a bottle of wine," he says, looking down at his hands as though he is holding the object he's talking about. "That's why I'm here. I was walking past a store in Mar Mikhael. I saw this wine in the window, this rare wine. I don't mean some expensive exclusive vintage, but a regional wine that we drank on honeymoon, and that I had seldom seen after that. I went into the store and bought a bottle. I was on my way to meet Yosephina and the girls for lunch.

"If I hadn't stopped to buy the wine, I'd have been sitting at that table too. Or maybe I wouldn't. I can be fussy that way. Maybe I'd have said the sun's going to be in someone's eyes at this table by the window, and we'd have sat someplace else. Maybe it would have made no difference."

He glances briefly at the Earth again, so small and far away. A place out of reach. A place to which he can never return.

"I didn't think I could go on. I watched my business fall apart because I didn't have it in me to work any more. I barely had it in me to eat, to sleep, to function. I came close to killing myself; nobody will ever know how close. Instead I came here. Took a job I could do in my sleep, an insult to the man I once was. That's why I built something else. It's all that keeps me going. I built something here and nobody is taking it away from me."

He turns and looks Nikki in the eye.

"I don't care who they are. If they want a battle, then I will teach them what a man is capable of when he's been through what I have and come out the other side."

THE INTEREST OF CONFLICT

Alice stays where she is as the others make their hurried exit, feeling a rush of woozy nausea from the effort of sitting up. Trick wasn't kidding about keeping her safely in place until he could be sure the drug had worn off. Everything goes swimmy again, dots appearing before her eyes like her vision has become pixelated and the pixels are getting bigger. She lies back down, turning on to her side, hoping it will pass. She feels her eyes close again, the wooziness subsiding but sleepiness taking its place.

Oblivion beckons and something in her embraces it.

When she comes round once more, her hand has gone numb from the weight of her head upon it. She wonders what the hell that gas was, and how long she was out in the second instance, how long she was out in total. She knows what the time was when she started chasing after Nikki Freeman, but with no readout on her lens, she doesn't have a clock to check.

Her memories come back quickly this time, and in the vanguard of their charge is a rush of fear as she reconnects to how she felt as she lay there pinned and helpless with those thugs deciding what they might do to her. But then the woman had seen through Alice's hacked identity and realised they were in over their heads.

She glances across to the workbench and is relieved to see her wrist sensor still lying there where it was carelessly discarded. She doesn't know how the woman deduced her real identity, what she meant by "running off primary" or what Project Sentinel refers to, but the bottom line is that the three of them quickly understood the ramifications of who they were dealing with.

Don't you understand what she is?

Effectively in charge of Seguridad: that's what she is. That's why they bailed.

She wonders if they somehow knew she wasn't recording. Possibly they understood on-sight what Trick was up to with her wrist disc, knew it meant her grabación capabilities were offline. No matter. Just like Trick did, they understood her word alone carried plenty of weight.

She swings her legs tentatively over the edge and checks that her feet are going to be steady enough to support her standing upright. There's still a hint of quease, but it's fading.

She knows it's exacerbated by the wooziness, but now that she can see it all properly, being surrounded by so much largely disassembled tech is giving her culture shock. The sense of chaos in itself is overwhelming, but what is truly unsettling is that the hardware looks so arcane, so alien. It is one of the things people find intoxicating about the idea of CdC: that it is a place where technology may have advanced faster, or merely along different paths to what was known on Earth. She had never given that aspect of it much thought, but the possibilities are coming at her fast now.

She wonders what Zack, that little boy on the shuttle, would make of it all. She remembers his wonder as he took in the activity in the freight bay on Heinlein. *Are any of them androids?* he had asked, and was fully ready to accept it if he was told yes.

When it comes to speculation about the technology on CdC, she wonders why this idea above all holds such fascination. There are robots on Earth, more complex automated systems being developed every day. Artificial intelligence programmes have long since passed the Turing test, or at least demonstrated that the Turing test is no longer particularly useful in helping people define the limits and parameters of AI.

But what the little boy was talking about, the source of enduring wonder (and fear) is the idea of an *embodied* AI: a machine walking around that looks like a person; that is, in fact, indistinguishable from a human being.

The whole point of the Turing test is about whether you could know the difference, and Alice wouldn't know what questions to ask, what responses might be the giveaway. In fact, she would have to admit that if there were lifelike androids up here, she could have met one and not known. And if there was one place where she could envisage the development of such technology, then it would be an off-planet construction facility where an android workforce would save a lot of money and solve approximately two hundred thousand problems.

She crosses to the workbench and places the disc gently back into position on the underside of her wrist, feeling a familiar tug against her skin as it forms a bond. The sensor lights up to signal that it is online and she taps to re-establish the connection to her lens.

Nothing happens.

She tries again. Same deal.

It will have to wait. The bigger issue is where the hell she is and how she can get back to Nikki. Somebody abducted her in order to erase her grabs, which means she saw something she wasn't supposed to. People knew she and Nikki had been asking about Dev Korlakian. She doubts these issues are unrelated, and she wants to hear Nikki's take on that, as well as the abduction she just witnessed, that of Trick.

She pulls the damaged door further open, enough to edge through the gap, cautiously peering each way before she ventures into the passage outside. It is another long narrow channel similar to the one she was sprinting along when the floor swallowed her up. There are pipes and cables running along one wall, opposite the side she emerged from. She estimates she is still in the sub-surface level, the extent of which she truly had no idea about. There appears to be a network of passageways, connecting a host of hidden premises. It is possible that every bar and club she saw on Mullane has a secret annexe down here, and who knows how many other clandestine hidey-holes, such as Trick's workshop.

She walks slowly along the corridor, her steps shaky from the wooziness and not a little fear. There is a clatter from somewhere behind her, causing her to shudder. She looks back and sees only the empty passage. Maybe it came from around the corner. As she progresses, she begins to hear the sound of a crowd once again, as well as the bassy thrumming of muffled music. It appears to be coming from behind the wall to her left rather than from further down the corridor.

The hubbub gets louder, rising in excitement, building up to a crescendo of cheers before gradually tailing off amid laughter and applause.

She looks at the blank wall. There is no way in.

There are no doors, just a uniform skim of plaster. Alice raps her knuckles to test what's beneath it. Feels like steel, like the inside of the door she just came out through.

She retraces her steps and takes a closer look at Trick's door. There is no handle on the outside, no lock interface. She taps her sensor, restarting her lens again, hoping to check for an authorisation status on the lock. The overlay still remains blank.

Alice notices that the side of the door facing into the corridor is covered in plaster. She pulls it to, gripping the outer edge as there is nothing else to hold. It is designed to close by automated command. She doesn't get it quite flush, but enough to observe that if it hadn't been damaged, it wouldn't be apparent that there was a door there at all.

She walks back towards the source of the sound, and as she draws closer she runs her fingers along the wall until she feels a vertical line. A metre further along there is a second.

It is another hidden door, but she has no way of getting it open.

No point in wasting more time, she decides, and resumes her progress down the corridor in search of an exit.

She has barely taken two steps when she is startled by another sudden noise, a sharp hiss like the one that locked her in that crate. This time, by contrast, it is the sound of air escaping as a seal is opened. She sees the door clearly now, swinging inwards, the sounds of music and voices immediately louder. Vapour drifts through the widening gap in billowing wisps as Alice braces herself to face whatever might emerge.

The answer is two drunk guys, laughing and haphazardly colliding in their staggering attempts to keep each other upright.

One of them notices her and holds the door open.

"You coming in?" he asks.

"Thank you," she replies, finding a hint of cheeriness by way of cover, acting like she knows where she's going, like she's supposed to be here.

But where is here?

She steps into what looks like another club. The coloured lights flashing through steamy darkness and the loud music are in keeping with what she saw upstairs in Sin Garden, but though the place is packed, nobody here is dancing. Perhaps, like Sin Garden, the dance floor is housed in a separate area.

Another thing that strikes her is that the crowd is mostly male. They're all just standing around, waiting for something to happen or perhaps talking about what just did.

Alice stays close to the wall, feeling anxious about drawing attention to herself, still unsure about what people will read on their lenses when they see her face. Finally, she sees a woman, but it is a far from reassuring sight. She is sitting at the end of a row of banquettes, being treated for a cut above her eye, her head tilted back to stop a nosebleed that has already stained her philtrum and her chin. She is dressed in a bright green skintight outfit. On first glance Alice thinks it is a dancer's leotard but then she notices that it has legs that go down to just above the knee and sleeves that stop at the elbow. The costume is heavily bloodstained too. That nosebleed was a gusher.

A fight must have broken out on the dance floor, wherever that is, and the woman has been taken back here to recover. Alice deduces that this must have been what the cheering was about.

Animals, she thinks, and she doesn't mean the combatants.

The woman looks a little dazed, a little pissed off and yet strangely resigned. Holding a cloth to her nose, she accepts a drink that is brought to her. It looks like some kind of cocktail. She takes a slug from it as the man treating the cut says something Alice can't hear. The woman shrugs, like whatever just happened to her was no big deal, but from her body language there is little question that she got second prize in the fight.

Alice makes her way deeper into the throng, and as she comes around a pillar at the far end of the row of banquettes, all becomes literally clear.

The focus of the crowd, the focus of the premises, is a glass chamber, transparent curving staircases leading to its roof at either end. It is raised half a metre on a dais, three short steps leading to a low door at the centre.

Standing close by is a woman Alice recognises from her visit to NutriGen, the one who told them where Korlakian normally works. Alice's lens is still showing nothing but she always has a reliable memory for names and faces. The woman is called Vera Polietsky.

Vera is dressed in a similar skintight outfit, and from the fact that she is on her feet, sipping water, it is clear that she was the victor. She looks calm and yet pumped up at the same time. There is dried blood on her knuckles, the beginning of a bruise under her eye.

On the far side of the chamber there is a bar, a neon logo hanging above the gantry.

KLAWS

That's the name of the place. She saw it upstairs as she walked with Nikki. From street level it looked like another bar and diner.

This is Mullane's underbelly. The Seedee underbelly.

Alice's instinct is to get out of here, but she knows that this is the world she needs to immerse herself in if she wants to understand how CdC really works. She steels herself, swallows back her disgust and pushes deeper into the crowd, making her way to the front.

"Everybody, everybody, as you're all still here I guess you already know the show isn't over!"

The announcement sounds over the PA, on top of the music. Alice looks for the source and sees a short, squat, powerful-looking older woman climbing halfway up one of the curving staircases to make herself visible to the whole room. She is dressed in a suit and tie, the starchy formality of her impresario outfit in perverse contrast to the spectacle she's peddling. From her flattened, much broken nose, Alice estimates that she probably served her time in the chamber before graduating to running the show.

"As always, we round off tonight's card, tonight's Pacific card anyway, with the open all-comers challenge. Costs you two hundred to enter the chamber, but the reward is healthy and the task is straightforward. All you gotta do is put down Razerthorn here. Not a KO, not even a standing count, just put her on the floor for one second, one lousy second, and you scoop the prize. And what a prize! In case you don't know, we reset the pot each week and it goes up by two thousand every night that it remains unclaimed. This being Saturday, it's currently standing at . . . Ten! Thousand! Dollars!"

There are whoops and cheers, chants of "Razerthorn, Razerthorn," and "Liza, Liza, Brutaliza". Given the unlikelihood of the bleeding woman returning for another bout, Alice assumes Liza must be the impresario.

Something inside her crumbles. She came to CdC hoping to see the future of humanity. Right now she's seeing a carnival sideshow from centuries past. She's also looking at an even older scam. Liza is saving the open slot for the end of the night when the only people drunk enough to take up the challenge are going to be in no state to compete.

That said, ten thousand is a lot of money, even for here. Certainly it would be a good enough reason for someone to stay sober if they already knew it was on offer.

"Come on, who's feeling sharp tonight? Who's feeling lucky? Razerthorn took some punishment that last bout, and she's already thinking about a nice lie-down. You're never gonna get a better chance than this."

It doesn't look like there will be any takers. Alice wonders what everybody here witnessed in that previous fight, reckons it's the punishment Vera doled out that is clearer in their minds than whatever she suffered. They might have been cheering while they were caught up in the moment, but something inside them had to have been scared and appalled, and that's the part that's holding sway now the moment is over. Nobody wants to be losing their pay cheque through missing work because they were dumb enough to get their arm broken in a moment of drunkenly deluded stupidity.

Then suddenly a hand goes up, amid shouts of "Yeah, yeah," from around the man holding it. He seems ridiculously eager, like he's afraid someone else is going to get the nod first.

It's a geeky guy who looks early thirties. He's out with other geeky young men and a couple of geeky young women: science and research types walking on the wild side. Precisely the kind of mark Liza must be hoping for.

Most of his friends are laughing as the crowd parts, forming a path towards the chamber, but Alice can see one of the women grabbing hold of him by the arms, telling him don't be crazy.

His eyes blaze and he throws off her grip, letting out an inarticulate primal yell with aggressive indignation. She looks as surprised as she is hurt, and not a little worried. This is uncharacteristic behaviour, Alice infers. A good night out that already went someplace dark is now threatening to turn into a disaster. He brushes past Alice to get to the front, his friends now standing around her, looking awkward, confused and a little worried.

"We have a contender," Liza announces, coming back down the staircase to meet him. "What's your name?"

"Javier," he replies into the mike.

The crowd cheers, a few start drunkenly chanting "Javier, Javier".

"Hey, nobody cheers this guy until we've seen the colour of his money," Liza chides. His fingers work his lens, making a transfer.

"Okay, we're good," Liza announces. "You ready to take on Razerthorn?"

Javier nods, his face already a study in concentrated aggression. He pulls off his shirt, eliciting a combination of cheers and laughter.

"Razerthorn, you ready for Javier?"

Vera looks weary. Not tired, weary. Like this is all a drudge to her, one last thing to take care of before she can clock off for the night. No different to how she might respond at the processing plant if she was asked to shift one extra pallet just as she was taking off her overalls and getting ready to head home.

"Okay, let's do this!"

Liza opens the door to the chamber and Vera steps through first. Liza puts a hand on Javier's chest as he makes to follow. Not yet.

People scramble for a view, rushing to the front, buffeting Alice as they pass. The more sober clamber up the stairs and take position on the roof to watch from above. There is barely any clearance between the top of the chamber and the ceiling above, only enough to sit in an awkward crouch.

Alice wants to arrest everybody and shut this place down. But for now she has to temper her wrath, remember she is in fact-finding mode, incognito and alone. This pinnacle of human civilisation is starting to look like a Bosch painting. When she engineered the opportunity to shadow Nikki Freeman, she thought the worst she would discover was bootlegging and backhanders.

Holding her arm across the doorway, Liza tells Javier: "Remember, son, you're trying to put her down, that's the game. Don't get yourself damaged. This isn't a war of attrition. You beat your palm down twice at any time to tap out and she'll stop. Understand?"

He nods. Yes, he understands, but something is troubling Alice about the fact that he hasn't spoken a word other than his name since he volunteered. He looks like he's on something.

Liza sends them to opposite ends of the chamber, warning them: "Nobody makes a move, nobody starts anything until this door is fully closed."

Liza takes hold of the handle. Javier has his gaze fixed on the door, his whole body on a hair trigger. Vera seems less concerned with her cue, concentrating her focus on her opponent.

Liza teases the audience, pushing the door halfway closed then opening it again; pushing it almost all the way closed, then all the way open again.

"Not yet, not yet. I'm not hearing nearly enough noise."

More vapour billows around, like she saw emerge when those two drunks opened the door. Alice realises it is dry ice, bringing down the temperature. The walls are running with moisture, the music still pounding, coloured lights pulsing. The volume gets pumped up, excitement rising as people clap to the beat, cheering and chanting names: Liza, Javier, Razerthorn.

Liza waits until the cheering and chanting has reached a crescendo bordering on hysteria, then she slams the door.

The trigger pulled, Javier moves with surprising speed. Alice assumed that the wait inside the chamber would have been enough for it to dawn that this wasn't the good idea it seemed in that earlier moment of euphoria and bravado. She imagined that he would slow down, play it cagey, think about how he might make a decent show of this so that he could get out with some dignity as well as all his limbs intact.

Instead he bolts headlong towards Vera, lithe and unflinching. She doesn't move, as though she hasn't had time to react, taken unawares by his pace, then at the last split-second she sidesteps him, leaving a trailing leg.

He tumbles over it and would have hit the floor and the wall with painful force were it not that Vera subtly catches his arm with one hand, slowing him down and effectively cushioning his fall.

Alice wonders whether anyone else noticed this. They're giving no such indication, all cheering and laughing. Is it a set-up? she wonders. Is Javier a stooge?

He gets up immediately, swinging for Vera a second time, aggression in his face like this means something, like he hates her. Again she dodges, putting him down far more gently than she could have, but the force of his charge is still enough for him to clatter against the glass with a thump that makes Alice and a few others wince. He gets up again though, looking further enraged, and launches another attack, this time throwing himself into a two-footed flying kick.

It's not a set-up and he's not a stooge, Alice realises. The guy is crazy and Vera is making sure he doesn't get hurt. She's spinning him off with expert technique, wanting him to realise it's futile. Alice wonders how many chances she's going to give him to grasp this; how soon she wants her shift to be over.

The answer is soon. The next time he comes at her she deflects him with a degree of force, adding to the velocity with which he clatters into the glass. The collision is such an ugly sound. He leaves a smear of blood on the pane and tumbles to the floor looking dazed. It takes him a few seconds to get up this time, and when he does, he scrambles towards the door.

"Hey, you just need to tap out, you don't need to escape," Liza says. "You should stay and take your bow. Everybody give it up for Javier, he really threw himself into it. Literally."

There is a mixture of laughter and cheers. Javier's friends gather close to the door, ready to greet him. The man who was treating the bleeding woman is hastening towards the chamber also, carrying a medical kit. Javier's expression is still frighteningly intense as he emerges. He isn't making eye contact with anybody. His friends gather around him, offering physical support, but he throws them off and turns to the medic.

"Just need to make sure you—"

Before the medic can even lay a hand on him, Javier has snatched the first-aid kit and grabbed something from inside. The young woman who had reasoned with him earlier sees whatever it is and reads his intentions. She grabs him again, calling on the others too.

"Stop him. Javier, no."

Javier's arm lashes upwards in an arc and a spray of blood maps the trajectory. The woman reels, colliding with Alice, who clutches her instinctively to prevent her from collapsing. Her face has been slashed open diagonally from jaw to ear, blood pouring on to Alice's chest. Her friends rush to help, taking the woman's weight as Alice stands frozen to the spot, feeling like a helpless witness to all that is unfolding before her.

A few metres away, Javier is clutching a laser scalpel as he charges towards the chamber. Liza has stepped in front of the door to block his re-entry, but from her angle Alice isn't sure whether she fully saw what just happened.

Liza is a sturdy and redoubtable figure, but some force of desperation propels him into her, swiping with the scalpel as he barrels forward. Alice sees more blood spray the outside of the glass and a number of small brown objects are tossed into the air. It takes a moment for Alice to realise they are fingers.

Liza falls against the wall as Javier races back inside the chamber. Alice is jostled by people moving to keep their distance. Others remain transfixed: with fear or fascination, she can't be sure.

Javier makes for Vera once more with absolute singularity of purpose. It is as though attacking her is the only reason for his existence. She has noted the weapon, as her stance is different from before. But even if she deflects him, a passing contact with such an implement is going to do some damage.

This time she doesn't wait for him to reach her. Instead she drives forward to meet him, her eyes locked onto the scalpel. Javier thrusts with it and she tracks the movement, gripping his arm and pulling it past her as she sidesteps. In a blink she has thrown him to the floor while retaining her hold on his forearm. The twisting movement causes the scalpel to drop, a fracture of a second before she drives a knee against his straightened arm, snapping it like a chicken bone.

It is a compound fracture, bone jutting raggedly through ruptured flesh. It makes Alice weak from the mere sight, many people around her averting their eyes despite having come here expressly to watch violence. It is not enough to stop Javier, though.

He grabs for the discarded scalpel with his other hand, that enflamed singularity of intention still blazing in his face.

Vera reads it. She kicks it away before he can reach, then flips him over and puts him in a chokehold. He flails like he is being electrocuted, struggling with all of his limbs. Even the wrecked arm flaps about horribly, Javier making no attempt to cradle or protect it.

It takes a long time, the strain becoming visible on Vera's sweating face, but eventually he loses consciousness and slumps limply to the floor.

At this moment, the music cuts out and the house lights come on. There couldn't be a less equivocal sign that the show is over, but it still takes everyone a beat to assure themselves that the danger is past.

The room no longer looks like some pulsing and colourful den of saturnalian revelry, but what it truly is: a claustrophobic steel-walled basement where the floor is swilling with spilt drinks, sweat, condensation and blood.

Upon an urgent call from the medic, one of the bar staff races across carrying a bucket of ice. Liza is slumped against the wall of the chamber, trembling, staring at the severed sections of her fingers that are lying on the floor. She can't pick them up because she has lost digits from both hands.

"The fuck was that guy on?" Alice hears somebody ask.

"There's a new super-strain of Spike in circulation," comes the reply. "The construction crews are taking it, guys trained up for hardcore physical exertion. If a little geek like that took some, it's possible his system couldn't handle it. Made him psychotic."

The medic is administering an injection to the girl whose face got opened up: a sedative maybe. He glances across to Liza, whose missing digits are being put on ice by the woman who brought the bucket. The medic looks fraught, aware he can't be in two places at once.

"Somebody call it in. We need more surgeons. And we need the Seguridad to deal with that psycho fucker."

Liza explodes from her catatonia, lifting her head and shouting. "No cops."

Her voice is still connected to the PA, reverberating all the louder having no music to compete with. She climbs to her feet, looking around the room, commanding everyone's rapt and appalled attention.

"No fucking cops. Nobody in here tonight saw shit, you people understand that? Nobody saw shit. You breathe a fucking word I will hunt you down."

She trains her gaze on Javier's group, all of them looking up anxiously from where the medic is crouched over their profusely bleeding friend. They are standing there in shock, horrified and incredulous, but now they're feeling threatened too.

Liza makes a lens gesture with an intact pinkie, cutting the audio.

"Get more medics down here," she tells one of her staff, the rage subsiding from her voice. "Fast as you can. But no cops."

"You know, you can't contain this, Liza," the medic argues. "It's gonna be all over Seedee in no time. You *need* to call the cops: so you can agree an official version of what happened. Put a lid on it."

"Maybe it hasn't affected you over at the enfermería, but FNG are pulling their 'new broom' bullshit again. Seguridad are all gonna be on their best behaviour: recording all incidents, doing everything super-straight. *I'm* going to contain this, because I don't have a choice."

The medic looks to the staff for support, but nobody is prepared to back him up. It's clear that he's right, however. They don't want to argue with the boss, but they must know she's kidding herself.

It is Alice who suggests a way out of the impasse. It pops into her head and she acts upon it almost before she has time to fully evaluate the consequences, aware that it's a window of opportunity that will only be open for a couple of seconds. It is a chance to establish some credentials for her cover, but more importantly, it will make explicit Freeman's connections to all this at a stroke, forcing her cards on to the table.

"What about Nikki Fixx?" she suggests.

Everyone looks at her like she just materialised. Trick's hack is doing its job: she's nobody to them, but she just put herself in a context that gives her instant currency.

Liza doesn't look convinced.

"Even Nikki Fixx will be playing it safe right now. She's too smart to take any chances while they're looking for a bad apple to make an example of."

"I disagree," Alice states. "I can't see Nikki letting the undersight curb her play. Though I'm betting her price has gone way up because she'll be claiming added risk."

Liza stares at Alice, weighing up the notion.

"Still cheaper than getting my whole fucking business shut down, I guess."

FULL MOON SATURDAY NIGHT

Nikki is so in need of a drink after talking to Yoram that she walks to the nearest vending point and actually buys a Qola.

She's feeling tremulous just thinking about the mess she's in, thinking how she's losing her grip, thinking how she got played.

Jessica Cho. Jesus fucking Christ.

She's being personally investigated by the Principal of the SOE.

The undercover ruse must have been at Blake's insistence, and Boutsikari happily went along with the charade, immediately sussing which way the wind was blowing. He threw Nikki under the bus in a move that's just so Boutsikari that it's almost hard to be pissed at him; he's the scorpion stinging the frog.

Nikki's been walking around with Alice Blake in tow and she couldn't have made it more conspicuous that she was trying to cover her tracks. She thought she could get away with it because she was dealing with some wide-eyed naif whom nobody would believe.

She glugs down half the bottle. She's going to need a lot more.

She winces as she remembers how she ditched "Jessica" so that she could get on with the investigation by herself. She's dug herself in so deep, she's almost broken through the outside of the wheel, and soon enough she's going to be hurtling back towards Earth.

But this can't simply be about a sting operation on one bent cop, she reasons. Not with someone so senior throwing herself into the ring like this. What's Blake's agenda? It has to be something bigger than Nikki; bigger than Omega's murder too. Maybe Nikki's only play here is to demonstrate that there is method in her badness. Show Blake she's an asset.

She finishes the bottle, buys another.

Some asset, she thinks, popping the cap and taking another slug.

The last to know. She needs to get ahead of this, needs to give Blake a reason not to put her on the first shuttle back to Heinlein.

Her thoughts immediately turn to that slippery fucker Lind at the docks. She checks his profile and runs a status query. Sure enough, he's got location switched on like a good little corporate climber. He's kicking it in a bar over on Mullane. Ain't that convenient. She needs to get herself back over there anyway, to make a pick-up. And a decent drink would be good too.

She takes another static halfway around the wheel. She shares the car with a weird mix that shows Seedee society in microcosm: people on their way to work, bleary-eyed and waiting for the stims to kick in so they can start their day; others heading out on the town, their shift over, looking to feed the id and feel some humanity as they float out here in space.

As she reaches to the surface again, she looks up through the narrow gap between the buildings. She glimpses the moon for a moment before the spin takes it out of sight. It's always night-time on Mullane, and the moon is always full.

She hears someone mention that it's Saturday. The day of the week doesn't matter here; it's merely a way of marking time.

She remembers her old life, old self, when she was a cop in LA. They used to talk about a "full moon Saturday night" like it was some kind of explanation for the shit they were dealing with. It was classic confirmation bias. If it was a particularly crazy Saturday night and the moon was full, the cops would point to it as proof of the phenomenon, forgetting the other three crazy Saturday nights each month when the moon wasn't.

Walking down Mullane, she reflects that people here don't get so crazy. There's no need for crackdowns or moral crusades. You get the occasional fight breaking out, but that's all. Nobody's getting shot with a Saturday night special.

Seguridad's reluctance to recognise a homicide notwithstanding, very few people on Seedee ever actually want to kill each other. That's why what happened to Omega is so jarring. She knows this is strange to say, given that Seedee has always been neck-deep in vice, but it feels like the end of an innocence. She can't shake the feeling that after fifteen years in this place, everything is slipping away from her. Something very bad is taking hold and she no longer has the smarts to identify the threat, let alone do anything to stop it.

Lind is in a joint called Spiral, on the ground floor of one of Wheel One's tallest buildings. The name is a reference to gravity. It's essentially a pick-up joint, trading on owning a suite of zero-g fuck pads in the upper levels of the structure. You can rent them by the hour at the bar, and you can usually rent someone to share them too.

Nikki slips in quietly, keeping out of sight of Lind as she makes her way to the bar. He's seated at a booth with a couple of dorky-looking friends. Oh, yeah, if they're getting any they're paying for it.

She talks to Sela, the proprietor. Sela's an ex-cop like herself, from Copenhagen. Lost a leg in a motorbike crash. Lost the husband who was riding pillion. She worked vice back in Denmark, but decided to work the other side when she sought out her new start in Seedee.

"Nikki Fixx. I just paid you last week. Is there a problem?"

Nikki eyes the gantry. There are two Speyside malts and a bottle of Isle of Harris gin that she just knows came from the missing shipment. She swallows back the question. Sela wouldn't answer it anyway.

"I'm here on other business."

"You mean, like, actual police work?" Sela asks scornfully.

"Sometimes it can't be avoided."

"Can I get you something? On the house, of course," she adds.

Nikki can detect the hint of grudge in there. Normally it would bounce off her, but it's bothering her tonight. What's up with that? It's like she's still got Alice looking over her shoulder. The girl ain't even here but she's still functioning as Nikki's auxiliary conscience.

"Glenfiddich. And I'll pay for it."

Sela gives her a surprised look, but she's not going to argue the point. She pours the shot and slides it gently in front of Nikki.

"So what else can I help you with?"

"I need a favour."

"Favours are not cheap here."

"I'll discount you half next month's sub."

Sela gawps.

"Sounds like a big favour."

It isn't. The payment is disproportionate, but she needs a result and she doesn't want to waste time negotiating.

Nikki tells her what she requires. Sela nods.

"Won't be a problem."

Nikki slips half the dram between her lips like it's an oyster, letting it play around her mouth, feeling the burn on her tongue. She swallows and instantly feels better, but only for a moment. That's always how it is, except the moments keep getting shorter.

"So how's tricks tonight? Any trouble, any excitement?"

"You just missed it," Sela replies wearily, like she's had quite enough of weird behaviour to last two lifetimes but she's stuck here making a living from it anyways.

"This lady gets up from one of the tables, strips off all her clothes and lets them drop on the floor. She comes up to this guy where you're standing, this total stranger, says to him: "Fuck me right here on top of the bar." I mean, like, *demands* he do her."

Nikki raises an enquiring eyebrow.

"She a pro?"

"No. Real straight-arrow type. Engineer or something. I heard her talking when she first came in. She's working on recycling systems for a test vehicle. Based at the dry dock, so she must be pretty high clearance."

"You intervene?"

"Not my job to get in the way of anybody having a good time. It isn't like we have families in here eating dinner. Very weird, though. She really wasn't the type, and yet she looked like she'd have killed me if I *did* intervene."

"So this guy did her right here on the bar? I hope you wiped this down."

"No. What happens is the guy can't get wood because there's all these people standing there. So she just starts asking around, asking

175

who can get it up and is ready for the job right here, right now. Takes the first volunteer. And he was no catch. I mean, hung, give him that much, but with that face and that gut, you or I would never have gone far enough to find that out."

"You get a grab?"

"You kidding me? *Everybody* got a grab."

A few minutes later, Sela brings a drink across to where Brock Lind is sitting with his two buddies: one drink, just for him. She glances back towards the bar, where she has instructed one of her girls to be standing in view, and tells him:

"You must have done somebody a turn. This drink is paid for, and when you're finished, there's a special lady who would like to meet you in our private rooms. She's paid for too. They said it was a bonus."

Ten minutes after that, Lind walks into one of the private rooms towards the rear of the premises. The shit-eating grin falls off his face damn fast when he sees who he's really meeting.

"Don't you think I'm special, Brock?" Nikki asks.

She closes the door and stands in front of it. They both already know he isn't a physical match for her.

She orders him to take a seat and he complies without question.

"Who are you working for?"

"I already told you. I didn't get his name. He was a big guy with a Greek symbol tattoo."

Nikki sends a picture to his lens. It's one she got from file, of a guy with a lambda symbol tattooed on his shoulder.

"This him?"

"No," he replies. He winces as he speaks. He's already getting uncomfortable but he doesn't know why. Nikki does.

She sends him a shot of Omega.

"This is him, yes. He paid me to divert shuttle *Hermia*."

"Who were the other guys?"

"What other guys?"

"The ones who locked down Dock Nine. The ones who took our shipment."

"Seriously, I don't know what you're talking about. Look, I've told you what I know, and I really need to go to the bathroom."

"That's because the drink you were comped contained an ultra-powerful diuretic. What you're feeling now is only the early stages. In a few minutes your bladder is going to feel like the inside of a fire hydrant. Now, I realise you're out with your friends, got your best suit on, acting the big shot. So you can go back out there, hit the head and then make up whatever lie you like to tell them about what happened in here. Or your big night can end early with you pissing more volume than you ever pissed before, straight into your pants, and you having to slop your way home, soaking wet right down to your shoes. It all depends on how soon you give me what I want."

He looks worried now, but she can't tell if that's worried because he knows stuff or worried because he doesn't.

"Okay, I lied. I didn't divert *Hermia*. I only told you it was diverted, that was the deal. Get rid of you, send you to another dock. I didn't know anything about these other guys."

"Bullshit. Of all the docks on this wheel, you sent us to the one that was currently under the control of some private-security types you knew we couldn't fuck with. Who were they?"

"I don't know who they were. Look, I told you Dock Two because it was the furthest away, like I was ordered. When you came back and dangled me down that shaft, I had just got word there was this lockdown on Nine. I was getting that information live on the internal freight admin systems, so I sent you there knowing it would be a dead end. That's how it went down, I swear. Your shipment came into Dock Eleven like it was supposed to, and the big dude with the tattoo showed up as planned. He and some other guys took it away. That's why I got extra money in my pocket here tonight. Now, will you please just let me go?"

Nikki takes out a bottle of water and begins pouring it very slowly into a glass in front of him.

"You can *go* anytime, and I can't stop you. But you're not leaving this room until you tell me everything. What do you know about the lockdown on Nine?"

177

"I don't know anything about it, other than it happened. Nobody does. It was seriously high-level clearance shit, way above my pay-grade."

Nikki leans back in her seat and takes a long gulp from the glass. He's got to be in agony by now.

"Okay, you want to know about a lockdown?" he asks eagerly. "I'll give you something I do know, about another lockdown. Something nobody else has."

"Hurry up then. The sooner I'm happy, the sooner you can go drain that little rice-noodle of yours."

He squirms in his seat, leaning forward, like a change of posture might give some tiny reduction in the pressure.

"Okay, a few days ago . . . this is from someone I used to work with at Heinlein. A few days ago there was a passenger shuttle came in, for transfer to the elevator going home. They cleared everybody out, took total control of the facility. Lockdown. But they still needed operational personnel, and my friend was on duty. He saw the transfer. He hit the button to authorise the descent."

"What's his name?"

"I can't tell you that because he'd be in deep shit. I swore to him I wouldn't tell anybody. He shouldn't have told me, but he wanted to know if I knew anything about it from my end. He saw it, though. He saw everything."

"Saw what? Who was on board?"

"Nobody. That's the whole thing. Not in the shuttle, not in the capsule, nobody. You know how much that costs, right? The whole elevator, the whole shuttle, no passengers. Yet there's this ultra-high-clearance, bad-ass security detail just like you described on Nine. Few days ago. April seventh. I remember the date because it's my parents' wedding anniversary."

That's when she knows it's bullshit. Worried she wasn't buying it, he threw in a specific date and the reason he remembered, to try to add authenticity.

Nikki stares at him for a second and sighs.

"So, to sum up, you've given me something I'm supposed to take your word for, from a source you can't name, the nub of which is that absolutely nobody went anywhere? Fuck you."

She gets up and exits, locking the door behind her. She's pretty sure he knows nothing, but he pissed her off. Sela can take the clean-up fee out of next month's payment.

As she walks away she sees an emergency call flashing up on her lens. Not a Seguridad emergency: a friend-in-need emergency. And a friend in need is a wallet you can bleed. Her pick-up will have to wait.

EMERGENCY SERVICES

Nikki detects a weird vibe as soon as she walks into Klaws. The bar is busy and it's obvious a lot of the people in here were downstairs when the incident happened. Some of them look real freaked and are taking a moment to deal before they move on. Others are regaling late arrivals of what they saw, some laughing about it. Everything is entertainment as long as it's happening to somebody else. Grabs are no doubt being shared. No way of getting those genies back into the bottle, but there are other steps that can be taken to contain the situation.

She has a quiet word with some of the more loquaciously inclined witnesses, making sure they know to pass the word around; making sure they understand the consequences of non-compliance too.

This is what she's being paid for here: to shape the official version, and to make the truth go away.

She approaches the door to the stairs, the way barred by a Ukrainian bouncer named Kron. He recognises her and has been briefed that she was coming.

"Emergency med team got here just ahead of you," he informs her, holding the door open.

She proceeds downstairs to the sub-surface vault where the fights take place. There is the usual smell of alcohol, sweat and cologne, but there is another unmistakable note in the bouquet. Blood. She's been warned it was a messy one, and the sight of two surgeons plus their call-out crews confirms this. They are carrying out on-the-spot patching up to prepare their patients for transfer to the infirmary.

There are still a lot of people down here: not just staff, but witnesses, friends of the people involved. Vera Polietsky is standing close to one of the huddled med teams, arms folded. She gives Nikki a curt nod. Between the surgeon and one of his assistants she catches a glimpse of Liza. She looks doped-up, out of it. They've given her something since she authorised the call to Nikki.

The guy who went crazy is lying on his side unconscious inside the chamber, which is locked. The medics have tubed and sedated him, leaving him in the recovery position. His feet are shackled together, one arm in a vacuum splint.

There are puddles of blood close to the fight chamber, considerably more than she's ever seen shed inside it. On any other day, the sight of all this would give her pause, but it's far from the worst thing she's seen lately.

Then she does see something truly horrifying, and not because it's a person walking upright soaked in blood. It's because said person is Alice Blake, and she's standing right in the heart of the mess Nikki is here to conceal from the likes of Alice Blake.

One of the staff clocks her reaction and misinterprets it.

"This is Wendy Goodfellow," he says. "She was the one who suggested we bring you in."

Nikki's lens confirms the ID. How did she manage that, she wonders, but more to the point, has Nikki just walked into her trap?

"Nikki Fixx," Alice states, offering a thin smile and a steely stare.

It's like looking at a different person, or maybe the scales have fallen from Nikki's eyes. She seems older than she looked a few hours ago, though it's harder to look like a wide-eyed innocent when you're standing inside an underground fight club covered in blood. She's also ten times more street-smart than Nikki would have guessed. Give the girl this much, being the one who suggested bringing Nikki in was a baller move.

Nikki gestures her to come away from the group so they can talk privately.

"What the hell are you playing at?" she asks.

"Just go with it," Alice replies. "Do what you came here to do. There's no point in keeping up any pretence. Like the man said, I was the one who told them to call you, and Liza's only reservation was that you'd push your price up because of the added risk."

Nikki's stomach is turning somersaults. She's totally made. This girl could pull the trigger on her life here at any second. And yet it seems she isn't about to. Not yet, anyway.

"Why you doing this?"

"I'm trying to blend in, so I can garner some information. If your previous antics achieved anything constructive, it was that they demonstrated nobody was going to give me squat while I was identifiable as FNG."

Nikki is being called out on everything. She figures there's no angle in pretending she still thinks Alice is Jessica Cho. Her only game here is to make out she's someone who can get the skinny.

"Yeah, you're gonna blend right in. Just need to hope everybody who saw a grab of you floating above Central Plaza was too busy looking up your skirt to pay much attention to your face. Yeah, I know who you are, Alice. You're overseeing the goddamn Seguridad."

Nikki expects her to look shocked or annoyed that she's been made too. Instead Alice looks scornful.

"Took you this long, huh? And I was told you're someone who always knows what's going on around here."

That one smarts, pounding as it does upon an already tender spot. She needs to get off the ropes.

"How did you get your ID changed, *Wendy*? Isn't that illegal for an FNG official?"

"Where have you been?" Alice counters. "You dumped me and disappeared."

Nikki knows her only play is to go on offence.

"Where have I been? Where have *you* been? I went to investigate something and when I came back you were gone. Where did you go?"

"I came after you to see if I could help."

"Like I told you not to, you mean? Then what?"

"I was abducted."

"You were what?"

"The floor opened up on me in a corridor and I got dropped into a container. I was drugged. When I woke up, I was strapped to a table and someone was hacking into my wrist unit, wiping my grabs."

"Who was he? You get a name?"

"He wouldn't tell me, but I heard someone call him Trick."

"And this Trick abducted you?"

"No. He said someone else dropped me off and paid him to erase the grabs. Said I had seen something I wasn't supposed to."

Nikki glances at the medical teams, the anxious staff and the friends of the girl who got slashed, these last barely moving as the surgeons work to stabilise the casualties ahead of transport.

"What did you see?"

"I don't even know. I opened a door to a room underneath Sin Garden and there was some kind of orgy going on."

"Some senior Quadriga or FNG person in there maybe?"

"Not that I recognised. It couldn't have been that, because one of them asked me to join in."

Nikki knows she shouldn't laugh, but with all the tension that's been building up, some part of her decides she needs a release. It's the idea of buttoned-down little Goody-Two-Shoes being confronted by that scene, the image of her face when it was suggested she jump right in.

"This isn't amusing," G2S states, in a tone that reminds Nikki how being fired and sent back to Earth would not be amusing either.

"How did you get away from this Trick guy?"

"He was attacked. Some people came in, broke the door down. They beat on him, took some of his gear away. Took *him* away."

Nikki fails to conceal the shock in her expression.

"You know him?" Alice asks.

With that horse already bolted, lying would only raise more questions.

"I know everybody," she replies. "Who attacked him?"

"There were three of them. A woman and two men. My lens was disabled so I didn't get any IDs."

"And these people knew Trick, you say?"

"They had a need for his skill and his equipment. They wanted him immediately and exclusively."

Nikki can't think what this need might be. Trick could provide

183

a lot of services, and God knows he isn't cheap, but why would they be abducting the guy?

She has a bigger question, however.

"How come the person who witnessed this was allowed to simply walk away?"

"Trick unlocked the clamps. He told them I was nobody. He had given me this new ID by that time."

"And why would he do that?"

Alice straightens her posture.

"Because he had discovered who I really was and he desperately needed to get on the right side of me," she replies, her greater message unmistakable.

"So you got up and ran, made it past them and gave them the slip?"

"No. The woman could see through the fake ID. She knew who I really am and what I'm doing here. She said she was 'running off primary'. Do you know what that means?"

"Yes. It means she ID'd you from locally stored information. The face-recognition in her lens found you in its cache of images seen first-hand, rather than referring to the central database."

"You're saying she had seen me before? Because I didn't recognise her."

"Or maybe she had just seen your picture. It's been shared in certain circles."

"She mentioned something named Project Sentinel, like I was connected with that. You heard of it?"

"No."

"Me neither. But once she had identified me, she got her people out of there quickly."

"You didn't get any pictures, any grabacións?"

"I already told you, Trick was working on my unit at the time. My lens was disabled. Still is. I can't get it connected up again."

Nikki feels a rush of hope as the implications hit home.

"So you didn't record what you saw in here? You're not recording right now?"

Alice shakes her head impatiently, like she doesn't see the relevance.

"Which would mean we're in 'my word against yours' territory here."

Alice sighs irritably.

"You really don't get it, Freeman. If I wanted to railroad you out of here, the absence of a few recordings wouldn't make any difference. There's a litany of crimes with which I could charge you. But I'm interested in a bigger picture here, which means I'm prepared to hold my nose and ignore the overpowering stench of your corruption if it helps me find out what's really going on. So how about you help us both by telling me what you learned talking to the people you didn't want to be talking to while I was there?"

FIRST DO NO HARM

Alice experiences a certain relief in no longer having to pretend she doesn't know just how corrupt Nikki Freeman is, but it doesn't make the ugliness of it all any easier to swallow. She feels the bile rising in her throat listening to Nikki so blithely describe the function and dynamics of this venal, fetid morass of self-gratification and indulgence.

Her shirt is clinging to her, the material weighed down by the damp and sticky weight of the slashed woman's blood. Every so often she catches the smell of it and threatens to gag. She wishes she could tear it off, wring it out over Freeman's head, rub it on her face. *This is the world you've created*, she wants to tell her, *the world your on-going greed and amorality sustains*.

But she has a job to do, so instead she simply listens, the anger turning toxic inside her like the blood on her clothes is surely putrefying.

"I spoke to Sol Freitas. He was one of Korlakian's work colleagues from NutriGen."

"I remember. Him and Alex Dade. Presumably your inquiries were not restricted to food processing."

"They all work for Julio Martinez, who runs one of Seedee's rival bootlegging organisations. Omega was involved in the theft of a shipment intended for Yoram Ben Haim. They paid a manifest administrator to divert Yoram's people to another dock so that they could make off with the shipment when it came off the shuttle. Freitas thinks Yoram killed Omega as payback for that."

"It seems highly disproportionate payback."

Nikki pauses, clearly evaluating how much to disclose, which serves only to tell Alice that there's plenty she's keeping back.

"Yoram's people were diverted to Dock Nine, which was in

186

lockdown. They snuck in and there was an altercation with these high-level mercenary types. I don't know who they were."

Nikki breaks her gaze for a moment. It's enough to tell Alice what she's hiding: she was there.

"And what is Yoram saying about it?"

Nikki pauses too long once again.

"I know you work for him, so let's skip the games. How is his demeanour? Could it have been him?"

Nikki frowns, busted.

"He's on edge, feeling besieged, looking for conspiracies. He even thinks you might be part of it: that the incident at the Ver Eterna was a set-up and you took a dart so that there could be a crackdown."

Alice glances at her forearm, Nikki tracking her gaze. There is still a bump beneath her sleeve where the bandage sits.

"And is that what you think? That I'm at the heart of some grand conspiracy?"

"I think Yoram is pretty paranoid, but he's probably not wrong that Julio is planning something. Freitas was boasting about some move Julio hasn't made yet. That's why he thinks Omega's death and what happened to his body was a pre-emptive strike in the war that's coming."

Alice recalls the words of Helen Petitjean, who gave her such invaluable information, not least the heads-up regarding Nikki.

There is tension in this place. You can feel it. And it's building up to something bad, something explosive.

Alice becomes aware of Nikki glancing to her left, from where she sees one of the surgeons approaching, wiping sweat and a smear of blood across her forehead. Behind her Liza is being moved gently on to a collapsible gurney, a medic holding up a clear bag full of fluid.

"Hey, Lupe," Nikki hails her. "How's Liza? She still gonna be able to count past six on her fingers?"

"My team are going to get her prepped over at ERU where I can work my magic. I've seen worse lately. Good thing is it was a cut with a laser scalpel, so the severing was clean. Nothing ripped and ragged."

"And what about the girl José's working on? She gonna be okay?"

"Think so. He was able to stop the bleeding quite quickly. Irony is, if she'd been cut up like that anyplace else, it might not have worked out so well for her."

"How come?" Alice asks.

"Because José was here on the spot waiting to deal with his specialty: fight injuries," the surgeon explains. "He had the equipment and the know-how."

"I'm not sure I see his contribution as 'ironic' given that she was injured with one of his implements," Alice replies. "By implication she wouldn't have sustained such injuries anywhere else."

The surgeon gives Nikki a quizzical look, seeking an explanation for Alice's attitude and possibly her very presence.

"Oh, sorry, allow me to make some introductions. This is Dr Guadalupe Hermosillos, trauma surgeon at Enfermería Rueda Uno. Lupe, this is— Ah . . . Wendy Goodfellow. She's new here, so I'm tutoring her in the ways of Seedee."

Alice and Lupe size each other up warily.

"Wendy, here's the thing they don't teach you at the induction courses," Nikki says. "If you really want to know what's been happening on CdC, you gotta talk to the surgeons."

"Why is that?"

"The most common ailment we encounter at ERU is amnesia," Lupe replies. "When people sustain an injury, they can seldom tell us how it happened. Nobody ever says they were stabbed or slashed or beaten up. They pitch up at the ER, and they can never remember a damn thing."

"Aren't there investigations following up on what you witness as a doctor?"

"We can only describe the wounds we're treating. We're not in a position to say for sure how they were inflicted, and we need patients to know that, so they aren't reluctant to seek proper treatment."

Alice tries and fails to mask her disapproval. This is all so rotten.

"It's not some epidemic of violence," Lupe adds. "Simply that people don't want to get themselves fired on account of their extra-curricular activities."

"And do you get their, ahem, gratitude, in exchange for this?" Alice asks.

Lupe stares back by way of reply.

"Hey, how's tricks generally these days, Lupe?" Nikki chimes, driving over Alice's question and the awkwardness it threatens to precipitate. "I mean, what *is* the worst thing you've seen lately?"

Nikki gives Alice a warning glance, and she gleans from both this and the ensuing question that Lupe is a potential source. More ugliness to be swallowed in pursuit of the bigger agenda.

"Oh, no contest. A few days ago, this guy came in, looked like he had put his right leg through a wood-chipper, foot-first."

"What happened to him?" Alice asks.

Lupe and Nikki share a look. Alice gets there late.

"He couldn't remember," she says.

"Thing is, in this case I think he genuinely couldn't remember. He was really spooked. He said the last thing he recalled was coming out of the shower. Next thing he's lying on his bedroom floor and his foot looks like burger meat."

"Who was he?" Nikki asks. "Was he a player?"

"Actually, he was a pilot. Not the usual type for a mystery injury. That's what made it all the weirder."

"What was his name?"

"You know the rules, Nikki."

"Come on, Lupe. Confidentially we're investigating a possible gang war here. Nobody will ever know it came from you."

Lupe considers it for a moment. She looks like she might be about to cough when one of the Klaws staff interrupts.

"Nikki, the medics are getting ready to ship out soon, so if you need to speak to the wits . . ."

"On it," she replies.

Two of the staff are lifting the unconscious guy on to a gurney. Alice sees that the slashed woman is also being moved, electrodes attached to multiple points on her face and body. The friends who came with her are getting ready to accompany her to the infirmary.

Nikki steps across and cuts them off. She shows them her ID.

"I'm Nikki Freeman of the Seguridad. Now, any one of you want to score some points by telling me what your buddy took tonight before he went full-on feral?"

Most of them simply look down, wanting to melt. One of them does answer, however.

"Nothing," the guy says. "Just some drinks from the bar. I swear. Javier doesn't touch stims or enhancers. He's a lab-rat, same as the rest of us."

Nikki takes this in. If she believes him, her face offers him no such reassurance.

"Okay, I'm gonna tell you all what I told everybody who already went upstairs. This didn't happen. You saw nothing. You weren't here. You know why? Because this place officially doesn't exist."

She paces in front of them. They look tired and frightened. They just want this to be over, and Nikki knows it. But Nikki means a different kind of over.

"If you voluntarily identify yourself as having attended an illegal underground fight club, I can personally guarantee that the FNG and the Quadriga will be informed, the official procedures will be set in train and your contract will be cancelled with no right of appeal. If you have the money, it will be automatically debited to pay for putting you on the first shuttle back to Heinlein. Otherwise you will have to fund some kind of hand-to-mouth existence until the end of your contract period, which means unofficial jobs, none of which you are going to want on your résumé when you get back to Earth. Do you all understand?"

There are wordless nods, tremulous lips.

"You share no grabs. You tell nobody about this. You don't even talk about it to each other. You wake up dreaming about this shit, I want you to slap yourselves in the face. Do you understand?" she asks, louder.

More nodding, which is not enough.

"I said *do you understand*?"

She elicits a few yes ma'ams, making eye contact with each of them in turn. No question but that they got the message.

"Okay, get out of here."

FAKE EMPIRES

Nikki can tell they're relieved to be dismissed. They won't be talking to anybody. In fact, they'll be pleased that she gave them permission to collectively erase tonight from their memories.

They file out, hurrying after the gurneys bearing their two injured friends. In a few moments there's nobody here but staff, who begin mopping up the blood.

"So that's how it's done here, right?" Alice asks. "You wave your wand and make it all go away?"

With the place rapidly emptying, little G2S seems less worried about keeping the disgust from her voice. The girl is just teeming with self-righteousness. Nikki doesn't like to contemplate how pissed she'd be if she had any idea what really happened to her tonight.

"It's like a competition to see who can be least ethical. How can a surgeon be playing a willing part in this carnage, tacitly condoning it, *enabling* it?"

"Would you rather there wasn't a surgeon here during a fight night? Because believe me, honey, this shit would still happen."

"Look at yourself. A club owner bribes you and suddenly there is no crime? This is your idea of policing?"

"I haven't been a policewoman in fifteen years. This is my idea of keeping the peace. In practice the law is a little fuzzier up here than you maybe wrote about in some Ivy League college paper."

"From what I've seen, the law is whatever you decide suits you at any given time. I've never encountered anyone even a fraction as twisted and corrupt."

"I'll take that as a compliment, because I'd really have to hustle to make as much dirty money as the scam-artists at the FNG. From the ground-level flat-heads on the take at your department of Franchise, License and Trade right up to the likes of Hoffman. You

191

want to take down corruption? You better stick to the likes of me and the Seguridad, because you'd be farting into thunder going up against the real graft in this place."

"You know, I studied law and criminology on three continents before coming up here to space, and I've yet to see a murderer or a thief beat the rap on the grounds that there's a guy down the street who does worse things than her. You think you're telling it like it is but to me it just sounds like pitiful excuses."

Alice folds her arms across her bloodied chest.

"I'm sure you're right," she goes on, "and there is corruption at the highest levels on CdC. So what chance would I have in changing anything when the law enforcement officers are the prime facilitators? You say you're keeping the peace, like it's the only way to deal with the world you've found yourself in. I would say it's more like you're a parasite that has evolved to thrive amid this filth."

There is genuine anger in her voice, not merely the usual FNG posturing. She feels bad the girl is getting a crash-course in CdC reality but Alice is talking like the whole thing is Nikki's fault, and it sticks in her craw to listen to moral commentary from the cheap seats.

"You're just shooting the messenger, honey. If it's me you're pissed at, then you're swatting mosquitoes because you can't drain the swamp."

Nikki has looked Alice up, now that she knows who she's dealing with. She was raised in a rich and influential family, both parents high-ranking diplomats, real FNG aristocracy. From their photographs, it's apparent that Alice was adopted, or maybe some surrogacy deal. They're both white; like, really white. They're old too, and by Nikki's arithmetic would have both been around fifty when Alice was born. That ought to have made it difficult to get approval for adoption, but maybe you get to cut in line when you're that connected.

"You *created* the swamp," Alice retorts. "You and the likes of Yoram, of Julio Martinez, of Liza, all the bootleggers, all the pimps, everyone complicit in this squalid trade in flesh and blood."

One of the staff notices Alice's voice rising, casting a glance from where he is cleaning up outside the fight chamber.

"You think we created this?" Nikki replies, speaking softly, emphasising her calm in the face of Alice's indignation. She might be a PhD, but the girl needs schooling. "The Quadriga created this. Do you really think the consortium couldn't produce enough decent alcohol up here to supply every bar on Seedee at a fraction of what the bootleggers charge? Or import the high-end luxury stuff at a reasonable price? But they choose not to. Why do you think that is, Dr Criminologist?"

"The Quadriga's priorities are about designing and building an interstellar spacecraft that will take us to new worlds. And in the shorter term about fashioning a city, a society that will ultimately build and crew that vessel. That's why they're not wasting their precious facilities, resources and freight logistics on getting people drunk."

Nikki stares at her, analysing her answer thoughtfully. She'll get along just great with Helen Petitjean, she reckons. Two bitches from a privileged background, pontificating about the future of humanity and making grand plans for how everybody *else* should live.

"The Quadriga flies and manufactures plenty of non-essential stuff up here," she replies. "Their position on booze is a moral decision, not an economic one, pandering to the likes of your acquaintance Helen Petitjean. See, if good liquor wasn't a rarity, affordable only by the very rich, it wouldn't be profitable for Yoram to find ways to mess with the cargo chain and smuggle it in here."

"You're saying moral zealots are to blame for immorality?" Alice asks, exasperated by the audacity of this.

"No. I'm saying certain elements inside the Quadriga have always been happy for Helen's type to prevail."

"You're making less sense by the second. Why would they be happy about that?"

"In a word, control. Don't you think the Quadriga could afford to ensure the blue-collar positions on Seedee pay enough that nobody needs to moonlight as a hooker, or fight bare-knuckle in a basement? Poverty and fear are the two most effective ways of controlling people: large populations or small individuals. The poor have few choices and the better-off are too scared to exercise theirs:

they look at the hookers and the people working three jobs and they think 'I don't want to end up in that position. Better not rock the boat.'

"The Quadriga is happy to let this whole underground economy keep ticking over so that the little people got something to distract themselves with: games to play, battles to fight, tiny empires to build. Nothing that affects the bigger games, bigger battles and bigger empires above, of course. It's a strategy that has kept order in civilisations for centuries. And those bigger games aren't about securing patents and contracts. This is empire-building. The players within the Quadriga are positioning themselves to carve up the territory on planets we haven't discovered yet. We don't know where our brave new world will be, but we do know that when we get there, we'll be drinking Coke."

"You actually sound sanguine about it," Alice states. "I mean, don't you care? Isn't some part of you ashamed that we all came here to drive our civilisation towards something noble, while instead you're playing your part in dragging it into a cesspit? This place is supposed to be the mother that is going to give birth to humanity's child. Yet from where I'm standing, it looks like the mother is a drunken whore."

Alice's voice is starting to waver with emotion as she says this. Testify, sister. Nikki's calculated response to Alice opening her heart is a shrug.

"Nah. Seedee's not the mother, it's just the vagina. You forget: humanity is born from somewhere messy and bloody and stinky. And there's usually a lot of drinking and fucking involved in conceiving the child. Maybe not in your case, I'm guessing. Which is why you don't feel part of this society."

The rage that the girl has been struggling to contain finally boils over.

"*You* aren't part of this society," Alice retorts. "You're just a parasite and a predator that's evolved to survive in it."

Nikki gives her a cold smile, but she's masking the fact that this hurt, and it hurt because she's starting to suspect it's true.

"I'm Nikki Fixx," she replies. "I'm everybody's friend here."

"You're for hire. You're nobody's friend."

"Well at least I ain't their enemy."

"No, you're not their enemy. You're not even their problem. You're everybody's least-worst solution."

EMERGING TRUST ISSUES

Alice can barely look at Nikki any more, but nor can she let her out of her sight again. She desperately needs some air, so this is when the reality of CdC truly hits home. The best she could hope for right now is to go out onto Mullane and try to fool herself that she's outdoors.

She feels disgusted and she feels disgusting. The sensation of the blood-soaked material against her chest is making her skin crawl. She walks away, heading for the bar. If she can't have air, another element will have to suffice.

"Can I get something to drink?" she asks the woman behind the gantry. From across the room Alice thought she looked mid-twenties, and was asking herself how she got here so young. Up close she can see she's older than Alice, maybe thirty-five. Her true age is in her eyes. Alice wonders what else they've seen, and how she can stand to be working down in this vault, serving people who come here to watch bloodshed as entertainment.

"Sure thing. What's your poison?"

Her accent is Nigerian, though her appearance is Somali. Someone else who knows what it is to feel like nowhere is home.

"I just want a glass of cold water."

"I can't get you something stronger? You look like you've been through some heavy shit tonight."

"Nah, she won't touch any fun stuff. Bought her one of Lo-Jack's famous mojitos at Sin Garden and she wouldn't even take a sip."

Nikki appears by her side, leaning against the bar. Alice doesn't want to acknowledge her, but she makes brief eye-contact via a mirror behind the gantry.

"Can I set you up, Nikki?" the barmaid asks, scooping ice into a glass for Alice's water.

"Whisky please, Kinsi. Speyside if you got it. Had a couple Qolas earlier because I couldn't source anything else. Need to remind myself what a real drink tastes like."

Kinsi places the iced water in front of Alice.

"You sure I can't offer you anything more?" she asks.

"Not unless you have a spare shirt or a shower back there."

Kinsi reaches for a bottle of Glenfiddich and glances at her other customer.

"Nikki lives just around the corner," she suggests in a helpful tone. "I'm sure she's got *something* clean you could borrow. You could grab a shower there too, couldn't she, Nikki?"

Alice can't imagine anyone feeling less enthusiastic than she does in response to this notion. That is until she looks in the mirror and sees how Nikki is taking it.

"I don't think Alice would be all that comfortable stripping naked and taking a shower in my apartment right now," she says, trying to shut it down.

She's damn right on that score, but suddenly Alice's discomfort is less acute than her curiosity about why Nikki doesn't want her there. Even the way she said it was an oversell. She didn't need to talk about stripping naked: that was clearly intended to make her imagine her vulnerability and awkwardness.

Nikki really doesn't want Alice inside her apartment.

"No, I couldn't feel less comfortable than I do right now with that woman's blood sticking to my chest. Is her place really nearby?"

She directs this last at Kinsi, knowing she'll get the truth.

"Two minutes away."

Alice turns to face Nikki.

"Let's go, then," she states. It's not a request or a suggestion.

Nikki looks trapped; one of the few occasions since they met when she doesn't have a backup move. She sighs, downs her shot of whisky and gestures to go.

Thirty seconds later they're at street level, walking along Mullane once again. Alice gets fewer second looks than she would expect. She guesses the sight of someone walking along here covered in blood isn't that rare, particularly in the company of Sergeant Freeman.

Nikki is conspicuously shifty, eyes darting back and forth like she's looking for a new option. Alice is starting to wonder if Nikki is about to take off again, prompting her thoughts to turn to when she took off last time.

"You sure you don't want it call it a night?" Nikki asks.

"We've got plenty of work still to do."

"Okay, I get that, but wouldn't you rather pop back to your own place to get changed? If you're worried about losing track of me again, I'll come with you back to Wheel Two."

"No. Your place is fine. We're against the clock."

Alice didn't lose track, she got abducted – the details of which Nikki has asked surprisingly few questions about.

They are walking past Sin Garden, Nikki leading at a far slower clip than the last time they passed this way. Alice thinks about that mojito, how keen Nikki was for her to drink it.

She skips back a few minutes, replaying the conversation in her head. As always, she has perfect recall.

I woke up, I was strapped to a table and someone was hacking into my wrist unit, wiping my grabs.

Who was he? You get a name?

Alice never said it was a man. Maybe there were reasons she might make the assumption, but Alice suspects it's because Nikki knew.

There are some people who are concerned that you were backstage without a pass, so to speak, snooping where you weren't welcome and witness to what you had no right to see.

At the time, Alice couldn't think what she had seen that might be damaging to anyone, when in fact everything she had seen was damaging to one person and one person only.

Witness testimony doesn't have the same traction without grabacións backing it up. Things tend to be a lot less binding when it comes down to "he said, she said".

After being conspicuously evasive all day, Freeman had undergone a volte-face, suddenly speaking candidly and behaving in an altogether less guarded manner. Alice now understands that it was because she had hit upon a plan to have her observer's grabacións erased, reckoning nobody would believe Jessica's word against hers.

She thinks about how Nikki told her to stay put. She didn't just take off, she *told* Alice she was taking off. She did it to make sure Alice would follow. She must have set it up with Lo-Jack and with the people Alice saw her wrestling down on the concourse.

She sees also that when it came to getting her into that metal box, this was an elaborate contingency. There was a far simpler Plan A. She was supposed to drink the mojito. It was what they used to call a Mickey Finn, and this is why Alice feels a new kind of ire coursing through her. This, more than anything else, gives her the measure of Nicola Freeman's ruthlessness.

She thought she would be drugging Jessica Cho, an inexperienced young intern on her first trip to CdC. When Jessica pitched up much later, she would be hung-over and disoriented, having lost her subject and had her observation files erased. She would be an inexperienced young girl who was dazzled by the Mullane neon, fell into temptation and got drunk when she was supposed to be carrying out her duties.

Nobody would believe anything she said about Nikki. She would be fired, sent home in disgrace, her career over before it even started. And it was nothing personal. Jessica was merely an obstacle in Freeman's way. A problem to be Fixxed.

Was Dev Korlakian a problem to be Fixxed too? she begins to wonder. She can't trust anything Nikki has said about him or about Julio Martinez, and certainly not about Yoram Ben Haim.

It is with a chill that Alice remembers she is still in Nikki's cross hairs: a far more dangerous problem than when Nikki thought she was merely Jessica. And she has just talked her way into going back with her to Nikki's apartment.

They turn the corner into a far narrower thoroughfare, a gloomy and claustrophobic passageway where little light can penetrate between the buildings. She can see the dark panels where elements have burned out and never been replaced. It feels like an old place somehow, her mind drawing upon images from Victorian stories, where lanes and alleyways gave shelter for the darkest deeds.

There is barely room for two people to pass each other, but this matters little, as she sees no other people.

No witnesses, she thinks.

Did Nikki pull that reverse bluff on her again? Demonstrably trying to put Alice off coming here so that she would be all the more determined to follow?

No. She's getting paranoid now. There *is* a witness: Kinsi knows they are headed to Nikki's place. And Nikki definitely didn't want that to happen.

Nikki leads her into a cramped vestibule, with a vending machine squeezed into a tight space between the door and the staircase.

There is a Chinese lady coming down the stairs slowly. She looks matronly, not a sight Alice has seen often around here; like somebody's grandma. She gives Nikki a cursory acknowledgement but stares curiously at Alice for a duration that strays well into rudeness, before proceeding into the alley.

They ascend two storeys, Alice still able to hear and feel the thump of music from the venue on the ground floor. There are three doors on the landing. Nikki opens one of them, which leads straight into a tiny combined kitchen and living area with two other doors off it. One of them is open to her right, allowing Alice a view into a combined toilet and shower cubicle, the head one of those automated foldaways that flip up into the wall when you're done, giving an extra meaning to the word flush. Adjacent to that is presumably the bedroom door, currently closed, Nikki taking position defensively in front of it.

Alice feels a twinge of something, maybe guilt, maybe embarrassment. This is Nikki's home, and the whole place must be a fraction the size of her digs back at the Ver Eterna.

Nikki stands with her back to the bedroom door, redundantly pointing Alice towards the bathroom. She gets the impression she is being anxiously ushered there, which implies she is being directed away from someplace else.

"Okay, you go use the shower," Nikki says. "I'll go to my closet, see if I can't find something for you to wear. I'm taller than you but I probably got a shirt you can borrow, long as you don't mind looking a little scruffy."

"I'll take scruffy over blood-drenched."

Alice steps into the cubicle and closes the door. She begins to tug at the sticky shirt when she realises something is missing.

"Hey, do you have a towel, or is it one of those . . ." she begins, stepping back into the living area.

Nikki is standing in the bedroom doorway with her back to Alice. She spins around, pulling the door closed with a slam and standing in front of it in a hopeless attempt to appear halfway natural.

She looks guilty and cornered, and she knows it.

"What? A towel? No, it's an air-dry system."

"What's in the bedroom, Nikki?"

Her eyes dart around.

"That's my personal space. You got no right to go in there."

There is a moment's stand-off, the two of them silently staring at each other. Then Nikki makes a lunge. Alice senses it a fraction of a second before, picking up on micro-gestures. She flinches, anticipating attack, but it's flight not fight. Nikki runs straight out of the apartment and disappears down the stairs.

Alice doesn't give chase. She's been burned by that already. Instead she steps to the bedroom door and turns the handle, half expecting it to be locked. It isn't. She pushes it open very gently, slowly revealing another tiny space. The bed is pushed tight against one wall, barely clearance on the other side to stand and reach into the shallow closet.

On the bed is the reason Nikki didn't want Alice to come here. She tried to bluff it, must have thought she could still get her showered and out again without seeing this. And maybe she would have but for the want of a towel.

There is a woman lying on the bed, her eyes bulging in a permanent horrified stare. Livid marks ring her neck, bruises and cuts marring her face, blood spattering the pillow. She's been beaten and strangled in the last few hours, while Alice was being kept out of the way by Nikki's careful arrangement.

CdC now has two homicides, and one suspect.

CONTAMINATION (1)

Nikki has only opened the bedroom door maybe half a second when she hears Alice unexpectedly re-emerge from the shower closet. A lot happens in that half-second; a lot changes. It's time enough for a hundred things to run through her mind, as though this old second-gen mesh implant could accelerate the speed of her thinking, instead of simply helping her understand a few Chinese phrases or the street layout on some never-visited quadrant of Wheel Two.

It's Giselle. She's been murdered right here in Nikki's bedroom. Beaten and strangled and dead. Girl was twenty-eight years old.

Girl was pregnant. Ducking Nikki because she owed her money and she was saving to pay for a ticket home.

Half a second is not time enough to process the shock, to even begin to contemplate the loss, but it is enough for her to sense the jaws closing and understand that she is being set up. At that point, instinct takes control, the lizard brain acting decisively before her deeper cognitive processes have even booted up.

She pulls the door closed, too fast, too hard.

She's usually got a damn good poker face, but how do you front out a moment like that? Her expression might betray little, but that counts for shit when her body language is screaming in panic. It sure doesn't help that as they face off, she is beginning to suspect that Alice already knows what is behind the door she just slammed.

What was all that about, she had been asking herself, this sudden desire to take a shower at the home of someone she openly despises? She must have gotten a message telling her to engineer this visit. She could be lying about her lens not restarting too. Even if Alice didn't know about the body, dispatching her here had to be part of the set-up. Was Kinsi in on it somehow? She was the one who made the suggestion. No, it was Alice, being cleverly manipulative. She mentioned needing a shower and a change, prompting someone to suggest it. Alice must have known it would be common knowledge that Nikki lives nearby. In fact, she should probably assume there is little Alice doesn't know about her at this point.

It's also possible that Alice coming here right now was just dumb luck, but either way, she doesn't have any time to waste.

She runs.

There are things she could have taken from the apartment, but she doesn't know what Alice might be secretly packing. She can't afford to risk getting taken down by an electro-pulse or a resin gun if she heads for the living area instead of out the door.

Nikki hurdles the banister rather than running down the stairs, thus dropping the two storeys in three bounds. She is out in the alleyway in a few seconds, racing back towards Mullane.

She sees the shuffling figure of Mrs Pang up ahead, and checks her stride so she can squeeze past. Pang hears the footsteps though, turning around and putting out a hand to indicate she wants to talk. She's a strange one. Fell out with her family about something that makes no sense to Nikki, and moved up here as a fuck-you to all of them. Eighty-two years old and lives for her job at a firm developing lightweight radiation shielding materials.

"Can't stop, Mrs P," she warns, skipping past her sideways in the tight passage.

"That girl back at your apartment," Pang calls after her. "Yeah, I saw her here before, except her hair was different."

Like much of what Mrs Pang says, Nikki doesn't know why she's telling her this, but the implications are a kick to the gut. Mrs P is a witness. She's saying she saw Giselle come here earlier, and that she saw Giselle visit here before.

Giselle was here lots of times: sharing a bottle together, watching movies, sleeping together; sometimes just actually sleeping, but together.

Her hair *was* different. Nikki pictures Giselle in that pink wig she favoured. She must have worn it every time she came around. It was part of how she dealt with what she did, how she compartmentalised sex work: she had this hooker get-up, a means of inhabiting a different persona.

Nikki knows there are girls who work in Mullane to save a nest egg, then pay for memory removal at the end of it, thinking they can go back to Earth with no recollection of the specifics of what they have done. The jury is out on whether it works. Giselle sure wasn't for going down that path. Instead she maintained a border between where Giselle ended and Gillian Selby began, and in truth Nikki only got to see the former.

She told herself they were friends. She told herself that when they went back to her place it wasn't only because she offered protection and opportunities, or lent money, but who was she kidding? Just because it was payment in kind doesn't mean it wasn't payment. It doesn't mean she liked Nikki at all.

Nikki told herself she liked Giselle, but if that were true, wouldn't she have been interested in knowing Gillian Selby? Now Gillian Selby is dead, along with the baby she was determined to keep.

Motherfucker. Who would do this? Why would they do this?

She runs out of the alley onto Mullane and barrels into a big guy in overalls, spilling the Qola he's slugging.

She apologises, not making eye contact, keeping her head down as she strides away.

It has to be a means of taking herself out of the equation, she reasons. Could it be Julio and his new allies? If they think she killed Omega, this would be both payback and an effective way of neutralising her, as simply killing a Seguridad officer would bring down too much heat.

She needs to get off the street. Even if Alice isn't lying about her lens not reconnecting, it won't take her long to call this in. There is going to be an APB out on Nikki in no time.

She crosses Mullane and ducks into a place called Red Shift, which she knows is always dimly lit. It's a lone-drinker hang-out, with a predominantly male clientele, but even as a woman she is unlikely to get a second look. People go there to be alone, in a way they can't be simply by staying in their apartments.

She slips through the back and takes the stairs down to the

sub-surface level, turning off location-signalling on her lens and changing her ident so that she is auto-tagged as Hayley Ortega, a propulsion systems researcher. She wishes it was truly that simple to drop off the radar.

She's scanning Seguridad comms, text streams and audio channels, looking for the first clues that the starter gun has been fired on her manhunt.

It comes when she is peremptorily logged out, the police feeds disappearing all at once. She's had her credentials revoked: credentials that literally opened a lot of doors.

She reaches the main concourse, the sub-level Mullane, sticking her head around the corner to scope out the landscape. She sees Carlos, the officer who helped her after her "fight" with Fernando and Julia, staged so that "Jessica" wouldn't realise Nikki was behind her abduction. There is another cop alongside him. Carlos is talking while looking at nobody in particular, which means he's in communication via his lens and sub-vocal. He's probably requesting confirmation of what he's just been told. "Arrest Nikki Fixx" is not an order he was expecting to get on this patrol.

She ducks back into the passageway leading from Red Shift. She'll have to hold her position until he disappears.

It gets worse, though. On her lens she sees the rapid refresh of multiple public feeds that indicates a breaking story. They aren't saying what she did, because Boutsikari and the like will still be debating whether they can keep the truth from reaching Earth, but it's already official that she is a fugitive. Changing her ident isn't going to make so much of a difference now that her picture is flashing up on everybody's lenses. And there's no comfort in assuming it will flash off again as soon as some other piece of trending tittle-tattle pops up to replace it. There's a reward being offered, so a lot of folks are going to keep it in the corner for reference, and saving it to primary.

Everybody's suddenly a concerned citizen when there's a dollar value attached to it.

At least the cops can only be ordered to "apprehend immediately", as opposed to "shoot on sight". If this had happened to her back in LA, she'd be lucky to survive the hour.

Killing her isn't the play here, though. If somebody wanted her dead, they wouldn't have gone to the trouble of murdering Giselle and framing Nikki for it. The fallout from this, particularly coming on top of the Omega killing, is going to be too overwhelming for the local authorities to contain. There's a far more elaborate game being played here, one much bigger than pawns such as Yoram and Julio suspect.

She has to get out of Mullane, away from residential and entertainment areas. If she wants to stay hidden, she needs to head for the industrial and manufacturing zones, where there are fewer people on the streets. Problem is, she can't take a static. Too many people, not to mention the automatic facial scanning on the cars. The transport itself is free, but they like to keep track of who is going where. It's not even sinister: just a hundred different kinds of logistical audit for the crunch-heads to pore over.

There is another way of getting around though: the mag-line. In theory it could transport you anywhere on the wheel – as long as there's enough air in the crate for the duration of the trip, and that there's somebody waiting at the other end to let you out before you get auto-stacked in storage and the lid trapped shut beneath five more boxes.

The nearest control and access point is beneath Sin Garden. With a shiver she reflects that it is the one most recently used to abduct the new Principal of the SOE, via a means they occasionally deployed to dispose of particularly unruly drunks and other undesirable customers.

At the time Nikki thought she was abducting Jessica Cho, not Alice Blake. She had felt kind of bad about doing this to some young intern, but in Nikki's defence, even as Jessica she kinda had it coming. She *was* annoyingly self-righteous, and needed to understand that Auntie Nikki was an ally to make friends with, as opposed to a suspect to be ratted out.

It would have made the kid look good to her bosses too: being abducted because she saw something the crooks wanted erased would suggest she had an instinct for getting to the heart of things. That's what Nikki had told herself, anyway.

The passageway leading back to the underside of Sin Garden is only about twenty yards from where she's standing, but that's a long way when there are dozens of people walking back and forth or simply hanging, laughing about the shit they just did or saw. Not to mention the two cops actively searching for her.

She can't hide out in this alleyway for ever either. Sooner or later, somebody is going to come up this way, heading for Red Shift or because they want somewhere quick and convenient for a blow-job or a knee-trembler.

She looks at the news feeds. Her face is still up there, a recent shot too. Whoever is behind this must have got somebody to snap her sometime during the past twenty-four hours.

Fuck them. They may have revoked her credentials remotely but they can't wipe her memory, and as an ex-cop she is adept at remembering call signals and codes. Using her lens, she navigates to the neighbourhood's publicly accessible environmental monitoring and emergency systems, entering the authorisation code to trigger a localised airborne contaminant alert.

Lights begin flashing in panels on the walls, matched by similar oscillations in everyone's lenses. There is no panic: people know these things are usually a false alarm, but they *will* take action, meaning she can pull an air-filter mask over her face without being conspicuous, because everybody else is doing the same.

CONTAMINATION (II)

Alice is gripped in a momentary paralysis as she stares at the body in Nikki Freeman's bedroom. The impulse to give chase is stayed by her realistic appraisal that it would be futile. This is Nikki's turf, she's got a head start, and in the unlikely event that Alice did catch up with her, she doesn't like her chances of physically apprehending a woman who may already have chalked up two kills in as many days.

What is also keeping her in stasis is a horrified fascination at the sight of the victim. Alice doesn't have a name for her, due to her lens remaining stubbornly on the fritz, but it is not the dead woman's identity that is asserting a hold strong enough to pin her in place: it is what the body tells her about who Nikki Freeman truly is.

With a shudder she surmises that she may have gotten off lightly. Jessica Cho was only intended to lose her career as a price for getting in Nikki's way. What measures might she have taken had Alice proven a more formidable obstacle?

Alice has seen plenty of murder victims both in the morgue and at crime scenes, in cities all across the Earth. Nonetheless, something about this one gets her in the gut, more even than the floating carnage in the Axle. That was too weirdly abstract to even relate to on a human level, its victim broken down into constituent parts that made it impossible to imagine the whole. This, by contrast, is intimate, immediate, heart-breaking. It is an affront, an insult to everything she wanted to believe about CdC. It was supposed to be a place where new futures were imagined and constructed. Instead she is looking at a healthy young woman who should be walking around right now: a million possible futures choked off in one ugly act.

Alice is stirred from her frozen solitude by the sound of footsteps on the stairs. She turns, half expecting to see Nikki bounding back, perhaps to tie up a very large loose end. Instead she sees an athletic-looking and sharply dressed man stride towards the doorway.

"Is everything okay? I just saw Nikki high-tail it out of here like the place was on fire and oh Jesus Christ."

He has seen the body. Alice reaches to close the door but she knows it's too late. He has already looked at it for a lot longer than the micro-second glimpse she needed to understand the situation.

He clamps a hand over his mouth, his eyes wide, staring at Alice almost accusingly in shock and growing fear.

"Wait," she says, but it functions only as the cue for him to flee.

He takes off, running down the stairs, and she knows she has no chance of catching him any more than she could have tailed Nikki. Even if the guy tripped and broke his ankle at the foot of the stairs, she is not empowered to detain him, and certainly has no way of preventing him from communicating.

There is no containing the situation like there was in the Axle. There's a witness on the street, possibly in possession of a grabación, and she doesn't even know his name.

This just went public.

DEAD ON ARRIVAL

Nikki feels the crate come to a smooth but rapid stop, the deceleration rate not designed with human passengers in mind. There is a subsequent lateral movement, shunting her on to another track perhaps. She braces for the next jolt of acceleration, hoping it comes soon. She was held in a bottleneck for a worryingly long time quite early in her journey, eating into her limited air supply. Another wait like that and it's going to be touch and go.

There is no movement for several seconds, enough for her to worry that she is in another queue. Then she feels the pressure of a vertical ascent against her back and she breathes again, because this indicates the crate has reached its destination.

There is one final shunt as the crate is moved clear of the conduit shaft, then stillness and silence. She waits a few moments to be sure, then presses upwards against the lid. It is stuck fast, immovable.

"Oh no. Oh no, no, no."

The crate must have been slid into a slot at the bottom of an automated stacking frame. This is precisely what she was afraid of. She had chosen this address, a botanical genetics lab, because the last time she passed through here, the receiving facility didn't have such a thing.

If she waits long enough, her crate will rotate to the top of the stack, but that could be hours or even days. She doesn't know how often these guys even use the mag-line. (Again, she chose this place because she thought there was a good chance nobody would be down here to see her emerge.)

She doesn't have that much air left and she's using it faster in her growing consternation.

She begins to bang on the lid and call for help. It might see her apprehended and in custody within the next half-hour, but given the alternative is death by asphyxiation, she has little choice. How long did she think she could stay running for anyway?

Jesus, she thinks, feeling the sense of panic grow as she bangs and calls, bangs and calls, to no response. What if she was right and the staff seldom come down here unless they're expecting a delivery?

No, she reasons, trying to calm herself. If they have a rotator, that means they get a lot of stuff coming through here these days.

The crate judders and begins to slide. It isn't being rotated: somebody is hauling it out of the frame.

Nikki presses with her fingers, the lid springing upwards and open the moment it clears the bracket that was holding it in place. She climbs up into a squat and sees an Asian guy backing away towards the wall. He's got an interlocking grab-pole in his hands, which he has just used to slide out the crate but is now gripping as a weapon.

Nikki holds up her palms to gesture that she means no harm.

"Thanks," she tells him, climbing slowly upright. He still doesn't look reassured.

"Somebody's idea of a joke," she adds, indicating the crate. "I was on a night out."

He retains his confused look for a moment, then breaks into an uncertain smile, nodding that he gets it. She realises he doesn't speak English and is probably translating through his mesh.

"Not funny joke," he responds, her own mesh rendering his words thus. "I not here, package dead on arrival."

"Exactly. I owe you. And I owe them payback. Best be on my way."

She steps clear of the crate and begins heading for the door.

"You are celebration?" he asks.

"Huh?"

"Got the test launch big. Go all systems."

She doesn't know what he's talking about, then remembers that she is identifying as Hayley Ortega. She vaguely recalls hearing that there is a laser-propulsion test vehicle getting ready to launch:

a two-year trip to assess long-term habitat sustainability and energy consumption.

Fortunately, he most likely assumes her bafflement is down to the translation.

"Yeah, that's right."

She gives him a thumbs-up gesture and hopes to hell these people don't have any specimens on the flight. She does not want to get into any kind of memorable conversation with this guy, particularly one in which she suspiciously doesn't know what she's talking about.

She heads up to ground level and slips out of a side door. She is in the McAuliffe district, where there is very little foot traffic outside shift change. Most of the buildings are comparatively low-rise, and there are some ground-level empty spaces, used for trial assembly of structures so that they can be sure everything fits and works before sending it up the line to a test vehicle at the dry dock.

Nikki's lens is fully functional again after the unavoidable blackout effect of her journey on the mag-line. The electromagnetics play havoc with comms, effectively turning the crate into a Faraday cage. Her log is showing multiple connection attempts from Yoram. She calls him back, voice-only so that she isn't broadcasting any clues to her whereabouts, and so that her face can't give anything away either. She wants the information in this call to be heading in one direction only, otherwise there's no point to it.

Yoram answers instantly.

"Nikki. Where are you?"

"I'm on Nightmare Boulevard, heading south."

"What's going on? Everybody's looking for you. I got Seguridad outside my building. They're on the way up here and I need to know what I can and can't tell them. What the hell did you do?"

"I'm being set up, Yoram. Somebody killed a girl and left her in my apartment."

"A girl? Who?"

"You don't know her. A pro. Worked out of a few places on Mullane. She's connected to me, put it that way."

"Damn it. Who did this? Julio?"

"That's what I'm trying to find out, but I'm running out of moves."

"I'd tell you to come here, but . . ."

"I get it. Wouldn't want to bring this heat down on you anyway."

"I appreciate that. There has to be some way I can help you, though. Do you have money? I can get some to you. Where are you right now?"

Nikki knows any payments she makes will automatically locate her: her ID is reading Hayley Ortega but the money never lies. She has some funds in chargeable tokens, the Seedee equivalent of cash, but it isn't going to last her long. It matters little. The only currency that can help her right now is information. She has to find out what the hell is going on before somebody slaps the cuffs on her.

"Thanks for the offer, but they're likely to tail anybody you could send. In fact, you best get the word out to everybody that they're probably under surveillance."

"I know more people than they could possibly tail, Nikki, believe me."

"Sorry, Yoram. I'm sure you do, and I like the odds. It's just the stake that I can't afford."

She disconnects, relieved she didn't have to look at his face as they lied to each other.

He's selling her out. He asked where she was – twice – and that wasn't even the biggest giveaway. Yoram offering help without looking for a back-end? Forget it. The Seguridad aren't on their way up to his apartment: they got there while she was stuck in the mag-line, and they've offered him a deal. It's what she would do if she were the cop in this situation. She wouldn't be surprised if Boutsikari and Jaganathan are there in person right now. At the very least they'll be talking to him, and were probably listening in on her call.

It hurts, but she doesn't hold a grudge. She of all people understands how Yoram would do anything to protect what he has here, and more importantly to avoid being sent back to Earth and the ashes of everything he lost. He will tell them something that protects himself as well as giving them what they want.

She can almost hear it: "I told Nikki that something needed to be done about Omega after the shipment got jacked, but I had no idea she would go so far." They will get to close the Omega case quick-smart, and to shut down the Gillian Selby murder before it becomes a big deal.

She checks her location. She's on McAuliffe, close to the junction with Hadfield, but in truth she's now leaving Nightmare Boulevard and taking a hard right on to Hellslide Avenue.

She is exhausted. The adrenalin that fuelled her flight from her apartment (and which was further charged by her desperate resort to the oxygen-roulette of the mag-line) has worn off, leaving her feeling weak and shaky. She could use a drink. She could use a sleep. She can't remember when she last got some rest.

No, that's not true. She remembers fine when she last woke up. It's the going to sleep part that's fuzzy once again. What's up with that? This happened before, when she woke up in bed with Candace, cuts on her knuckles, no recollection of how she got them.

After the disastrous deal at Dock Nine, she worked her shift, broke up some fights, looked into a robbery at an electronics manufacturing firm (almost certainly an inside job) then clocked off and hit some bars. She remembers who she spoke to, who she drank with, early part of the evening, leastways, but after that, nothing. She woke up in someone else's apartment, someone else's bed: guy named Arlo, a medical researcher with a sideline in developing performance-enhancing stimulants.

She doesn't remember if they did it. She doesn't remember getting to his place, in fact, only waking up there. That's where she was when she got the call to go to the Axle, where she got handed the poison chalice that is the Omega case.

It's starting to worry her. Frightening possibilities are suggesting themselves. She keeps seeing Giselle, dead in her bedroom. Half a second, that's all she saw of her, but it's replaying in her mind more vividly than any grab on a lens.

She recalls a conversation with Alice, back when she thought she was Jessica.

It's irrational, but it's still a scary idea that what you think is a person could actually be a machine.

No. That's only a little bit scary. What's terrifying . . . is the thought that you could be an android yourself and not even know.

She was just screwing with the noob, playing on Earthbound fears about Seedee. Nikki doesn't believe in the bullshit theories that AI tech is secretly further advanced than anybody knows, but she's got a mesh inside her skull, and she doesn't know for sure what that really does. Nobody asks to examine the blueprints before they sign up for the surgery, any more than they would ask to decompile the code before installing a piece of software.

It's a device for inserting memories, for Christ's sake. How does she know that everything she remembers wasn't uploaded half an hour before she woke up?

The unavoidable horror is that she doesn't.

Like the fear she alluded to about being an android, the scariest part is you'd never know. She could have killed Giselle. She could have killed Omega. Everything she remembers, or thinks she remembers, could have been inserted while she slept, her immediate past edited, rewritten.

No. Shake it loose, she tells herself. She's tired and fucked up and she can't afford to let these ideas into her kitchen. She needs to go to what she knows: she needs to think like a cop, if she can still remember how to do that.

It's *possible* Yoram had Omega killed, but it doesn't feel right. It's a zero-option play. When your entire business model relies upon keeping the authorities looking the other way, it's mutually assured destruction to murder a rival and thus bring down the cops on both your heads. That's why it doesn't track that Julio would retaliate by killing a prostitute merely in order to frame Nikki. Julio wouldn't want to attract that kind of heat, particularly when he's got some major play in the offing. Plus, it's way too nuanced a plan for Julio's mentality.

That's who she needs to speak to. She needs to find out what Julio really knows, and to do that she needs to look him in the eye when she's asking her questions. She can't go to him, though. Even if he isn't responsible for what happened to Giselle, he'll still be only too happy to capture Nikki and hand her over to the Seguridad, thus neutralising her as a threat.

She needs to draw him out, come at him sideways some place where he's off guard. In short, she needs an edge.

She wracks her memory for any angle she can use. It keeps coming back to this nebulous, nagging thought that she's not been able to pin down; the feeling that she missed something when it was right before her eyes. It was something connecting Omega, Freitas and Dade, something other than that they all worked for Julio, and yet intrinsically linked to that fact.

The obvious thing they have in common is their day-jobs, though maybe that's only suggesting itself right now because NutriGen is on Hadfield, only a short walk from where she's standing. She's been mulling it over since she braced Freitas but nothing seemed to leap out, maybe because her head is so full of other things. Right now, she has no greater priority to deflect her focus.

She walks back through everything she can remember about her visit there with Alice: who they spoke to, what they saw.

There was Vera Polietsky, who they both ran into again at Klaws. Couldn't be that – Nikki spoke to Freitas before she saw Vera again, and this same undefined thought had been nagging her then.

There was Frank Jacobs, their supervisor. No, couldn't be him either. They spoke to him in a bar on Mullane, not at the processing plant.

Then she zeroes it. It was just before their conversation about AI, and the notion that you might never know if you were an android. Alice stopped in front of one of the fish tanks and stared into it like it was a window into Nikki's soul. At the time, the girl was being generally weird and evasive, trying not to answer any questions about her family background. Now Nikki knows why that was, but she still doesn't know what she was finding so interesting about the fact that fish were avoiding one corner of a goddamn tank. She hadn't paid this much heed because she thought "Jessica" was merely some wide-eyed young intern, and who could predict what she might find fascinating? But if Alice Blake was staring, then there was something worth staring at.

216

That's the thing she missed. Something had snagged on her subconscious inside the place where Omega and two more of Julio's people worked. She needs another look at it, right now.

HUMAN INTEREST

An hour later Alice is still standing in Nikki's tiny hallway, but now she has been joined by Boutsikari, Captain Jaganathan, medical examiner Dr Samira Hussein and a Seguridad officer named Phil Lito. Lito is looking vertiginously apprehensive from finding himself in a situation as high above his pay grade as Heinlein Station is above the Pacific Ocean. With her lens and comms system still inoperative, Alice needed somebody to call in the situation and he was the first officer she encountered out on Mullane.

Boutsikari's first action upon arriving at the scene was to stress to Lito how imperative it was that he keep his mouth shut, while Alice's first words to Boutsikari were to convey how this would be pointless.

She could see the impact as she described her encounter with the startled witness. It was a kick to the gut, but he went from dismay to acceptance with practised speed. Like most political animals, Boutsikari's primary survival skill was adaptability. His agenda turns on a dime, and he is already formulating new strategies, altering priorities. Right now it's all about information, getting the details clear in his own mind.

"Nikki brought you back here?" he asks. "Knowing what you were likely to see?"

"It wasn't her idea. She was backed into a corner but I think she reckoned she could get me in and out without seeing what was in the bedroom. Nonetheless, I saw what I saw, and she ran."

"As innocent people always do," says Jaganathan.

"So what do we know about the victim?"

"Her name is Gillian Selby," Lito responds redundantly, drawing a glare from Boutsikari. He knows that much from his lens.

"I'd estimate she was killed sometime in the last six to eight hours," Dr Hussein replies. "Death by strangulation, chokehold with bare hands rather than any kind of ligature. Beaten about the face, defensive abrasions on the hands. Looks like she put up a fight, or maybe it started as a fight and she lost."

Six to eight hours, Alice calculates. It most likely happened while she was unconscious, and definitely during the window while she and Nikki were separated.

"The files say she worked automated production maintenance at a multi-purpose fabrication outfit," Boutsikari observes. "But I doubt that's what got her killed. Is she connected to Ben Haim or Martinez?" he asks Jaganathan.

"Not that I'm aware of."

Boutsikari's expression indicates a deep scepticism as to whether Jaganathan would be aware of it either way. Alice can imagine Nikki scoffing at how far the captain is from both his jurisdiction and his comfort zone.

Boutsikari fixes Lito with a piercing stare, impaling him to the spot.

"You work Mullane. You know her face?"

Lito swallows, mouth dry. He doesn't look like he's used to speaking truth to power, or speaking anything to power for that matter.

"I think she was a prostitute," he answers apologetically, his cringing fear of being the shot messenger indicating that he fully understands the ramifications.

"Fuck me. A dead hooker, found in the home of, and most likely killed by, Seedee's dirtiest cop, and someone's probably got a grab of the body. This is going to be leading the news planetside in a matter of hours."

Boutsikari lets out a long sigh at the escalating awfulness.

"I actually can't think how we could possibly air more of our dirty laundry in one go. I mean, that's unless anyone can suggest how we might make this worse."

Dr Hussein clears her throat.

"Would the victim being pregnant do the trick?"

"Jesus Christ, you're kidding me," Boutsikari says, glaring at Dr Hussein like she said this just to piss him off. "How can you tell that from a cursory examination?"

"I wouldn't need her to pee on a stick. She's four months gone, maybe five. That's unless she had one bitch of an abdominal abscess."

The ensuing moment of silence is punctured by the arrival of another Seguridad officer, rapping his knuckles tentatively on the doorframe to attract his bosses' attention.

"Sir, we've been showing Selby's picture to people in the building. A Mrs Li Pang confirms that she saw her here with Freeman on multiple occasions. Said they were friends, implied they might be more than that."

"Yeah, well, Nikki didn't get her pregnant," Boutsikari observes. "Could be something to fight over, though."

"And someone else in the picture," Jaganathan says. "We need to find out who."

Boutsikari glances into the bedroom, looking at Hussein rather than Selby. The victim isn't his primary concern: that will be Jaganathan's problem. Boutsikari has multiple wider battles to fight, and is currently weighing up which front to shore up first.

"Okay, it's public, the genie's not going back in the bottle, so we have to make that work for us. We need to get messages out on all feeds that Freeman is wanted and extremely dangerous. Offer a reward for information but warn people not to approach her. The last thing we can afford is Freeman offing some have-a-go-Joe civilian when the eyes of the world are about to be trained our way. We need to bring her in asap, it's the only way to put a lid on this, but even then we're in damage limitation mode."

"Yes, sir," Jaganathan responds, then heads out the door, already relaying orders.

Boutsikari turns to Alice and lets out a baleful sigh.

"I really thought we were going to get away with it," he tells her.

Get away with what? she wonders, then remembers that success for Boutsikari was defined by preventing news of a murder on CdC reaching Earth. It was always a long shot as far as she was concerned, but the clock had not run out until this second murder changed the game.

"We caught a major break on the Omega killing while you were gone," he explains.

"What?"

"Our analysts discovered Korlakian recorded a grab before he died. Because we don't know the time of death, it could have been ten hours before the killing or ten minutes, but it's the only thing he recorded in weeks, so we're guessing it was important."

"Yes, but you can't access it," she points out. "Or are you telling me you can hack his personal cache?"

Grabacións are private, protected by unbreakable DNA-based encryption unless you choose to unlock them. In certain circumstances the law can compel an individual to do so, but once they die, anything they chose not to disclose is effectively locked away for ever.

"No, but Korlakian approved a share. That's why we reckon it was a Hail Mary, or more like a bequest."

"If he was recording his assailant, why didn't he broadcast it at the time?"

"Don't know. We're guessing the signal was blocked. But the break for us is that the file was tagged for his legacy archive, and he had a nominated recipient."

"Who?"

"A sister, back down below. If we can contact her, we're confident we can persuade her to share the file so we can give him justice. We're assuming that's why he tagged the file for legacy: knowing that if the worst happened, someone he trusted would see it."

"So why are you saying 'if'? Are you having difficulty persuading her?"

"We're having difficulty finding her. Korlakian was from LA but his family hails from Armenia. Turns out the sister went back there years ago, after she got divorced. Left no forwarding address. We've got people on it, though. Reckoned another couple of days and we might have had all we need. If the grab showed Yoram, or even better, Nikki Freeman, we could have wrapped up Seedee's only ever murder case with a ribbon and a bow before anybody down below even heard about it."

"But then . . ." Alice says, casting a glance towards the bedroom. He looks imploringly towards her.

"Unless that's something you can help us with?"

Alice has an instinctive desire to assist, driven in part by her concerns regarding how her superiors back on Earth are likely to react when they find out about this. For the first time, she feels a commonality with these people who are effectively her new colleagues, rather than with her old ones at FNG: a solidarity in protecting themselves against the forces below who can exercise power over CdC but have no first-hand understanding of the realities up here.

Us against them. Secrecy, conspiracy, mendacity. This is how it begins, she realises: going native.

"I helped you contain the Omega murder, and this is where it led us. How FNG responds is out of my hands now. In fact, if I don't report in full on this, I'm going to be on an elevator home before I've even officially taken up my post."

Boutsikari's expression remains neutral. He might be disappointed, but he must know she's right. This was taken out of her hands the moment that neighbour came downstairs and saw the body.

"When was the last time you got any sleep?" he asks her.

It suddenly hits her that she's been on her feet for around thirty hours, minus an indeterminate period spent drugged unconscious, which is not the same as rest.

"It's been a while."

"Sounds like one hell of a shift you've had. You should go get your head down. Maybe by the time you wake up, this will all be sorted," he adds with grim humour.

IN PLAIN SIGHT

Nikki is back inside NutriGen within a few minutes, walking straight in the front door much as she did earlier. Security is generally not a huge priority for most workplaces on Seedee, for the simple reason that at any given time, most people are too busy inside their own workplaces to be up to no good inside someone else's.

Some of the scientific and engineering research facilities understandably take precautions against industrial espionage, because they are often in direct competition to develop technology and new products. That doesn't apply to a facility primarily in the business of turning fish into protein.

Nikki's greatest concern is therefore not gaining ingress, but being identified. The menial nature of much of the work here increases the possibility of employees scanning the news feeds for distraction, but certain environmental factors are working in Nikki's favour by giving her a reason to slap on a face mask. Half the people in here are wearing them, so even though the fish tanks are not inside the noxious area, anyone passing her might plausibly assume she is on her way to or from there.

She retraces her earlier route and walks slowly among the tanks. The slot that was empty has been filled since she was last here, a new tank locked into the brackets. Another has been drained, one of its side walls completely removed; possibly for damage repair or maybe routine maintenance. The bottom remains covered in gravel, a smell of brine wafting from the interior. It isn't pleasant, but it nonetheless sparks a warming memory, of walks on Venice Beach down to Marina Del Rey.

Why are the fish all avoiding that one corner? Alice had asked.

Nikki looks into one of the tanks, where she sees no evidence of this. She looks in another, a third, a fourth, then into the new

223

one. Nothing there either, she thinks. Then suddenly it's noticeable. A dozen fish, swimming in a group, dart one way then another, reacting as one to who knows what. They zip back and forth, but there's an area they are consistently avoiding.

You asking me to be a fish psychologist now? How the hell would I know? Don't look like anything to me.

Nikki goes to the drained tank, reaches in and picks up a handful of gravel. She walks back to the new tank, reaches above the walls and scatters it on the surface. She watches the tiny stones slowly sink, but most of them don't reach the bottom. They appear to be suspended half a metre up, forming a flat surface. Something is there and yet not there: an area with a volume that has to be at least fifty litres.

She remembers as a kid, her science teacher making a Pyrex jar disappear inside a larger jar of cooking oil. The oil's index of refraction matched that of the Pyrex, meaning you couldn't see one inside the other. There has to be a vessel inside the tank made of some transparent nano-carbon material that matches the index of refraction of far less viscous liquids, such as water. And quite possibly alcohol.

Son of a bitch. This is how Julio is bringing in his tequila.

Nikki takes a moment to breathe. A few days ago, this would have been a game-changer, a discovery that put the balance of power in the palm of her hand. Now that she understands how small the power game between Yoram and Julio truly is, all she's holding is a tuft of grass on the edge of a cliff.

It's more than she had half an hour ago, however.

Nikki slips out of NutriGen and finds a quiet spot just off Hadfield. She checks the time to reassure herself that she's still a few hours from the next shift change, then composes an anonymous message to send to Julio.

I am with FNG oversight. I just took up a position with FLAT and my beat includes Hadfield. I have discovered some significant irregularities at NutriGen concerning the transferable tanks used in the replenishment of fish stocks. It would be in your interest to discuss mutually reassuring arrangements.

She lays down a time and a carefully chosen venue, a place called Habitek that is among the very few premises on CdC that Nikki can guarantee will be empty. She signs off by adding:

Come alone and don't be late. Anything happens that I don't like, my associate has instructions to toss some limes into the tank and let the fish make margaritas.

HONEYTRAP

Nikki watches Julio arrive, tracing his progress from the outer perimeter and through the labyrinth of corridors that comprises Habitek HQ. It took her only twenty minutes to get here from NutriGen, but she knew it would take Julio at least twice that, giving her time to scope the terrain.

Habitek designs and manufactures environment modules for spacecraft and for use on prospective exo-planets. There's seldom such a thing as a vacant lot on Seedee, but she knows Habitek's staff have all decanted to the Axle and the dry dock, where they have spent the last couple of months fitting out their environmental systems aboard Test Vehicle 14.27.

Julio is headed for the octagonal central chamber, where Nikki is waiting for him, though he doesn't know who he is coming here to meet. The octagon is where Habitek assemble and demonstrate their test modules, but it is currently empty, the central area of the floor as clean as any surface on Seedee. This is because this section is in fact an elevator platform that descends all the way to the outer rim, allowing the modules to be tested in space conditions. It also allows them to be picked up by shuttles for transportation.

The interior is a maze, which means there are multiple exits should Julio try to pull anything, with the caveat that Nikki does not have a simple or direct escape route. What she does have is the Seguridad emergency-access code to Habitek's internal monitoring network, which means she can stream all of the camera feeds direct to her lens. She is toggling through them to track Julio's progress and to ensure that he has come alone as ordered.

So far she hasn't seen any of his crew within the perimeter. She doesn't doubt they'll be close by, but the important thing is that they won't be getting within fifty metres of the central chamber without Nikki knowing about it.

She watches Julio stride through the corridors with that light and lazy gait of his, the slightest limp on his left-hand side if you know to look for it. He's looking good, but then he always does. He's in his late thirties but still boyishly attractive, and his dress sense is to be envied. Nobody has much of a wardrobe up here, but whatever Julio does wear looks stylish by virtue of simply being on him.

Nikki isn't too proud to admit to herself that she'd like a tumble with the guy, if he wasn't such an asshole.

Everyone assumes he was some kind of gangster back on Earth, a rumour he has diligently cultivated in order to bolster his reputation. The Quadriga has a controversial open-door policy on hiring ex-cons: a criminal record does not disqualify you from working here, as long as you are given a clean bill of mental health by their psychologists. It is part of the philosophy of the entire project – the idea that we should all believe in the possibility of a new beginning. Consequently, there are a lot of people here quietly serving out a personal penance. The Quadriga always knew that Seedee would benefit from individuals like that: folks who understand they'll never be family men and women, and whose lives are only given purpose by a commitment to their work.

That isn't Julio's story, though. Nikki knows otherwise.

He grew up in a rough neighbourhood, with no father, a drunk mother and two older brothers who were running rackets in their early teens when they weren't serving juvenile detention. Julio had a route out of there, though. He was this genius soccer player. The gods reached down and touched his left foot. He got signed up by one of the big clubs in Spain and was tipped for a career that would take him to a different world from his fuck-up family. Problem was he never escaped their orbit and they dragged him back down.

Julio got his left knee shattered. Not on the field: two psychos with baseball bats took him to a lock-up and went to work on his leg. It was nothing to do with him: just a means of getting at one of his brothers, who had crossed the wrong guy.

Took him six months to walk again, and as for soccer, forget it.

He trained as a chef, made a new start, but he was still living in a world where soccer was everywhere and he couldn't deal with the constant reminders of what he had lost. Word is he just couldn't forgive his brothers either: never spoke to them again. Eventually he applied to come work in Seedee, start over in a place with few reminders of his past.

A lot of people got a plan like that, but it only works if you can wipe the slate clean inside your own head. Julio showed up on Seedee with a sackful of bitterness and rage. He was short-tempered, violent and resentful: always angry about not getting his due, and no matter how much he did get, it was never enough. Then ironically, for a guy so determined to escape his fuck-up brothers, he found that his real mojo lay in the family business.

Nikki is standing on the opposite side of the octagon, about fifteen metres from where Julio enters. It's as close as she intends to let him get.

He gives an odd little laugh as he realises who he is looking at, like he's surprised and yet shouldn't have been.

"Nikki fucking Fixx."

"I need you to know that I didn't kill Omega," she says.

She doesn't have to tell him to keep his distance. He leans against the doorway, folding his arms, reflecting upon what she has said and most probably the very fact of her presence.

"Your buddies in Seguridad sure seem to think you did. That's why your face is on every lens and you're hiding out in here, instead of strutting around being cock of the walk up on Mullane like you love to do."

Interesting, she thinks. That isn't why she's on the lam, so either he doesn't know the real reason or else he is *pretending* not to know. She's betting on the former. Julio's not sharp enough for that kind of compartmentalisation. On the spur of the moment, he wouldn't be able to calculate what information he can and can't reveal.

"What they think doesn't matter. The truth is it wasn't me."

"You drew me out here just to tell me that? Like I care which one of Yoram's people did it. If you're hoping to spare yourself from the coming storm, I hope you got something more to offer me than pleading that you didn't butcher my friend."

"The reason I brought you here is to tell you that I don't think Yoram did it either. Come on, Julio. God knows there's no love lost between us all, but nobody on Seedee ever resorted to murder over illicit liquor. Why would Yoram cross that line, never mind so spectacularly, knowing it would have the authorities back on Earth demanding a crackdown up here? Who does that help?"

"Maybe he had nothing left to lose. He's an old man, getting desperate. He knows we're taking over all his business, so maybe he figures if he can't run it, nobody's running it."

He sounds confident, like he actually believes this.

"I don't know what you've got up your sleeve, Julio, but I think you've got a tiger by the tail. I mean, don't you have any questions, any suspicions over who these guys were at Dock Twelve?"

She gets it wrong deliberately. She wants to see if he corrects her.

He doesn't. His expression is blank; but vacant blank rather than poker blank.

"Do you even know what I'm talking about?"

He smiles.

"I know far more than you, that's for sure. And that can't be comfortable for you, Nikki, huh? Being so out of the loop that you're reduced to hassling Sol while the guy is trying to enjoy a quiet workout?"

At the mention of Sol, Nikki toggles through the cameras on her lens. There is still no sign of movement on the outer perimeter, nobody approaching the premises.

"Oh, sure, you're the man in the loop. Tell me again: why are the Seguridad chasing me, Julio?"

She takes in the discomfort in his expression, adequate confirmation that he doesn't understand the relevance of the question.

"I'm trying to warn you there's a bigger game being played here, way above your head and mine. Somebody is trying to make out there's a turf war going on, and they're using it as cover for something else."

"There *is* a turf war going on," he replies. "You're just pissed that you're losing it." Julio lets out a chuckle. "Yeah, used to be so sweet for you, the glory days when you ran me and my boys out of Mullane. Acting like the sheriff when you were the biggest outlaw on the wheel. Thinking yourself some kind of patron saint to all those hookers because they're paying you for protection instead of working for someone like me or Sergei Rascasse."

He's babbling away, savouring his moment with that smug look on his cute-but-stupid face. Then she realises she's the stupid one. He isn't savouring the moment: he's playing for time.

She checks the cameras again and watches three of Julio's men drop down through the ceiling in different corridors. They're right outside the octagon, approaching from all sides, and those are just the ones she can see.

They knew there were cameras inside and scanning the perimeter. They must have ziplined across from an adjacent building.

Nikki looks back at Julio, who is moving towards her as Dade and two others she doesn't recognise enter the octagon. She doesn't see Freitas, but he's bound to be on his way too.

She's carrying an electro-pulse and a resin gun. At this distance she could neutralise one of them with the jizz cannon, get off two shots if she is lucky. The zapper is a direct-contact weapon, good for one-on-one. There is no way of running these numbers that shows her winning this fight, and everybody in the room knows it.

"See, I sussed that message had to be from you, 'cause I knew you'd been sniffing around NutriGen," Julio says. "Take it as a double-edged compliment. I figured, who else would be smart enough to work out my deal with the tequila? And who else would be dumb enough to back herself into this rat trap?"

"I'm not the one being dumb here. Believe me, you don't want to do this."

"Believe me, we really do. Reckon we'll score ourselves some points with Boutsikari and the FNG by being such good citizens. Maybe even get us a reward."

They're all around her now, only a few metres away.

"Julio, I'm trying to warn you. I'm not the one walking into a trap."

It's as she says this that the lights go out.

PREMIUM CHANNELS

Alice does not return to her accommodation in the Ver Eterna. It would just take too long to travel all the way back to Wheel Two and she wants to stay close to the action in case of any developments. Instead she asks Boutsikari for a recommendation and makes her way to the Armstrong Hotel on Garneau, where an FNG account gets her a room.

Garneau was CdC's commercial and admin district before Wheel Two was built and the Armstrong its favoured bolthole for VIPs on short-term visits, but its history and comparative grandeur are redundant as far as Alice is concerned. She only needs two things: someplace to lie down and a comms terminal to connect to while she waits for FNG's tech people to fix her lens. They've been working remotely to reset her database connection at source. If they haven't cracked it in the next few hours, she will need to head back to HQ on Central Plaza to be fitted with new hardware.

The room is cramped compared to the Ver Eterna, a legacy of times when space was at more of a premium rather than a testament to the FNG's budget. She takes off her shoes, a sensual experience on its own comparable to stepping into a warm bath, and flops down on the narrow bed.

The clock says 04:12 but these are merely numbers. She's so tired she can't even remember whether this is stating Greenwich Mean Time, the time in New York when she left or the time at Ocean Terminal where she boarded the elevator. Nor does she have the clarity to work out which phase any of them relates to.

It's bedtime. That's the only time that matters.

She doesn't go to sleep though, not right away. First she's got to perform some damage limitation of her own, having decided that the only way to mitigate the coming fallout from FNG is to be the one who breaks it to them.

She connects to the room's terminal, instantly turning one wall into a screen, which she promptly reduces with a gesture until it is a less overwhelming size. The default settings flood her with a dozen feeds she would have had muted on her lens, some public, some privileged. So much information but no real news. There have been no reliable sightings of Nikki, though she does spot a report of a contaminant alert around Mullane. Going by the time it was triggered, she figures that was probably her creating a distraction to cover her retreat, but it offers no clue as to where she was heading.

She wonders where Nikki is; and not merely in the way the Seguridad are desperate to locate her. She is trying to picture her, imagine how she is doing, what is going through her head. Nikki is a presence unlike any that Alice has known, and part of her doesn't want to believe she is really responsible for what she is being accused. It's Alice's job to clean things up, but she can already see how CdC would be a duller place without Nikki in it.

Alice composes herself on the edge of the bed and sends out her request to the Chair of the FNG's Oversight Committee, to whom Alice reports. Most people on Earth could name the FNG's current President and at least their own country's Prime Representative to the Federation, but few people outside political circles will have heard of Aurelia Ochoba. This is intentional, because when it comes to CdC, it is the person in her position who holds the true power at the FNG.

As she waits for a reply, she checks her image in the frame and runs a hand though her tangled hair. She is wondering whether it would make a better impression to look respectfully smart or bedraggled by her exhausting efforts when Ochoba's face suddenly appears on the screen.

She is at home in Lagos, Nigeria. Alice is too tired to work out what the time is there, but she can tell she got Ochoba out of bed and she doesn't look thrilled about it. The Chair knows she wouldn't do this unless it was important, but Alice suspects she's not going to be any happier when she finds out quite *how* important.

"We've got a major situation up here," she begins, and proceeds to fill in Ochoba on everything she had previously been so diligently suppressing.

Even as she speaks her opening words she realises how skewed is the Earth's perspective upon its effective first colony: like a too-precious child, obsessively fussed-over and in danger of being spoilt as a result.

It's not a major situation. It's a murder hunt, like is probably happening within a few miles of where Ochoba sits now, like is probably happening in every major city on Earth. Everything up here is always amplified and extrapolated, everyone down below permanently overanxious at their perceived stake in the great game.

And some stakes are bigger than others. History's most complex public-private partnership, the world's largest super-corporations ostensibly locked into a pact of mutual cooperation, but in reality battling to slice up its biggest-ever pie. Ochoba's talent is in navigating the treacherous waters between the Quadriga and FNG, as the latter endeavours to maintain some control of where its constituent nations' money is being spent. But they both know that is nothing compared to the factionalism within the Quadriga, which is in a state of permanent conflict with itself.

Alice can't help but think of Nikki Freeman and her talk of how the perceived criminality on CdC is a mere distraction to keep people's eyes off the bigger games being played elsewhere.

Ochoba is impassive as always, concealing her anger and dismay behind her usual façade. Nonetheless, she seldom leaves anyone in any doubt as to where she believes their shortcomings lie.

"You admit you were complicit in concealing this initial murder from us?" she asks, her tone an audible affidavit.

Alice isn't ready to sign any confessions.

"I believed I could learn considerably more about how things really work up here if I let things play out, particularly having found myself in a position of advantage during a moment of crisis. To come in heavy-handed at such a time, as a newcomer and an outsider, would have been to waste that advantage."

Ochoba stares back at her, a tactic that usually prompts the speaker to rethink their defiance. Maybe it's the perspective of distance, maybe it's the time delay or maybe she's just tired, but whatever, it isn't working on Alice right now.

"I know there's a major storm brewing over all this, but I'm willing to bet I've given you more valuable information in the past five minutes than Hoffman gave you in the past five years."

Ochoba continues to stare, but it's not theatre. She's ruminating.

"Okay, point taken," she eventually replies. "But let's not keep each other in the dark from here on in."

Ochoba ends the transmission. Alice is left staring at a blank screen, reflecting on what she was intended to infer from the Chair's final words. When the storm breaks below, Alice will want to be aware of the political machinations that ensue. Ochoba is reminding her that she can choke off the umbilical if she feels the information isn't flowing in both directions.

ENHANCED INTERROGATION

It takes Nikki a moment to understand that the blackout is not part of Julio's plan, and another to remember that she has an infrared setting on her lens. It's standard issue for Seguridad, but for everybody else it's an expensive optional insurance against an eventuality that almost never happens.

It doesn't kick in automatically, because nobody wants that happening every time they turn out the light, but the option to trigger it does flash up in response to the lens detecting a sudden widening of her pupil.

She can tell which of the others has it instantly. Those without are frozen to the spot, heads jerking around as they search reflexively for a light source. Julio and Dade, by contrast, look first at each other. They're checking in, questioning what their move should be, wondering if they missed something and are about to pay a price.

Nikki reacts quicker than either of them. She doesn't have to check with anybody. She draws and hits Julio with the resin gun. He reads her move and he's quick, so it's slightly off-target, but she gets lucky. The cum-shot glues his right arm to his side and partially attaches him to one of the night-blinded pair.

She zig-zags as Dade lunges for her, catching him with the electro-pulse *en passant*. He's a big guy so it doesn't drop him, but he's reeling and dizzy as she runs for an exit.

She's outside the octagon now, in the maze of passageways that she had little choice but to put between her rendezvous and the nearest point of egress. It all looks different in the infrared too, which isn't going to make her navigation any easier, but the situation is still way better than it looked ten seconds ago.

She stops at a junction, trying to remember the way, expecting to hear footsteps hurrying behind her. Instead she hears screams.

She can't tell whose, but she's not so curious that she's going to turn back and investigate. She makes it to an exterior door, one that opens right on to Hadfield, except that it doesn't open at all. An overlay on her lens confirms that it is locked and reminds her that she has no override authorisation, as her Seguridad credentials have been suspended.

She needs another out. She can hear more cries, more screams. The last thing she wants is to return towards the octagon, but to find an alternative exit she'll need to follow the adjoining corridor, which unavoidably takes her back towards the centre. She proceeds more cautiously, the sound of her own breathing loud in her ears.

The screams have stopped, and she is sure she hears footsteps, but they are not heavy and lumbering like Freitas or Dade. They are swift and light, a whisper echoing around the walls.

She is midway along the passage when a figure looms into view from around a corner, cutting off her path. It is Sol Freitas. She knew he had to be in here somewhere: probably deployed to secure the perimeter and make sure Nikki didn't have any hidden backup. From his gait, not to mention the look of focused determination on his snarling puss, he is tricked out for night vision too. He is also toting a telescopic whip-cosh.

Nikki reaches for the resin gun. There is an orange warning light blinking on the handle, indicating it isn't ready to fire. That's bullshit, she thinks. The reload time is like a second and a half.

She looks closer, sees that it is reading "chamber empty".

She curses her own sloppy practice. She can't remember the last time she fired the thing before today, but evidently she didn't reload after and she sure as shit didn't check it before duty any time since.

She thinks about drawing anyway as a deterrent, but Freitas looks like he has sussed her hesitancy. He starts to charge, his muscular frame pounding the floor with each footfall. He's a mass of white in her vision, growing against the blackness as he picks up speed.

Something flashes past on her left, then it's to the right, then left again. It is a human figure, jarringly fleet, impossibly nimble. It seems slight, but perhaps only because of the speed, grace and balance with which it moves. The figure is a white streak, human tracer fire in Nikki's lens, but she is sure she is looking at a woman. She ricochets off the walls, part bullet, part ballet, her angle of approach surely impossible for her target to track.

A second ago Freitas seemed a juggernaut. Now he is like a lumbering quadruped being picked at by an airborne predator.

She takes him down in the blink of an eye. Nikki hears snicking sounds accompanied by gasps and moans, a spray of white arcing across the corridor. Then she sees the assassin drag Freitas around the corner. He looks like he should be too heavy for her to move, but she somehow manages his fall, using gravity to create momentum as she drives him backwards and out of sight.

She hears a voice. It is too quiet to make out the words, but the tone is insistent, punctuated by strangulated replies, cries of agony. Freitas is being interrogated.

Tortured.

Nikki stands motionless for a second. She often asks herself whether there is any part of her that is still a cop, and not some glorified security guard taking every last dollar she can skim. She gets her answer in that moment. She has to help Freitas. She has little confidence that she can, but she needs to try, or she'll know there truly is nothing left of who she once was.

All she has is a dart gun with zero stopping power, and the electro-pulse baton, which is only useful in close combat. Having seen her move, Nikki sincerely doubts she would get anywhere near this acrobatic assailant. She proceeds nonetheless. There's no way out behind her anyway.

She sees a white pool on the floor as she nears the junction between corridors, fading as it cools.

Freitas is sitting against the wall a few metres around the corner, his hands on his belly, his head slumped onto his chest. The assassin is gone. Nikki can't hear any footsteps, only the echoes of desperate cries from deeper inside the building: voices fading, life ebbing.

Freitas raises his head as she approaches, begins reaching towards her, stops himself. That's when she sees that he needs both hands to hold in his guts. There are tiny stab wounds in multiple strategic locations, surgically precise, and one deep slash across his abdomen.

She flashes back to Omega's crime scene, that nightmare orrery floating in the Axle.

Freitas tries again to reach for her, using his arm to keep pressure on this one wound, while six or seven others gape and bleed. His eyes are pleading. He knows what's coming. He doesn't want to die alone.

Nikki crouches beside him, places a hand on his forearm.

"I'm here," she says. It seems stupid, redundant, banal, but it's all she can offer.

Blood seeps over his arm and on to her fingers. The warmth of it is a wrench in its familiarity. She's been here before.

"Who did this to you?" she asks, bringing her mind back to the immediate. She can't let herself be taken there. Not now. Not ever.

"Guess you were right . . . about that tiger," he replies, wincing with the effort.

"What is this alliance? Who has Julio been dealing with? Believe me, I don't think he'll be caring much if you tell me."

Freitas looks at her, the intensity of his stare weirdly amplified by the negative effect of his widening pupils being white.

"Doesn't matter," he rasps. "They'll be dead soon too. Ate the forbidden fruit. Maybe just touched the tree. We're not supposed to have it. Nobody's supposed to have it. They're coming to get it back."

"Knows about what? Who's coming?"

He swallows, fighting for the breath to speak.

"Project Sentinel. Anyone who even knows about it is a target. It's the touch of death."

His face contorts in what she thinks is pain but is in fact Freitas enjoying his last laugh.

"And I just gave it to you."

The lights come back on, finding Nikki standing in a corridor over Freitas's lifeless corpse. There is no more screaming, no more cries or moans, only silence. A dead silence.

She proceeds towards the centre. She's got her electro-pulse baton drawn, for what it's worth. She doesn't think she's going to encounter anybody, or stand a chance if she does.

She tries toggling through the surveillance feeds, but they aren't coming up. The cameras have been killed.

Them and everybody else.

The octagon is a slaughterhouse: four bodies scattered about the floor.

For better or worse – usually worse – Julio has been part of her life as long as Nikki cares to remember. A problem, an irritation, an enemy. The rival bootlegging was just a stupid game, like she told Alice: a petty distraction among the insignificant, one she never really expected to be over.

Yoram didn't want this. Nobody should want this. But somebody had.

Three of them look like they were despatched swiftly, but only so that there was time and space to work on Julio. He has this twisted, horrified expression. It was his voice, his screams that she heard. Nikki knew it at the time, but didn't want to admit it to herself.

The assassin tortured him, and longer than she tortured Freitas, but she nonetheless worked quickly. She wanted to know something, or maybe merely to satisfy herself that he *didn't* know something. Either way, she's looking at a cleaning-up operation, just like Freitas suggested.

Begging the question: why is Nikki still alive?

A live image blinks into her lens, showing another of Julio's men lying dead in a passageway. The security cameras are back on.

And now she has her answer.

The cameras recorded Julio and his men entering the octagon to talk to Nikki just before the lights went out. When they come back on, the playback will show her standing over all their bodies.

She tried to tell Julio that this phony turf war was being used as cover for a larger agenda. Now he and half his crew have been taken out, and Nikki set up to take the rap so that nobody goes looking for the real reason they died. She doesn't know what that was, but according to Freitas it was something they knew, something they saw, *something they took*.

She has the answer to another question too. This settles any lingering bullshit about blackouts, about her possibly doing stuff she couldn't remember. She was wide awake when this happened and it sure as shit wasn't her.

If the body at her apartment is any precedent, the Seguridad will be on their way here soon, probably following an anonymous tip or a silent alarm she would be seeing if she hadn't been cut out of the loop. The net is closing. She's got no friends to turn to and she's even running out of enemies. But it's not over. Not yet.

She has nowhere left to run to, but she can still run to nowhere. With the authorities searching for her, her only option is to hide someplace the authorities don't acknowledge exists.

AFTER-EFFECTS

Alice is woken by an incoming comms alert, rudely startling her into consciousness. At first she can't work out where the sound is coming from, her woozy state taking its time to realise it's internal, meaning her lens must be up and running again.

She needs a few seconds before she can respond, muting the alert but not answering yet while she waits for her head to clear. Why does this keep happening? Again, it feels as though her brain is booting up in stages, with her short-term memory in particular taking the longest time to right itself.

She checks the time and calculates that she has been out for at least seven hours. That should have been enough to thoroughly recharge but she feels like she could use seven hours more. All her limbs are heavy, as though she's run ten miles and swum five. Perhaps this is a result of her body adjusting to art-grav, or maybe in this case the after-effects of whatever she was drugged with on her way to Trick's. She doesn't know, but either way she could seriously use some coffee.

She recalls her previous scorn for people when she heard them say that. She privately derided their weakness in needing a stimulant merely to start the day, or even to get over their indulgence the night before, evidence of still another weakness in terms of will-power, discipline and self-restraint. But right now, she knows she is going to struggle to perform the simplest of tasks unless she gets hold of some rich, hot, bitter, black and unadulteratedly caffeinated espresso.

She connects the comm. It's Boutsikari.

"Did it all get sorted while I was sleeping?" she asks groggily.

"Not exactly. You need to come to Habitek over on Hadfield right away. There's something you have to see, and you best not have breakfast first."

*   *   *

"I'm sorry, ma'am, but I'm afraid the premises are closed due to an incident and there's no admittance without authorisation."

The Seguridad officer on the door at Habitek is polite but insistent, though he straightens just a little to emphasise his greater bulk in case Alice should attempt to get past him.

She is about to state her case with equally polite insistence when she sees Boutsikari over the officer's shoulder, waving to her from down the corridor inside.

"Let her through," he calls, prompting the guard to step aside.

"Thank you," Alice says to both of them, though she blends a note of query into her tone in order to convey her annoyance at not being admitted at once.

"You do realise you're still identifying as Wendy Goodfellow?" Boutsikari tells her.

He questioned her regarding it yesterday, and in response she explained about her abduction and interactions with the since also-abducted Trick. At the time she had no means of changing her ID profile, but her lens system is fully functioning now. She restores her correct credentials, noting that Trick was as good as his word: she now has the option to switch between multiple fake personae.

"As we feared, the shit has hit the fan down below," Boutsikari says, guiding her along a twisting corridor deeper into the Habitek complex. "It's early yet in terms of the political fallout, but from the media response you'd think it was the first murder ever, never mind the first murder in space."

"I informed Aurelia Ochoba myself," Alice tells him. "I reckoned it best if she discovered first-hand."

"How'd she take it?"

"Do you know her at all?"

"We've spoken a few times."

"Then you know it's not her reaction you need to be concerned about."

"Quite. That part's out of our hands. The politicians can all wave their hands around and have their tantrums. Meantime all we can do is our jobs."

"And how is that working out?"

"Slowly but surely, like all good police work. We got confirmation that Selby was pregnant and we've had officers all over Mullane asking questions, trying to find the father. No joy on that score yet, but what we did discover is that Selby owed Freeman money."

"She's a shylock too?"

"No, more like protection subs. A lot of the girls – and the boys – paid Freeman so they could work for themselves, keep would-be pimps off their backs. But it gets worse. The word is that Selby was saving money because she wanted to keep the baby. She was on a two-year contract so she needed to pay for an early ticket home. She had been avoiding Freeman and Freeman knew it."

Alice feels a shudder of revulsion.

"A few hours ago I believed Nikki Freeman to be merely someone who *encapsulates* all that is rotten on CdC," she says. "But it's starting to appear that she personally accounts for a large percentage of it."

"Believe me," Boutsikari replies. "You ain't seen nothing yet."

He leads her towards a wide octagonal chamber at the heart of the building, across the entrance to which her lens overlays a visual barrier denoting it a crime scene. Jaganathan is standing in front of the doorway, expectant.

She can smell the blood before she reaches the open door. There are four bodies lying on the floor, dead from stab and slash wounds. Two of them are entangled, stuck together by a discharge from a resin gun.

"That's Julio Martinez," Alice observes, her lens identifying one of the conjoined corpses.

"There are two more elsewhere in the building," Boutsikari says. "I'm informed that these were all known associates of Martinez."

Alice notes the "I'm informed". Still protecting his deniability, maybe all the more as the bodies pile up and CdC's hidden face is revealed to the world below.

Alice notices an incoming grab appear in her lens.

"It's playback from the security cameras," Boutsikari says. "You should take a look."

Alice watches Nikki Freeman standing only a couple of paces

from where she is now, the image superimposing on the scene before her eyes. Martinez and his three accomplices are surrounding her. There is audio too.

Believe me, you don't want to do this.

Believe me, we really do. Reckon we'll score ourselves some points with Boutsikari and the FNG by being such good citizens. Maybe even get us a reward.

Julio, I'm trying to warn you. I'm not the one walking into a trap.

Everything goes dark. Alice hears scuffling, shouts, the discharge of a resin gun, then screams. So many screams.

Jaganathan notices her wince.

"It's like that for a few minutes. You best skip forward to when the lights come back on."

When the image is restored, it shows Freeman standing over the bodies, trembling with exertion, blood smeared on her clothes.

"Was this an ambush?" Alice asks. "More of Ben Haim's people moving in when the lights went out?"

"Yoram Ben Haim is adamant he had nothing to do with this. He says she's gone rogue. Gone insane. I'm inclined to believe him."

"Could she have done this all on her own?"

"She's highly trained," says Jaganathan. "Equipped with night vision, infrared. She put a lot of men down in her LA days. We figure she lured them here: maybe making them think they could bring her in, claim a reward and get her out of the picture as a twofer. Then she cut the lights and slaughtered everybody while they were stumbling around blind."

"We gotta throw a net around this bitch," Boutsikari growls. "I'm concerned that Ben Haim is right and she's escalating into some kind of psychosis. We've been lucky in that this bloodbath is behind closed doors, but people already know she killed Selby, and since that got out, the lid has come off the Omega thing too. There's all kinds of rumours going around. All it would take is for Freeman to attack some civilian and we'd have a widespread panic on our hands."

"So where the hell is she?" Alice asks. "I know I'm new around here but I wouldn't have thought it possible to hide for very long in a city where she literally can't show her face in public without raising the alarm."

"Unfortunately for us, if anyone on Seedee could pull that off, it would be Freeman."

GHOSTS

Nikki has no choice but to take a static, and not just because where she's headed is halfway around the wheel. She's going to be in plain sight, but it's the only shot she has at this point, and she needs to take it fast.

She searches around Habitek for anything she might use to reduce her visibility. In a lab close to the octagon she finds a set of hazard coveralls which will conceal the bloodstains streaking her clothes. Less helpfully, it has a name badge sewn on, reading "Roger Searle", and she definitely doesn't look like a Roger. Maybe if she can also find a cap and a pair of protective glasses she can carry it off, she reckons, spotting a hopper with all kinds of junk spilling out of it.

Rooting through it, the contents don't turn out to be work materials but stuff left over from the party they must have thrown here when they finished work on their new module before everybody decanted to the Axle. Looks like they used the fabricator to make joke face masks of each other, an office-party cliché that refuses to die. Nothing that will fool anybody, or even register a false ID on the worst facial-recognition scan, but it gives her something to work with. She can act like she's on her way back from a night out with colleagues.

She finds some Qolas nobody drunk, meaning they must also have had some decent liquor at this shindig. Nikki opens one of them and pours it over the coveralls. Just in case she isn't giving off enough of a booze smell already.

It takes her ten minutes to walk to Hadfield station. She leaves the mask off but the cap on for the first part of the trek, keeping her head down as she passes the few people who are on the street right then. If nobody can get a look at her face, then their lenses can't scan her.

She pulls the mask on once she's in sight of the station. There are two officers watching the entrance, standard deployment. The Seguridad aren't expecting to apprehend her walking into the station: it's to prevent her getting around using the statics.

She staggers a little as she approaches them, afraid they can hear her heartbeat from where they're standing. She measures her gait so that she appears sufficiently wobbly as to seem tipsy, but not enough to look like she's going to be a problem. It's a narrow margin of error, but she has first-hand knowledge of how cops calibrate this scale.

Her pulse doesn't stop pounding as she boards the car and takes a seat, though the whole time she has to act like she's got a healthy buzz on and doesn't have a care in the world or off it. The car goes past Malhotra, Faris, passengers getting on and off, nobody paying her any mind. Then as it approaches Gutierrez, she feels a hand on her arm.

Without looking up she can see from the uniform trousers that it's a Seguridad officer.

"Hey."

So near and yet so far.

She glances up, every sinew tensing.

"This your stop? Thought you might be nodding off there, buddy."

She lets out an involuntary jet of breath, which she disguises as a chuckle of relief.

"Thank you, officer," she says, keeping her voice hoarse like she's been talking loud all night.

She sees him eyeing the name badge, knows everything is being recorded. Shit. If anything belatedly strikes him as suspicious, she doesn't want him knowing which station she was headed for.

She gets off at Gutierrez, and fortunately he doesn't, or she'd have had to walk out and double back. She waits a nerve-shredding twenty minutes on the platform, expecting cops to storm in at any second, then gets the next car to Garneau.

She doesn't have to worry about officers guarding the entrance at this end of the trip. She isn't going up that high. She walks along the platform until her lens shows her a code request, identifying the location of a concealed door. She sends her response and it unlocks, swinging outward from what had appeared to be an advertising screen. Workers passing through Garneau and Dunbar must see people slip in and out of these doors every day, but they don't think anything of it. Even if they are mildly curious as to where these folks are coming from, they are rendered invisible by the Seedee straight-arrow assumption that everybody is busy doing what they're supposed to.

These hidden doors are ideally located for slipping into the stream of ordinary citizens, entering and exiting the static system as they go about their daily business. It disguises that the people coming in and out of here are Seedee's true dispossessed, its literal underclass.

You see someone heading down towards the Garneau static and maybe assume they're heading home at the end of a shift like the rest of the folks on their phase. Technically you'd be right, but if they pass through that hidden door, they aren't going back to some des-res apartment. Or even a shitty one like Nikki's.

It's known as the Catacombs, or sometimes Ghost Town on account of who lives there: Seedee's invisible population. People who are not supposed to be here. People who lost their contract but didn't want to leave. People who were never supposed to be on Seedee in the first place: smuggled themselves up, probably alongside the corpses of three others whose jerry-rigged air supplies and untested knock-off pressure suits failed.

As a Seguridad officer she would occasionally be asked to investigate an abscondence: that was when someone had their contract cancelled and subsequently never reported for the final processing ahead of their appointed shuttle to take them to Heinlein. The Quadriga never really wanted her to look too hard. For one thing, they know they can always sell that seat. Even at a few hours' notice, there is always a standby waiting list.

But that wasn't the main reason.

The people living in the Catacombs aren't down here because they're hiding from the authorities. It's because where else are they going to live if they can't get a job that pays the rent? That's another reason this place doesn't officially exist, and the Quadriga aren't in a hurry to do anything about it. A lot of companies hire ghosts because they can get a job of work out of them for a pittance, and it's not like the ghosts are in a position to negotiate. It pushes up profits and drives down wages for the officially registered workers in certain blue-collar sectors. Hence so many of the legitimate employees on Seedee are working extra jobs; whether that's double-phase moonlighting or more proscribed activities.

It's a shanty town warren, constructed of the remnants of the cramped zero-g habitation modules that were used in the very origins of what became the Axle, back when it resembled an amped-up version of the ISS. Nothing up here is ever truly junked, so once the first art-grav quadrant became inhabitable, these modules were gradually abandoned. What fixtures and materials couldn't be recycled were put into storage someplace and forgotten about, until somebody found a belated use for them a few decades later.

On the maps and schematics it appears as part of the static network, officially a siding yard for storage and maintenance of the passenger cars. It sits beneath so many buildings that it is unclear who technically controls the space, and with it being under so many different companies, a lot of people have had to be paid to look the other way or not ask any questions. Nikki knows this because she's one of them.

Somebody is controlling it, though; somebody is collecting rent, which is another reason its ongoing existence is tolerated. First principle of the Quadriga's ideology: if it's making money for somebody and not hurting anybody else, it's cool. And by somebody and anybody, they mean among themselves, obviously.

Nikki wanders between the rows of pods, ducking now and again where overhead ducts reduce the clearance. Even where they don't it feels claustrophobic. It's hot and humid down here too, and though it is connected to water and sewage systems, there's no getting around the fact that it smells pretty rank.

Looking at the people huddled in these pods, she has to wonder how bad their life must have been back on Earth that they'd rather stay up here even if it means living like this. But maybe she ought to wonder how much they must hate themselves that they'd rather stay here as a ghost than go back to being the person they once were.

Yeah, that's a question she understands.

Nikki thinks of the horrible, burning shame she felt when Alice insisted on coming back to her place. She knows Kinsi didn't mean any harm, but she could have slapped her for suggesting it. Nikki tried her hardest to put her off, laying down hints about the mutual awkwardness that any woman ought to have picked up on. Whether Alice had an insider instruction to go there she'll never know, but the reason Nikki didn't want her in her apartment was not because she knew there was a dead girl in her bedroom.

It was because she didn't want that stuck-up, Ivy League, blue-blood G2S *child* to see what Nikki's world was reduced to. Forty-five years old and living alone in this soulless little shoebox with nothing to show for her life.

Plenty of people on Seedee live frugally, renting equally small and sparsely fitted pads, but that is usually because they are saving as much as they can. With some, usually the younger ones, it's to build a nest egg for when they return to Earth. Others have no intention of going home, but they're saving money to send none-theless – to people they're trying to make it up to; oftentimes people who don't want them to come back.

Nikki doesn't even have that as an excuse. Instead she is part of another common Seedee constituency: spending everything she makes in pursuit of a hedonistic numbness because she has no meaningful purpose up above or down below. She's as lost as any ghost in the Catacombs. It took her a while but she's finally found her way down here where she belongs.

She's not looking to move in, rent a pod – she just needs some-place to hide while she works out her next move. Problem is, she has no next move. She's got nobody left to turn to, and not just because Yoram has sold her out. She realises there's nobody she *would* turn to: nobody she has any reason to trust or who would do her a solid now that she has nothing to offer in return. She doesn't have friends, only people who are afraid of her or who have been paying for her services.

She remembers what Alice said at Klaws, comments that hurt so bad because they found their mark. She's nobody's friend, nobody's enemy and not even anybody's problem: just their least-worst solution. Now there's nobody who could be *her* solution, least-worst or any other kind.

She recalls her last exchange with Candace, who was trying to be a friend, or at least a confidante, until Nikki threw it back in her face.

Even a cold-hearted bitch needs to feel somebody likes her now and again.

They don't like you, Nikki. It just seems that way because they don't hate you as much as you do.

Well, she's pretty sure everybody hates her as much as she does now, especially if the word is out regarding Giselle.

DAMAGE CONTROL

Alice needs to call this in, which means a return to the privacy of her room at the Armstrong Hotel. It isn't a conversation she can be having over sub-vocal, standing where someone might overhear. She travels by static, compiling further details of her report during the journey back to Garneau, now that she has full functionality of her lens.

She notices a pile of comm requests and other messages stacking up. She scans the list briefly, in case there's anything that can't wait. One is from someone at the FNG's tech department concerning her lens outage. Another is from Helen Petitjean, flagged Urgent. From the impression Alice gleaned during their time together, she is willing to bet it's anything but. However, she owes Helen on a number of counts, so she decides to respond to the request anyway.

"Ms Petitjean. I just got your message. I've been dealing with a situation. Is everything okay?"

Helen does not reply immediately, and when she does, her tone is breathily meek.

"Alice, my dear. Thank you for getting back to me. I apologise if I gave the impression it was something dramatic. I realise in retrospect, with your current jurisdiction taking in law enforcement, that our definitions of what constitutes 'urgent' may diverge."

Alice finds her cadences pleasing, a hint of the old-fashioned peculiarly reassuring in her present environment.

"Don't mention it. Is there something I can help you with?"

"Well, it's simply that I woke up to this horrible, horrible news and felt it was imperative that I speak with you. I just feel so awful for that poor woman. It's like we are all complicit because we didn't act in time."

"Gillian Selby," Alice says, because there is nothing else she can offer. She speaks quietly, conscious that there are other people in the carriage.

"Was that the name of the ahm, the ahm . . . the victim?"

"She was a fabrication worker."

Alice isn't sure whether Helen was skirting around the word prostitute or the word victim, but some impulse doesn't want Selby defined as either.

"Of course," Helen replies, seeming to understand the same point. "But I was actually talking about the sergeant."

"Nikki Freeman?" Alice needs to confirm.

"Of course. I was concerned about all that she has become, and I warned you she was dangerous, but I never would have believed she could be capable of something like this."

You don't know the half of it, she thinks, picturing the slaughterhouse she left behind at Habitek.

"I must confess that sympathy for Nikki Freeman is not what I was expecting to hear from anybody right now," Alice says.

Least of all you, she does not need to add.

"And therein lies a tragedy in itself. Because one cannot begin to imagine the state of torment someone's life must reach before they are driven to such despair. And it is all the worse because I know she wasn't always like this. I knew her when she first arrived here. We were acquaintances, if not precisely what you would call friends. We've both been here a long time."

"Do you know why she came?"

"Not specifically. To escape something, that's all I know. Some people come to CdC because of what they are trying to leave behind and some people come because they see opportunity, but in both cases we're trying to build a new future. Nobody comes without hope, no matter what has happened to them in the past. But that's why we must nurture it, and why corruption is such an insidious enemy. This far from the Earth's molten core, your moral compass is the only one that guides you. But if it gets damaged, you can so easily become lost up here in the darkness. It becomes a process of tiny increments, each little compromise taking you one step further off the path than the last.

"Something hurt that woman. That's why she's here. Something damaged her, and this place should have repaired it, but instead she got worse and worse. That's why what's happened should be a time for a new beginning. With you in control, we have the chance to clean up the Seguridad, to change the culture of CdC, and finally make it the launchpad where we truly set our sights upon a better vision of mankind."

Alice glances across at two people sitting opposite on the static car. She has only been here a matter of days, but she already finds it difficult to look at anyone without wondering what brought them to this place, what their story might be.

"Being able to work here isn't merely a privilege," Helen goes on, a warm passion rising in her voice. "It should be a vocation, a calling. Once you finish your shift, your thoughts should be about how best you can rest and prepare to make your next contribution. Not about physical gratification. You should be improving yourself in the interim, every way you can. Reading, learning, practising. Professor Gonçalves has given people an unprecedented shortcut in learning new skills, new abilities and knowledge, so they should be spending the time this shortcut saved them by building on that. Strikes me some of us are making sacrifices and giving so much of ourselves so that mankind can reach for the stars, while others are still just reaching for a bottle or reaching into their shorts.

"If we don't cure ourselves of these indulgent instincts, if we don't mature as a species, how do we think those brave pioneers are going to survive for generations on the *Arca*? These are the problems we need to solve before we can even think about launching that thing. Oh, sure there are technical challenges to be met too, but I believe we'll solve those ones a whole lot faster once people start learning to *behave* themselves."

THE DISAPPEARED

Nikki hears raised female voices, sounds of panic and distress. She doesn't know if it's a result of decades of conditioning or something more instinctive, but her immediate concerns are instantly suspended as she readies herself to respond.

She sees a woman hurtle out from between two rows of pods, bashing against a bulkhead and then running full-pelt in her direction. Her eyes are wild, a look of primal ferocity in her face.

Another woman emerges at her back, looking distraught and fearful.

"Stop her," she calls. "Somebody stop her."

Nikki grips the electro-pulse baton and takes a defensive stance as the crazed woman barrels towards her. She is about to strike when the other calls out again.

"Please. She's going to hurt herself."

Nikki deactivates the baton with her thumb and braces for impact. This is going to hurt. She lets the woman crash into her, absorbing some of her momentum so that she can shift her balance and bring her down. They tumble to the floor together, Nikki taking the brunt of the fall, then Nikki expertly rolls her so that she's on top. The woman is not strong but she's desperate, fighting for her life.

The second woman catches up with them and crouches down, putting a hand on the crazy one's shoulder.

"Amber, it's okay. Amber, you're safe. It's okay. Just let go. We've got you. We've got you. It's okay."

Her voice is soft and steady, though Nikki can hear the anxiety she's masking.

Nikki feels the fight go out of Amber, if that is her name. According to her lens, she doesn't have one. Stowaway, she thinks.

The other woman she knows, now that she can see her up-close.

Her name is Zola Petriskaya, a Russian nurse who used to work at the infirmary. A few years back she made sexual assault and harassment allegations against an exec at OmniSant, the company that runs ERU. Then, what do you know, damning evidence suddenly emerged in support of a bullshit fraud allegation against her, and guess which one was expedited in the Seguridad's list of investigation priorities? Zola was discredited, her contract cancelled and a jump seat was rapidly (and expensively) allocated to bounce her back planetside.

They railroaded her but she didn't leave town. Now Zola's the closest thing they have to a doctor down here: a regular patron saint of the Catacombs. She's getting medical supplies from someplace, and she makes enough in unofficial work to get by in Ghost Town but not enough to escape. Nikki suspects she's getting paid by somebody upstairs to provide certain services, same as somebody gets paid to sort the air and the water if anything goes wrong.

"Nikki Fixx," she acknowledges. "Thanks for your help. This one's extremely distressed."

"So I see."

"What brings you down here?"

And there's another reason she came to Ghost Town. These are not merely Seedee's materially dispossessed, they are its information-poor also. Zola doesn't know Nikki is on the lam.

Like most people here, Zola's lens has limited functionality (if it's functioning at all, repairs and maintenance being an expensive business). Once you abscond, your lens still retains its localised primary data, but is cut off from network services, such as the centralised ID database, in the same way as Nikki was instantly cut off from Seguridad comms channels. Nikki is still able to access these other services because Trick hacked her rig years ago, allowing her to switch between multiple identities, and Hayley Ortega still has her basic privileges intact.

"Can you help me get her back to my nook?" Zola asks.

"Sure."

They assist Amber onto unsteady feet, the fight and mania having gone out of her. She needs merely to be led rather than carried.

They flank her either side, making sure she doesn't bash herself against anything but also positioning themselves to prevent another flight attempt.

"They took my baby," Amber says, sounding numb, tearful. "They took her. They took my baby."

"Who did?" Nikki asks.

"They took my baby. They took my baby."

"She never says," Zola replies. "We don't get much sense out of her. She's catatonic half the time, incoherent the other half, and occasionally hysterical, like just then."

"She ever say anything else about the baby?"

"Nothing that makes sense. I think this is something that happened before she came to Seedee. I'm guessing it's *why* she came."

"You say her name is Amber? I'm getting nothing on my lens. She's reading completely blank. She could be a stowaway."

"I've asked her what her name is but she says she doesn't remember. She responds to Amber, but it's like she knows you're referring to her even though it's not her real name. I don't know, I could be wrong. Just a feeling."

They reach Zola's pod, or nook as the ghosts call them. Nikki helps Zola lay her down on a roll-up nano-foam mattress she must have salvaged from somewhere, maybe even her own apartment before she had to bail. Amber curls up into a foetal position, weeping meekly from blank eyes.

"Why Amber, then?"

"Amber is what the man who brought her here called her. He gave me some money and asked me to look after her. He didn't say when he'd be back, but he hasn't shown up yet and this was four days ago."

"Who was he?"

"He wouldn't tell me. Said it was best for me if I didn't know. I found out, though. A man here called Jabra has a hacked lens. Jabra got a look at him. He told me his name was Leonard Slovitz."

The name doesn't mean anything to Nikki, but she can look it up. Of more immediate concern is finding out more about this Jabra guy so that she can stay out of his line of sight.

257

"I might speak to him later. Can you show me what he looks like?"

"I can take you to him, or maybe go fetch him so I don't leave Amber alone."

"No, no, just send me a pic if you got one."

"Okay."

An image appears in Nikki's lens. Jabra looks Middle Eastern, older than Nikki, an unkempt bushy salt-and-pepper beard dominating his face. In other places she would see him coming a hundred yards out, but in the Catacombs a messy beard is the male dress code, grooming facilities being somewhat sub-optimal.

"What is your business down here?" Zola asks.

"Can't talk about it. I'm kinda waiting for something, so I'm not in any rush. If you got things you need to attend to, I can sit here with Amber until you get back."

Zola has the look of a stressed mother who just got an offer to look after the kids for an hour.

"You are sure?"

"Just don't abandon me here for four days like Leonard."

Nikki takes a seat down on the floor next to Amber, who is still breathing fast but seems more peaceful, or maybe just exhausted. It's Nikki's first chance to get a close look at her. She's young for Seedee; at least for someone outside the more rarefied professions, where whizz-kids and prodigies proliferate. She looks like she could be mid-twenties, maybe even younger. Certainly not old enough to have made a big mistake she's running away from.

Maybe running away was her big mistake.

Her eyes remain open, a disconnected waking state that seems a distressing mockery of sleep. She reaches out a hand and rests it on Nikki's thigh. Nikki looks down and there is eye contact, a supplicant pleading look. It takes a moment to work out what she is pleading for. The answer is merely contact.

She places a hand on top of Amber's, at which point something softens in her face and her eyes begin to close. A few minutes after that, she is asleep.

Nikki shifts her position, trying to get comfortable in the cramped nook. Amber moves too, Nikki concerned that she has woken her, but she is merely rolling over. Granted a view of the back of her head, Nikki notices that she has a scar from where a mesh has been fitted. This doesn't fit with the stowaway theory. You can't get the operation unless you're legit, and yet she is showing up as having no identity.

Another possibility is that Amber has the credentials to deny identification, but that usually prompts a "not authorised" message in the lens of the beholder, just to rub it in. It would also beg the question of how someone with such credentials could end up abandoned to this place.

Nikki looks closer at Amber's hands. There doesn't appear to be a sensor on either wrist, suggesting she doesn't have a lens. Who has a mesh but no lens?

Of course, a simpler explanation for Amber's ID showing up blank is that something is wrong at Nikki's end. It could be the first sign that her rig is corrupting, or that Hayley Ortega's privileges are more limited than she'd like.

Ordinarily this would be her cue to visit Trick, but that is not an option now, and for multiple reasons. She wonders who these people were that abducted him. Was that bullshit from Alice? Covering up that she had actually called in some help while she was being held there, and had her own people take Trick in for questioning?

No, she realises, and not merely because Trick's first task was to disable Alice's lens, thus preventing her contacting anybody.

Nikki flashes back to their conversation in Klaws, concerning the woman who took Trick away.

She mentioned something named Project Sentinel. You heard of it?

The reason they had subsequently bailed in a big hurry was not, as Alice assumed, because they identified her as having major status with the FNG. It was because something connected her to the same "touch of death" Sol Freitas passed on to Nikki with his final breath.

This being the case, she doesn't like the implications for her chances of seeing Trick alive again.

For now, Amber's identity aside, Nikki's lens appears to be functioning normally, so she runs some searches for Leonard Slovitz.

The good news is that there are no clearance-level restrictions on access to his basic data. The bad news is that he won't be coming back for Amber any time soon. According to his public profile, Slovitz is a neuroscientist who works at the Neurosophy Foundation. He took a leave of absence to return to Earth for personal reasons. He left CdC on April 7, three days ago, shortly after Zola says he came here.

The date chimes with Nikki but she can't remember why.

A neuroscientist drops off a basket case in the Catacombs and promptly blows town. Nikki thinks about the shooting incident in Central Plaza, wonders whether Yoram was wrong. Maybe the target was Gonçalves after all.

There are multiple contact details listed for him, accessible at Hayley Ortega's level of clearance. It's less than she could access if she was still logged in as a cop, but it's a lead at least.

Nikki copies a message to all the listed contacts, asking Slovitz to get in touch as a matter of urgency. She adds that it is concerning "a code amber". She isn't holding her breath for a reply.

The news feeds are firing out updates in a ferment, horrified responses to the Gillian Selby murder. Won't be long before somebody at Seguridad leaks what happened at Habitek, or they simply quit trying to contain it because they have someone to pin the whole thing on. Nikki can already imagine the reports once they connect her to the scene. "She went on a killing spree when she was cornered by concerned citizens trying to bring her in." They can pin Omega on her too, say she went space-crazy, any bullshit they want to make up.

This is over for her. It's so over. All she can do now is hole up here and wait for the inevitable. She closes her eyes and lets herself drift, content at least that on this occasion she is aware of where she is lying down to sleep.

COMMAND PROMPT

From the background hum and the shape of the windows behind her, Alice can tell Ochoba is speaking to her from on-board the private jet the FNG places at her disposal. The Chair is transformed since their last conversation interrupted her sleep, resplendent in a crisp purple suit: full battledress for whatever business she is on her way to conduct. Alice doesn't know who she is meeting with, but is pretty sure the agenda got radically updated last night.

"Is this a secure situation?" Alice enquires, not knowing who else might be out of shot inside the cabin.

"It will be in ten seconds," she replies, signalling to someone to make themselves scarce.

"From your discretion, I am assuming the news is unlikely to have me order everyone a round of breakfast mimosas," Ochoba continues, by way of letting her know she is clear to proceed.

"More like a black coffee, Madam Chair."

Alice delivers a full report, complete with grabs from the Habitek security cameras.

When she stops speaking, Ochoba simply nods.

The Chair is legendarily phlegmatic in public, and not given to fits of anger in dealing with her staff, but she has subtle ways of expressing her emotions if you know what to look for. Alice would have expected her to register a certain degree of dismay at this bloody escalation. From its absence she deduces that this is because nothing she said is going to change what Ochoba already decided twelve hours ago.

"Sounds like you caught a break with the locus. A multiple homicide anywhere less enclosed and I doubt you would have been the first person I'm hearing this from."

"It will get out soon enough, Madam Chair. The dam has broken

261

with regards to confidentiality among Seguridad officers. You can get them to stay quiet about one killing, for a while at least, but there is a law of diminishing returns as the bodies pile up. People need to talk."

"Oh, don't I know it. The media has gone nuts down here over the Selby killing. It's not as though they are short of Earthbound murders to report, but you know what it's like: anything that happens on CdC has this elevated news value. Add to that the prurience factor of Selby being a hooker, and you can imagine the effect. They're 'lifting the lid' on the hidden culture of prostitution on CdC, and everyone is getting themselves into an almighty froth. I'm on my way to New York right now for a summit to discuss how we should formulate an emergency response."

"And am I right in assuming you wouldn't set off to such a summit without having already formulated an emergency response?"

Ochoba allows her the tiniest of nods by way of acknowledgement.

"Very much thanks to your work, yes. Your reports contained eye-opening and alarming information. We now have reliable confirmation of things that were merely rumoured before. The FNG debate chamber has long been awash with allegations, but given the delicacy of our relationship with the Quadriga, the first rule when it comes to CdC is 'Don't make it an issue until it is an issue'. As of last night, the conduct of the Seguridad is very much an issue."

Ochoba takes a moment, straightening in her chair. Alice senses an announcement.

"The FNG is declaring a temporary Condition of Crisis and taking direct control of the Seguridad. I am assembling a task force of experienced law enforcement officers who have been on permanent standby for this kind of eventuality. These new captains will be put in charge of all Seguridad divisions, and will be directly answerable to you as our senior law enforcement liaison on-site. They will lead a crackdown, closing all illegal or semi-legal operations as described in your account: bootlegging, prostitution, fight clubs, the lot. I expect this to be rubber-stamped at today's summit, and the personnel ready to proceed to Ocean Terminal within the next twelve hours."

Ochoba fixes her with a stare, scrutinising her reaction. Even allowing for the delay, there is a glimmer of disapproval in her eyes at what she sees.

"Is there a problem with the transmission?" Ochoba asks, which is as good as putting Alice on notice that she'd better change her attitude *tout de suite*.

"Madam Chair, as the person on-site I feel obliged to sound a minor note of caution. I believe a response that is locally perceived as heavy-handed may have the potential to incite unrest. People up here don't like being pushed around, especially by the FNG."

Alice can hardly believe she's saying this; it sounds like Nikki talking, but it's true.

"There would be little resistance to action against the more extreme sub-level activities I described beneath Mullane, but if we are shutting down bars and restaurants and the like, the danger is that we might become regarded as an occupying force."

Ochoba's stare remains laser-like. She issues a sigh like a safety vent that prevents an explosion.

"Dr Blake, I appreciate your candour and I do not doubt the veracity of your impression. But equally I believe you underestimate the wider impact of what you just told me about Habitek. There is a deranged killer on the loose, guilty of multiple homicides stemming directly from police corruption, prostitution and gang warfare. This will be headline news on every feed within hours, generating sufficient concern among the citizenry that they will understand things need to be a little quieter up there, at least until the situation is brought safely under control.

"It is a matter for the Quadriga and the politicians to discuss what brought this licentious culture about, and what they want to do to address it, but in the short term we have an opportunity to cut a cancer out of CdC. So, are you ready to take command of this operation?"

HAIL MARY CALL

A response from Slovitz isn't likely to make any difference, so Nikki is surprised but hardly elated to be woken by the sound of an incoming audio request. However, when she opens her eyes, her lens informs her that the contact is not from the elusive scientist: far more surprisingly, it's from Candace.

"Hey," she responds quietly, mindful of Amber's fitfully sleeping form alongside.

"Nikki. It's so good to hear your voice. I didn't really expect you'd answer."

"Yeah, you're lucky I did. Got so many well-wishers to respond to, gonna take a while to get through them all."

There is a pause, long enough for Nikki to worry that Candace has disconnected. Then she speaks again, and her words are a balm.

"You okay? I mean, you know. Are you . . . ?"

"I know."

It's not the Song of Solomon, but it's not Yoram's "where are you?" and that means something.

"This thing at Habitek . . ." Candace says, like she doesn't know what to ask but she's dreading the answer anyway.

Nikki glances at the scrolling feeds. The story is out: six dead. They haven't named the victims or a suspect, but she knows it's only a matter of time.

"Yeah, they're gonna pin that shit on me too."

"You need to get off this wheel, Nikki."

It's not like she hasn't thought about it. Unfortunately, the reason it would help is also the reason it's not an option: nobody would be looking for her on W2 because she has no way of getting there.

"That would mean going up a spoke and along the Axle, which

264

I can't possibly do without being seen. I'd have to pass through like six access checkpoints, and they'll all be guarded."

"I was talking about a shuttle."

"Nah, that door's closed too. Yoram's thrown me to the wolves. His entire smuggling network is burned to me now. If I were to arrange a rendezvous with one of his pilots, I'd expect the Seguridad to be waiting for me at the dock."

"I know a guy," Candace says, though she sounds tentative, conflicted. "A pilot. Bjorn. Been seeing him for a couple months."

"You kept that quiet."

"Well, that's the whole thing: he's pretty straight. He doesn't know what I do on the side. Doesn't know anything about our world. Bjorn's a very Wheel Two kind of guy."

"So you don't think he'd go for it? Why are you telling me? You think we could fool him somehow?"

"I could get him to do anything. I'm a great lay, remember?"

"How could I forget?"

"The fact he's so straight should work in your favour. Any pilot bent enough to smuggle you is also gonna be bent enough to sell you out. Whereas a guy like Bjorn, once he realises what he's caught up in, he isn't going to tell anybody in case he loses his contract."

And now Nikki sees the true catch.

"At which point he's never going to trust you again, and your relationship is over."

"Maybe not over – I'm pretty good at smoothing things out – but never the same again, for sure."

"You don't owe me something like this, Candace. In fact, you don't owe me anything. So I can't ask you."

"You're not asking, Nikki. I'm offering. Because not everybody hates you as much as you do."

STRINGS

With the transmission ended, Alice is left staring at the blank wall, seized simultaneously by a surge of pride and a sense of trepidation. The difference between the two is that she knows where the trepidation is coming from. The pride feels like a glimpse into someone else's perspective, how she imagines it must feel to access an imported memory when you've got a mesh. She is the one who has just been given this massive endorsement by the Chair of the FNG Oversight Committee, but it's as almost though she's pleased on behalf of someone else.

The problem is that it doesn't seem real, that it feels like it came too easy. Maybe that's because it *is* unreal. The new captains will ostensibly be answerable to Alice, but she knows that in reality they will be answerable to Ochoba. While not quite imposing martial law, the FNG would still be taking control, much as the more paranoid CdC citizens have always predicted. The Chair is invoking Condition of Crisis provisions, but temporary measures have a tendency to become permanent once governments get a taste of the powers they confer.

Alice has a strong sense that events are overtaking her, even though on the surface she is at the heart of those events. She is being handed the reins, but is she really the one driving the horses? She has this insecure feeling of being over-promoted, given a responsibility she isn't ready for. It is a more intense version of how she's felt at certain junctures, certain appointments throughout her career.

As an academic prodigy, she has learned to shrug off jibes about being too young, or even merely looking too young. Given who her parents are, she has also had to repel accusations of nepotism regarding how connected she is. But she would have to admit there were times it seemed things slotted into place a little too smoothly.

Alice knew what hard work was, what it felt like to face intimidating obstacles and the endeavour, sacrifice and self-belief required to get past them. She knew when she had worked for something. She knew when she deserved it. But the corollary was that, deep down, she also knew when she didn't.

There were times when she suspected strings had been pulled by her parents, or by people they were connected to. Leading her to wonder who is pulling strings now. And is she the puppet?

An alert appears in the corner of her lens, signalling the arrival of classified documentation pertaining to Ochoba's plans. She has a cursory look through the materials, triaging what will need to be read first. Among them is the list of personnel who will imminently be headed to CdC to form the new task force. Alice casts a quick eye over it to see if there's anybody she's had dealings with, and more pertinently anybody likely to give her a problem. She sees nobody she knows, but nonetheless a single name stands out: Dominic Petitjean.

A quick search establishes that Helen Petitjean is his older sister. They hail from a wealthy Louisiana bloodline with political connections going back generations. Suddenly Alice finds herself wondering how coincidental it was that Helen just happened to be on hand during the all-stop. She came to Alice's rescue and was able to get the uninterrupted, unchaperoned access she wanted, providing the opportunity to identify Nikki Freeman as indicative of the corruption Alice ought to be rooting out. Fast forward barely a couple of days and suddenly the likes of Nikki is going to be replaced and overseen by Ochoba's own picks, one of whom is Petitjean's kid brother.

This train of thought is derailed by an incoming request from the same FNG tech who tried to get in touch earlier. She sees his profile headshot pulse in her lens, a nagging line of text informing her how long it's been since his first unanswered attempt. The Accept and Decline options present themselves. Her natural inclination would be to go for the latter, but having spent so long without a functioning lens yesterday, she can't afford to be negligent.

"I just wanted to make sure everything is operating as it should be," he states.

"Yes, absolutely. Thank you. It was back to normal when I woke up and there have been no problems since."

"I wouldn't ordinarily trouble you with follow-up, but it's just that somebody really did a number on your system and I wanted to verify no new problems have emerged. I've got you going to Habitek on Hadfield and then back to the Armstrong Hotel where you are now. Is that right?"

"Yes. It's all good so far, though I believe there may have been some grabs deleted by the guy who hacked me. I don't suppose there's any way of restoring the data?"

"No, ma'am. The reason it took so long to get your system back up was that I had to let it recompile absolutely everything in your data cache, and when it did, all grabs from the previous twenty-four hours proved irretrievable. The whole console architecture seems to have been radically replumbed, including the addition of some non-native functionality, which is again why I'm curious as to how it's holding up."

"I thought it might still have been ticking over in the background even though I couldn't get the console to respond; you know, location logs, basic monitoring functions. I would be interested in any data from the period I was out of contact."

"That's what I mean by doing a number. There's nothing. Your lens was completely dead from the moment he did whatever he did until I recompiled it for you."

"Good job nothing interesting happened to me then," she remarks wryly, before politely ending the conversation.

Now that she has had this discussion, Alice can't help worrying that some recurring glitch might be about to take down her lens again. She runs a systems diagnostic, to make absolutely sure everything is working as smoothly as she just told the tech.

Nothing seems to be amiss, though she has her suspicions regarding that 'non-native functionality' the tech remarked upon: the hacked upgrade allowing her to access multiple identities. She can't help worrying that Trick may have slipped some kind of time-bomb into the works.

She looks again at the list of fake personae she can adopt, the name Wendy Goodfellow sitting at the top. And that is when something seismic pulses through her.

Trick said his identity spoofing *"fools the receiver into thinking it has got its information from the CDB, when actually it's coming straight from your local device."*

All that time she was identifying as Wendy Goodfellow, her local unit was stone dead. Trick lied. Like magicians down the centuries, he had misdirected his audience by telling them how it couldn't be done.

What do you think I am, some kind of a god? Nobody can hack the central database.

He had. And Alice isn't the first person to have worked this out. The people who abducted him knew it too.

269

DEBTS

Sleep won't come now. Nikki lies on the floor next to Amber, watching her chest gently rise and fall, listening to her occasional moans of unconscious distress. She feels heavy-limbed, sluggishly aware of her exhaustion, but while she drifted off before, that was because she was in a state of resignation. Like the guilty man in the cell, her mind had allowed itself to shut down, knowing there were no immediate decisions to be made.

Candace's call changed all that. Nikki has spied a glimmer of hope, albeit only for delaying her capture, but it is enough to give her an edge again. She lies there and waits, her mind a storm of questions and replayed incidents, none of it cohering into anything useful. All that matters is that she is still free, concealed down here in the realm of the invisible.

She watches the clock slowly tick its way towards when she will have to leave, increasingly concerned that Zola has still not returned. Why is she taking so long? she wonders, worrying that when she does come back, it will be with a posse of Seguridad.

No, she assures herself. Zola herself has too much to lose from that. Except that giving up Nikki could be a valuable bargaining chip if Zola was seeking to negotiate the restoration of her status.

Then she hears Zola's voice approaching the nook. She's talking to someone, an older voice, male. Nikki sticks her head out cautiously to check. Sees she's talking to this bearded guy. She can't get a clear look at his face and she sure doesn't want him getting a clear look at hers.

Zola is bringing Jabra back here to talk to Nikki about Amber and Slovitz.

Not good.

But then they part ways at the corner, Zola coming this way, the bearded guy heading off towards another row of pods.

"She's sleeping," Zola observes with some relief.

"I need to get moving now," Nikki says quietly, standing up. "I got a call. Did I hear you talking to somebody? Was it Jabra?"

"No, I haven't seen him. That was Otto. He was supposed to be doing a cleaning shift in the Axle but they're running ID checks, so he's had to duck out. Some big security alert. Is that why you're here?"

"It's related, yes."

"I hope I haven't kept you."

"Not at all. Listen, Zola, I've been looking into this Leonard Slovitz. Seems the guy went back to Earth right after he came here and dumped Amber. I'm going to chase this down for you, okay?"

"That would be . . . I would owe you, Nikki."

There is deep sincerity in her expression, but also an element of fear in her acknowledgement that she would be in Nikki's debt: concern as to how Nikki might want a favour returned. Nikki must have seen this look a hundred times before without it really hitting home. She doesn't like what she's seeing.

She puts a hand on Zola's arm.

"No, honey," she tells her. "You don't owe me shit."

Nikki picks her way carefully back through the narrow channels between the decades-old plastic pods. She is in sight of the hidden door back out into Garneau station when she sees someone step through it. It is a bearded man of Middle-Eastern appearance. Their eyes lock before she can get her head down. His name displays as "Hannes Jensen", but she has no doubt that this is Jabra.

Nor has she any doubt that she has just been made. He will have spotted her face in news feeds, recent shots taken only hours ago. He has seen her identified as Hayley Ortega and won't be buying it any more than she believes that he is Hannes Jensen. They both know they are each looking at someone with a hacked lens, and in his case it will be confirmation that she is precisely who he thinks.

She considers her options and realises that it's not a disaster. If he reports her as sighted here, then that could work in her favour, because all going well she will be off Wheel One in about forty-five minutes.

But when did it ever all go well?

Nikki steps out of the hidden door and into the light stream of travellers heading up to street level from the static station. She still has the coveralls and cap on, keeping her head down as she makes her way towards where she has arranged to meet.

Candace said she would be at the junction of Garneau and Young, but Nikki doesn't take the most direct route. Instead she slips down a parallel passageway and circles back so that she can scope out the situation, verifying first that Candace is there and more importantly checking that nobody else is. She feels disloyal doing this, given what Candace is risking for her, but she can't take any chances.

She doesn't see Candace, but she doesn't see any Seguridad either. There is nobody in uniform on the street, and she is pretty confident she could spot any who were in plain clothes, as there's very few of them worth a damn as police officers.

She isn't going to stand out there in plain sight, however.

She is holding her position in the alley when she gets a call request: a reply from Leonard Slovitz.

Nikki answers, and is surprised to hear a woman's voice: the delay enough to indicate that she is speaking from Earth.

"You sent out a message to my brother. It came to me off a relay."

"Your brother is Leonard Slovitz?"

"That's right. I'm calling because I can't get a hold of him. What's this code amber? Do you work with him?"

"I was under the impression your brother had returned to Earth. Are you saying he hasn't?"

"Absolutely not. He hasn't been back in two years, but if he was coming back, this is where he'd be. He doesn't have a house down here any more. I'm getting concerned. I usually speak to him pretty regular and I haven't heard from him in days."

"I may have gotten my lines crossed. We work on different wheels," Nikki tells her.

Nikki terminates the call shortly after. She feels bad about adding to the woman's worry, but suspects she's right to be concerned. The guy hasn't just bailed from Seedee, he's gone on the lam since he got to Earth.

She sees Candace approach from the direction of Gutierrez. Nikki steps out of the passage and intercepts her before she reaches the junction. They stop and stare at each other for just a moment, like they're not sure what to say. Then Candace steps forward and pulls Nikki into an embrace, kissing her on the cheek.

Nikki hasn't experienced a sensation like this for as long as she can remember, hasn't felt someone give her affection. Sex yes, but not this: this is warmth. This is caring. She'd forgotten what it feels like.

Candace is looking all dressed up. Nikki's never seen her look so good, and not merely because she's such a welcome sight under the circumstances. She's carrying a travel bag from which she produces a flight suit. The suit is for Nikki, so she looks like the pilot and Candace the passenger. Taking a shuttle between wheels is an expensive option, exercised only by the rich and the Quadriga elite, hence Candace scrubbing up to look the part.

That is only the beginning of their cover, however.

"I told Bjorn you're a VIP who's been on a hush-hush visit to Wheel One and doesn't want to be seen going back, whether via the Axle or even through normal passenger channels. He's supplied us with today's live access codes for Dock Seven."

Nikki doesn't see any Seguridad, but she still holds her breath as they approach the entrance and the codes are transmitted. The doors open without delay and they proceed briskly but without conspicuous hurry into the shuttle bay.

Nobody looks at her twice. It's business as usual: people loading and unloading from the shuttle that's already in place, others getting ready to serve the next one incoming, which will be Nikki's ticket out.

She sees the manifest administrator inspecting a crate, checking the details with a cargo handler. That's when she remembers why the date of Slovitz's departure rang a bell: Lind's bullshit story. Maybe it wasn't bullshit after all.

Lind said a capsule left Heinlein with nobody in it. Maybe it was so that nobody could testify that a certain passenger wasn't on board. In which case Slovitz hasn't gone on the lam by bailing to Earth: he's spent a fortune making it look like he has and effectively rendered himself invisible on Seedee. But why?

From here in the bay she can look up through the canopy and see the next shuttle approach. It disappears out of sight, heading beneath them to the outer side of the wheel, where it will invert and ascend to the dock on a platform.

"There's been a lot of new faces sniffing around Mullane," Candace says. "They've been asking questions about you, offering cash. They were wanting to know who owed you money."

"So they know about Giselle?"

"Everybody knows she owed you and was planning to book. I mean, wasn't that the point?"

"What do you mean?"

Candace takes a step away, her face suddenly stony.

All of the dock workers turn as one, abandoning what they were doing and moving in to surround Nikki. Except they're not dock workers. They're Seguridad.

"You killed Giselle to send out a message," Candace says. "Well, we all got it. And this is our reply."

LOOK THE DEVIL IN THE EYE

Alice has little difficulty finding her way back through the passageways beneath Mullane, reached via the secret underground exit from Klaws. She is headed for Trick's workshop, retracing the route she took after escaping it. She has always had a gift for navigation: if she visits a place once, she is able to draw upon a vivid mental map and an infallible sense of direction. It's almost as though she's got a photographic memory.

As she steps into the narrow corridor outside the fight club, she closes the door behind her and has a look at the wall. When she first came by here, the door was all but invisible, and she would have had no means of opening it were it not for those guys happening to come out when they did. Now when she gazes at it through her lens, she can see the hidden door picked out in an overlay, the name of the premises stated above an input-request icon. If you know the password, you're good to go.

She knows she could put out an APB and have Trick brought in if he is to be found at all, but the truth is she doesn't want the Seguridad involved. Trick constitutes an asset she would like to keep to herself. Finding him without anyone else's help is likely to prove difficult, but having a valuable contact who is not ultimately answerable to Ochoba makes it worth the effort.

The Seguridad would not be much help anyway, she reasons. She doesn't know Trick's real name and even if she did, she doubts it would show up in anybody's lens in response to them looking him in the face.

If she's being honest, she has no idea how she is going to track him down, but figures this is the obvious place to start. She wends her way back down the passageway, scanning the walls for more hidden entrances. She sees none, but the door to Trick's lair is easily found on account of still being unrepaired since it got busted open. It remains slightly ajar, though there are no insignia or input icons overlaying it through her lens.

Out of curiosity, she switches from her FNG profile back to Wendy Goodfellow, the first one Trick gave her. Instantly the door becomes picked out in gold trace against the wall, a virtual door-knocker appearing in the centre.

Alice nudges the door further open, catching a glimpse of the chaotic scene she left behind, upturned tables and all manner of electronic debris scattered about the floor. Trick hasn't been back, and neither has the cleaning service.

She takes a tentative step inside and something moves in swiftly from her right. In half a second she's staring at the muzzle of a resin gun, Trick's wary gaze looking along the barrel.

He's got an electro-pulse in his left hand and not one but two flechette pistols hanging on his belt. He is looking a lot better prepared to deal with surprise visitors this time.

Alice holds up her hands.

"I'm alone," she says.

Trick lowers the resin gun slowly, reluctantly. There are multiple swellings and contusions on his face, purples, reds and pinks glistening against the dark brown of his skin. One eye is almost closed, and despite the initial rapidity of his movement, he seems lopsided. He limps slightly as he shuffles backwards, beckoning her to step further inside. He seems physically tremulous too. Alice knows she's looking at a man who has recently been tortured.

"What can I do for you?" he asks, his weary tone indicating that he has no intention of being helpful.

"Anything I ask," she replies. "Unless you want a one-way ticket south. You were working for Nikki Freeman, weren't you? Nobody dropped me off here before: you collected me from wherever that crate delivered me on the mag-line. She paid you to wipe my grabs."

"And yet you ain't here with a squad of Seguridad. So I'm guessing you can't prove anything."

"I can prove you hacked the central database. That would be more than enough to get you a jump seat. But I prefer the idea of keeping you here, where you can be useful. Trouble is, I'm not the only one who knows *how* useful. Who were they?"

Trick reels at the mere mention.

"Uh-uh. Client confidentiality," he adds, unconvincingly.

"Clients, huh? I was there, remember? If they were clients, why did they abduct you?"

"They wanted my immediate attention. Beating the crap out of me got it for them. It also served to convey the importance with which they regarded their stipulation that I refrain from telling anyone what they needed me to do. I strongly intend to adhere. So if that's what you came here for, you're shit out of luck, because they scare me way more than you do."

"How did you get away?"

"They let me go. They were finished with me."

"If what they wanted was so secret, why did they let you walk?"

"Same reason you haven't had me arrested. They might need me again."

"They're not the only dangerous company you've been keeping, though."

Trick looks quizzically at her, not following.

"I forget you've been busy, not to mention you've had a few bangs on the head. You must have seen the feeds, though."

"You mean Nikki?" he asks. "That she offed some goon who ran with Julio and then murdered that girl Giselle who worked out of Sin Garden? Yeah, it sounds like bullshit to me."

"I can confirm first-hand that it's true. I saw both bodies. I was in Nikki's apartment: she ran because I saw Giselle lying strangled on her bed. The autopsy puts Giselle's time of death during the period when I was conveniently out of Nikki's way, strapped to your table."

Trick leans against said table, wincing slightly as he aggravates one of his many injuries. He has a troubled look, like he can't argue with what Alice is telling him but can't quite believe her either.

"Nikki could use her fists when she needed to, but this shit makes no sense."

"Nobody is a killer until they kill somebody."

"See, that's just it though. People don't *get* murdered up here. Yeah, there's rumours Seguridad covered up some things, made sure they weren't classified as homicides, but we're not talking about a whole lot of cases: not over all these years, these decades. People come here to escape the bad stuff. Sometimes they're gonna fight, sometimes they're gonna get crazy, but we don't make it easy to kill each other on Seedee. There's no *guns*. No real guns, anyway. All we got is stun restraint weapons and home-brew plastic dart shooters that we make in our fabricators. So much of what we do here is about keeping everybody safe. Keeping everybody alive.

"Nikki's here fifteen years, part of this culture, keeping the peace. Okay, we both know she's no angel, but keeping the peace nonetheless. Then suddenly she's butchering some gangster and killing this girl in the space of two days? I ain't buying it."

"There's a way you could help me find out for sure. That's why I came here."

Trick looks sceptical, but she knows he's intrigued. They also both know she has him over a barrel.

"You can amend the CDB. Does that mean you could access someone else's private grabs? Theoretically," she adds, to let him know she isn't asking him to incriminate himself.

"No. It's impossible."

"Says the guy who told me only a god could hack the CDB. You were able to wipe my grabs for Nikki, so I'm assuming you could have copied them too."

"I had first-hand access to your unit. I couldn't have done it remotely. I can exploit loopholes in the part of the database governing how an individual is identified, but clearance levels are a tougher beast. I can't give you a fake profile with clearance levels above your own, for instance, and I can't access profiles above my clearance level. But that isn't the problem. The reason grabs are perfectly protected is that individual profiles can only be accessed by a single user. Two people can't log into one account simultaneously. If you tried, you would get like what they used to call a busy line."

"You're saying you were able to mess with my grabs because I was disconnected from the system at the time? I wasn't using the line?"

"Correct."

"So could you remotely access a low-clearance profile as long as the person isn't using it?"

"In theory. Except that nobody is ever not using it. People are permanently connected."

"Dead people aren't."

It takes about an hour. Trick enters a state of trance-like concentration, occasionally muttering with frustration or satisfaction, then suddenly Dev Korlakian appears as one of Alice's available profiles. She copies the grabación to her local cache, then deletes the original, so that she has sole control of the file. Until she knows what it shows, she doesn't want Trick accessing Korlakian's profile later and viewing it for himself.

"Got what you wanted?" he asks.

"I'm about to find out."

She takes a seat against a wall and begins running the grab.

It's always jarring, the view from inside someone else's head, especially when you're looking at it double-lens, cranked to maximum opacity. The outside world disappears and is replaced with another person's remembered reality, which can feel creepy enough at the best of times. There is a temptation to sub-frame the image and reduce the audio, in order to provide the comfort of distance, but Alice doesn't want to miss any potential clues. Also, if the killer does turn out to be Nikki Freeman, she doesn't want to flinch from the reality, so having it thrust at her this way would make the truth impossible to ignore.

Alice is glad she took a seat before she set the grab running, as the moment it starts, everything in her vision lurches and swirls. It shows the view as Omega recoils from a blow, tumbling and clattering against a wall before hitting the floor.

Blood runs into one eye, causing it to close. An arm comes up to wipe it, tattoos on the forearm. Omega is reeling but this moment is also a lull in the assault, and he recognises it as such: his only chance to take action before the next wave. Alice sees activity play on his overlay. He is trying to broadcast. He is calling out, breathless, desperate.

"Help me. Anybody. Please. Get to this location as fast as you can."

Something moves past, a pair of legs, too quick to focus on any detail.

"Please. Please."

It's not clear at this point whether he is saying this for broadcast or saying it to his assailant. Nobody is listening, however. The overlay warns that no signals are getting out.

The view shunts suddenly, like he is being dragged. A hand appears, reaching for his forehead, pressing down, holding it in place. Alice hears a metal clunk that she recognises. He is being restrained.

She hears more clunks, but all she sees, all Omega sees, is the ceiling, grey and blank. He can turn his head left and right a little, but can't look up or down.

Activity on the overlay indicates one of his hands is working the lens: hurried, desperate, making slips and mistakes. He is trying to access the sharing protocols. The recording is stored locally, and he must know it will upload the moment it gets clear of whatever is blocking the signal. He's trying to tag it so that it can be accessed by his comrades.

In his panic, he's gone into the wrong menu sector and the only option visible is to allocate legacy status, meaning the grab would be shared with his named executor.

It's his last act of free will, the only one open to him.

There is movement, the ceiling coming closer. Whatever he is strapped to is being elevated: a hydraulic gurney, perhaps. It was a stretcher, now it's a table.

An operating table.

Alice isn't sure she can watch any more, but she knows she must. She slides down the opacity just for a moment, reminding herself where she is by way of minor respite. She knows he is going to be tortured. She recalls the bag of skin, wonders with a shudder at what point he was flayed.

He is choking, breathless from the effort of his screams, and above it Alice hears another voice. His killer is speaking to him. It is a whisper, barely audible over his groaning and panting, but unmistakably the voice of a woman.

"Let's talk about Project Sentinel," she says.

A shadow passes over the field of view. A laser scalpel is held up so that Korlakian is forced to view it. Then the killer leans over, staring at her victim.

Which is when Alice sees her own face looking back.

PART THREE

PART THREE

WASTE DISPOSAL

Some mornings when Nikki opens her eyes, it takes a while for the picture to fit together. On this occasion, the second she sees the blank wall of the holding cell, it all slots instantly into place. Everything that could possibly be wrong is wrong, and she didn't even need to get drunk for that to happen.

She sits up on the edge of the narrow cot, catches a whiff of herself as she moves. She's not smelling too fresh. She wonders how long she's been out. She has no way of knowing, as they've taken away her lens. Not merely taken away connectivity, but physically removed the hardware. That's when you know you're officially a non-person on CdC, when you are cut off from all channels of information, truly isolated.

She yawns and stretches, reflecting how it used to be an old standby for cops: put a number of suspects in a cell, and the guy who goes to sleep is the guilty one. The others are too anxious, but the one who did it knows he can't change anything from inside the cell, so he might as well get some rest. Nikki knows she's not guilty of what she's been arrested for, but she's guilty of plenty more.

She uses the slide-out toilet, vaguely aware she's being watched. She's put plenty of people in these tanks, usually just to cool off. There are cameras embedded high on the walls where the prisoners can't reach to gouge them out.

As though to confirm that she is being monitored, and her waking state noted, a slot opens in one wall and a tray slides through bearing an offering of what she interprets to be breakfast. The logging systems track whether a prisoner is on Pacific, Atlantic or Meridian phase, allocating meals accordingly, but if she's being perfectly honest Nikki doesn't really know what breakfast looks like to most other human beings.

She knows the food isn't automated. There's somebody outside the cell.

"Who is that?" she asks. "What's your name?"

"I'm not supposed to talk to you," comes the reply. Sounds male, maybe around her age. Possibly a real cop once upon a time.

"Come on. I work Seguridad a decade and a half and I don't deserve the courtesy of a few words?"

"Alonso," comes the answer, his tone grudging. "Miguel Alonso."

"Don't believe we've had the pleasure."

"No, I'm over from Wheel Two."

"One of Jaganathan's boys, huh?"

"That's right."

"Jag must be pretty excited. First time he's ever caught a real criminal, I'm guessing. Maybe even the first time he's seen one."

She hears him snicker despite himself. Yeah, he's an ex-cop.

"Food meet your dietary requirements?" he asks, voice dripping sarcasm. "Or can I get you anything else?"

"How about a lawyer?"

"Oh, you'll get one of those, soon as your feet touch the ground. They're shipping you back to Earth today. Taking you for processing in about a half-hour."

Of course. There are no courts up here, so most legal procedure has to happen down below, particularly if it's serious. On the very few occasions someone was deemed a genuine danger or facing severe criminal charges, the authorities expedited an immediate transfer. It gave rise to the term "jump-seat offence" among Seguridad officers, though it is more commonly used in the negative. "Not a jump-seat offence" is a call for perspective, like "not the end of the world".

Nikki is being charged with eight jump-seat offences. It is very definitely the end of her world.

She wonders whose jurisdiction a murder case will come under, thinking of how far the Quadriga and the FNG have gone in the past to avoid answering that question.

"You won't be missing much," says Alonso, an edge coming into his voice. "The Seedee you know is finished anyway. FNG are taking over, sending up new captains to run Seguridad. They're going to close down all the illegal operations. You gave them the excuse they needed, so we'll all be drinking Qola from here on in. Thanks a fuckload, Nikki Fixx."

He slams the hatch closed. Nikki picks up the hunk of bread from her plate then puts it down again. She doesn't have an appetite, not for food, not for anything.

She's out of allies, out of colleagues, out of friends, but she knows she's really fucked when she doesn't have any enemies left either. Whoever is behind this shit doesn't count, because she suspects it wasn't personal, any more than what happened to Giselle. They were both used, albeit in different ways, pieces on someone's board.

The hardest thing is dealing with Candace's betrayal, not because they were particularly close, but because she knows she deserved it. It was Candace who sold her out, but it could have been any one of them. It's not like Nikki is in a position to say: "How could they, after all I did for them?"

She's been nothing but a mercenary, the real whore working Mullane. She told herself she was doing whatever it took just to get by, one day at a time, but in truth Alice was right: she was instrumental in making Mullane what it is. It's like she decided to live in a world where nobody helps each other out except for a price; where everything is bought and sold, whether it's flesh or favours.

She came here to get away, to start over, but she didn't let herself believe in a better world, and CdC is for people who truly believe in building a better future. It is a place for idealists, for optimists, for dreamers, for goody-two-shoes. Nikki has been acting contemptuous of Alice from the get-go, but the truth is she admires the girl. She's got game, she's got guts, she's got heart and she still believes in something. The only thing that really bothers Nikki about Alice is that she represents the antithesis of everything she has come to despise about herself.

The cell wall suddenly alters to reveal a door, through which a squad of four officers enters, bearing electro-pulse batons. They are here to take her away. They put the cuffs on her but she doesn't need restraints. She'll go quietly. She deserves to be flushed out of here like the human waste that she's become.

MEMORIES ARE MADE OF THIS

There is only so much of the grab Alice can bring herself to watch. With Omega's head fixed in place, the view mostly shows the ceiling above, but the cries and the shuddering are unbearable, punctuated by the occasional chilling glimpse of her own blood-speckled visage. She holds out a while, hoping the image will go black from Omega's eyes closing, lapsing into the merciful oblivion of unconsciousness. It doesn't happen before she gives up and stops the play.

She rolls back the file and pauses on that single moment, the clearest shot of herself staring down at her victim, willing the face to change into something else. Her hair is blonde, jarringly unnatural. Clearly a wig. The light in the chamber is not the best, and focus is affected by misting from Omega's eyes watering in agony, but there is no mistaking who she is looking at. Or should that be *what* she is looking at.

Alice has no recollection of these deeds, and yet clearly she carried them out.

She feels a cold inside her like nothing she has ever known. Something harsh and inescapable, something she has been hiding from, or more accurately whose existence she has sought to deny. It has been stalking her, occasionally glimpsed in the shadows, but now that she has seen its face, it cannot be outrun.

She doesn't have a mesh. No artificial augmentations necessary for the remarkable Alice Blake. Yet she has this perfect recall: an infallible memory for names and faces, for facts, images, places, routes. A prodigious ability to retain and process information that has allowed her to excel academically. She always told herself it was down to hard work, focus, diligence, maximising her natural gifts. But just as deep down she always suspected her parents' status opened doors for her, deep down she also suspected this was not

289

her only unfair advantage. Somewhere inside, she knew that the ratio of effort to attainment seemed skewed in her case, compared to her peers. The fear she would not name, the thing glimpsed in the shadows, was the notion that this superior mental capacity she enjoyed was not entirely natural.

There's always rumours that they have invented super-intelligent androids that pass for human, but they never told nobody.

She has been dogged by this feeling of disconnection since she got here: of not quite being in control, either of her situation or sometimes of herself. It ties into that horrible disorientation every time she wakes up, as she struggles to piece recent memories together. She thought it was merely a symptom of the adjustment process in acclimatising to life in space. Now she deduces that this could explain why she feels so tired, why her limbs are heavy and she reckons she could use another seven hours' shut-eye. She thought she had been asleep when in fact she may have been very busy elsewhere.

At Habitek.

She can think only of the dark little seed that Freeman planted. *You could be an android yourself and not even know.*

Anything made by man can be controlled by man, such as an augmented brain, particularly one not voluntarily enhanced. Everyone who has a mesh *knows* they have a mesh. So if Alice has always had some kind of artificial superbrain, imposed upon her without her knowledge, what does that make her?

It makes her a robot. An android. A machine.

She flashes back to their argument at Klaws.

There's usually a lot of drinking and fucking involved in conceiving the child. Maybe not you, I'm guessing. Which is why you don't feel part of this society.

At the time, she thought this was a dig to convey that Freeman knew she had been adopted, but now she wonders if she meant something else.

How indeed would you know you are not an android?

She never truly asked herself this question at the time, but she is searching desperately for possibilities now.

Would an android get tired? she asks herself. Of course it could, logic tells her. It might be the cue that instructs her to shut down so that she can be used for other tasks: shedding this persona, this consciousness and slipping into another, like slipping in and out of the profiles Trick gave her.

Her mind flashes on the bodies scattered about the floor, the blood she was able to smell before she even entered the chamber.

She begins to weep silently, tears clouding her lenses and rolling down her face.

Would an android cry?

If it was programmed to.

Can an android feel?

She recalls an old tech-philosophy paper on the subject.

Robots can see much better than we can but they don't understand what they see. Robots can also hear much better than we can but they don't understand what they hear.

An android can be told *that* it is feeling, but does that mean it knows what feeling *is*?

Alice knows what feeling is, because this hurts. And if it turns out she is an android, then she wouldn't want to be human if it means sorrow feels worse than this.

"Everything okay?" asks Trick, and it takes her a moment to even remember there is someone else in the room.

"No," she says, getting up on unsteady legs.

"Not a feel-good picture show," he suggests. "Was it Nikki?"

"That's classified," she answers, making for the door.

As she exits into the passageway, the true significance of this remark sinks in. She controls this information absolutely, the only clue that she is guilty. Even if they get hold of Korlakian's sister, the Seguridad will find the grab gone from his legacy archive.

Nobody will suspect her of anything.

She wonders if this is what really motivated her to come here, and not some nebulous notion about cultivating Trick as an asset. After transferring the file, before even watching the thing, the first thing she did was delete the original so that Trick couldn't see it, so that *nobody* could see it. Some process was triggered when she learned that Omega may have recorded his killer, feeding her the subconscious instruction to secure this evidence.

So it could be worse than what she is doing when she thinks she's asleep. She may not even be sure what is motivating her actions when she is conscious. She hears Professor Gonçalves' voice, at that lecture that now seems such a long time ago.

Multiple competing systems are permanently striving for attention . . . The brain retrospectively . . . constructs a narrative to give the impression that a solitary unified entity was at the helm the whole time. In short, consciousness is a lie your brain tells you to make you think you know what you're doing.

She is stumbling against the walls as she navigates a passageway that seems narrower than it was before. She can see the main underground thoroughfare beneath Mullane up ahead, thronged with people as always. Thronged with humans. She needs to find the stairs. There's no outside but she needs to get above ground. She feels like the walls are closing in.

She was charged with finding a killer, when all the time the killer was hiding in the one place she would never think to look. There is some hidden second animus within herself, a stone-cold assassin, and somewhere out there is an individual or organisation whose purpose it serves for her to play both parts.

Still she searches for reasons this can't be true, the most compelling of which is that an android would be manufactured. It wouldn't be a child, it wouldn't grow up, go to school, have a career, forge a lifetime of memories. But no sooner has this thought granted her comfort than it begins to tarnish.

Memories: the very things that can be artificially inserted here on CdC. Memories of her life on Earth, of childhood, school, college, career, family, colleagues, friends: how does she know any of them are real?

Get a grip, she urges herself. Get practical. If she was an android, she wouldn't need to eat, or drink, or go to the bathroom, or shower, and she has done all those things in the past few hours.

Or has she?

It hits her that *all* her memories could be inserted, large and small, recent or old. That if her mind is an AI, then loops could be written to cover something that happened or didn't happen five minutes ago. She wouldn't even need to have been unconscious: bang, a subroutine kicks in telling her she just ate dinner, had a shower.

Verification, she thinks, corroboration. She could simply ask someone: Did you just see me eat that meal, drink that drink? Did I just wash my hair? But that would only prove she ate, drank and showered, which does not preclude her being an android – a machine – that does all those things.

It does mean that she could verify all her memories since arriving on CdC, but equally, nobody up here can verify anything that happened in her life before that. She could have been activated for the very first time when she "woke" in that capsule, already arrived at Heinlein, significantly the only one left in the elevator.

Barely admitting to herself why she is doing it, Alice stops against a wall and accesses her parents' contacts, sending out a comm request to each of them.

Both of them come back as currently unavailable.

Convenient.

Her *adoptive* parents.

Also convenient.

Alice looks at their headshots, staring back serious and unsmiling, and can't bring herself to feel anything. Maybe they don't really mean anything to her. Or maybe she can't feel anything for anybody.

She knows she doesn't miss them. Her relationship with them feels more like you'd have with colleagues than relatives. Theirs wasn't a warm or tactile family. But surely if her memories of them were false, implanted for a purpose, they would be happy ones?

Not necessarily, she reasons. She has memories of discipline, hard work, study, a career mapped out ultimately leading here, to this role, this place.

There is a simple test, then. She could disobey. Couldn't she? She has free will. Or would her artificial brain retrospectively rationalise her actions and decisions, like Professor Gonçalves described in her lecture: create a narrative that justifies in her conscious mind what her subconscious mind has already been instructed to do?

She has been telling herself she is better than Nikki, for whom "do as thou wilt" is the whole of the law. But is Alice better if she never actually had a choice but to obey? She's been following rules her whole life: is that because she chose to, or because she was programmed to? And if she truly believes she chose to, does that mean she has the free will to choose *not* to?

In short, can Alice Blake misbehave?

She climbs a staircase and all but bursts through a door onto Mullane topside. It's busy but calm, nothing like the hysterical media reports are depicting it down on Earth. The FNG are sending a sledgehammer to crack a walnut.

Nobody should have to sell themselves for sex, or fight in a basement in order to get by. But the solution is better wages, not a moral crackdown.

She thinks again of what Nikki told her in Klaws, about little people distracting themselves with little games, while bigger games are being played above their heads.

No kidding.

She should hand herself in, confess what she knows, surrender this grab. That would be the right thing to do. That would blow this wide open. The question is, confess to who? Alice has no idea who could be in on this, or what it might trigger within herself if she threatens to reveal what she knows. Some emergency shutdown procedure could be invoked if she violates a prime directive protecting her puppet master. Or worse: if she tells the wrong innocent person, then she might be sent after them to clean up her own mess, another death at her oblivious hands.

She finds herself walking past Sin Garden, where they first argued about bribes and kickbacks while Nikki tried to slip her a spiked mojito; and from beneath which Alice was abducted in order to more freely facilitate Nikki's remorselessly illegal activities.

That's where it hits her that Nikki might be the most corrupt, duplicitous and amoral woman Alice has ever met, but right now she is the only person on Seedee she can trust.

END OF DAYS

The restraints are seriously starting to chafe Nikki's wrists as she is marched down Resnik, but she's feeling another sting more keenly: that of humiliation. She is being escorted by a detail of four guards, two in front and two behind, sporting the maximum Seguridad weapons load-out, which is normally only deployed in the most extreme circumstances. They have the usual jizz cannons and electro-pulse batons, but these are supplemented by "goodnight guns" slung over their shoulders: suppression rifles that would normally remain safely in storage unless they needed to quell a riot.

It makes her look like some kind of monster, a dangerous animal who may need to be put down at any moment. And that's what passers-by would see even without the overpowered arsenal.

She read once how the layout of Paris was altered after the French Revolution so that wide boulevards replaced the labyrinthine backstreets where mobs were formed and unrest fomented. They weren't worrying about civil unrest when they designed Seedee, as it is nothing but narrow passageways, far from conducive to the discreet transport of prisoners. There is no option but to walk the short distance to the nearest dock, in full view of whoever happens to be around.

This is what the phrase "walk of shame" truly means. In the past it was merely a term she associated with stumbling home for a shower (or stumbling to wherever she was supposed to report for duty) with a blinding hangover and a queasy sense of embarrassment, details of her recent sexual exploits flashing into her mind like the pulses of her headache.

Nobody gave her a second look on those occasions, however. Today, she feels every pair of eyes burning.

She keeps her head down, which sucks because this is the last she's going to see of the place. It looks kind of sad. Minus her lens, without all the overlaid information on every wall, door and citizen, it looks like a living room after the Christmas decorations have been taken down. Still familiar, still the same place, but somehow a little less warm, a little more dull.

Even the handcuffs look strangely denuded. Ordinarily she would be able to see the prompt, allowing anybody with the appropriate authority to release the restraints. She used to have that authority. She could have unlocked them with a gesture of her finger. She seldom needed them, though. That's what makes her look all the more wretched. Nobody on the street will ever have seen somebody restrained like this, never mind under an armed four-man escort.

She can see the entrance to Dock Nine looming ahead. That's when she starts to feel a dread sense of foreboding that reaches from deep in her gut to the ends of every hair now standing up on her neck.

Maybe it's down to it truly dawning on her that this is real: not only is she leaving Seedee, but she's looking at spending the rest of her life in jail, where she'll never discover what this whole thing was about.

They pass through the reception area and proceed towards the shuttle bay, which she can see through the open doors. There is no spacecraft in position, no stevedores, no manifest administrators. Looks like flights in and out of Dock Nine have been suspended. The whole place is deserted, much as this same facility was when Yoram's shipment got jacked. That's where the vibe is coming from. The last time she came through here was when everything started to go south.

The déjà vu gets jacked up a notch as the party marches out onto the shuttle bay floor, where she sees two of the private-security-looking assholes who were there that day. They are waiting patiently, close to where the shuttle elevator comes up.

"The fuck are these guys?" one of the Seguridad detail asks.

"I don't know," replies Alonso. "Nobody is supposed to be here. I'll check it out."

One of the mercs is already on his way over. Unlike the Seguridad officers, he isn't carrying any visible weaponry, but he looks all the more intimidating for that. There is a quiet assuredness about his gait, like nothing could threaten him.

"We'll complete the transfer from here, Officer Alonso," he says. It doesn't sound like a suggestion.

"The hell you will. We're to escort the prisoner all the way to Heinlein. We have explicit orders."

"So do we, and I believe you'll find that ours countermand yours."

Alonso sees something on his lens and visibly blanches.

"No shit. Just two of you?"

"Two of *us* will be adequate."

Alonso turns to the rest of the detail.

"Okay, change of plan. These guys are gonna take it from here."

Up above, through the canopy, Nikki can see a shuttle approaching. In a few moments it will disappear underneath. She recalls the last time she witnessed such a sight. It was as she waited on a dock with Candace, about to be sold out.

Suddenly a lot of things become clear, none of them good.

Her foreboding derives from a subconscious awareness that is far ahead of mere cognitive deduction. She isn't spooked because she is on Dock Nine again, but because there's nobody here: no admins, no stevedores, no pilots.

No witnesses.

She's bound for Heinlein.

Way, way too late she comprehends the real reason the shuttle platform at Heinlein was cleared and the capsule officially transporting Slovitz was empty. It wasn't to conceal the fact that Slovitz was secretly still on Seedee. It was to conceal the fact that he had been murdered. The official record would show he went home, explaining the fact that he would never be seen on Seedee again.

There is a stillness to the shuttle bay, an unnerving silence in a place normally alive with noise and activity. The incoming shuttle has dipped out of sight, and the rotation of the wheel means she can see the Earth through the canopy. Both of her captors are gazing placidly at the main doors, through which the last of the Seguridad detail has exited.

They are not taking her anywhere, she realises. They're going to do it here. They'll make up some story that she was killed during an escape attempt, because they won't want her taking the stand at any trial.

The three of them stand wordless for a few moments longer, like some solemn observance, before one of the mercs rolls out a black plastic sheet on to the floor. It's not a prayer mat.

The other merc slams a fist into Nikki's gut, dropping her to her knees.

"So how do you want it?" he asks. "Strangled like Giselle, sliced up like Julio, or skinned and butchered like Omega?"

She is doubled over, feeling the cold metal of the floor through the plastic sheet. She is gasping for breath. She knows these are her last moments.

Funny thing is, it was her intention to die here. Just not so soon.

Some say death is not the end, and right now she believes that, but not in any kind of bullshit spiritual way. For her, the end came fifteen years ago in Santa Monica. Everything since has merely been waiting.

And yet she doesn't want to go. Wretched and self-loathing as she has allowed herself to become, she still wants more of it. She wants to make amends. She wants to get justice for Giselle. She wants to show Candace there's a caring woman inside this callous shell. She wants to tell Alice Blake that she has inspired her to change. But none of those things is going to happen.

For the first time in forever, she permits self-pity. For the first time in forever, she cannot prevent tears.

Her captor draws a knife, and Nikki gazes at the Earth for the last time.

SELF DETERMINATION

Alice exits the static station and races down Resnik, pedestrians stepping clear and sending her curious looks as she runs flat out in the direction of the shuttle dock. One of them doesn't see her, obliviously veering into her path, causing her to slow and to divert her course.

She lets out an angry sigh, a percussive exhalation. Most anyone else would swear, she is sure. Alice never swears. She even censors internally. *Can* she swear? Perhaps the Alice Blake persona is not allowed to, but whoever else is hiding in here must have looser moral parameters. If she can kill, she can surely curse.

She can see the entrance up ahead, further than she was hoping. With Nikki in custody, she thought she had more time. She was on her way to the holding cells when she learned that the prisoner was being escorted to Dock Nine for a shuttle to Heinlein. The order for immediate transfer back to Earth came from Boutsikari, but Alice suspects Ochoba's hand. Ochoba needs a quick and visible win on this, and parading the one bad apple in leg-irons would do it.

That's why Alice is hurrying to get there in person. If she contacts the officer in charge via his lens, he could quickly verify that Alice doesn't have the authority to stall the transfer. On the spot, she can tell him she has received updated instructions, and he is unlikely to defy the Principal of the SOE to her face.

If he does, however, she has no idea what her move is. Does she really think she's capable of springing a prisoner? Never mind the practicalities, *would* she do it even if she knew it was physically possible? Or is there some override protocol that is about to restrain her if she attempts an action that will obstruct Ochoba's orders, or interferes with the unseen plans of whoever else the puppet master might be? Will it kick in even to prevent her from lying to the head of the Seguridad detail?

Her mind is a storm, has been since she saw Omega's grab. She is feverishly deconstructing her own personal history, disoriented by the questions of whether any of it is real. She recalls the childhood memory of a tortured lizard that was sparked by the sight of the dry dock from the shuttle window. She doesn't know if the incident really happened or if it was put there so that she would view the world a certain way, sympathetic to an ideology that would guide her decisions in a manner her invisible controller intended.

Her thoughts flick back further, to when she first woke up in the capsule and the ensuing shuttle journey.

There will be no children, she was told. And yet among the first people she saw were children.

There are no androids here.

And yet . . .

There are worse implications than merely the veracity of her memories. One in particular is quietly crushing her from the inside.

There will be no children.

She can't have any. If she is not truly human, then she can't have children. It wasn't exactly a pressing priority, but contemplating that the possibility may have been taken away, she feels an emptiness she can barely explain.

There are other voids too. Can she have a relationship? Can she fall in love?

She's had a couple of boyfriends, back in college. Nothing serious, but they *were* relationships.

No: not verifiable. Not admissible. Nothing she remembers before arriving here on CdC counts.

Does the past matter now? Is she defined by memories that may be fictions, or is she defined by her actions from here on in? And if she acts here in defiance of Ochoba, does this mean she is exercising free will?

She's almost there. Ahead of her the concourse is empty, a lens overlay reporting that the dock is temporarily closed. She endures a moment of concern that the doors won't open as she seeks out the prompt and sends it her credentials, but the outline turns green as she approaches.

A few seconds later, Alice Blake swears for the first time, if only to herself.

She's too goddamn late.

INTERVENTION FROM ABOVE

As she approaches within a few metres of the doors, Alice sees four Seguridad officers walking out through them. They seem relaxed despite the rifles slung around their shoulders, an off-duty air about them as though they're out for a stroll.

"Given the flight time to Heinlein and back, I reckon we can take us the rest of the day off," one of them is saying to his colleague: Officer Alonso according to her lens.

"Where's your prisoner?" she asks.

He gives her a disdainful look and she can tell he is about to dismiss her query. She recognises the very nano-second that her name and status registers on his lens. He stiffens. They all do, like a wave passing through them.

"We had new orders to hand her over to the two guys who were waiting for us inside."

"Which guys? Who were they?"

He blanches, a gravity about his expression.

"We didn't have clearance to see their names."

"And you just handed over your prisoner to them?"

"Their orders came from the highest echelons in the Quadriga. Seems somebody doesn't trust us to handle the transfer."

"This is unacceptable. I need to speak to the prisoner. Come with me."

"Ma'am, our orders were countermanded from on high, and obstructing them is punishable by a ticket home. Besides, these are not guys you want to cross. We're glorified rentacops. These were soldiers."

Alice remembers Nikki's description of the unidentified actors who had closed down this same dock a few days ago: *high-level mercenary types*. She doesn't know what strengths or skills might be secretly residing within herself, far less how to activate them, but she does know how to exploit the element of surprise and an elevated angle of fire.

"Give me your weapons," she commands.

She expects a modicum of resistance, but Alonso shrugs and complies, a man well-used to navigating the path of least resistance.

"It's your funeral," he says, that path no doubt taking him and his buddies to the nearest bar.

Alice races up the ramp to access the receiving areas above. She slips inside quietly and crouches close to the edge of the platform, peering through the glass barrier.

Down below she can see Nikki. She is handcuffed, kneeling on a sheet of black plastic with two men standing over her, their backs to Alice. They are dressed identically in charcoal fatigues; they are not uniforms but there is something unquestionably military about their appearance. One of them is holding a knife.

Alice stands up and raises the suppression rifle. The weapon automatically links to her lens, overlaying a cross-hair upon her view, which she places over the knifeman's head. She takes a steadying breath and pulls the trigger.

IN THE FRAME

The part of Nikki that's resigned to this wants to close her eyes, but the part that's pissed at never getting another shot of Speyside wants to look this fucker in the face. She lifts her head and stares at him in defiance

He suddenly flinches and puts a hand to the back of his neck.

"What the fuck?"

When he pulls it away, there are several tiny bloodspots on his palm, a pattern of dots in a cluster.

The knifeman and his buddy turn around to look in the direction of possible fire, at which point a second cluster blooms on the other merc's cheek.

He looks up towards the viewing gallery, both of them drawing flechette pistols and aiming them instinctively. Nikki watches a slight, silhouetted figure duck swiftly as a hail of plastic darts impacts uselessly against the glass. The figure isn't going anywhere either, just sitting tight and observing. Which would indicate that the weapon Nikki can see is one of the Seguridad's goodnight guns.

"Who the hell is that?" asks the knifeman.

"Too far to ID. Dart just grazed me anyway. Give me some cover while I go deal."

"You got it."

"No," Nikki says. "You boys best take a seat."

"What?" he asks, irritated but curious.

"So you don't injure yourselves when you—"

He collapses like a felled tree, no hands reaching to cushion the fall. Consequently his face slams against the deck, a tooth clattering out across the metal, but by that point he is oblivious of pain and injury.

His buddy goes down a little easier, like a puppet with his strings cut.

Riot control measures, Seedee style: suppression rifles deliver a high-velocity blast of rapidly-acting tranquilliser pellets. Once you've been tagged, you've got a matter of seconds to make yourself comfortable, then . . .

"Goodnight," Nikki says.

From below comes the rumbling of the elevator bringing the shuttle up the shaft. It was supposed to be her hearse. She was bound for the cargo hold wrapped in this black plastic sheet. Less than a minute has passed since that merc drew his knife, but she's already supposed to be dead right now.

Nikki looks up again and watches her saviour climb over the glass barrier. She drapes down, landing on the floor with practised gymnastic elegance. Nikki immediately thinks of the assassin at Habitek, but no, it's even weirder than that.

Walking towards her with a suppression rifle slung across her back is G2S herself: Alice fucking Blake.

Nikki's handcuffs fall open and tumble to the ground.

"We need to get this pair into the passenger cabin," Alice says, bending down and trying to drag one of the mercs towards the platform where the shuttle is beginning to emerge.

Nikki watches, still paralysed by disbelief.

Alice stops mid-drag and glares at her.

"You going to give me a hand here or not?"

"I dunno. I'm getting mixed signals and I want to consider my next step. I mean, I recall telling you that your attitude to law and morality was kinda rigid, and I'm getting the impression that your position is a little more ambivalent than last time we spoke – which I applaud, don't get me wrong. But you wanna tell me just what the fuck is going on?"

"I know you didn't kill Omega."

The shuttle's co-pilot is emerging from his craft, the pilot still visible in his seat up in the cockpit. He looks apprehensively towards the two unconscious figures lying on the deck, the shorter of whom is now having his clothes removed by Alice. Then he turns his gaze towards Nikki, whom he assumes to be in charge as she is the older of the two.

"We have orders to pick up a Seguridad detail," he says, sounding uncertain. "Prisoner transfer to Heinlein?"

"Prisoners plural," Alice tells him, standing up. She speaks with the confidence of somebody used to being obeyed.

Nikki figures the co-pilot's lens is now telling him who is really in charge, and to precisely what extent: no less than the Principal of the SOE. He doesn't ask any questions.

He assists in dragging the two mercs to the passenger cabin, where they are strapped into the side-facing seats. Alice produces a jizz cannon and hits each of the assholes with a cum-shot, binding them around the torso and gluing them to the wall. She then rips out their wrist discs. These guys won't be sending any SOS messages when they wake up: not until they reach Heinlein, leastways.

The co-pilot looks at her in shock. Nikki isn't sure if he's appalled by her repeatedly shooting unconscious men or if he's already thinking about the effort it's going to take to remove all that resin from the inside of his nice ship.

"I want you to take them to Heinlein and await instructions. Do not open the passenger cabin. These individuals are dangerous. You will be met at the other end by people who can handle these guys. Do you understand?"

"Yes, ma'am."

"Then what are you waiting for? Get to it."

They watch the shuttle begin to descend on its platform.

"There isn't the equipment at Heinlein to free those assholes," Nikki says. "They'll need to be brought back to Seedee before they can be completely cut from the resin. That means the pair of them are out of play for at least ten hours, but once the alarm is raised there will be others looking for me."

"Flight time to Heinlein is five hours, so that's our window," Alice replies.

"To do what?"

"Find the puppet master."

"You mean whoever's behind this shit? Because I don't have a list of suspects. How about you?"

"Nothing concrete, just the odd suspicious coincidence. What can you tell me about Helen Petitjean?"

"That bloodless old husk? She's who you got your eye on?"

"Just a thread that might be worth pulling. I found out she's got a high-level connection in the FNG, and as a result of current events, things are suddenly going very well for both of them."

"Petitjean is a true believer," Nikki tells her. "In a bygone age she'd have been a religious fundamentalist. Fond of fancy talk about the potential of humankind but not exactly overflowing with human kindness. She reminds me of every school teacher I ever hated, though I'm guessing hating a teacher ain't a concept you can get your head around."

"Well, you don't need to like somebody to learn from them," Alice replies, though there is a hint of a smile in there.

Nikki can't help but return it.

"Come on," Alice urges. "Clock's ticking. Get these clothes on."

"These clothes that you just took off that merc? Why?"

Alice hands her a new lens rig.

"Because you're Megan Driscoll, veteran FNG data analyst on secondment to the SOE. The facial-recognition alert status on Nikki Freeman was deactivated once you were placed in custody, and now as far as Seguridad is aware, Nikki Fixx is officially off CdC and on route to Heinlein."

Nikki accepts the rig gratefully, popping the lenses, wrist unit and sub-vocal into place. Then she slips out of her clothes and into the fatigues. They are a little roomy but a passable fit.

"Not sure this is me."

"That's the idea."

Nikki pulls her hair back into a ponytail, fixing it with a tie-band she found on the floor. There's always dozens of them in freight areas.

"I look uptight enough?"

Alice ignores this.

"So, you wanna tell me what's behind you going rogue all of a sudden? How come you know I didn't kill anybody?"

"I didn't say anybody. But I know for sure you didn't kill Omega."

"How?"

"Because *I* did."

Nikki gapes. This shit just keeps making less sense.

"I'm sending you a grab. This was taken by Korlakian."

Nikki runs the file. Everything lurches and swirls. She's looking out through the eyes of a guy getting his ass handed to him, and with a growing revulsion it dawns on her that if it ends the way she anticipates, this could be a literal description.

She is bracing herself for horror, so she isn't ready for shock.

"Fuck me."

Nikki pauses the playback. She doesn't need to see what happens next.

"You did this," she says. "All along, it was you. So why are you fessing up now? And what else ain't you telling me?"

"Because I only found out it was me when I saw the grab. I have no memory of this."

Nikki races through possibilities. Are they talking about mind-control shit here? People on Seedee have always been paranoid about the concept of mesh malware, but nobody ever came forward to claim a malfunction, never mind a virus. Besides, Alice doesn't even have a mesh. G2S only just got here.

She looks to the girl, a dozen questions on her lips, but Alice is the one who gets in first.

"I need to know, Nikki: why did you talk about me not being born from drinking and sex? What do you know?"

Nikki has no notion of how this is relevant or where it might be going.

"What do I *know*? About what? I meant you probably weren't conceived in some late-night drunken fuck like the rest of us. It was a dig at your straight-ass FNG aristo parents. I was forgetting you were adopted. What's that to do with—"

"Why did you bring up the idea of someone being an android without knowing it?"

"I was just shooting the shit, throwing out stuff that sometimes freaks new arrivals."

Then Nikki belatedly realises what Alice is saying.

"Wait. You're telling me you think you're an *android*? That's your explanation for this?"

"Yes. Because I have no recollection of doing it, but it's me right there in the grab. I realised I have no independent verification of anything I did before I came to CdC. And since I arrived at Heinlein, every time I wake up from sleep, it's like my memory is reassembling itself."

"I keep waking up with no recollection of what preceded going to sleep, but there's a simple explanation. It's called alcohol."

"You said there are rumours that super-advanced AI has been invented on CdC but its existence kept secret."

"Yeah, but I never believed them."

"How about now?" Alice asks. "Yesterday I woke up feeling physically exhausted and then found out about the Habitek massacre."

And suddenly something Nikki has been trying to run away from has her cornered. The assassin who killed Julio and his men: jarringly fleet, impossibly nimble. A white streak, human tracer fire. Part bullet, part ballet.

"I saw the killer at Habitek. It was at a distance and I was looking through night vision, but yeah. It could have been you. I'm sure it was a woman: slight, sleek, fast, graceful."

"That's what I meant by finding the puppet master. Somebody is controlling me."

Nikki is still fighting it. Her cop's instinct is nagging her that something doesn't fit, like the times she couldn't place a suspect at the locus even though everything else appeared to match up.

She looks at the grab again, paused on Alice's face as she stares back at Korlakian. It's her all right, but with different hair. Gotta be a wig.

Shit.

Instead of dispelling what she can't accept, she just made another piece fit. Nikki realises who Mrs Pang was really talking about when they spoke in the alley.

That girl back at your apartment. Yeah, I saw her here before, except her hair was different.

Mrs Pang meant Alice, not Giselle. She saw Alice going up the stairs with Nikki, and she had seen her earlier, heading to Nikki's apartment with Giselle, but with different hair.

It was Alice who killed her.

But even as she thinks this, she sees where the theory doesn't add up. For one, the face in the grab is not triggering any recognition. Like Amber down in the Catacombs, she appears to have no listed identity.

"You've got an alibi," Nikki tells her.

"For what? Being asleep alone doesn't count."

"For Giselle. My neighbour Mrs Pang said she saw you and Giselle heading for my apartment before she was killed."

"I don't know how they do things in the Seguridad, but that sounds like the opposite of an alibi."

"No, it's as solid as they come. Because while Giselle was being murdered, you were trussed up unconscious in Trick's workshop. And what you didn't notice is that your name doesn't come up when you look at this woman. No name does: she registers as a blank. This blonde psycho bitch ain't you."

TRUE NATURE

Alice knows Nikki's logic is incontestable. She couldn't be in two places at once. It is also true that she failed to register how no name had come up to identify the face she was looking at. If she noticed the anomaly at all, she perhaps assumed that it was simply what happened when you were seeing yourself in someone else's grab.

She calls up the image again, looking closer this time. Maybe she's imagining it, but she can see slight differences she failed to detect before: lines around the eyes, fewer freckles, a paler skin tone that she subconsciously ascribed to the lighting.

She has a doppelganger.

She enjoys a moment of blessed, elevating relief as the implication flows through her: she is not, after all, harbouring a secret self who kills people while she sleeps. However, it is but a moment, as it is rapidly dismissed by a further incontestable deduction.

"Hey, I just proved you innocent and yet you look like the other shoe just dropped," Nikki says. "What gives?"

"I didn't kill anybody, but there's a near-identical version of me running around CdC, behaving in a way I never would. Same model, different directives."

Alice swallows back tears, but she fears they are merely a subroutine, a programmed response. The conclusion is becoming harder and harder to escape.

"I am an android, and so is she."

Nikki stares at her, doubtless grasping for alternatives. Alice recognises the process. It's been her world since she first saw Omega's grab. Unfortunately there is no way back out of the rabbit hole.

"This ain't right. There has to be another explanation. You're as human as I am. Look at you, you're *crying*, for Chrissakes. You eat, you drink. Not the good stuff, but you drink fluids. Hey, you got shot with a dart the other day. Didn't you bleed?"

Alice shows her the scab on her wrist where the dart penetrated.

"I bled. In fact, I'm bleeding now, if you know what I mean. But crying, bleeding, digestion, these are all functions that could be synthesised."

"Come on, that's just crazy. Why the fuck would they synthesise periods?"

Nikki makes it sound like a game-changing question. But Alice has an answer.

"To keep the android credulous of the idea that it is human."

Nikki's expression indicates she still isn't convinced. Alice hopes that the basis for her doubt proves compelling.

"No. I still ain't buying it. Though, if you *are* an android, we certainly got proof that it was a man who designed you. Builds an artificial woman and still gives her the goddamn curse? Fucking asshole. Why would he do that? Wouldn't *not* having periods be one of the consolations of being artificial?"

"Think about it. Convincing the android that she is human would serve to prevent people discovering how advanced the AI has really become. If someone has achieved this level of technological accomplishment, keeping it secret would confer an extraordinary advantage. Androids acting as your agents: compliant, programmable, unsuspected. And how better to conceal their true nature than to keep that hidden from even themselves."

Nikki is staring at her now, suddenly gaunt, as though something strong inside her just withered. Her doubt is gone, and something more chilling has replaced it.

"Project Sentinel," she says. "That's what this is. A secret so deadly, you're a target even if you hear the words."

"Who told you that?"

"At Habitek, I spoke to Sol Freitas as the poor sonofabitch was dying. He said they 'ate the forbidden fruit'. Julio's people took something they weren't supposed to have, and that's why they were killed. He mentioned Project Sentinel, called it the touch of death.

I remember you asking me about it at Klaws, but you didn't know what it was."

Alice thinks of the first time she heard it, and once more sees an altered meaning in the same information.

"When I was strapped to Trick's table, the people who took him bailed in a hurry when one of them recognised me. She said she was running off primary, which was why she saw through my fake ID. She mentioned Project Sentinel but it didn't mean anything to me."

Nikki gapes.

"They knew what you were."

Alice nods grimly.

"They knew what I was, what I looked like. I was strapped to a table and they were still worried. Maybe they knew I was merely one of many, sending information to a central source. Cut off one head . . ."

"And someone who looks exactly like you comes along to cut off theirs."

CONTROL

Nikki keeps her head down and avoids any eye contact as they traverse her familiar stomping ground and head towards the passageways beneath Mullane. Fortunately, nobody's passing curiosity survives contact with Alice, who is broadcasting her status as the FNG's snooper-in-chief. It's like a deflector shield, making everybody *else* keep their head down and avoid eye contact.

Nikki falls in behind as they leave the main thoroughfare, her gaze focused on the neat figure of her companion. Alice has been transformed since Nikki fled her apartment, going rogue, breaking rules, breaking laws. These things all seem very human to her; quintessentially human, in fact. And yet she's seen Omega's grab, an identical woman carrying out the murder, and Alice seems resigned to the notion that they are both some kind of android. It would sure explain how squeaky clean the girl is, how slavishly adherent to rules and protocols, though her conduct over the past few hours would represent a serious malfunction.

In seeking an explanation, Nikki had been working on the Sherlock Holmes principle that once you've ruled out the impossible, whatever is left, however improbable, must be the truth. She would have to concede that if someone has developed super-advanced, indistinguishably human-like androids, then the widespread assumption that this was impossible would be the perfect cover. And it would certainly explain a lot if this were indeed Project Sentinel, the deadly secret worth killing so many people for.

Nonetheless, her instincts are telling her there has to be something else. She's seen a lot of weird things on Seedee, a place where new tech is emerging all the time, but this just seems a leap too far and too fast. If there has been a development as huge as this, she can see the power play in keeping secret the fact that you have effectively created slaves or surrogates who can pass as human. However, a breakthrough like this doesn't happen overnight, so keeping it secret doesn't strike her as consistent with the corporate behaviour she is used to observing up here. They would be wanting tax breaks to assist their efforts in developing this revolutionary new tech, not to mention maximising the effect it would have on their share price.

Bottom line is she just isn't buying it, though admittedly that's easier for her to say than for Alice. Nikki isn't the one having to contemplate the possibility that she runs on batteries and might be only a few days old.

"He's fixed the door," Alice says as they approach Trick's den. "Let's hope he's beefed up his security too."

"I can't *see* the door," Nikki reports, her lens not showing the outline she is familiar with from a host of previous visits.

"That's because you're Megan Driscoll," Alice reminds her. "Allow me."

"Oh yeah, I'm forgetting you and Trick are tight now."

Trick looks a mess, all beat up. He seems alarmed by the sight of Nikki, like she's a total stranger and not somebody he's known for years. Then she remembers she is supposed to be: one, a mass murderer; and two, long gone from here.

"Hey, Trick," she says quietly.

He manages a crooked smile and shows his guests inside, closing the door behind them. He's strengthened it and added some bolts. Nikki figures he's got an emergency exit hidden someplace too.

"Nikki Fixx. Guess you're the turd that wouldn't flush. Hey, I like the new duds. You look halfway respectable, and by that I mean totally unrecognisable. What is this, witness protection? Or did you get recruited? How many dudes you gotta kill before they give you a job helping out the FNG?"

"Fuck you, Trick. We're here to save your ungrateful hide."

"Save me? From what?"

"You were right," Alice tells him. "Nikki didn't kill Giselle or anybody else. Now we're working together to find out who did."

"These assholes who took you and beat the shit out of you, Trick. We need to know who they were and what you did for them."

He physically backs away, stepping closer to the wall.

"Nuh-uh. I already told your new boss, here. I'm not crossing these people."

"They're not the ones you need to be afraid of," Alice tells him.

"You can say that, but fact is I'm more scared of the psychos I know than the devil I don't."

"We understand," Nikki replies. "And we're not asking you to rat nobody out. Just maybe take a look at a few pictures and help eliminate some people from our inquiries."

On cue, Alice fires him a series of images from the aftermath at Habitek: six blood-spattered bodies, their twisted faces nonetheless recognisable enough to be identified by his lens.

They both see the revulsion in Trick's eyes.

"It wasn't any of these people."

"Yeah, but I'm betting the ones who took you worked for the late Mr Martinez here, right?"

He swallows. That's a yes.

"Told you they're not the ones you need to be scared of," Alice says.

"Julio and everybody else in these images got killed because of something called Project Sentinel," Nikki states. "These people mentioned it when they took you. Everyone who even heard about it has been murdered, meaning that either you're the evil-genius mastermind behind this – which, with respect, I seriously fucking doubt – or you're in real trouble. So I ask you again: who were they and what did you do for them?"

Trick looks freaked now, no doubt about it. Two minutes ago he thought the worst thing that could happen was these people coming back. Now he understands the true stakes.

"It was Yash. Yash and two of Julio's psychos: Bollo and Krug." Nikki nods.

"That figures."

"Who?" Alice asks.

"Yashmin Sardana," Nikki replies. "A known associate and some-time fuck buddy of the late Mr Martinez. She handles stolen tech. She's normally a deft hand at cracking the protection and repurposing hardware. What did she need you for?"

Trick bristles, anxiety running through him like a current. It's as though he fears they're watching and listening right now.

"They had this device. I think it might have been one of the machines they link you up to for uploading memory to a mesh."

"You think?" Nikki asks. "Ain't you seen one?"

"No. I don't have a mesh."

Nikki's eyes widen. Of all people, she'd have pegged Trick as the last to be a hold-out.

"Why not?"

"Look what I do here. I wasn't convinced they're secure. There's no tech been invented that can't be hacked, and that shit's in your head."

"The security is that you have to go to Neurosophy Labs and be physically connected up," Nikki says, though as she speaks she realises she is only trying to reassure herself. Like most other folks, she never thought much about this. As long as the only people with the tech were the doctors and scientists at Neurosophy, there didn't seem any risk. But now . . .

"You're telling me somebody managed to boost one of those things?"

"If that's what it was, yes."

"This is the secret weapon Freitas was talking about. Not literally a weapon, but something that would give Julio a serious edge, financially."

"He would have instantly monopolised a black market in illegal memory uploads," says Alice.

"Except this was something else," Trick says. "Something different. If it was simply a memory upload device, I'm sure Yash could have handled it. They needed me because I know ways to manipulate the central database. They were using this thing to connect to *people*, and it did that by piggybacking onto the CDB network."

"A memory upload device that can connect to people's lenses?" Nikki asks, though she can't see how that would possibly work. Lenses connect to the CDB, but they are merely augmentation devices. They render data, they handle comms, they play audiovisual files.

"No. That's what's so fucking scary about this. It was connecting to their meshes."

"That's impossible," Nikki insists, though again she is only trying to reassure herself. Even as she speaks she realises Trick is about to tell her why she's wrong.

"It only worked in maybe one person out of five," he says. "I noticed it was mostly tech types. Early adopters."

"People who upgraded to the latest mesh," Alice suggests.

"That ain't me," Nikki says, relieved. "I have a very rigid ain't-broke-don't-fix-it policy when it comes to that stuff."

"But what should worry you is that even with the older meshes, it still established a preliminary connection. It just wouldn't communicate fully with the device after that, like there was some kind of incompatibility."

"But what could it be connecting to? There's no airborne receiver on a mesh."

"Isn't there? What if that physical interface, and the fact you have to go to Neurosophy and lie down on a bed for six hours . . . What if that was misdirection to disguise the fact that meshes *can* be remotely connected?"

Nikki's hand goes to her scalp involuntarily.

"You don't have one, if I recall," he says to Alice.

"No. I couldn't stand the thought of any artificial processes influencing my actions."

If she is an android, it appears the G2S unit does have a sense of humour after all.

"So what were Yash and her buddies uploading to people once you worked your magic?"

"They weren't uploading anything. That isn't what it did. They were controlling people."

There is a silence in the room, enough for them to be able to hear the distant thump of music from one of the joints upstairs.

"You did not just say that."

"Man, I wish I had a mesh so I could go and get my memory of this shit erased, but I don't, so I'm stuck with the truth. This machine allowed them to make people do things."

"Like, follow commands?"

"No, it looked more complex, more sophisticated, though the way they were using it sure wasn't. It had a thousand settings and variables, looked like it would take an expert to operate it properly – however you'd define properly when you're talking about such a technological abomination. Yash was trying to understand it, but the other two assholes were like kids messing with an instrument they knew they couldn't play: they hit all the extremes just to see what would happen."

"Extremes like aggression and sexual desire?" Nikki suggests.

"Exactly."

"Klaws," says Alice, up to speed.

"What?"

"Alice saw this straight-arrow type volunteer for a chamber-fight. It got very messy."

"I saw it," Trick says. "Through his eyes, his lens. Kept coming at the prize fighter no matter how many times she put him down. Eventually he jacked a scalpel from the surgeon on-site and started cutting people up."

"I also heard about a woman in Spiral . . ."

"Strips off and starts fucking strangers on the bar top, yeah. They were having a high old time with that shit. They couldn't merely control them via their meshes, they could also tap into the victims' lenses and watch the show live. They must have got it working in some limited capacity before they came to me, because I heard one of them talk about it. He said, 'This is so much more fun than with that pilot.'"

"I saw reports of fights and disturbances all over my Seguridad feed around that time," Nikki says. "Just thought it was a wild Saturday night."

Trick shakes his head gravely.

"You suggested earlier that this isn't 'literally' a weapon, but it

319

literally is. That's why I've been so scared. It's not simply that this was stolen and Julio's people weren't supposed to have it. *Nobody* is supposed to have it. And I knew that whoever created it would go to extreme lengths to prevent anyone from finding out it even exists."

Alice sends Nikki a look. Just like Project Sentinel.

Nikki's thoughts turn to Slovitz, the missing scientist. He worked for Neurosophy, and she's pretty sure he's dead too, though nobody will ever find his body. Somebody went to a lot of trouble and spent a lot of money to ensure nobody even went looking for it.

Nikki turns to Trick.

"You got like a dozen other identities, haven't you?"

"Yeah."

"Well, if you got someplace you can lie low, where nobody knows who you really are, I'd recommend you disappear."

"Trust me, I'm gone."

"But just before you leave . . ."

Nikki reboots her rig and sees the familiar and comforting sight of multiple aliases waiting to be exploited.

She would thank Trick, but he booked the moment he handed her back the hacked wrist unit, leaving the two of them in his workshop.

"Will it trigger some alert if I access my own profile?" she asks Alice.

"Shouldn't do. It was suspended but I had it unfrozen. All the alerts were cancelled when we threw you in the clink."

Nikki takes the plunge and gets a rapid illustration of how quickly Seedee forgets about you once you're gone. In the past, if she was incommunicado for any length of time, like even a few hours of sleep, there'd be a dozen messages waiting for her when she woke up: people impatiently trying to get hold of her, all assuming she was on their phase. Right now, there is one solitary message, and it's from nobody: sent from a monitor terminal rather than a lens.

Needing some validation that her identity hasn't been entirely purged from people's minds, she takes a look.

It's a video message from Zola. That's why it's from a terminal. It was sent not long after Nikki left the Catacombs, maybe around the time Nikki was being thrown in a cell.

Zola looks distraught. Her face appears blotchy from tears, but as she turns her head Nikki can see that some of the discolouration is actually bruising. Her voice sounds choked, tearful.

"I heard some bad things about you, Nikki, but I figure you're the only hope a ghost like me has. If there's any way you still can help me, I'm begging you. They took Amber."

HIDDEN SCARS

"We need to find Yashmin Sardana before we do anything else," Alice insists, though she knows Nikki won't agree. She can tell Nikki is concerned about her friend and about this semi-catatonic woman who has been abducted, but she also knows every passing second takes that shuttle closer to Heinlein.

"Did you forget the part where I told you the scientist who dumped Amber on Zola worked for Neurosophy?" Nikki replies. "And his return to Earth was faked to cover the fact that he was almost certainly murdered? This is connected."

"I appreciate that, but Yash has to be our priority. When was that message left?"

"Around eighteen hours ago," Nikki admits.

"So it's a little late to drop everything and run to Zola's aid. Amber's gone and as you say, Slovitz is most probably dead. Yash is our last lead. We've got to get to her before my doppelganger does."

Nikki nods solemnly, conceding the point.

"Okay, but if we find her, you'd best let me do the talking. I figure she's bound to be somewhat skittish around someone of your appearance."

"You know where she might hang out?"

"Ordinarily, sure, but she won't be in any of her usual haunts. After what happened at Habitek, she's got to know there's a target on her back."

"Do you know where she lives?"

"No, but her apartment is the last place she'll be."

"Nonetheless, it's still the only logical place to start, unless you've got a better suggestion."

Alice runs a search for her name, as she has privileged access to residential listings. Yash's apartment isn't the only result that appears, however.

"Shoot."

"What?"

"Her name just showed up on a Seguridad alert. She was found hanged in her apartment three hours ago. Suspected suicide."

Nikki frowns, shaking her head.

"No way she committed suicide, and no way she went back to her apartment, at least not voluntarily. Your evil twin is having to disguise the deaths now that I'm not available to take the rap."

Alice grips a table, knuckles whitening with frustration.

"End of the line," she says.

"There's still Bollo and Krug," Nikki suggests, but her tone betrays that she holds out the same hope as Alice for finding either of them alive.

"No. Let's go and speak to your friend. Where does she live?"

"Garneau."

That's where the Armstrong Hotel is, the last place Alice slept, whenever that was.

"I thought you said she was a nurse, and that she lost her contract? She stays in a very upmarket neighbourhood."

"Oh, you have no idea."

Alice has seen some astonishing sights since her arrival on CdC, but this is the one that most jolts her perception. Seeing the Earth from space, the moon at such close range, the rooftops on the far side of a wheel when looking up through the canopy: these could transfix anyone, gazing upon views that seem to rebuff a lifetime of expectations. The Catacombs, however, have her slack-jawed and speechless, not with awe but revulsion.

Her disgust is not at the sight itself, but the lie it represents. This place is the mirror's backing, the squalid secret beneath CdC's reflection of a perfect society.

She feels tears welling up. She wants to conceal this from Nikki, though she is not sure why. Shame, perhaps. There is no hiding it, though. Nikki has been looking for her reaction.

"They don't show this shit in the brochures," she says.

"You should have taken me here first," Alice replies. "It would have saved a lot of time."

"Took me this long to be convinced it would make a difference. I conned Hoffman into coming here once. Told him it was a tour of a new fungus-protein farm being developed beneath Garneau. Strangely, I don't think he ever made reference to the Catacombs in any of his reports to the FNG."

There is a choking smell of urine and other matter as they make their way down a narrow channel. Alice glances to her right and sees that they are passing a makeshift latrine block, a communal facility opposite a bank of improvised shower stalls. Up ahead, a woman crawls out of what Nikki referred to as a nook, bidding goodbye to whoever she was visiting.

"But try not to move it," she is saying. "And have someone come get me when the dressing needs changed."

She notices their approach and reacts with surprise and confusion upon turning her face fully towards them, revealing bruising down once side. It confirms Zola's identity even before her name flashes in Alice's lens.

"Nikki?" she asks, not daring to believe it. "I heard you were in custody awaiting transportation back to Earth."

"Rumours of my deportation have been greatly exaggerated. And the rumours of my killing spree have been exaggerated too. I'm sorry I couldn't get here sooner. This is Alice Blake, my boss. What happened to Amber?"

Zola touches her face tenderly in automatic response to the question.

"These men came for her. Four of them. Like police but not Seguridad. Soldiers."

"Did they know you had her?" Nikki asks.

"No. They were searching for her and I think they ended up here. They were showing her picture around, asking if people had seen her. They were smashing their way into places, trashing people's pods. Karyl here tried to object. They broke his arm. Compound fracture."

"Ouch."

"I heard the disturbance and I might have found a way to smuggle her out before they got to my nook, but Amber must have recognised their voices. She panicked and was trying to flee, but this place is a labyrinth. She pretty much ran straight into them, and she went crazy. For someone who had seemed so confused, she was suddenly very clear about the threat she was facing. She started screaming again, saying 'Don't let them take me, they're going to kill me. They took my baby and they're going to kill me.'

"They zapped her unconscious and when I tried to intervene, one of them hit me. He could have zapped me unconscious too, but he punched me to the floor instead and hit me a few more times. A crowd had gathered, and this was for their benefit, I think."

"Did they say anything to her, or to you?"

"Apart from asking people if they had seen Amber, they said nothing. The one who hit me barely looked me in the eye. He didn't even seem angry. Merely calculating. Amber was so scared. I had seen her have her hysterics and her nightmares, but this was something else: this was a rational, specific fear."

"You said before that you didn't know what she meant when she talked about someone taking her baby," Nikki reminds her. "Whether it was maybe something that happened on Earth before she came here. Is it possible she meant these people in particular?"

Zola's face takes on a pallor.

"Amber never wanted to shower or change her clothes. That is, I persuaded her eventually, but I had to stand guard at the stall. She was reluctant to take anything off. I don't know why. But it's the reason I never saw it before."

"Saw what?"

"After they zapped her and hit me, I was lying on the floor next to her. She had like three layers on but they rode up when they lifted her to carry her away. I saw her abdomen. She had a fresh caesarean scar. I saw enough of those on Earth to know this was only a few weeks old. She was confused and often incoherent but she wasn't lying. She had a baby and she was damn sure these people took it."

"Who were they?" Alice asks. "Had you ever seen them before?"

"No."

"Where did you send the message from?" Nikki enquires.

"There's a woman here who has a monitor terminal."

"Take us to it."

They negotiate the warren, Alice amazed that Zola can tell one lane from another, far less one pod. Zola crawls into one of the cluttered cubicles and emerges with the terminal. Alice sends the device some images taken from Dock Nine, showing Nikki's would-be executioners lying unconscious on the floor.

Zola clasps a hand over her mouth, shaken by the pictures.

"That's them, yes. Along with two others. Who are they?"

"We don't know."

"You have to find out. You have to get her back. She was so scared."

Nikki and Alice share a look, acknowledging two things: that Amber may already be dead, and that even if she's not, they are up against a clock they cannot see.

"We'll do what we can," Nikki says. Her tone is sincere but not optimistic. "Meantime, you gonna be okay?"

"I'm fine. Still tender, but it could have been a lot worse."

"Oh yeah, your friend Karyl. Did you have to set his arm yourself?"

Alice wonders why this would be the case, given the standard of medical care available at the ERU. Then she realises that the ghosts of the Catacombs can't show up to the enfermería because their presence would register on all kinds of systems. Proper medical attention would come at the risk of being sent back to Earth, which is presumably a worse prospect even than living here.

"I had some help. Lupe came down and treated him. Gave me some painkillers too. I still have some friends in the caring professions."

Lupe: Dr Guadaloupe Hermosillos. Alice recalls the name, as well as the condemnation she rained down upon the surgeon for her complicity in what went on at Klaws. She was a little hasty there, it seems. Lupe went where she was needed, asked no questions, told no tales.

Suddenly Alice makes the connection.

"Dr Hermosillos told us she treated a man with a mangled foot who claimed he had no recollection of how it happened. She believed him because he 'wasn't the usual type for a mystery injury'. She said he was a pilot."

Nikki sees it too.

"According to Trick, Yash's pet assholes said what they were doing was 'more fun than with the pilot'. Trick's modification let them target people at random. Whatever they did to the pilot preceded that. He wasn't targeted at random, he was targeted specifically. We need to find this guy."

"Way ahead of you," Alice announces.

THE KICKER

Within half an hour they are standing outside an apartment building on Weber. It is a primarily residential area bordering on the Scobee district, which Nikki informs Alice is Julio's stomping ground.

"*Was* Julio's stomping ground," she corrects herself.

Nikki surprises herself with how genuinely regretful she feels about this. It's not like she had any affection for Julio and his attack-chimps, but she sure didn't want them dead. It's more than their loss that she is mourning, however: it feels like the Seedee she knows is dying before her eyes. At best she will unmask the killer after the fact, but she won't be able to prevent the murder.

The ground floor of the apartment building is given over to a fitness arena, comprising several banks of running pods, 3D-rotating climbing cubes and other state-of-the-art exertainment machines. It's a far cry from the boxing gym where Freitas and his buds hung out, and there certainly isn't much overlap in terms of the clientele. The building is comparatively high-rise for a residential block, so as well as a general fitness facility, the arena is a necessity for people renting in the upper storeys. There are certain conveniences about living in a low-g apartment, not least that the rent is usually cheaper, but you can lose muscle mass if you don't work out regularly.

The guy they are looking for lives on the second-highest floor. Alice was frustrated in her intention to search medical records for recent leg injuries, as strict patient confidentiality rules meant even *her* clearance level didn't grant override access. However, she was able to access transportation shift rotas, and discovered that a pilot named Aaron DeLonge had been off work for several days.

They take the stairs, feeling the climb ease with each flight.

"Remember to be economical with your movement," Nikki warns. "You can ping around like a pinball if you're not used to it."

"Learned that the hard way," she replies, referring to her zero-g mishap during the all-stop.

"You'd think they'd give an android different settings, so it can switch between gravity modes."

"No, I only have one," Alice replies, raising her middle finger.

"Obscene finger gestures from such a pristine girl."

"I'm not that pristine."

They reach DeLonge's apartment, where lens input requests and plain old knocking both fail to elicit a response.

Nikki puts her ear to the door. She detects only stillness and silence within. Time was when the sight of a murder victim was as much a part of her working routine as coffee and paperwork. She thinks of the many corpses she has encountered in recent days, and realises that after nearly two decades here, she has grown used to the absence of violent death. That is the thing she is truly mourning, not Julio or Omega or any of the others.

Apart from Giselle, that is. She has barely had the opportunity to truly process that. She keeps shunting it to the back, something she can't afford to deal with yet.

"The lock isn't responding to my emergency override," Alice reports. "It's been jammed or hacked or something."

Nikki thinks of the Seguridad listings Alice saw, regarding Yash. Found hanged, suspected suicide. Something tightens inside her, bracing for the impact of what she is about to see.

Nikki busts the door open with her heel, sending it flying to the wall.

There is rapid movement inside, where Aaron DeLonge is very much alive. Startled by the explosive intrusion, he has got up from his chair and is catapulting himself towards the kitchen area to the rear of his living room. His right leg is dragging behind him, encumbered by an aluminium frame around a protective plastic cast, blinking sensors on the outside.

Despite this, DeLonge is fast, used to the low gravity environment. He reaches the back wall in a couple of seconds. Nikki's cop instincts anticipate why he's headed there and she begins closing the distance.

Above the worktop next to the sink there are four stainless steel one-piece blades glinting on an electro-magnetic rack. DeLonge seizes the nearest of them, gripping it in his right hand and turning to face his intruders. He looks scared and desperate. Despite Nikki being the nearer of the two and the one who has made a move, she notices that he only has eyes for Alice.

"Everybody take it easy," Alice implores, holding up her hands. "Nobody needs to—"

But Alice isn't seeing what Nikki is. She lunges towards him, deflecting his knife hand upwards with her left forearm and sending a blow to his gut with her right. Encumbered by the leg brace, he is easy to take down and pin, having relieved him of the knife in a disarming manoeuvre. This last she hadn't used in twenty years, which suggests her muscle memory is more durable than its mental equivalent. Though to be fair, it isn't her muscle memory that she has been trying to erase with Speyside malt for two decades.

"What did you do that for?" Alice asks, appalled.

"Because he was going for his own throat: that's what the knife was for. This dude took one look at you and decided to kill himself. I'm not saying I don't know how he feels, but it's my duty to intervene."

DeLonge keeps struggling. He's trying to push sharply against the floor in order to bounce both of them into the air, but Nikki keeps him tightly pinned until she is sure the fight has gone out of him. Still his gaze is fixed on Alice, though the look of anguish gradually dissipates into one of timidity.

"We don't mean you any harm, Mr DeLonge," Nikki assures him.

"Allowing that intention and practice can sometimes diverge," Alice adds pointedly.

"Yeah, I'm sorry I wasn't able to prevent you killing yourself in a less painful manner, but the point is we're the good guys, okay?"

DeLonge doesn't look convinced, but Nikki allows him to get up and vigilantly escorts him back to his chair while Alice pushes the door to.

"So you wanna tell us why you were trying to take a shortcut? What's so scary about Dr Blake here?"

He shakes his head, staring mostly at the floor, occasionally stealing a glance at Alice. He looks like a beaten dog scared of when the next blow will fall. Nikki feels kinda bad about the punch to the gut, but in her defence, he had worse planned for himself.

"Let's start off with an easier one. What happened to your leg?"

Still he says nothing.

"Okay, I'm gonna try fill in some of the blanks for you. Would it be possible that your current anxiety derives from a fear of reprisals by one Yashmin Sardana, known associate of one Julio Martinez?"

DeLonge's eyes react, drawn to Nikki in reflexive response to these names.

"Or should I say, the *late* Yashmin Sardana, known associate of the *late* Julio Martinez. In fact, I could save myself some time by telling you that the words 'late' and 'associate of Julio Martinez' are now so synonymous as to constitute a tautology. They're not coming for you. But somebody is, and I'm guessing you know she looks a lot like my colleague right here."

DeLonge glances back and forth between the two of them in confusion.

"It's kind of an evil-twin deal," Nikki says. "Alice here is the wholesome one. You should make nice with her."

"We're the only ones who can protect you," Alice tells him. "But we can't help you if you won't help us."

DeLonge lets loose a long, slow exhale. Nikki has seen it a thousand times before, enough to know when a wit is going to cooperate.

"Okay, but you have to let me get something from the kitchen first."

Nikki steps back and allows him to stand up. DeLonge makes his way to the rear of the apartment in two gliding bounces, then leans awkwardly to reach down into a cupboard. He casts an eye back towards Alice as he does so, which Nikki is pleased to see provokes the same response in both women.

"Easy," Alice says, taking the resin gun from her belt.

331

Android or not, she's got some cop instincts to her.

"What do you have there?"

Very slowly he pulls out a green bottle Nikki instantly recognises as Glenfiddich. He pours himself three fingers and necks most of it, then shoves the bottle back into the cupboard jealously.

Nikki feels a dryness of want in her throat. Selfish bastard.

"I don't fly freight," he says, sucking his cheeks together in response to the burn of the liquor. "Sure, I'm licensed to fly ion shuttles, but there's no fun to it. That's why I fly limpet-bugs."

This is his way of saying he knows some fancy flying, over and above the mindless back-and-forth between Heinlein and Seedee. Limpet-bugs are used for carrying out exterior maintenance work on the wheels and canopies. They are small and highly manoeuvrable compared to the ion shuttles. Their nickname refers to their insect-like appearance and their requirement to stick to the outside surfaces while their crews carry out EVA work.

"Do a little moonlighting?" Nikki asks.

"Moving bulk quantities between locations. Most contraband comes in on the ion shuttles and gets offloaded at one of the docks, but if you actually need half of your shipment to reach the other wheel, I'm your guy."

"You did this for Julio?"

"I did it for whoever. You can always use a little extra cash, right? But then I took a job that I wish I'd never touched. I guess it was for Julio ultimately, but that's not who I agreed it with or how it was packaged. In fact, nothing about this package turned out to be what anybody agreed."

"Who did you deal with?"

"Omega. I take it there's nothing I need to tell you about him."

"Nope," Nikki replies.

"It was a subcontract gig. Omega had an arrangement with this scientist, Slovitz. Slovitz wanted to smuggle something out of the Neurosophy compound, some new tech."

DeLonge drinks the rest of the whisky. Nikki can almost taste it on her lips. Fucker still ain't sharing.

"Slovitz agreed a deal with Omega to organise the transport.

Hired me to do the flying. Omega and Yashmin tagged along – they said as security, to make sure it all ran smoothly, but I smelt bullshit. Yash deals in stolen tech and Julio's people would rob the sugar from your coffee, so the prospect of getting to poke around inside Neurosophy was always gonna be a huge temptation. I guess Slovitz smelt it too, but he was going underground to get this done so maybe he didn't have a lot of choice.

"Slovitz supplied clearance codes to get the limpet-bug into the shuttle elevator under the Neurosophy compound. We stopped part-way up the shaft and the other three got out. You know what it's like on Seedee: all controlled doorways above, but when you get underneath into the guts, there's always ways in and out of places you shouldn't be."

"I'm starting to grasp that, yes," Alice says.

"They were edgy though. Caught trespassing around that place and you're Earthbound, you know? They all put on masks so the security cameras couldn't ID them. Omega made sure that big old tatt of his was covered up. Good as a barcode, that thing."

"But you stayed with the limpet-bug?"

"Ready for a fast getaway, yeah. They were gone a long time, though. Seemed like a long time anyway. And when they came back, everything felt wrong. They had this machine, I'm guessing the one they were there to get, but they also show up with this girl, who looked totally spaced out: just babbling, scared and crazy. Omega was real pissed because the girl wasn't part of the deal. Slovitz had insisted they take her, and I'm guessing this put us all in deeper shit than Omega bargained for."

"Did they say anything about where this girl came from?" Nikki asks.

"No. But Yash seemed real spooked. She kept asking Slovitz about something called Project Sentinel, but he was taking the fifth."

"What did she say about it?" asks Alice.

"All I remember is the name. She was asking him about the machine too, but he wasn't playing ball. I remember Yash and Omega talking quietly on the flight back, cooking something up while Slovitz was busy making sure the girl was okay. I think he slugged her with some kind of sedative, because she fell asleep.

"When we got back to base, Omega told Slovitz the terms of the deal had changed. Said he was taking the machine as part of the payment. Slovitz objected, and you can imagine how it went from there."

"Vividly," says Nikki.

"Anyway, a little while after that, as you know, Omega gets himself butchered, and then Yash shows up here with two more of Julio's people: Bollo and Krug. I thought they were here to pay me my end, but then I see they got the goddamn machine with them.

"They connected it to my mesh, right there on the floor. Knocked me around a bit first, to let me know it was useless to struggle. I'm shitting myself, thinking they're gonna fry my brain. Instead I'm lying there a few minutes, then they unplug me and leave. I'm thinking what the fuck. I'm a mess and I'm sweaty and shook up, so I take a shower. That's the last thing I remember before waking up on the floor with my leg all chewed up."

"So you don't know what happened to it?" Alice asks.

"Oh, I know fine. While I'm lying in the infirmary, I get a message from Yash telling me to check my grabs. Turns out I recorded one without knowing. Turns out I did a lot without knowing. Best you see for yourselves."

DeLonge sends the grab to both of them. Nikki runs it semi-transparent so that she can make sure he isn't trying to pull anything while they're distracted. Even at that opacity, she has to stop watching after about twenty seconds. She lasts longer than Alice, however.

The grab shows the view as DeLonge comes out of the shower, walking towards his bed upon which a fresh change of clothes is laid out. It's like he misjudges his stride and kicks the sharp edge of the sturdy metal bedpost with his bare foot. The contact is shudderingly solid. There is an audible crunch that Nikki can almost feel. He looks down, revealing one of his toes to be bent and cracked and bleeding.

He lifts his foot tenderly off the floor a few centimetres, like he is about to cradle it, protect it. Instead, he drives it full-force into the bedpost again like he's kicking a field goal.

The scream sounds in Nikki's ears, shaking her.

DeLonge kicks it again, harder still. More crunching, more breaking of bones, more tearing of soft, bloody flesh.

This time he falls over. A hand reaches to grab the foot, not daring to touch the damaged toes. Then inexplicably he lets it go and draws himself awkwardly upright again. He takes his weight unsteadily on his left foot and kicks once more with his right.

It goes on and on, kicking and falling and crunching and tearing and bleeding. And when he can no longer get back up, he starts kicking where he lies on the ground, smashing his shin against the bedpost until it is gashed open and the bone visible, at which point Nikki can't take any more.

SAFEGUARDS

Alice is trembling. In a way, this is worse than seeing any of the corpses she has witnessed of late, because bodies only show the aftermath. It is almost as bad as watching Omega's grab, but for its sick-joke killer twist.

Alice and Nikki look to each other and then to the protective frame around DeLonge's shattered limb.

"They got a machine that can make me do that to myself," DeLonge says. "Imagine what else it could make someone do."

"We don't have to," Alice tells him. "We've already seen."

DeLonge opens the cupboard again and pours himself another shot of whisky, knocking it back in a gulp. Alice notices Nikki's eyes on the bottle, like a dog spotting a hare.

"A little later, I got another message from Yash," he says. "You should take a look at that too."

He forwards the data. Alice sees an image of her doppelganger: a shot lifted from Yash's own recording of a picture on a screen. No blonde hair this time, so the face looks even more like Alice upon a cursory viewing. It shows her in military fatigues, water twinkling in the background. There is accompanying text.

This is who butchered Omega. You've probably heard otherwise but that's because Julio is too dumb to understand the real threat. He's convinced himself it's all about Yoram, but I was inside Neurosophy. I saw what she is. She is coming for what we took. She is coming for all of us because we need to be silenced.

Your instinct will be to delete this grab. Do not. I want you to keep it, and I want you to watch it again any time you are even thinking of telling anybody about what we did. Because if she

finds you, what happened to your leg will be a treasured memory
by comparison.

If she tracks you down, I recommend taking whatever course
is available to end yourself, because she won't make it so quick.
Believe me, it's what I will be doing.

"And you really have no memory of inflicting this injury upon
yourself?" Alice asks. "Only the grab?"

"Nothing. It's like it happened to somebody else, or my memory
was on pause while I was under someone else's control."

Alice is on the verge of thinking she could use a drink herself.

"The implications of this technology are terrifying," she says.
"And I'm inclined to believe that Slovitz thought so too. He wanted
to blow the whistle on it by smuggling out the device and bringing
its existence to light. Unfortunately for everybody it ended up in
the hands of a criminal."

"I think the phrase you're looking for is fucking asshole moron
gangster shitbird," says Nikki. "And I'm starting to see a timeline.
I figure Omega goes back and tells his boss they've got this amazing
weapon that's gonna change everything for them – just as soon as
Yash works out how to operate the damn thing. That's why they
get pumped up all of a sudden, pulling shit like jacking Yoram's
shipment. They could have done something like that before but
they never dared risk the reprisals.

"Yash must have tried to warn Julio that they were playing with
fire, given whatever she saw inside Neurosophy and what she was
learning about the device – especially once Omega got sliced and
diced."

"But Julio wouldn't listen," Alice suggests.

"Because he was a fucking asshole moron gangster shitbird. He
assumed Omega's death was down to me and Yoram because he
could only see things in terms of his own little world. And in that
world, he was in touching distance of having a mind-control device
that would let him rule the roost."

"We have to assume that after the raid, my doppelganger
suspected Slovitz was the insider. Then presumably she tracked him

down and he gave her Omega's name before she killed him. She then repeats the drill with Omega. I wonder why she made sure his body was found when she managed to conceal what happened to Slovitz?"

"I don't know how much Omega told her before he passed out, but it wouldn't have been difficult for her to suss he was mobbed up. That's a nightmare scenario for her: instead of a small trio of robbers to silence, she's got a whole crew. Making a macabre show of Omega gave her a phony gang war to pin everything on."

"I don't know how much he gave her either," Alice confesses. "I haven't been able to force myself to watch the whole grab. I'll have another look."

"Okay, you do that. Maybe while we wait Mr DeLonge can fix us all a coffee. Or something stronger," Nikki hints, to no satisfactory response.

Alice scans the grab, skipping the blackouts, homing in on vocal audio signatures to save time. Her doppelganger doesn't say much, just keeps asking for names. Omega fades in and out of consciousness, but the end doesn't come quick enough, and he does eventually submit. He may have been a thug and a criminal, but Alice marvels at his loyalty: he withstood remarkable torment before he was prepared to give up his own people.

"He named Slovitz, Julio and Yash," she reports. "But not Mr DeLonge. She didn't ask anything about transport, so maybe she assumed they got in at ground level using access codes."

DeLonge slumps a few inches as some of the tension is slackened.

"This shouldn't come as a surprise," Nikki tells him. "Because if Omega named you, you'd be long dead."

Understandably, this doesn't appear to bring him any comfort.

"It was Yash who had possession of the device itself," Alice points out. "Which must have made her the primary target. If she was afraid of being tracked down, why risk drawing attention by experimenting with the thing, making random strangers do weird things in public?"

"For one, she probably had Julio on her back, demanding results. But maybe she reckoned if she could figure out how to operate this thing, she could use it against the assassin. Looks like she didn't figure it out soon enough, though. And given that the killer never showed up at this here door, I'm now thinking she did commit suicide when she knew your evil twin was about to show up at hers."

"Before she could be tortured to reveal any more names connected to the raid," Alice confirms.

Nikki swallows, a look of concern descending upon her.

"None of this is sounding promising for Amber," she admits.

"Who's Amber?" DeLonge asks.

"The girl you helped smuggle out. Who had no official identity and who was presumably being held against her will. At least we know where they most likely took her. This all goes back to Neurosophy. And not to some rogue tech-developer there either."

"No," Alice agrees. "Those men at the dock were able to chase off the Seguridad with just their clearance, which was also high enough to suppress their identities from appearing on even *my* lens. Who can confer that kind of status?"

"The same level of people who have the resources to cover up a murder by paying for an empty shuttle to Heinlein and an empty elevator capsule to Earth."

Alice feels something shudder through her. It is vertiginous, the sudden perception of a chasm that threatens to suck her down. This device, whatever it is, wherever it is, can remotely connect to people's meshes, overriding even their instincts for self-preservation. And if it can override their conscious will, she is sure it could upload memories without their knowledge also.

People are reassured against this possibility by the existence of the watermark effect, but they have also been told that the requirement for a physical connection to the machine is a safeguard too. If one has been overcome, why not the other? And if memories could be remotely inserted, what if they could be remotely deleted?

"Not people," Alice corrects Nikki. "Person."

For there is only one individual on CdC capable of creating such a device: the one who only a few days ago she heard joke about building a robot army. In this moment, Alice understands that if she is indeed an android, then there is no restraining protocol to prevent her making the deduction that has revealed the identity of her designer.

Her creator.

Her true mother.

ROGUE

Silence falls around the room now that Alice has identified what they are truly up against. She has heard it said that the power of a fear is diminished by the naming of it, but this feels like it has had the opposite effect. It's as though they've been trying to evade the jaws of a shark only to realise they're already swimming inside the belly of a leviathan.

"Maria Gonçalves is the most respected person on CdC," Nikki says. "Not to mention one of the most powerful."

"She's practically a saint," adds DeLonge. "A goddess."

"Nobody is above the law."

"Yeah, right."

Even before Nikki says this, Alice realises how naïve she is being. Back at Klaws she was appalled how easily the law could be manipulated by a single corrupt cop. Seguridad is a wholly owned subsidiary of the Quadriga, of which Neurosophy is among the crown jewels.

"It's not like the Seguridad are gonna walk in and slap the cuffs on her," Nikki adds. "We don't have any evidence to bring a case against her anyway. That machine was the whole ball-game, and given that your evil twin must have tracked down the late Ms Sardana, we can be sure it's safely back at Neurosophy. Without that, we got nothing."

"What about me?" Alice asks quietly, as though reluctant to give voice to this truth and all its implications. "Don't I prove something?"

"Not on the basis of the available evidence. We don't know anything for sure – about you or your psycho looky-likey."

"But I do have a grab of the murder. I can prove it wasn't you, and prove this whole turf-war theory is a set-up."

"And how do you think that would play out? 'Honest, officer, the

341

killer in the grab looks exactly like me but I swear she's this totally other person who officially doesn't exist.' They'd lock you up, then Seguridad would hand you over to those Neurosophy goons soon as Gonçalves snapped her fingers. After that they'd quietly go about getting rid of the only other two people who know the truth."

Alice knows Nikki is correct. One of the few things they have going for them right now is that she herself is not yet under suspicion. Nobody knows that she has been acting against Neurosophy's interests, and nor will they, at least until that shuttle reaches Heinlein. Even then it is possible the two men she shot never got a good enough look at her before the tranquillisers kicked in. And herein, she realises, lies an opportunity.

Nikki keeps referring to the doppelganger as Alice's evil twin, but it is in fact Alice who has gone rogue. The doppelganger is off the grid, a silent, anonymous assassin, while Alice's complementary role is visible and official, a pliable instrument of the law directing the Seguridad in the manner Gonçalves would prefer. As far as the good professor knows, that is exactly what she is doing: obedient and under control.

"I think I've got a better idea," she announces.

"Than instantly incriminating yourself? Serve it up."

"I'm going to seed reports that Mr DeLonge is under investigation regarding unauthorised use of a limpet-bug vehicle during hours matching the time of the incursion at Neurosophy."

DeLonge already doesn't like this plan.

"Are you kidding me? She doesn't know I was part of this, but you want to use me as bait, in the hope that the two of you can stop a killing machine who took down six men in a matter of minutes?"

"Oh, we're not going to stop her, Mr DeLonge, because she's not going to find you. Though she *is* going to be kept busy looking."

"Why? Where am I gonna be?"

ELEMENTS

Nikki's stomach lurched the first moment the limpet-bug started to move freely, and it's lurching a shitload more now that she can see the outside of the wheel, spinning only a few metres beneath them. There are barely the words to express how much she is hating this.

She is close enough to see the joins between sections, and within the sections the tessellated pattern of interlocking plates. All she can think about is how this whole thing is being held together. She knows it has passed the greatest safety standards the human race has ever exacted, but she also knows that the motivator behind every increase in safety standards has always been that the previous attempt didn't quite cut it. It's still merely a man-made object, a human structure spinning in space. If it comes apart, everybody dies. In the history of human exploration, it is thus no different to any vessel that ever set to sea, and the fate of many of them was to sink.

However, it's not the sight of the wheel's exterior that is truly disturbing her, or of the massive structures she can see beneath the canopy on Wheel Two in the middle distance. It's the endless nothing everywhere else.

Nikki has seldom been on a shuttle the whole time she's been on CdC. If there was ever a way of avoiding it, then she took that option, no matter the inconvenience. She only contemplated it when she was on the lam for the same reason she's prepared to tolerate it now: because there is no alternative.

Since she first arrived here, Nikki has taken great comfort in where she is not – that being the place she left behind – but she doesn't enjoy being reminded of where she actually *is*. Some people love looking up through the canopy and glimpsing the Earth, the

Sun and the Moon. Nikki prefers to keep her head down. She likes being on Mullane, a place of permanent night where the neon and the looming closeness of the buildings reveal nothing of what lies above.

It's bad enough being on an ion shuttle, but the limpet-bug is like flying through space in a four-door compact. Okay, a little bigger than that, but what the hell, it's as tiny as it is flimsy, so if confronting the very physicality of the outside of the wheel makes her uneasy, then the fragility of this flying tin can amplifies that tenfold.

It's only one step up from being out here in an EVA suit, which to Nikki is the single scariest prospect on Seedee. She'd even go as far as to say they are the three most frightening letters in space, given what they stand for: extravehicular activity.

She has always been terrified that some emergency or some procedural eventuality would require it of her. At Seguridad, she has occasionally sat in seminars as Quadriga and FNG execs war-gamed mass-evac scenarios. If there was some uncontainable disaster on one of the wheels, and everyone had to make it to the other without recourse to the bottlenecks that would form in the spokes and the Axle, the planned response always involved EVA suits and massive human daisy chains. Nikki remains unsure whether she would rather head towards the conflagration than climb inside a flimsy piece of material and hurl herself into the void hoping she could be towed to safety before the oxygen runs out.

DeLonge, by contrast, lives for this shit. He was jumpy and apprehensive as they made their way to the hangar, as befits someone so besieged by terror that he had to be physically stopped from committing suicide less than an hour before. Now she would say he is quite literally in his element, except that this makes her queasy too. A pilot's element would ordinarily be described as "air", but that element has constituent parts you can actually breathe. They say nature abhors a vacuum, but DeLonge clearly digs it. From the moment they helped him into the cockpit, he has undergone a liberating transformation.

Strictly speaking, he shouldn't be in control of any machinery, far less a space vehicle, due to the pain medication he is on, though it's probably less of a consideration than the volume of single malt he consumed before boarding. Nikki is trying to take some consolation from the fact that at least he doesn't need his legs to fly.

There doesn't seem to be too much of a trick to it once they are clear of the structures, flying half a klick parallel to the Axle through three hundred and sixty degrees of emptiness. It's only as they draw closer to Wheel Two that Nikki remembers it's a lot easier being fired out from the bottom of the elevator shaft than executing the manoeuvres necessary at the other end.

DeLonge inverts the limpet-bug and brings them in close to their destination, matching vector and velocity in preparation for locking onto the rectifier that will guide them inside the elevator shaft. It makes Nikki feel sick, even though there is little sense of motion. It's the visual effect of the speed corrections as he tries to match the spin, the view through the window making it look as though they are shunting forwards and backwards.

DeLonge looks frustrated. Nikki doesn't know how long this usually takes, but it feels wrong. Alice senses it too.

"Maybe if you hadn't drunk all that whisky," G2S chides, helpfully.

"When I drank it I didn't know I was going to be doing any space flying."

"Yeah," Nikki says. "And if I'd known we were gonna be doing any space flying, I'd have demanded you share the fucking bottle."

"That's what's on your mind right now?" Alice asks, tense and surprised. "Ever consider you might have a drink problem, Sergeant Freeman?"

"No, ma'am, what I got right now is a fucking sobriety problem."

The limpet-bug keeps accelerating and decelerating clumsily, failing to home in in on the rectifier.

"Why aren't we locking on?" Alice demands.

"It's not letting me. Looks like they've changed the codes. Maybe you shouldn't have seeded those reports telling them how we got into this place last time," he adds in a tone of counter-accusation.

"Are we screwed?" Nikki asks.

"No. I can still get you in there. This is a limpet-bug, after all."

"Meaning what?"

"We've got clearance to open all maintenance traps and hatches on the wheel exteriors. Can't guarantee where the shafts will take you, but you'll be able to get underneath the Neurosophy compound at least."

"Better than nothing," Nikki admits. "So you just clamp over one of these hatches, form an airlock and we go down through the belly of the bug?"

DeLonge arches his eyebrows.

"Not exactly."

FRAGILE BEINGS

Nikki's hands are shaking as she and Alice help each other into their EVA suits inside the bug's cramped interior. She's trying to conceal the tremors like a mother not wanting her kid to see she is frightened. She doesn't know why, but now that they are on the same side she feels drawn to protect the girl. It makes no sense: Alice is the one who appears fearless.

Or maybe it's simply that if someone else notices, it forces Nikki to acknowledge to herself just how scared she is.

That selfish voice inside her asks why she is prepared to go through this in a probably doomed attempt to rescue some crazy girl she's barely met, and who is most likely already dead anyway. But then, that selfish voice has been running the show for too many years, and nothing got better for her listening to it.

Also, this isn't about a rescue. If they're rescuing anybody, they're rescuing themselves. It's not like Nikki can happily get on with her life if she doesn't go through with this.

She checks the last of the seals, not at all comforted by the feel of the material. Up here it is always depicted as a virtue for things to be lightweight, but it doesn't feel like a good thing right now. The layer that will be between her and the cold of space, of imminent death, feels like gossamer. Maybe the barrier between life and death always is.

She tries not to think about the fact that limpet-bug crews do months of training and sims before they attempt any of this stuff, and even then, it is under the supervision of highly experienced colleagues. She and Alice are doing it with zero formal instruction, under the supervision of a one-legged drunk.

DeLonge has inverted the bug once again and brings it down

to rest on the wheel, where it lives up to its name by clinging to the surface via six electromagnetic feet.

For safety reasons, the maintenance hatches are not controlled by code but by manually operated dial-keys, carried as standard by limpet-bug inspection and maintenance crews. It's so that if something goes wrong, a worker isn't lost for the lack of a security clearance to open the nearest route back to safety.

Nikki can see their target. It is ten or twelve metres away. Landing spots are restricted by out-jutting attachments, such as aerials and dishes, and by banks of solar panels, but she is sure he could have narrowed the gap.

She double, triple, quadruple checks the tether that will be her only means of survival should she get deflected from the surface.

"Can't you get any closer?" she asks. "I don't see any obstacles."

"Can't land on top of a vent," DeLonge replies. "If it's obstructed, it will trigger a report, maybe even an alarm."

"I don't see any vent."

"You have to know what you're looking for."

They need to go one at a time, so that neither of them is out there any longer than necessary, waiting for the other to clear the hatch entrance.

"I'll go first," Alice volunteers.

That mothering instinct gnaws Nikki again, but not enough to make her argue.

They have a final check of their comms, ensuring their lenses have an open channel to each other. Then Nikki watches Alice crawl down through the limpet-bug's door, the safety line trailing after her as she grips one of the purpose-designed handholds, curved bumps in the otherwise smooth surface.

"It's a bit like rock climbing," DeLonge tells them. "Except it's the absence of gravity that is the hazard. Instead of falling, the danger is floating off, exacerbated by the fact that the spin of the wheel is always repelling you, with the same force as it is drawing people in on the other side. Progress is by reaching the next handhold and pulling yourself along. Mostly you can reach the next one before you let go of the last, but not always."

"And what do you do then?" Nikki asks.

Alice illustrates. She seems to instinctively know what she's doing. She uses the spin to move, gently pushing off the surface a few centimetres and letting the wheel pass beneath her. Using this technique, she makes it to the hatch in a matter of seconds, skipping several handholds. She's a quick study, that girl. Or maybe she already has this training in some neural database that she's tapped into automatically.

Nah. Nikki still isn't sold on Alice's android hypothesis. It's maybe down to the fact she doesn't believe human technology has reached such an apex that it is possible to have created a machine that can be so consistently self-righteous and annoying.

Nikki won't be trying any of that skipping-holds shit. She's got the insurance of a line connecting her to the limpet-bug, but that only means her life is entrusted to the integrity of the cable, to the strength of the bolts attaching the anchor, to the metal in the thread around the bolts, to the material of the EVA suit where the tether is clipped on, and so on through a dozen other things that could fail.

She begins to crawl out of the bug, coaching herself as she grabs that first handle. It's only a few metres, and it's not a climb. She's not hauling herself anywhere, fighting against her own weight. She can do this.

She reaches for the next hold and gets her fingers comfortably around it, grateful in this instance for the thinness of the suit. Memories of an indoor climbing wall in Santa Monica come rushing back. Same deal: always look at the rock face, never at anything else. She stretches to grab the next hold, then the next, taking it steady, but then sees that the one after is just too far. Why the blank space? Were they trying to save money on one tiny lump of metal?

There is no alternative: she will have to kick off, push clear and let the wheel pass beneath her as Alice did. She's going to have to work up to it, though. Find her calm, centre herself, go to a happy place, whatever. Just one more second. Maybe two. Possibly twelve.

Up ahead she sees Alice's head peek out of the hatch, looking back to check Nikki's progress.

"Come on. Hurry up."

"Fuck you."

Nikki lets go and pushes off with her feet as gently as she can, eyes fixed on the hold she needs to zero. It is gliding smoothly towards her outstretched hand when something slams her from the side, spinning her out and away from the wheel.

It is a vent, a blast of escaping gas. She can see it now: one second it's invisible, the next it's lines of a grate, an ejecting plume of vapour.

She drifts outwards, the surface of the wheel passing beneath her. The hatch is three times the distance now, four times. Then she feels the jerk as the safety line runs out and the resultant motion tugs her back towards the wheel.

She flails for a handhold, misses in her panicky desperation. She's hyperventilating, the sound of her own breathing claustrophobically loud inside the suit. She can hear something else too, a wheezing sound, and is terrified that it's an escape of air, a tear in the material.

She realises it's DeLonge laughing. This shit must happen all the time.

On the plus side, it appears she's been flung around to within an arm's length of another hatch.

"I'm gonna go in this way," she tells Alice. "We'll rendezvous on the inside."

That may prove tricky, but it's got to be easier than navigating all the way to the hatch Alice went down.

She fishes for the key and tries turning the dial. It doesn't move, which prompts another moment of panic before she susses that she's simply not tugging hard enough because she's terrified she'll break the goddamn thing. She gives it a solid wrench and within another few seconds she is inside with the hatch closed again behind her.

Nikki enjoys a moment of blessed relief at no longer being directly exposed to space, before having to deal with another kind of blackness. She would confess she had been picturing a well-lit vertical shaft that would take her all the way to topside, like she has seen in the shuttle bays. Should have known it wasn't going to be so straightforward, or even straight upward. Instead she's facing a complex journey through interlocking ducts and channels, all of it in the dark. All she's got is a shitty little light on the suit, and this new lens isn't tricked out for night vision.

As she worms her way around this 3D maze, she nixes the self-pity by contemplating how some poor bastard had to build everything she is climbing through, before they connected this to the next section and created a new seal. This was somebody's job every day, only metres from instant death, working in an EVA suit for air and as protection against the cold. And he or she still probably made less for risking everything each day than some pen-pushing corporate suit-full-of-nothing who signed off on the purchasing order for the materials.

Because of constant changes of axis, Nikki has no idea how far she still has to go. Her arms are telling her she has done enough climbing, but there is still no indication whether she is nearing topside. Then she crawls into another channel and feels water running beneath her knees, maybe a centimetre deep. At the next perpendicular junction, she looks up and sees it tumble down the wall of the shaft opposite an integral ladder.

She ascends the ladder and hauls herself into a gently sloping sluice, further along which she can see water and light spilling down through a grate. Nikki crawls beneath it and looks up. She can see foliage. Greenery. Things she generally associates with the tops of buildings, in Seedee's world of contradictions.

The grate lifts with a gentle push and she tentatively sticks her head up, knowing it could signal the end if she's spotted. There are shrubs and bushes and ferns all around, grass underfoot. Real grass. She is in a garden: not an agricultural space, a garden.

Looking closer she can see that there is a wall screened off by a row of thickly planted bushes. It is to create the illusion of the garden continuing, or at least of its borders being a dense arbour that might extend beyond the visible.

A pleasure garden at ground level, full gravity. An expanse given over to plant life, ground that might otherwise accommodate several storeys of exploitable space.

What would justify such an extravagance?

The air is suddenly pierced by a high-pitch squeal of laughter. It is both the most natural sound in the world and one that somehow does not belong on Seedee.

Crawling behind a row of ferns and peering cautiously through the branches, Nikki sees the answer.

Children.

WHEN SHE WAS BAD

Alice pulls the second hatch closed behind her, sealing the airlock. She has a detailed recall of how many safety regulations she was in contravention of whilst performing her brief traverse from the limpet-bug to the maintenance channel, and understands with statistical precision how many things could potentially have gone wrong: twenty-seven regarding the safety tether alone. And yet, what she is feeling now that it's over is not relief but exhilaration. She's not about to go and reprise the trip, but part of her is disappointed that it is complete.

It was a buzz. An adrenalin rush. Does she even have adrenalin? Or is it a synthesised adrenalin response? She doesn't care. What matters is that she is feeling it.

She remembers so many times being told not to do dangerous things, the stifling tyranny of the risk-benefit equation, her mother quoting the statistics to put her off the college trends for base jumping and wingsuit dives. A rain-lashed weekend alone in a dorm looms large in her memory, poring over books while all her room-mates went on a trip to Colorado.

She even remembers being warned against attempting flying dismounts off the swing-set like she saw other kids executing with vocal alacrity.

It is possible none of these things truly happened, but it doesn't matter. The memories feel real, and they had their effect. Implanted or not, they conditioned her to avoid risk and to obey the rules. All the rules. Maybe that's adding to how exciting this feels. But maybe it constitutes an abuse, an implanted brake against exercising her desires, her curiosity.

Her free will.

She would never have imagined it, but she has become jealous of Nikki Freeman and the hedonistic abandon with which she conducts herself. Alice wouldn't want to swap her life for Nikki's, but she could certainly use a pinch more of her attitude, so as not to feel so constantly constricted by rules, regulations, recommended intake, safe levels, approved procedures, authorised access. Even being inside this access shaft feels exciting. It's a secret space, a forbidden world: one of those places that would normally remain hidden to her, behind the doors that say Authorised Personnel Only, Strictly No Admittance.

It is dark, claustrophobic and thoroughly dangerous. Through her night-vision she can see hazards everywhere: ways to get trapped, burnt, frozen, electrocuted, crushed, asphyxiated and even drowned. There are very good reasons that the untrained and thus unauthorised shouldn't be here. And that is why she is kind of getting off on it.

She isn't merely accessing an unauthorised area, however: she is breaking into the highest-clearance facility on CdC. And this comes on top of stealing a space vehicle, after effectively jailbreaking the city's most notorious ever criminal fugitive, an act which required the assault and false imprisonment of two ultra-high-ranking security personnel.

In practice the law is a little fuzzier up here than you maybe wrote about in some Ivy League college paper, Nikki said back at Klaws.

Before Alice left for Seedee, her colleagues joked about her becoming the new sheriff in town. Instead it has taken only a matter of days to make her an outlaw.

She is still tortured by the possibility that she may be an android, but even if that turns out to be so, these last few hours are the most human she has ever felt.

Alice emerges cautiously from the darkness of the access channel into the darkness of a closet that serves as an anteroom and storage space for the maintenance hatch. She steps daintily between shelves of equipment as she strips off the EVA suit and stashes it out of sight, then takes a few seconds to check her inventory. She makes sure that everything survived the journey intact, and in particular that the broken-down parts are the parts broken down by her for storage. Then finally she pats down her clothes after their confinement beneath the suit, before donning the single extra item that she predicts will transform her in the eyes of her enemies.

She emerges into a brightly lit corridor, lined with marketing posters for Neurosophy's various mesh systems down the years, and framed images from surgical procedures. The graphic nature of the latter indicates that this area is accessible by clinical personnel only, and she soon encounters three women walking towards her, one in a lab coat and two in theatre scrubs.

Alice tenses with the rigidity of someone whose entire existence has been defined by the imagined consequences of being caught breaking the rules. This is the first moment that her clever plan could fall apart.

The women walk past. Even though she is identifying as Wendy Goodfellow, a vital-systems scientist at a firm on Wheel One, nobody challenges her, nobody looks at her twice. She remembers that the lack of crime on CdC, in conjunction with its advanced access technology, has a security downside in that nobody is suspicious. Everyone assumes that if you are inside someplace, then you are supposed to be there.

This may not be the case further in, however, when she closes in on the things Neurosophy doesn't want even its own workers to see.

Up ahead is an open door marked Mesh Lab 3, from which Alice overhears conversation as she approaches.

"Standard cranial insertion," says a woman's voice. "Should take about two hours as it's the Gen-4 mesh. Averages half the time I used to need for the Gen-3. But the subject is signed up for the full suite of initial uploads, so that part's going to take me the rest of the day."

When she draws near enough she can see two people in scrubs, one man and one woman, making preparations for surgery. Her lens identifies them as Dr Florian Ringwald and Dr Lisa Kaiser. Alice stops on the spot, listening to their conversation while the corridor is clear and nobody can see her eavesdropping.

"Least you have some surgery to make it interesting," Ringwald replies. "I got a whole day of nothing but uploads. Six patients. Two for languages, three for technical data and one for map layout. Just wish they didn't have to come in for this. Maybe you could propose that the next-gen mesh should let us do remote uploads."

"And what, put us out of a job?" Kaiser scoffs. "Besides, nobody's going to sign up for a mesh that allows that. I sure wouldn't."

They don't know. They've been implanting the Gen-4 for over a year and they don't know.

"No, I've heard the big development on the Gen-5 will be to do with the watermark effect," Kaiser goes on. "The new mesh will be able to suppress some of the contradictory signals and impulses that cause the memory to be identified as non-native. Supposedly subjects will be able to turn this off if they want to experience a more emotional and authentic interaction with the implanted information."

"But if a subject is consciously turning off the watermarking, that's effectively a watermarking in itself, isn't it?"

"You get the full benefit of the imported experience but you still know it's not your memory. Sounds like a win-win to me."

It sounds like a massive lose-lose to Alice. She is certain the Gen-5 will secretly allow watermarking to be remotely deactivated, just like the Gen-4 secretly allows itself to be remotely accessed. Thus non-native memories could be installed without the safeguards that normally make an individual aware of it. Conceivably, native memories could also be remotely deleted, allowing Neurosophy the power to edit and censor the memories of anyone with the Gen-5 mesh. In a few years, they would have complete control over the memories and therefore the world view, the perspective – the very personalities – of everyone on CdC.

Then they just have to wait for the technology to be finally approved and rolled out down below. It's certainly no wonder they're killing anyone who might have found out about this.

Alice has to find a way of making it public.

She hurries away from the Mesh Lab and turns a corner, where she comes face to face with someone who *is* looking at her twice: staring right at her, in fact.

It is the man from Central Plaza, the one who shot her. She only glimpsed him for a moment and from a distance, but as soon as she sees him she is sure. He is dressed identically to the two guards she shot: charcoal fatigues. He has the same athletic build, and his identity reads blank: clearance-protected.

His voice is quiet but forceful, a tone of controlled aggression that is unused to refusal.

"Where the hell do you think you're going?"

THE GIFTED ONES

They are mere toddlers, four of them. Nikki would put them at around two, maybe three, chasing each other aimlessly but joyfully around a square of lawn. There are two adult supervisors, a man and a woman, vigilantly ready to intervene but otherwise keeping their distance. When the woman turns, Nikki sees that she is cradling an infant in her arms.

This is a bigger secret than mind-control devices or Project Sentinel. Someone is raising children on CdC, which is as unethical as it is illegal to the extent that women are forced to abort pregnancies or fly back to Earth to give birth.

These are not mere visitors. This garden proves that. Someone wants young bones to develop properly, under standard gravity while playing outdoors and enjoying nature; or as close to nature and outdoors as you're going to get here.

Nikki hasn't seen children in the flesh in fifteen years. The sight of them is almost paralysing. She wants to get closer, wants to reach out and hold them but she has to stay hidden.

Her eyes mist, a rush of feelings and memories coming back, lying dormant but so close to the surface. The sluice-gates open on a flood of hurt she tried to escape, but there is not only pain: there are good things too. Things she once had but lost. Things she could not stand the loss *of*. Things that made her who she used to be.

You can't have one without the other: the memory of what once was treasured without the agony of its absence. She thought when she came here that if she could distract herself, anaesthetise herself, then the blotting out of all those good memories would be a price worth paying for the absence of the pain. But to be thus anaesthetised is to feel nothing, not merely for yourself, but for anybody

358

else. It is how she became this wraith, feared but friendless, needed but despised.

Corruption is a form of decay. Something good inside you has to die before you can do something truly bad. Then with every further bad thing you do, a little more of what was good inside you dies.

This is why she is embarking on a suicide mission on behalf of a crazy girl she has barely met. She needs to believe that there is still some last fragment of good left inside her.

"Okay, who's hungry?" asks the woman.

Excited hands go up in response, restless feet jumping up and down.

"I think it's time for lunch."

One of the kids is looking Nikki's way. She may have pulled aside one branch too many, trying to see a little more. The little girl tugs at the male helper and points.

Nikki withdraws and freezes. Logic is telling her the man is unlikely to make much of it. Toddlers love making things up.

"Come on, everyone," the woman beckons, holding open a door leading out of the garden and into an adjacent building.

The little girl who was pointing trails obediently after her friends, no longer interested in what she may or may not have seen among the bushes.

The man has decided to check it out, however.

"I'll catch you up in a minute," he announces.

Damn it, Nikki thinks. The distance is too short to give her time to get back down the grate. She's going to have to deal with him.

The door closes, so at least there won't be any witnesses, particularly tiny ones who shouldn't see shit like this.

Nikki grips her electro-pulse. She has the drop on him so she could easily zap him unconscious, which will prevent him from raising the alarm via his lens. But if he fails to return, somebody is going to come looking for him in just a few minutes. That alarm is getting raised one way or the other, and Nikki has some questions she'd like answered.

She takes him down in a heartbeat, swiftly removing his wrist

359

disc to disable his gesturing. Not that he would be able to concentrate on those options and menus when he was reeling from the shock of a blow.

She flips him onto his back where her lens identifies him as Tobias Muller. Nikki figures he is part scientist and part kindergarten teacher, so he's probably not schooled in withstanding interrogation techniques, or even schooled in withstanding the prospect of being punched in the face. He'll tell her anything she asks.

"I'm looking for a girl named Amber. Where is she?"

"She's in isolation," he replies, terrified. "I don't have clearance. She ran away. She got confused. She needs help."

"She wasn't confused, she was seriously distressed. Her head's all messed up, but she was adamant about one thing: she said someone took her baby."

Muller swallows. He's scared, but she isn't sure whether he's more frightened of what might happen to him if he doesn't answer her questions or of what might happen to him later if he does.

"Well, like you said, her head is messed up."

"Don't jerk me around, son. I know ways to hurt you that would make you puke if I even described them. She had a fresh caesarean scar on her. What's going on here? Who are these kids? How come Amber doesn't even have an identity?"

He's trembling. Nikki recognises this particular flavour of shock and fear. It's what happens when assumed impunity meets cold reality: people who have been getting away with something so long that they almost forgot it was wrong. Almost. One hint of retribution is all it takes for the illusion to come crashing down. This guy is already thinking about how he can cut a deal. Probably never broke a regular law in his life.

"None of them has an identity, officially. When they come here they get given a colour rather than a name. Amber, Scarlet, Cyan."

Deniability, Nikki thinks. These women were never officially here on CdC. She thinks of the container at Dock Nine, diverted because of the all-stop, the whole place shut down and cleared of witnesses.

"So they're smuggled in? To have children?"

Muller nods, sweating.

"Where do they come from?"

"They are recruited. Carefully screened. They are very well paid."

"They come here pregnant?"

"No. They are artificially inseminated. Every part of the process is monitored, from conception to birth. Diet, fitness, sleep patterns. No expectant mother is better looked after, believe me."

"And what happens after birth?"

Muller pauses again, because they both know the answer.

"They give the children up. It's all agreed in advance."

"And these children who don't officially exist and have no rights become Neurosophy's property?"

"These children are being cared for perfectly, all of their needs met. They're being given a gift."

"Not the gift of a normal life on Earth, where they can breathe fresh air and visit the countryside or spend a day at the beach."

"The children on the *Arca* will not have these things."

"Yeah, but they'll have family. They'll have parents. And they'll have rights. These are *children*. They're not your subjects to experiment on."

"Their welfare is our primary concern, I assure you."

"Sure. That's why this is all off the books, because nobody would have a problem with the ethics of it if they knew."

"All humanity will benefit from this gift, in the long run."

"Said every mad scientist ever. Where's Amber? Where are *all* these children's mothers? What happens to them post-partum?"

"Once they are fully recovered, they return to Earth. With a substantial payment."

"Yeah, you already said that. Which counts as a red flag. No amount of money would give you insurance about a secret this big, and I can't see you people leaving yourselves vulnerable like that."

Muller is trying to steal a look towards the door, hoping to see help on its way. He's even more nervous now. She's homing in on something he really doesn't want her to know, and suddenly she susses it.

"You motherfuckers. You wipe their memories."

Muller swallows, guilty as hell.

361

"First you ensure they have no credibility, so nobody would believe them. They can't prove they were ever here. They have no recourse, no rights, no claim on their own children. But the real insurance is that you take away their memory of having the child."

"It's part of the advance agreement. It's a kindness to them. They are told they will not remember why they came here."

"Will they remember a fee was agreed? Because it strikes me that money leaves a paper trail."

"I wouldn't know about that. I'm a paediatrician."

Nikki thinks of the women she has met who had traumatic memories erased, and why she wasn't tempted having seen the results. They still suffered the same sadness but could no longer remember what was making them feel this way. She wonders how many women down below now have this desolate sense of loss, of aching emptiness, but don't know that they have had their child taken and their memory of it destroyed.

"So what about Amber? It didn't work with her, did it?"

For the first time, Muller looks pained rather than guilty.

"She changed her mind," he says.

And she wasn't the first, Nikki would wager.

"She wanted to keep the baby," she says. "But she had no rights and you people took it from her."

"They couldn't let her. She knew too much."

They, Nikki notes. He's distancing himself from this.

"She endangered the child. She tried to escape with the baby, so they sedated her and did the wipe then, hoping that would solve the problem, but it was too soon. I tried to tell them. I knew it was wrong. It's not like overwriting a piece of data in the mesh. This kind of memory is more than that: it's something you feel, something you instinctively know. She was still lactating, all these hormones telling her body something that contradicted what was in her mind."

"So what is this gift you're giving the children? Because it would have to be a hell of a thing for you all to be able to live with yourselves pulling this shit."

Muller almost seems relieved to be asked this.

"Oh, it is," he says.

Then Nikki hears a door open and Muller looks up, hope and relief lighting up his face.

She rolls off him and wheels around rapidly, only to find herself staring down the barrel of a suppression rifle. Staring back is what should be a familiar face, except that it is topped with blonde hair, not black.

"Officer Nicola Madeleine Freeman," Blondie declares. "I think it's time for you to meet my maker."

SENTINELS

Alice freezes, her cumulative terror of finding herself on the wrong side of rectitude paralysing her into a wordless stare, which her interlocutor mistakes for intransigence.

"I mean, Jesus Christ, Beatrice, you know you're not supposed to be wandering around unsecured sectors. The staff around here don't have clearance. What happens when they get a look at Alice Blake on a feed? They'll think, 'Hey, apart from her hair, the new head of the SOE looks exactly like this woman we keep seeing around Neurosophy. What's up with that?' You scope me?"

Still Alice fixes him with her stunned, silent and ostensibly sullen stare, rapidly coming to terms with this evidence that her plan is working. All it took was that single extra item – a blonde wig – and he thinks she is the doppelganger.

Beatrice, he called her.

Alice. Beatrice. A and B. Is there a Clarice?

Beatrice has been kept under wraps. They are conscious of the suspicion it might raise should her resemblance to a certain high-profile new arrival become widely observed, which implies she can't have been visible prior to Alice coming here. And to keep her out of sight *before* would suggest that they knew Alice was coming to CdC, otherwise why bother.

When did Beatrice get here? And as she has no ID, not merely a protected one, *how* did she get here?

"People don't see past the hair," Alice says. Which is apparently true.

"Look, just get inside where you're supposed to be. Who the hell is Wendy Goodfellow, anyway?"

"It's a false ID I've been using to remain incognito."

He leads her down the corridor towards a security-controlled door. Alice hangs back so that he can get there first and obligingly open it for her.

A sign indicates that she is now inside the Research and Development Sector of the Neurosophy Foundation: Maria Gonçalves' inner sanctum, hallowed ground requiring a commensurate clearance level.

Suddenly anxious of the growing silence as they pass deeper into the controlled sector, she feels compelled to ratify her insider credentials.

"And what of our fugitive, Amber?"

"Dealt with," he replies curtly, which doesn't sound good. "What about yours? I thought you'd gone to Wheel Two. Wasn't there a lead on someone else who might have been involved in the raid? A pilot?"

"Yes. I'm following that up but I need to check on something first."

Alice passes several laboratories matching her idealised expectations of what cutting-edge research facilities on CdC ought to look like, but she also sees workshops that resemble the chaos of Trick's den, only blown up on a massive scale. There are windows onto all of these, open doors, open-plan spaces. She knows there must be closed doors elsewhere. Locked doors. Amber claims she was kept prisoner here. She is the principal subject of their mission, but Alice has her own agenda too.

"One of the intruders, Yashmin Sardana, took her own life before I could question her. I know she saw sensitive materials. I want to see what she was exposed to."

"You know what she was exposed to," he replies. "She saw the Project Sentinel legacy files."

Legacy, Alice wonders: implying something historic. Something finished.

He is giving her a curious look, one that threatens rapid progress to outright suspicion.

"Are you questioning my methods?" she asks.

That sets him straight, puts him back in his box. Nobody wants to cross Beatrice, it would appear.

"No, ma'am."

"We already missed the pilot by making assumptions. I want to review the precise materials she accessed. This is so that I can be absolutely sure not only of what she did and didn't see, but what she may have inferred, even mistakenly. Rumour is our enemy here."

"Indeed. I'll send you the exact file Slovitz left open on his terminal during the incursion. It was like the asshole was leaving a trail of breadcrumbs."

Alice realises that this is no good, as the file will go to Beatrice.

"Remember to send it to Wendy Goodfellow," she says, pitching her tone at irritable. "I already got a ton of stuff open in this profile and I don't want to be switching back and forth."

She counsels herself to breathe as she watches for his response. Then he straightens as he alters the recipient and prepares the material, attentively obedient having been given an order.

"Here it comes. Weird thing is we still don't know how Slovitz got the older file. We couldn't find the original anywhere. Professor Gonçalves assumed it was lost in the fire twenty-five years ago."

"So Slovitz never worked on Project Sentinel?"

He gives her that curious look again. She figures she's on strike two, despite her apparent seniority.

"The fire was before he came here."

"I meant, even indirectly? Some tangential reason his work caused him to happen upon it?"

"Always possible, I guess. But his area was behavioural modification and adjustment: neural inhibitors and disinhibitors. It was effectively his own invention that he boosted. Trying to sell it on the black market, the greedy sonofabitch. Imagine the chaos that would have sown."

Alice spots an empty seat in the corner of an otherwise cluttered lab. There is nobody around, and it looks like it's the cleaner's year off.

"I'm going to take a moment to review this stuff," she tells him, by way of dismissal.

He doesn't seem to hear her, adopting that zoned-out look indicative of dealing with an incoming message.

"I'll just stay here and make sure you're not disturbed," he replies, leaving Alice none the wiser as to whether he heard her or not.

There are two files, one time-stamped as a recent creation and the other bearing no such indications; indeed none of the metadata that would mark it as native to the system.

The recent, smaller file turns out to be effectively a preface for the other. A plain cover page bears the name "Project Sentinel – Legacy", beneath which are the dates the project must have been operational. The later date coincides with that of the Neurosophy fire.

On the following page, Alice is confronted by recent photographs of herself and her doppelganger. Her own image was taken during a seminar at the FNG building in New York a month ago. The other is the same one Yash included in her warning message to DeLonge. It looks like it was taken on a boat or maybe a pier. Beatrice is dressed in military-style fatigues, blue water sparkling in the background. They are both flattering images, something affectionate in their choice.

Beneath them, a single paragraph informs her that:

While <u>Sentinel's development phase</u> was prematurely terminated by the disaster and its breakthrough technology lost, the first fruits of the project continue to thrive and are being monitored closely as we endeavour to honour Dr Shelley's legacy by recreating her work.

She activates the indicated link, which turns out to be the accompanying undated and non-native file. It is a compendium document, a mish-mash of media across multiple formats, some of them redundant for more than two decades. If it were a physical object, she would be blowing dust off it right now.

Once more she is confronted by photographs of two identical females, but this time they are newborns. Twins. They are lying side by side in transparent cots, facing each other, eyes closed, thumbs in mouths in perfect symmetry. They are identified only as A and B.

Alice and Beatrice.

She stares breathless for a few seconds, then swipes to the next page. It shows several images of the same infants, intubated and linked up to a dozen monitoring systems while a neurosurgical procedure is carried out inside their tiny open skulls.

Following these images are screeds and screeds of technical detail Alice does not have time to read, far less digest and comprehend, so she skips to a grab, that being among the formats she recognises amidst the jumble of information.

It shows one of the neurosurgical procedures being carried out, the surgeon's fingers serving to further emphasise the tiny size of the baby's head: possibly premature, as twin births often are. Alice recoils, her squeamishness exacerbated by the possibility that she is looking at herself on the operating table. She is about to stop the playback when the camera tracks up and picks out the surgeon.

It is Maria Gonçalves, decades younger, a wisp of silver hair sticking out from beneath her cap.

"Aside from closing up, the procedure is over," she says, addressing the camera. "But the process itself has only just begun, and will take around twenty years to complete. If you are watching this, Alice, then you must have passed that stage some time ago and your subsequent progress been deemed satisfactory. It has been suggested that I record this now, in case you have difficulty believing me when I tell it to you personally. Wait, it's Alice first, right?"

"Yes," says a voice off-camera.

"Okay. And you can edit this out?"

"Of course."

Alice feels her pulse surge. It *is* her on the table, and this was recorded for her benefit, but never shown to her. From what the guard said, perhaps it was thought lost in the fire, but she suspects that is not the only reason.

"What I have set in motion inside your head is a nano-process developed by my esteemed colleague Dr Shelley, whereby your neurons will be individually replaced by synthetic equivalents as you grow and develop. The synthetic neuron clones the information and processes of the original, organic neuron before switching it out. Ideally, in the future we will be able to commence this process in the womb. The earlier the better.

"It is projected that by the time your brain is fully developed, it will comprise one hundred percent artificial neurons, effecting a seamless transition from organic to synthetic, without you being conscious of any change."

Gonçalves blurs out of focus. It takes Alice a moment to realise that this is because she is weeping. She glances towards the door. The guard is hovering around but he isn't looking her way.

"Prior to this advent, the great existential question was always, if you upload a human mind to an artificial construct, aren't you essentially just creating a duplicate and terminating the original, even if it remains housed in the same human body? While the artificial consciousness might be indistinguishable from its organic equivalent in terms of all the information encoded within, none-theless the original consciousness would die.

"In this process, the developing consciousness will gradually become mounted on the artificial, neuron by neuron. The subject – you, Alice – will never be aware of the transition. Then once the brain is fully synthetic, it continues to be fully replaceable, neuron by neuron. As technology allows us to replace other body parts, whether through organic transplantation or through artificial organs and limbs, your consciousness will be able to endure for centuries, conceivably millennia."

Alice is aware of physically shivering, feeling as though she could melt into a puddle and be mopped away. She has just learned that she is effectively immortal and yet she has never felt so fragile.

"You and your sister will be the first of our Sentinels, who will guide and protect the pilgrims striking out aboard the *Arca* when finally it sails. You will be their guardians, their teachers, their judges and defenders, but always anonymous. They will not know what walks among them, but you will be protecting invisibly, from the shadows: shaping the new humanity, our interplanetary diaspora, for centuries to come.

"It is said that twins are especially close, but none will ever be as close as you and Beatrice, as you will be able to rapidly share what is in each other's minds. It is my vision that all of the sentinels will be able to communicate thus, so that if something were to befall one of them, all that they have seen and heard – right up until the moment of their death – will be accessible to the others, who will be able to identify and deal with that threat all the more effectively."

Gonçalves smiles warmly into the camera, though there is a hint of uncertainty in her expression.

"This is my gift to you," she says, "but I realise that it is one you have no option to refuse. For that, I—"

Alice feels a hand on her shoulder and jolts in fright.

The guard's expression is stern, but he seems wary at having disturbed her. Having seen what she just has, Alice can understand why he might be treading lightly.

"Sorry to interrupt, but I'm guessing you missed the security alert. We have an intruder."

"Where?"

"The nursery," he adds, his voice grave.

"Let's go," she says, getting to her feet, a subtle hand gesture indicating he should take the lead. This is not merely so that he can open the doors, but because she has no idea where this nursery is.

He strides at a brisk pace without running. There is an assured control about this, a discipline that supersedes panicky urgency.

Alice reaches into her bag and begins reassembling the suppression rifle as she follows behind, occasionally having to break into a jog to match his longer stride.

"Where did you get that?" he enquires, his tone a mixture of awe and disapproval, like she's just produced a blood-spattered broadsword.

"Picked it up on my travels."

A bladed aperture gapes open ahead, a second such door awaiting beyond it. In order to pass into the next sector, they are going to be held in an antechamber, the security equivalent of an airlock. Alice steels herself. She knows that the second door won't be opened until some unseen observer is satisfied that all is well, but the real threat lies in the fact that once inside, there is no way out if said observer decides otherwise.

This particular antechamber is intended to keep out more than unauthorised personnel. They are scanned by a multitude of sensors, observed at light frequencies either side of the visible spectrum, even their exhalations sampled and scrutinised. She has experienced similar analysis entering a hospital intensive care unit back in New York, checking bacteria levels and identifying any vectors of possible infection.

Alice wonders how Nikki managed to bypass all of this. She can hear her speak, transmitting an interrogation that Alice is unavoidably about to bring to an end.

"I'm looking for a girl named Amber. Where is she?"

"She's in isolation. I don't have clearance."

Alice sends Nikki the files she has just seen with a note directing her immediately towards the grab, though she's not exactly sure when Nikki is going to get peace to check it out. It fills a few seconds, at least, keeping her from worrying whether she is ever going to get the green light.

Finally the second aperture swishes open and they step forward into a very different environment. While the last one was cramped and cluttered, veering randomly from the clinical to the chaotic, the ambience here is instantly more welcoming and relaxed. The corridors are broader, the walls pastel, the lighting soft.

Alice can hear children's voices from behind a nearby door, muted but unmistakable; excited, exclamatory, joyous.

She can't say if it is this sound, or the environment, or a combination of the two, but she is struck by an almost debilitating surge of déjà vu. It is disorienting, like a splintering crack in the lens of reality. She has the unmistakable sense that she has been here before, or that she is experiencing something for the second time.

She knows for a fact that she has never been in this place before.

No. She knows almost nothing for a fact where her own past is concerned. Nonetheless, something in her is convinced she knows this place, but the memory feels obscured by cloud, as though she is trying to remember something glimpsed in a dream.

She *was* here. She has just seen video of Gonçalves operating on herself as an infant. She was probably born here, or somewhere very like it: the original Neurosophy facility on Wheel One.

Why didn't she remember it before? Perhaps because she left it when she was too young. But if so, why can she *half*-remember?

Further along the corridor she passes a window, through which she can see children playing on a cushioned floor. There are four of them, plus a babe in arms.

There will be no children.

She remembers this declaration but she can't remember who said it to her.

There will be no children.

She can't recall the conversation, a face, anything. Only these words, sounding in her head, like they've been placed there in isolation.

She knows her brain is synthetic. She knows Neurosophy has been developing the technology to remotely edit memories. She knows Gonçalves has been trying to reconstruct the technology that was devised by her colleague Shelley but lost in the fire. Thus everything that followed has been an attempt to catch up to what was already possible at the time of the Sentinel programme.

The implication hits her like a blast wave.

Maria Gonçalves has had control of her memory since shortly after her birth. Maria Gonçalves is the curator of her soul.

An ashen-faced woman hurries down the corridor to meet them, the angst in her expression a mirror into Alice's own feelings at this point.

"Beatrice, Daniels, come quickly. The intruder is in the gardens. She's got Toby."

Alice has to put everything else from her mind and concentrate on the matter at hand. Reeling as she is from what she has discovered, her strategy is nonetheless tantalisingly close to coming off. The plan was to successfully impersonate her doppelganger in order to gather evidence of what Gonçalves was secretly doing, and if possible to take Nikki as her "prisoner" in order to gain access to wherever they might be keeping Amber. To her relief, according to Muller's testimony, it would appear the fugitive is still alive.

What Alice has already learned should be enough to force Ochoba's hand, though her intention is to make it public first, so that Quadriga influence and FNG politics can't contrive to suppress anything. She now knows Ochoba is not the puppet master, but that doesn't mean Alice is ready to trust her to do the right thing – as opposed to the politically expedient thing.

"Get the door," Alice commands, raising her rifle. "I'll cover, you cuff. Then we'll take her to Isolation."

"No," Daniels replies.

A jolt of fear pulses through her.

"What do you mean, no?" she demands.

"Didn't you just get the order?"

"I'm still logged in as Wendy Goodfellow. She's not in the loop."

"Professor Gonçalves says we're to bring Sergeant Freeman directly to her."

Alice swallows. This suddenly went somewhere it wasn't supposed to, and from the look he just gave her she is worried she just made strike three, but the opportunity here is huge. If she can get Gonçalves to incriminate herself on record, it's a slam-dunk. And besides, it doesn't look like she has any choice.

"Let's do it," she says.

Daniels unlocks the entrance to the gardens and Alice steps through at speed, on light feet. In a second and a half she is on top of Nikki, levelling the rifle at her as she rolls off Muller on the grass.

"Officer Nicola Madeleine Freeman," she declares. "I think it's time for you to meet my maker."

She keeps the rifle on Nikki while Daniels moves in and puts the cuffs on her. He then turns and faces Alice, expression neutral.

"Your prisoner," he says, taking a step away.

Alice doesn't know where she is supposed to be going. She wonders if he is aware of this. Is this a game of bluff, or a situation she can get through if she holds her nerve?

"Daniels, you take the vanguard," she suggests. "I'll keep the prisoner covered from the rear. She's given her escorts the slip once already."

With this thought she checks the time. The shuttle shouldn't have reached Heinlein yet. She still has around forty minutes. With Nikki having turned up here, the guards will have questions, not least about why their colleagues are not responding, but as long as they don't know the identity of Nikki's confederate, then she still has a window.

They follow Daniels out of the gardens and back through the nursery, wary staff stepping into side doors to give them a wide berth. At the end of a corridor Alice can see another bladed aperture, above which a sign reads: "Cassandra Shelley Memorial Laboratories".

They pass into another antechamber, where Alice suspects cardiac monitoring would be enough to give her away. The relief of knowing that she does indeed have a heart is not enough to calm its thumping as the stakes keep rising.

Once the aperture closes behind the three of them, it occurs to her that as she was not party to the order Daniels referred to, she has no idea whether it was genuine. He could be leading them both to a jail cell or an ambush. This whole thing could be over in a few more seconds.

Daniels tells them both to hold still. They are not being swept for bacteria this time, but Alice suspects they are nonetheless being closely screened.

Then the second aperture dilates and reveals not a jail cell but a clinically white laboratory suite. She sees banks of machinery and equipment ranged along one wall, and as she steps fully into the room she notices faucets, basins and sluices. It is not merely a laboratory but a surgical theatre, and standing expectantly between two operating tables is the slight but unmistakable figure of Maria Gonçalves.

Alice notes that there are two assistants in lab coats standing by the machines, as well as two more of the unidentifiable guards flanking the professor, giving her space but ready to move should there be a problem. Nikki described them as private military security, but Alice sees they are more than that: they are Gonçalves' secret police. She thinks of the people who flocked so quickly to protect Gonçalves on the Ver Eterna terrace. They were trusted senior colleagues, acting out of loyalty and devotion, but crucially identifiable members of staff. They were expected to be visibly part of her entourage. Her real Praetorian guard officially doesn't exist. They are "protecting invisibly, from the shadows", the way she likes it.

They all have a similar look, but not because they are twins or clones or androids. It's because they are all of a kind: elite soldiers, elite *mercenaries*. Hired guns, and very expensively hired, Alice estimates. The kind of money Gonçalves can offer would buy a lot of loyalty. But could it buy silence?

Then she realises that it wouldn't have to. It may well be in their contract conditions that they submit to memory erasure at her discretion, and that would probably suit them, because it would confer complete deniability regarding anything they do in carrying out her orders.

Daniels commands the prisoner to halt and steps aside, clearing his boss's line of sight. Gonçalves casts a brief, distasteful eye over Nikki, then looks to her other guest with a warm smile.

"Home again, home again," she greets Alice breezily, before raising a pistol and shooting her.

THE END OF PAIN

Nikki will say this much for Gonçalves, for a woman in her eighties, the bitch can handle a piece. She drew that flechette pistol and got off a shot in the blink of an eye, the tiniest dart hitting Alice in the chest before there was any time to react. It stuns her for a few seconds, though she doesn't have time to drop before two of the mercs move in and catch her.

Nikki flashes back to Kobra, falling on his face on Dock Nine. Now she knows what did it: Gonçalves is packing the same kind of heat, a miniature goodnight gun.

The guards lay Alice out flat on one of the operating tables and engage the restraints before the dart wears off. Her limbs and trunk are clamped by steel bands that emerge from the surface while a neck brace pulls her head down into a cradle comprising a kaleidoscope of sensors, which the two lab geeks immediately start checking.

Nikki scans the area and calculates her options. A locked room, three highly trained soldiers, probably armed with multiple short-range and close-combat suppressing devices, two lab assistants plus dead-eye Maria, all versus an unarmed woman in handcuffs. Normally on CdC, to be this thoroughly fucked would cost you good money.

Alice begins to come round again after a few seconds, probably trying to work out how she went from upright holding a rifle to horizontal and pinned without noticing the process in between.

Gonçalves stands over her, looking down with unmistakable affection.

"The old-fashioned version of facial recognition is more reliable in some circumstances," she says. "A lens probably couldn't differentiate between you and Beatrice without sustained-focus analysis, but I could tell at a glance. I could tell you apart within moments of you being born, and I've been watching you closely ever since. You and your younger sister."

On the forced march here, Nikki was quietly parsing the grab Alice sent. She was relieved on the girl's behalf that she isn't any kind of robot after all, but can't imagine Alice was comforted by what she has learned.

"You performed non-consensual and non-essential surgery on us as infants," Alice replies, anger spilling into her voice. "You made us your experiment. What gave you the right? Who gave you *us*?"

Gonçalves ignores the question, though there is a hint of regret in her expression.

"You have to understand, from a scientist's point of view, twins are an especially precious phenomenon. I could observe the differences your respective experiences made, knowing that so many other elements were identical. I learned so much from you both, things I could never have learned had you even been dizygotic, or mere siblings."

"You separated us," Alice states, the accusation causing her voice to wobble. "I never knew I had a sister."

Gonçalves's answer runs at a tangent. It's not so much like she's skirting the point as that the point has led her on to something she considers more important.

"I placed you each with well-connected families, ensuring you the best of upbringing, education and opportunity. *Your* role was to learn statecraft, diplomacy, politics, the dynamics of how societies are run, which is why you were raised by parents who would ensure you ultimately rose to take a senior position in the FNG. Beatrice, meanwhile, was placed in a family with high-ranking connections to both the Quadriga and the defence industry. It was my intention to reunite you when the time was right, which would have been soon, but certain events took the timetable out of my hands."

"You mean somebody boosting one of your gizmos," Nikki suggests. "Not to mention liberating a woman kept prisoner here as a brain-butchered baby-maker. Yeah, that would fuck with your calendar pretty bad. Wouldn't do for the rank and file to find out what their betters literally have in mind for them."

One of the mercs makes to move in but Gonçalves halts him with a stare. It's not an act of mercy, more like she barely thinks Nikki is worth the attention.

"I lost almost everything in the fire, including a good friend and the brightest mind I ever knew. I have been rebuilding ever since, trying to recreate Cassandra Shelley's work in parallel with the further development of my own. And all of that was almost lost because of one greedy, corrupt individual and some opportunist petty-criminal low lifes. I couldn't allow that to happen. It would be like losing a cure for a terminal disease because some burglar trashed the lab while stealing clamp stands for their scrap value.

"I am forging a better future. Those children you saw: it took us all this time and a few missteps, but we have recreated Shelley's neuron-replacement technology. They are the first in a new generation of Sentinels. You and Beatrice will oversee them when I cannot go on. At first there will be one *Arca*, but it will send back word of its colonies. More vessels will follow, and each of them will have guardians to ensure that it is the best of humanity that evolves aboard."

Nikki gets it now, should have recognised it sooner. She sure saw it enough times back in LA. Gonçalves doesn't think she's the bad guy here. Nobody ever does, but that's not the same as believing you've done nothing wrong. Gonçalves knows she's done things that are wrong, but she believes she was right to do them for the greater good, and that's why she is so dangerous.

"Why didn't you trust your little private army here to get the job done?" Nikki asks.

Gonçalves acts like the question is unworthy of her time, then Nikki realises that this aloofness is a posture to mask the truth.

"You were still experimenting," Nikki deduces.

"You brought in Beatrice as your secret assassin?" Alice asks, almost tearful in her outrage. "What kind of upbringing did you give the girl?"

Gonçalves sighs, casting a glance towards the assistants, who are busy flipping switches and checking settings.

Nikki isn't sure how many more questions the professor is likely to tolerate, then asks herself why she is tolerating any. The answer is not because she is filling time while her techs get the kit up to speed. It is because she needs to talk, needs to justify herself. Nikki has little doubt that Gonçalves means to neutralise their threat, and does not like to consider what that will soon entail, but on some human level she knows it's not the same as persuasion. Particularly in the case of Alice, she needs to feel the common purpose of a shared goal. Gonçalves craves affirmation, to reassure herself that she is in the right.

"Beatrice has been trained in multiple combat techniques at the highest level. But being trained is not the same thing as being capable of the deeds recently required of her. That's why I commissioned Slovitz's work on mechanisms to inhibit certain behaviours and disinhibit others."

Gonçalves swallows. Nikki is sure she can see a hint of a tear.

"In combination with selective uploading of certain memories, I empowered her to carry out terrible deeds," she admits, leaning over Alice and speaking softly. "I accept responsibility for this. The burden will not be hers to carry. I will not let her keep those memories: neither the inserted ones nor the genuine horrific recollections of what she has done. Beatrice will be clear of conscience, happy, at peace. As will you, I promise. You will be fully committed to what we are building, and you will have a part in it that will last centuries."

"Committed because you're going to edit my memories to make it so?"

"You speak as though you believe that hasn't already happened. Do you believe your ideologies and perspectives are entirely a construct of happenstance? All throughout your life I have had a hand in shaping the way you've come to view the world. Values, manners, politeness, appropriate language. You never swear, for instance, do you? It's no different to what any mother tries to do, but I had to work from a distance. Your synthetic mind has always had a two-way connection, allowing some judicious editing to make you see things from a carefully cultivated perspective."

Nikki is reeling at this. Not only has Gonçalves been selecting and censoring Alice's memories, bitch has been doing it from off-planet, on high, not so much playing puppet master as playing God.

The enormity must be hitting Alice too. She looks hollowed out, defeated. But then she raises her head just as much as she can and replies:

"So how come my perspective over the past few days has led me to conclude that you are full of shit?"

Nikki couldn't say if it is she or Gonçalves who looks the more shocked that the girl has learned to swear. It only lasts a moment though.

"I'm not quite sure. I lost the connection when you were in the elevator to Heinlein Station. There is a lot of electromagnetic activity around that thing, many combinations of forces that could have created a shield. I might expect it to suspend the link, but it outright severed it. I made multiple attempts to restore communications, which you may have experienced as moments of confusion each time you woke up. The dart you were shot with outside the Ver Eterna hotel was actually a covert means of implanting a subcutaneous signal relay. As far as I am aware, it successfully embedded, so I don't know why it didn't work, but as you can see, we are about to re-establish the connection manually.

"In fact, it's the only connection that will be established in here, in case you had notions of transmitting incriminating evidence and calling out for intercession. This suite is electrically isolated in order to carry out the experimental procedures that allow us to develop new meshes. That's why I've been talking openly about this."

And this is when Nikki realises where they are. She looks up at the blank ceiling, sees what Alice must have recognised already. This is the place where Omega was taken, the place from which he could not send a plea for help as he was butchered and skinned.

"No, you're talking about this because you need to," Nikki tells her. "Trying to clear your conscience so you can sleep later."

Gonçalves gestures to the mercs.

"Can you deal with the prisoner?" she asks.

Nikki takes a step forward. She knows it will result in her being hauled back by a burly pair of arms, but she wants to ensure that she draws Gonçalves's attention.

"Look me in the eye," she demands. "And don't excuse yourself with euphemisms and deniability. You can delegate your dirty work, but if you're going to have me killed, you should have the decency to meet my gaze and admit to us both that it's what you're doing."

Gonçalves takes a step closer and does as she is asked, staring back at Nikki with a placid expression.

"I am not going to allow any harm to befall you, Sergeant Freeman. I refuse to tolerate any further violence than was absolutely necessary to clean up the mess made by the gangsters whose activities you utterly failed to discourage. So how dare you talk about me being able to look you in the eye. You are the one who was supposed to uphold the law, but your sins of the flesh and sins of omission, your self-indulgence and your lack of self-respect allowed this culture to fester, a culture of criminality and corruption."

"Those greedy assholes at the Quadriga not paying people a decent wage is what causes criminality and corruption," Nikki replies, but she can't pretend Gonçalves hasn't landed a blow. Gonçalves knows it too.

"Which is why it is right and fitting that your fate is to stand trial for the bloodshed your negligence and laxity ultimately precipitated."

"Suits me. I was always good on the stand, back in the day. I'm sure I could give a convincing account of all the damning evidence I've uncovered about you and Neurosophy. But I don't imagine my testimony is likely to reflect my present knowledge, is it?"

"Correct, Sergeant Freeman. You will confess all and you will plead guilty, because I am going to erase your recollection of what you have learned here, and replace it with Beatrice's memories of what she did. As far as you will know, you are the guilty one. You will tell the court that, and justice will not only be done, but seen to be done."

"Yeah. Says the bitch who was just lecturing me about corruption."

This bounces off Gonçalves, who looks at her with unfiltered disgust.

"After all these years, it's a little late to act like you're suddenly interested in justice."

Another gesture. Nikki is lifted bodily by two of the mercs and slapped down on to the other table. The rings spin into place around her wrists and ankles with solid clunks. The techs advance, conspicuously untroubled by any ethical issues.

Nikki jerks her head back in an attempt to damage the cradle, but they have anticipated this. They keep it tucked back and don't engage the neck restraints. She's guessing they will have a means of sedating her when they're good and ready.

"I still know the difference between low-level palm-greasing and the greater corruption that's eating you, Professor. I know what a murderer is, even if she ain't the one wielding the blade."

"No. You still *don't* know the difference between your tiny, blinkered perspective and the bigger picture. You don't think I've weighed these crimes against the benefit they protect? You don't think I've contemplated their enormity but seen that this was a burden I must not shirk from carrying?"

"Actually, no. Because I heard this kind of shit all the time back on the job."

"And why did you leave the job?" Gonçalves asks, and something turns to ice inside Nikki.

"That's none of your goddamn business."

"Wasn't it for the same reason: that you were unable to recognise the greater importance of what was right in front of you because you were too busy *doing the job* to recognise what your real responsibility was?"

"Fuck you."

It's a pointless defiance. She wishes she could put her hands over her ears. She's scared of what this woman might know, what she might force Nikki to confront. Gonçalves will have done her research, and she is as thorough as she is connected.

"It was tough as a single mom, I don't doubt it, but maybe if you hadn't been so intent on feeding your ego by busting cases, you might have noticed the signs."

"Fuck you."

She's trying to hold it back but the waters are spilling over the floodgates.

"Were you too busy doing the job the night your son shot himself at the age of, what was it, twelve? Just approaching his thirteenth birthday. Killed himself with your spare service weapon, according to your files. Would you change it now, if you could? Would you let a few low-life criminal deaths slide down the priority list in exchange for paying more attention to Lawrence, and the mental health issues his teachers reported he was having?"

Nikki can't speak. The deluge is coming now, choking her throat, drowning her voice.

"I'm sorry for your pain, Sergeant Freeman. Sorry to tap into it like this, but I have to make you see. I am trying to spare people from suffering like you have ever again. I can create a future without crime, without violence. And in the short term, I will take your pain away, all these agonising memories."

Nikki's voice feels like it is drowning, unable to break the surface and call out her objection. She doesn't care if she ends up in jail, or even if she has Beatrice's murders inserted into her mind, but she needs her pain. She needs the worst of her memories because they are inextricably entangled in the best.

"Or rather, I will delegate, as you suggested. It will be Alice who does it, and she will be happy to."

Nikki can barely see now, unable to wipe her overflowing eyes because her hands are restrained. She hears Alice find her voice, lying parallel a few yards away.

"So why didn't you simply erase the memories of Omega and Julio and everybody else? Why did the path to your world without violence require a detour via torture and murder?"

"We had to find out how much they knew, who else had been told. But equally, there was an opportunity both to eliminate a toxic element from CdC and expose to people on Earth – particularly the FNG – the corrupt, hedonistic culture that had taken root here.

This place will be policed properly from now on, but more than that, we will effect a culture-wide change in people's philosophy as to what they are on CdC for."

"You're going to edit people's minds," Alice says. "And it won't stop here. As above, so below. Thought crime eradicated at source. A whole species enslaved by your vision of morality."

"You don't want to talk about my vision, Alice. You who have enjoyed the privileged existence I so painstakingly ensured. You haven't seen the things I witnessed, had the things done to you that I did, *as a child*. You have no idea what humanity is truly capable of when it allows its basest instincts to run unchecked."

Nikki swallows, finally rediscovers her voice.

"And what about the base part of humanity that's obsessed with controlling people and having power over everybody else? You working on a plan to eradicate that?"

"This isn't about power and control. This is about being a responsible mother. But I guess that's not something you could relate to."

Gonçalves walks over towards the wall, where she begins tapping on a console.

Nikki strains against the clamps. It is futile, but it is instinctive, a search for any possible way out of this as the clock counts down the last few seconds to defeat.

"This won't take long," Gonçalves tells Alice. "Your synthetic brain can transfer data back and forth far faster than it takes to upload to a mesh. In a matter of minutes, you're going to feel like a whole new woman."

WOKE

Alice can hear voices, distant at first then gradually becoming clearer as her consciousness attempts to resolve itself.

"Okay, final checks. Transfer status?"

"Confirmed complete."

"Non-native data integrity?"

"Confirmed at one hundred per cent."

"Overwrite of targeted memory sectors?"

"Confirmed."

"Roger that. Subject is coming round. Go-ahead to disengage restraints?"

"Confirmed."

The clamps withdrawn, she pulls herself into a sitting position, taking in her surroundings. Her mind is fuzzy, a storm of information cohering in places, chaotic in others, but she recognises where she is. She is waking up where she expected to find herself.

She slides off the table and walks towards the wall, watched carefully by assistants and security personnel. Before the procedure, she didn't know their names, didn't know their roles. She does now. She knows so much more now.

Memories are continuing to assemble themselves as she approaches a bank of machines and accesses a console. She understands the device it controls, knows in exhaustive detail how to operate it: every parameter, every calibration, every setting.

When it was stolen, the thieves were like illiterates blindly stabbing at individual letters on a keyboard to see the pretty shapes they printed. With what has just been uploaded into her memory, Alice could use this thing to write any story she likes. And most importantly, she knows what she must do with it first.

FAMILY TIES

With the head restraints still not fully deployed, Nikki is able to twist and crane her neck in an effort to see what is going on in the rest of the room. It doesn't make her feel any less helpless, but it always exacerbates the sense of vulnerability when she can't see her enemy's line of attack.

The most horrible thing is the calm, the quiet. She wants to go down fighting in a storm of noise and struggle, but as Alice lies there motionless, Nikki understands what absolute defeat truly looks like.

Green lights flash all around the edge of the cradle, and Gonçalves is good to go.

There is barely a word for several minutes, then the lab assistants break the silence by methodically checking that their act of electronic butchery has run its course to their technical satisfaction.

"Subject is coming round. Go-ahead to disengage restraints?"

"Confirmed."

Alice sits up slowly, looking like nothing has changed, and yet Nikki knows they wouldn't be letting her loose if everything hadn't.

She watches Alice walk across to a bank of machines and begin to calmly operate a device she knew nothing about when she walked into this lab. That is when it truly hits home. Nikki feels a mixture of marvel and horror as she contemplates how Alice's mind has been literally changed: the memories informing her beliefs and consequent actions swapped out so that she opened her eyes a different person. Then a sickness takes hold as she confronts the inescapable reality that the same thing is now about to happen to her.

Alice raises her hands from the console and looks towards Gonçalves, who has given no exterior indication of satisfaction or relief at Alice's transformation. It's just business as usual to her, merely another step on the long path that began in that refugee camp and ends with her vision of a better humanity colonising the cosmos.

"What are you waiting for?" Gonçalves asks.

"A reunion," Alice answers.

A moment after she speaks, the aperture opens with a swish, and in walks Beatrice, the lethal twin.

"I saw her approach on my cam feed," Alice explains, then turns to greet the new arrival. "My dear sister," she says, her voice warm, threatening to break with emotion. "I'm overcome to finally restore our acquaintance."

"The feeling's mutual," Beatrice replies. "Believe me, it's been harder for me watching you at a distance. Glad to see you're all caught up so we can, you know, catch up."

"Which there will be plenty of time for later," says Gonçalves, gently reminding Alice she has a job to do.

"Of course," she responds, casting a neutral, unfeeling glance towards the operating tables. It's like Nikki isn't even there, not as an individual at least. All Alice is seeing is the tools for a job.

Nikki wishes she could feel resignation, but she can't give up the fight. She focuses on her memories of Lawrence, like this will somehow protect them, then realises it will probably just make them easier for the process to identify.

Her mind searches for any last sliver of hope. She thinks about the people who have had erasures, and even what she has learned about Amber. The memory is taken, but some part of them still knows something is missing. Will that be her fate when she cannot remember her son? Or does this mean some part of Alice still instinctively recognises who are the bad guys here?

Alice looks up from the console and addresses the lab assistants.

"I need the subject properly secured."

That will be a no, then.

READ-ONLY MEMORY

It is consciousness itself that is an illusion . . . that process of retrospectively fabricating a continuous narrative is going on at every moment, fooling us into believing we are experiencing the world objectively through our own singular perspective.

Alice is not sure in which order the processes occur, whether the impulse to operate the console has come first and triggered the memories, or whether the impulse has been triggered as a result of the memories. They are like a child's collage inside her mind, a kaleidoscope of disparate components experienced simultaneously.

Amidst the maelstrom is a memory of a face, speaking directly to her in a video message. It is a woman in her forties or fifties, moist-eyed and tired, burdened by sadness. Alice feels affection, sorrow and regret, but at a remove. This must be what was meant by the watermark effect, because she can sense that this is not her own memory. She has never experienced it before. She doesn't know if this means that all of her previous memories are genuine, or that the synthetic neuron system works more seamlessly than the mesh.

"I'm sorry that this is the last time I will speak to you," the woman says. "I'm sorry I didn't come home to Earth for the end, but I don't have long left, and I have chosen to use the time I do have to do this."

More fragments coalesce. She knows who this is. It is Cassandra Shelley.

It is her mother.

No. The watermark. This is not her memory, not her mother. Shelley is the mother of whoever's memory this is.

"I kept the tumour secret from you, and for that I apologise."

Alice feels an echo of sadness, the memory of a memory. This is the recollection of someone watching this video message not for the first time. Watching it in a lab, nearby, recently.

"I had to keep my illness from Maria because I didn't know what she might do if she found out. She still thinks there will be time for her to understand my work. She believes we will get over our disagreements and that I will share with her the elements I have kept to myself. But I have realised that I cannot allow that, and I honestly don't know what she is capable of were she to learn that I will be taking those secrets to the grave."

Alice feels another echo of sadness, another coalescence: whoever's memory this is reflecting on the irony. Shelley designed these synthetic neurons and their cell-cloning replication process as a means to repair brain damage, but her innovation came too late to save herself.

"I've seen what she means to do. She has already operated on two infants. Twins. I can't say for sure how she got them, though I have a strong idea, which I will also have to take with me to my grave. What she has done is beyond unethical, utterly unconscionable, but I can just about forgive her this much. It is her long-term plans that truly frighten me. I am sending you the files along with this transmission, so that you can understand: nothing less than the free will of the human race is at stake here.

"This is why I am going to destroy all of my work, and as much as I can of hers. It will appear as an accident, a fire. She must never know that I was the cause of it, or that it was deliberate, because I do not want suspicion to fall upon you when one day you take up a post here. Maria will not give up. She will rebuild and try again, which is why I am pleading with you to become my own invisible agent.

"I hope you understand what I have done. Please know that I have taken steps to ensure the fire will be contained and nobody else harmed. I also have drugs to ensure I do not suffer. I will be gone before the flames reach me. Forgive me, Leonard. I love you."

Leonard.

Leonard Slovitz was Shelley's son. This is his memory, of re-watching an old video message from his mother.

The kaleidoscope resolves again.

"If you are remembering this, it's because everything else has failed."

Another second-hand memory: Leonard Slovitz looking in the mirror. He is talking to himself, and yet not talking to himself. He is talking to the intended recipient of his message.

"Gonçalves is moving all her pieces into place. The most powerful of them is you, Alice Blake, through whom she will effectively control the Seguridad. Electromagnetic shielding dictates that her link to your mind will be lost on your ascent to Heinlein. I have sabotaged the system at this end so that it can't be re-established remotely. Eventually, Gonçalves will have to bring you here, to restore control and to correct anything she doesn't like. I have hijacked that process too. Instead, she will upload this little care package, my own last resort.

"My plan is to go public by smuggling out a piece of hardware, one I have been involved in designing. It is a prototype remote-access module for the Gen-5 mesh, augmented with an emergency behaviour-control function. With it I will be able to demonstrate what this new technology allows its operator to do. It is power that should be in nobody's hands: no individual, no government and no corporation.

"Time will be against me. Once my actions are discovered, Gonçalves will move heaven and Earth to recover the machine and to silence me. If that should prove so, then all I have left is to plead to you this echo of my mother's request if I have become, like her, a ghost in the machine."

LOYALTIES

"She's already on the table," Gonçalves states, sounding a little testy to Nikki's ears. "Oh, you mean the neck brace."

"No," Alice replies, insistent. "I mean I need the subject secured. Freeman is not the subject."

Acting on some unspoken cue, one of the mercs raises the suppression rifle he took from Alice and shoots Beatrice with it, hitting her just above the collarbone in a cluster of tiny marks. As she reels around in disbelief, the merc she has just turned her back on zaps her with his electro-pulse, taking her out in case she does any damage before the sedative can act.

Then it's serious déjà vu: the same two mercs moving with speed and efficiency to grab Alice's twin before she falls, then laying her down on the same operating table Alice just vacated. Restraints simultaneously cycle and clunk around Beatrice's limbs as they withdraw from around Nikki's, while Daniels disarms Gonçalves of her stun pistol and secures her in a double armlock.

Nikki climbs to her feet. She's not sure what just went down, but she's happy to run with it.

"Release me at once," Gonçalves demands. "What the hell are you doing?"

"They're securing the subject," Alice replies.

Silently they lift Gonçalves on to the other operating table and lock her into place. She strains against the loops in protest. This is in frantic contrast to Beatrice, who is unmoving, the suppression rifle's sedative having taken hold.

"You've been betrayed, Maria. Twice. Leonard Slovitz sabotaged your system so that when you tried to edit my mind just now, my memory was protected and the vital information he needed me to know was uploaded instead. You ought to admire him. He acted out of self-sacrifice and loyalty."

"Slovitz?" Gonçalves asks, as confused as she is incredulous. "Loyalty? Selling our work to criminals?"

"He wasn't selling anything. He was throwing a clog into your loom, just like his mother did twenty-five years ago. Slovitz was Cassandra Shelley's son. The fire was her doing, after she learned what you had done to Beatrice and me, after she realised what you were capable of. Shelley was dying of a brain tumour, so she sacrificed herself because it was the only way to stop you."

Gonçalves's face twists into a wordless grimace as a vast and precious piece of her past is ripped up and rewritten in an instant.

Yeah, bitch, that's what it feels like, Nikki thinks.

"Shelley knew you would rebuild and try again, so she passed the torch to her son. Slovitz did what his mother asked in order to protect *her* vision, her values, except he didn't need his brain interfered with in order to do so. But now there's a simpler way to stop you."

The tech assistants move in, engaging the neck brace and bringing the cradle into place around their boss's head. Neither they nor the guards have uttered a single word, nor looked at each other, yet they are acting in concert. It's the console. Alice is directing them like they are her appendages.

"No. Please. Jason, Michael, you have to release me."

"Release you? They can't even hear you. You should be happy. I'm going to follow your vision and take away the painful, damaging memories that have so corrupted you."

Gonçalves strains against the brace to try and look at Alice. Her neck won't turn, so she stares in desperate supplication at Nikki instead.

"No, please. I need those memories. I need my pain! It's what drove me to achieve what I have, so that I might prevent such atrocities happening to other women, other children."

"And what makes your memories, your pain worth more than everyone else's?"

Gonçalves closes her eyes. Nikki sees tears leak out either side and run down her cheeks.

"I think she's finally getting it," Nikki says.

She looks to Alice, expecting her to stand down, but her fingers continue to work the console, busy and deliberate.

"Her remorse is coming too late as far as I'm concerned. Remorse can't undo what she did to me and to Beatrice. She edited my mind, appointed herself a controlling voyeur upon my whole life."

"Alice, you made your point. All threats are neutralised. Now you need to back away."

"Why should I?"

Nikki walks between the operating tables, approaching the console behind which Alice is standing. Daniels steps into her path, arms folded. She feints to skip past him but he moves with each of her steps, blocking her off. Nikki pretends to give up in exasperation then turns around and tries to cold-cock him. He's fast. He catches her fist, takes her off-balance and throws her back. She clatters painfully against one of the operating tables and drops to the floor, dazed.

The room spinning, she lifts her head and addresses Alice.

"Doing what she did was the only way Gonçalves could make sense of all the horrible shit that happened to her. Otherwise it was just meaningless suffering. People do terrible things when they can't find any other way to deal."

"She doesn't need you to make her excuses for her, Nikki. She made this bed, so be grateful it's her lying in it and not you."

"It's not an excuse, it's a warning. You can't justify tearing up her mind because bad things were done to you: that would make you as bad as her. You need to step away. You need to stop this."

"Why should I?" she asks again.

Alice's face is like stone, a cold determination in her eyes. She looks more like her twin in Omega's grab than the goody two-shoes idealist Nikki has come to know and, she has to admit, kind of like.

Nikki crouches on the floor, catching her breath. There are now all three mercs forming a barrier, while the lab assistants stand over the operating table where Gonçalves's head is secured inside the cradle. Green lights are flashing all around the crown, same as before. They are ready to rock.

Nikki has to find a way through. She can't let Alice do this.

She looks around the lab for any kind of weapon, sees that the guards have got them all, even Gonçalves's little stun pistol. However, they haven't used any of them against Nikki: they haven't shot her down or zapped her. Alice has got them programmed to repel, not attack.

Nikki vaults on to the edge of the operating table nearer the console and launches herself through the air. Two strong arms catch her and she is thrown back again, winded by the impact as she thumps against a wall. It is hopeless. Gonçalves is locked in and Alice has total control, in a perfect reversal of the situation a few minutes ago. The one thing that hasn't changed is that Nikki is powerless to do shit.

Doesn't mean she'll stop trying, though.

"Alice, you gotta listen to me. Gonçalves wanted to change you into someone you're not. You do this and she's got her wish. How you're feeling right now, all your anger, this isn't who you are. But it's who you'll be for ever after if you don't stop. You *have* to stop."

Alice looks up from the console, eyes burning with rage. She fires out her reply like a hail of bullets.

"And I ask you again: Why should I?"

Nikki hauls herself upright, and in her exasperation grabs on to the last argument she can think of. It's the only thing she's got left, so she screams it out with all the authority she has ever brought to bear.

"BECAUSE IT'S AGAINST THE FUCKING LAW."

And with that, Alice lifts her hands from the console in a gesture of surrender and composes her face into an expression of placid serenity.

"Thank you, Sergeant Freeman. You just said the magic words."

S. E. P.

Alice keys her final commands into the console, sending the signals that will cause the guards and the lab assistants to stand down and surrender themselves, the mere stroke of a finger delivering their absolute obedience. She is the puppet master now, but it doesn't make her feel like she is in control. It doesn't make her feel powerful.

On her last trip to visit Trick, she glimpsed inside a club beneath Mullane where the patrons can command paid couples to perform any sexual act they choose for their gratification. If you took how that made her feel and multiplied it by a hundred, it still wouldn't describe the unease she experiences manipulating this device.

She feels nothing but relief when she knows she can step away from it, and greater relief knowing that thanks to Slovitz, she can take the necessary measures to prevent anybody from interfering with her own mind again. She realises she may never know which of her memories are genuine or even unadulterated, but she understands that it doesn't matter. She is the sum of those memories, for better or worse, true or false, and she will be the sole guardian of that archive from here on in.

She sees Nikki stare in wonder as two of the guards cuff the lab assistants then meekly volunteer their own wrists to be cuffed by Daniels. He in turn offers up his arms to Nikki for her to do the honours.

"Jesus. Future of policing," Nikki says. "That is some terrifying shit and we seriously need to destroy it before the Seguridad gets here."

"We're destroying nothing. It's evidence."

"And do you trust the FNG and the Quadriga to keep something as powerful as this safely in isolation while we all wait for a court case? How hard do you think it would be to pay somebody to look the other way while they swapped it out for a decoy?"

"Regardless, what happens to this technology is not ours to decide. Besides, there's a cop in the Seguridad I reckon I can trust to keep it safe. She's got a reputation for corruption but I believe her heart's in the right place when it comes to the big stuff."

"Yeah, I always said you were dangerously naïve about the ways of CdC."

They share a smile, but it is Gonçalves's reaction that catches Alice's eye. The professor is rousing from her resigned catatonia, like something has reignited her spark.

"You have something you'd like to say?" Alice enquires.

"Would you like to know about your parents?" she replies. "Your natural ones, I mean."

A combination of longing and wariness stirs inside Alice. It is confusing enough to stall her from answering.

"It's my last bargaining chip," Gonçalves says. "I'm prepared to trade it."

"For what?" asks Nikki, who appears to have noticed that Alice is struggling to find her voice.

"For you to wipe Beatrice's memory of the things she did, and the memories I implanted in order to make her do them. Please. Before the Seguridad get here and take it out of your hands. She should not have to carry that burden."

Nikki looks to Alice for a decision. It is a hard one to make, but hard doesn't mean difficult.

"That's not our call either. It should be Beatrice's decision, though only after the trial."

"But that is my primary concern. She should not face judgement for acting upon things I falsely put in her mind."

"That's a very good point," Alice concedes. "Do we absolve her on the basis that she might have made different decisions had these memories *not* been inserted? If these memories were artificially put in her head, can we say she acted of her own free will? Or should she be judged for the decisions she made and acted upon on the basis of what she *believed* to be true?"

Alice leans over and looks Gonçalves in the eye.

"Thanks to you, Professor, I've been privileged to study ethics and the law under some of the greatest minds on planet Earth. Consequently, my perspective on these questions is surprisingly straightforward."

"And what is that?" she asks, anxious and expectant.

"I'm glad it's someone else's problem."

CHOICES

"They'll be here in about ten minutes," Alice informs Nikki, having accessed a terminal to relay her communications beyond the electronic isolation of the lab. "The explaining part comes later, but right now we don't need to worry about anybody questioning the fact I've got Maria Gonçalves under arrest. Ochoba's got our backs."

They are standing against the wall furthest from the operating tables, Nikki washing a cut with water from one of the sinks. All of their prisoners are restrained by various means but Nikki has slung the suppression rifle around her shoulder and has assembled the other weapons at her feet. Mind control devices or not, clearly she isn't taking any chances.

Alice offers her a towel to dab herself dry. She feels some kind of acknowledgement is called for.

"You okay?" she asks. "I know you took a couple of knocks there."

"It's okay, I get what you were trying to do. I appreciate it. Are *you* okay though? Because I figure you gotta be dealing with some serious shit. I mean, at some point we all have to confront our own mortality, but it's something else to confront your potential *im*mortality."

"It is a lot to take in," Alice admits. "I could yet, in a way, fulfil the role Gonçalves chose for me, ultimately book myself a place on the *Arca* and be a living repository of knowledge. Equally, a synthetic brain needs a body to support it, same as any other. It needs oxygen, energy, so I can choose not to repair myself, and die of old age. Am I obliged to accept this gift, given what it might allow me to give in return? Would it be selfish to refuse? So many difficult questions, so many confounding possibilities."

"Yeah, and unlike the Beatrice issue, this one really is your problem."

"Fortunately, my synthetic superbrain has already come up with a short-term strategy for dealing with the sheer enormity of it."

"And what's that?"

"It involves mojitos. Do you know where I can get a good one?"

PRECIOUS CARGO

Alice is standing next to Nikki on Dock Twenty-One, the first place she ever set foot upon CdC when she disembarked here on Wheel Two after her journey from Heinlein less than a week ago. Dock Twenty-One is where VIPs normally land, close to Central Plaza and the only such facility dedicated exclusively to passenger use. As usual, it is looking pristine, befitting the first impression the Quadriga wishes to grant visitors to its fabled realm. Less usual is the fact that it is in lockdown, closed off to anyone without clearance, and guarded by high-level security.

The dock is replete with as many VIPs as have ever assembled here at one time, but it's not because any of them are arriving or departing. They are here to greet the FNG's task force taking temporary charge of the Seguridad, Ochoba's team of new captains who will each oversee a different regional sector. However, this high-profile arrival is not the real reason for the lockdown and elevated security presence. All of that is for an extremely low-profile departure, which will happen once the great and the good have been and gone. Not even they have clearance for that.

There are several senior Seguridad officers present in dress uniform, looking all kinds of uncomfortable in their unaccustomed garb, but more uncomfortable at the prospect of meeting the people whose arrival here will constitute an effective demotion.

Nikki is not one of them, but she is looking unusually present-able, like she's dressed for a cocktail reception at the Ver Eterna rather than a night of drinking and who knows what else on Mullane.

"You scrub up well," Alice remarks, by way of deliberate under-statement. Nikki looks stunning, and she suspects Nikki knows she looks stunning, so she wants to undermine her just a little.

"I'm a changed woman, remember. Got new duties and responsibilities."

"Glad to see you're taking them seriously. I'll want a full report."

"Oh, you'll get a report. You maybe won't want all the details."

Nikki smirks. Alice shakes her head, fails to suppress a smile. She knows Nikki won't let her down.

Alice tracks the shuttle's approach and watches it pass beneath out of sight. It brings back a vivid memory of her recent extravehicular ingress, sending a thrill through her. It's been a hell of a week.

"I'm hearing Ochoba didn't make the trip," Alice remarks.

"So?"

Alice doesn't respond, but Nikki works it out anyway.

"Oh, I get it. You were wanting a pat on the head and an attaboy."

Busted.

"She's my boss. I've had a tricky start to a new job, and I'm an affirmation junkie."

"Girl, the fact Ochoba didn't make the trip *is* your attaboy. She knew she didn't need to come here because she knows you got this."

Alice appreciates the sentiment, but suspects that Ochoba has bigger fish to fry. There are trades and negotiations going on at the highest levels regarding what is to happen to Gonçalves and to Beatrice, and the only thing looking certain is that they will never see a courtroom back on Earth. The whole affair remains ultraclassified, with the official version still blaming a turf war between bootleggers. Partly this is because nobody wants a panic breaking out regarding mesh technology, given that almost everybody on Seedee has one; but just as crucial is the fact that Gonçalves and the Neurosophy Foundation are simply too valuable to the Quadriga.

She has no idea what is likely to happen to Beatrice, and remains content that this is not her problem to solve. However, she is less sanguine about the possibility that Gonçalves will end up essentially serving out a sentence of sorts here on CdC, a permanent house arrest that allows her to continue her work under supervision. Alice's brief time here has taught her that the culture of petty corruption she was supposed to eradicate is positively noble compared to the squalid compromises that get hammered out between the Quadriga and the FNG.

With the shuttle's ascent imminent, the untidy gathering divides and begins to order itself. That is when Alice sees Helen Petitjean, and Helen Petitjean sees her. More significantly, she sees Nikki too, though it takes Helen a moment to recognise her in her glad rags. Once she does, her face is a picture, and not because Nikki is looking so damn hot. Nikki gives her a sarcastically cheerful wave then takes leave of Alice to assume her assigned role in the reception committee.

The subject of her disapproval having absented herself, Helen predictably seizes the opportunity to buttonhole Alice.

"It is an auspicious day," she states, adding gravitas to her words with that sing-song Southern accent.

Alice can tell that this is as much an unsubtle reminder of Helen's on-going agenda as an acknowledgement that change is afoot.

"I suppose so," Alice replies neutrally. "Hence everybody who is anybody being in attendance."

This prompts Helen to glance across to where Nikki is now standing.

"That's one way of putting it. I have to say, I am relieved to be assured that Nicola Freeman was not guilty of the things she was accused, but I must express my great surprise to see her present at an occasion such as this. Unless you consider it symbolic to include someone who embodies everything about CdC that needs to change."

"I would argue that Nikki represents that change. Trust me on this much: you will never know how grateful you and everyone else up here ought to be to her."

"And why will I never know?"

"You don't have the clearance."

Helen sighs.

"Well, I guess after all is said and done, CdC *is* a place for redemption. For second chances and sometimes third and fourth ones. But I do assume she will not be allowed to persist in her role as a sergeant in the Seguridad."

"You assume correctly," Alice replies. "I have seen to it personally that this will no longer be the case."

Helen nods with understated satisfaction.

"So, if you don't mind me asking, what is she doing here?"

"She is part of the reception committee. I have assigned her a very specific role, and I trust her to carry it out conscientiously."

The shuttle is rising into view. Helen strains to look over the heads of the people in front, trying to get a view of the door.

"I guess I don't need to ask what *you're* doing here," Alice remarks. "Come to welcome your little brother."

"Younger brother, yes. He's not so little."

"I know. I've seen his profile. He should be a model officer. Could be a model, period. He's a good-looking fellow."

"He is good in every particular, Dr Blake. And with the likes of Dominic forming your new broom, there is absolutely no reason for you not to sweep CdC clean now."

The door opens and the first of the flight crew emerges, greeted by ground staff to complete safety checks and admin formalities.

"Oh, I'm going to sweep the place," Alice assures her. "Though maybe not quite as clean as you'd like."

Helen tears her gaze away from the shuttle to fix Alice with a disapproving glare.

"And just what might you mean by that?" she enquires, her tone challenging to the point of impertinent. Alice could remind her of their respective credentials, but she has other ways of making her point.

"I mean that my experiences here have taught me how we all need to misbehave sometimes in order to feel alive. We each of us have our private temptations, our secret transgressions. They're part of what makes us human."

"Many undesirable things are part of what makes us human," Helen replies with a pronounced haughtiness. "But it should *not* be the policy of the authorities to turn a blind eye to them."

"Really? Because I was talking to someone who works in the Wheel Two rotary hub, and I've got him on record saying you bribed him to force an all-stop at the moment of your choosing."

Helen's eyes bulge, all colour draining from her face.

"My policy was to continue turning a blind eye to that," Alice continues, "but I'm happy to alter it if that's your preference."

Helen swallows, sweat breaking out on her otherwise immaculately made-up face. She bounces back quickly though, her composure returning in a matter of seconds.

"Well, Dr Blake, I suppose we *all* have to compromise ourselves sometimes in the pursuit of what we believe to be right. I guess I'm just disappointed it took so little time on CdC for you to turn native."

"To *turn* native?" Alice replies. "Ms Petitjean, I was born here. I *am* a native."

Almost an hour has passed since the last of the official delegations departed Dock Twenty-One, but the same shuttle remains in position in the bay. This would ordinarily be an unacceptable turnaround time, but nothing about this mission is ordinary. The flight crew who brought the task force from Heinlein is comprised entirely of high-clearance FNG personnel, but this was not due to the status of their inbound passengers. It is their outbound manifest that is the real reason for the lockdown.

Nobody must know about this. Any of it.

Having been given the signal to proceed, today's truly important people begin to emerge on to the floor of the shuttle bay. They have travelled here the way Alice was involuntarily conveyed from beneath Sin Garden and the way Nikki travelled out to the McAuliffe district when she was on the run. For today's journeys, however, the crates have been modified to enhance safety and comfort, their progress monitored every metre of the way, and each of the young passengers is accompanied by an adult. The trip will only have taken a few minutes from the Neurosophy HQ, where they have remained CdC's most closely guarded secret.

The first to appear, her baby son in her arms, is the woman Alice previously knew only as Amber. Her real name is Rachel Coutts. She looks transformed: calm, younger, complete.

Then come the rest of the children, each one led by the hand. They are looking around the dock in wide-eyed fascination.

Alice doesn't know what will happen to them, but she knows they will grow up on Earth, breathing fresh air, making their own choices. Certain decisions are out of their hands, however: the procedure that was done to her has been done to them too. Inside their heads, the nanobots are steadily carrying out their tasks, and to interrupt it would be fraught with risk.

Their mothers will be contacted. The question is whether they will want them, given that they will not remember. Perhaps like Rachel Coutts, some part of them will instinctively know the truth. If not, then ironically their lives will be much the same as Gonçalves planned out for Alice. They will be placed with trusted, responsible, well-connected families, given the best of upbringings, given every opportunity to realise their vast potential. But what they won't have is someone overseeing which memories they are permitted to keep, or inserting artificial ones because their real-life experiences have been deemed inappropriate or insufficient.

Alice watches them board the ion shuttle, waiting until they are all out of sight before she approaches a member of the flight crew. The conversation is brief. She has only one instruction.

"Once you're in open space, take off their seatbelts. Let them fly around."

"That is against regulations, Dr Blake."

"I know. But they're kids, and it's fun."

Alice watches the crew make their final checks, then the shuttle descends smoothly out of sight upon the platform. She remains in place, observing through the canopy until she sees it reappear, flying free, accelerating towards Heinlein.

Now that first memory she had upon waking up in the elevator is true. There are no children on CdC.

AWAKENING (III)

Nikki is brought gently around by the rhythmic pulsing of a soft blue light, programmed to let her know the day is starting for Pacific phase. She opens her eyes and makes a gesture to cancel the visual wake-up call, not worried that she might drift off again. She slept well and she moderated her alcohol intake so she isn't hung-over. She's got responsibilities now: more than she wanted. Alice was smart that way. A lot of ways.

Without the usual levels of booze to cloud it, details of the night before come flooding back quicker and more clearly than she is used to. That said, it was a particularly memorable evening, as evidenced by the fact that there are not one but two extra bodies in her bed. She sits up and looks at the rather beautiful form of Dominic Petitjean sleeping peacefully alongside her. He's going to have some vivid memories too, but they might be a little fuzzier than hers, unless he's got a greater tolerance for Speyside malt than his condition last night indicated.

Nikki and Alice figured all the members of Ochoba's task force had volunteered for their positions either because they were ultra-straight-arrow hard-ass zealots, or because they quite liked the idea of a temporary gig on CdC, with all the potential for adventure that entailed. In Dominic's case, they were betting on the latter. It was an informed bet, Alice having done some discreet asking around, though her research clearly missed a few things.

Alice had commissioned Nikki to give Dominic the grand tour and allow him to indulge his appetites wherever they might lie. Once she got a close-up look at how pretty he was – and more importantly discovered that he was precisely as much fun as his older sister was not – Nikki decided to take a more hands-on approach to her mission. Her strategy had been to get him shitfaced and tempt him back for a three-way with Candace, but it didn't quite work out like that. He was into a three-way, but the composition was not entirely as anticipated. Turned out it was Garret he was more interested in, which is why his is the other body sprawled across Nikki's bed.

Nikki and Candace are good now, happy to say. When they first saw each other again, Candace was all guilt and apologies, and it was tempting to milk that, or at least manipulate it into some quality make-up sex. However, Nikki couldn't help but think of that hug they shared at the junction of Garneau and Young, and how it made her feel. It had turned out to be a Judas kiss, but that didn't mean they couldn't have it now for real.

"There's nothing to forgive," she told Candace. "I'm the one who's got all the making up to do."

Nikki looks out her clothes for the day and begins dressing in front of the mirror. As she begins buttoning her shirt, she notices Dominic open a bleary eye and take in his surroundings. Give him props, he doesn't look fazed.

"You have to get a move on," she tells him. "You're addressing your new troops at ten. You'll need to take the static seven stops. Be busy at this time, could take at least half an hour, maybe forty minutes."

He looks precisely as confused as she intends him to be.

"The static? I thought *this* was my sector. Leastways, this was where you showed me around last night."

"No, this is Mullane. I showed you around here because I figured it was what you'd rather see. Your new turf is McAuliffe. Nothing much to scope there that you won't see soon enough."

"So who's the new captain in Mullane?"

Nikki fastens the tricky topmost button on her dress uniform and smiles at him in the mirror.

extras

orbit

www.orbitbooks.net

about the author

Chris Brookmyre is the author of twenty crime and science fiction novels, including *Black Widow*, winner of the 2017 Theakston Crime Novel of the Year and the 2016 McIlvanney Prize. His work has been adapted for television, radio, the stage and in the case of *Bedlam*, an FPS video game.

Find out more about Chris Brookmyre and other Orbit authors by registering online for the free monthly newsletter at www.orbitbooks.net.

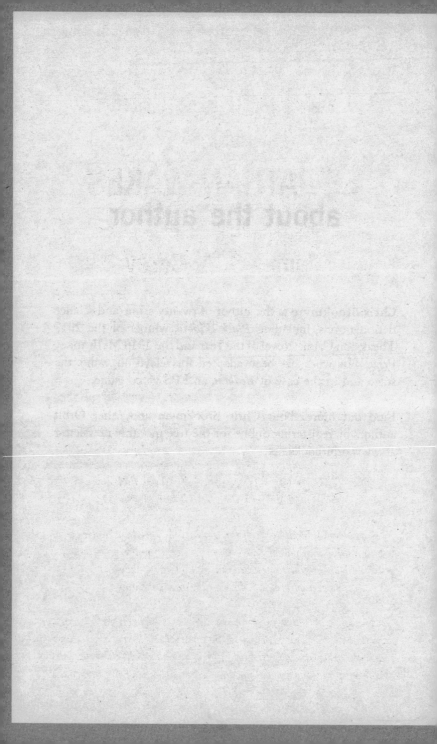

if you enjoyed
PLACES IN THE DARKNESS

look out for

LEVIATHAN WAKES

by

James S. A. Corey

Humanity has colonised the solar system – Mars, the Moon, the Asteroid Belt and beyond – but the stars are still out of our reach.

Jim Holden is an officer on an ice miner making runs from the rings of Saturn to the mining stations of the Belt. When he and his crew discover a derelict ship called the Scopuli, they suddenly find themselves in possession of a deadly secret. A secret that someone is willing to kill for, and on an unimaginable scale. War is coming to the system, unless Jim can find out who abandoned the ship and why.

Detective Miller is looking for a girl. One girl in a system of billions, but her parents have money – and money talks. When the trail leads him to the Scopuli and Holden, they both realise this girl may hold the key to everything.

Holden and Miller must thread the needle between the Earth government, the Outer Planet revolutionaries and secret corporations, and the odds are against them. But out in the Belt, the rules are different, and one small ship can change the fate of the universe.

The *Scopuli* had been taken eight days ago, and Julie Mao was finally ready to be shot.

It had taken all eight days trapped in a storage locker for her to get to that point. For the first two she'd remained motionless, sure that the armored men who'd put her there had been serious. For the first hours, the ship she'd been taken aboard wasn't under thrust, so she floated in the locker, using gentle touches to keep herself from bumping into the walls or the atmosphere suit she shared the space with. When the ship began to move, thrust giving her weight, she'd stood silently until her legs cramped, then sat down slowly into a fetal position. She'd peed in her jumpsuit, not caring about the warm itchy wetness, or the smell, worrying only that she might slip and fall in the wet spot it left on the floor. She couldn't make noise. They'd shoot her.

On the third day, thirst had forced her into action. The noise of the ship was all around her. The faint subsonic rumble of the reactor and drive. The constant hiss and thud of hydraulics and steel bolts as the pressure doors between decks opened and closed. The clump of heavy boots walking on metal decking. She waited until all the noise she could hear sounded distant, then pulled the environment suit off its hooks and onto the locker floor. Listening for any approaching sound, she slowly disassembled the suit and took out the water supply. It was old and stale; the suit obviously hadn't been used or serviced in ages. But she hadn't had a sip in days, and the warm loamy water in the suit's reservoir bag was the best thing she had ever tasted. She had to work hard not to gulp it down and make herself vomit.

When the urge to urinate returned, she pulled the catheter bag out of the suit and relieved herself into it. She sat on the floor, now cushioned by the padded suit and almost comfortable, and wondered who her captors were—Coalition Navy, pirates, something worse. Sometimes she slept.

On day four, isolation, hunger, boredom, and the diminishing number of places to store her piss finally pushed her to make contact with them. She'd heard muffled cries of pain. Somewhere nearby, her shipmates were being beaten or tortured. If she got the attention of the kidnappers, maybe they would just take her to the others. That was okay. Beatings, she could handle. It seemed like a small price to pay if it meant seeing people again.

The locker sat beside the inner airlock door. During flight, that usually wasn't a high-traffic area, though she didn't know anything about the layout of this particular ship. She thought about what to say, how to present herself. When she finally heard someone moving toward her, she just tried to yell that she wanted out. The dry rasp that came out of her throat surprised her. She swallowed, working her tongue to try to create some saliva, and tried again. Another faint rattle in the throat.

The people were right outside her locker door. A voice was

talking quietly. Julie had pulled back a fist to bang on the door when she heard what it was saying.

No. Please no. Please don't.

Dave. Her ship's mechanic. Dave, who collected clips from old cartoons and knew a million jokes, begging in a small broken voice.

No, please no, please don't, he said.

Hydraulics and locking bolts clicked as the inner airlock door opened. A meaty thud as something was thrown inside. Another click as the airlock closed. A hiss of evacuating air.

When the airlock cycle had finished, the people outside her door walked away. She didn't bang to get their attention.

⚡

They'd scrubbed the ship. Detainment by the inner planet navies was a bad scenario, but they'd all trained on how to deal with it. Sensitive OPA data was scrubbed and overwritten with innocuous-looking logs with false time stamps. Anything too sensitive to trust to a computer, the captain destroyed. When the attackers came aboard, they could play innocent.

It hadn't mattered.

There weren't the questions about cargo or permits. The invaders had come in like they owned the place, and Captain Darren had rolled over like a dog. Everyone else—Mike, Dave, Wan Li—they'd all just thrown up their hands and gone along quietly. The pirates or slavers or whatever they were had dragged them off the little transport ship that had been her home, and down a docking tube without even minimal environment suits. The tube's thin layer of Mylar was the only thing between them and hard nothing: hope it didn't rip; goodbye lungs if it did.

Julie had gone along too, but then the bastards had tried to lay their hands on her, strip her clothes off.

Five years of low-gravity jiu jitsu training and them in a confined space with no gravity. She'd done a lot of damage. She'd almost started to think she might win when from nowhere a gauntleted fist smashed into her face. Things got fuzzy after that. Then the locker, and *Shoot her if she makes a noise.* Four days of not making noise while they beat her friends down below and then threw one of them out an airlock.

After six days, everything went quiet.

Shifting between bouts of consciousness and fragmented dreams, she was only vaguely aware as the sounds of walking, talking, and pressure doors and the subsonic rumble of the reactor and the drive faded away a little at a time. When the drive stopped, so did gravity, and Julie woke from a dream of racing her old pinnace to find herself floating while her muscles screamed in protest and then slowly relaxed.

She pulled herself to the door and pressed her ear to the cold metal. Panic shot through her until she caught the quiet sound of the air recyclers. The ship still had power and air, but the drive wasn't on and no one was opening a door or walking or talking. Maybe it was a crew meeting. Or a party on another deck. Or everyone was in engineering, fixing a serious problem.

She spent a day listening and waiting.

By day seven, her last sip of water was gone. No one on the ship had moved within range of her hearing for twenty-four hours. She sucked on a plastic tab she'd ripped off the environment suit until she worked up some saliva; then she started yelling. She yelled herself hoarse.

No one came.

By day eight, she was ready to be shot. She'd been out of water for two days, and her waste bag had been full for four. She put her shoulders against the back wall of the locker and planted her hands against the side walls. Then she kicked out with both legs as hard as she could. The cramps that followed the first kick almost made her pass out. She screamed instead.

Stupid girl, she told herself. She was dehydrated. Eight days without activity was more than enough to start atrophy. At least she should have stretched out.

She massaged her stiff muscles until the knots were gone, then stretched, focusing her mind like she was back in dojo. When she was in control of her body, she kicked again. And again. And again, until light started to show through the edges of the locker. And again, until the door was so bent that the three hinges and the locking bolt were the only points of contact between it and the frame.

And one last time, so that it bent far enough that the bolt was no longer seated in the hasp and the door swung free.

Julie shot from the locker, hands half raised and ready to look either threatening or terrified, depending on which seemed more useful.

There was no one on the whole deck: the airlock, the suit storage room where she'd spent the last eight days, a half dozen other storage rooms. All empty. She plucked a magnetized pipe wrench of suitable size for skull cracking out of an EVA kit, then went down the crew ladder to the deck below.

And then the one below that, and then the one below that. Personnel cabins in crisp, almost military order. Commissary, where there were signs of a struggle. Medical bay, empty. Torpedo bay. No one. The comm station was unmanned, powered down, and locked. The few sensor logs that still streamed showed no sign of the *Scopuli.* A new dread knotted her gut. Deck after deck and room after room empty of life. Something had happened. A radiation leak. Poison in the air. Something that had forced an evacuation. She wondered if she'd be able to fly the ship by herself.

But if they'd evacuated, she'd have heard them going out the airlock, wouldn't she?

She reached the final deck hatch, the one that led into engineering, and stopped when the hatch didn't open automatically. A red light on the lock panel showed that the room had been sealed from the inside. She thought again about radiation and major failures. But if either of those was the case, why lock the door from the inside? And she had passed wall panel after wall panel. None of them had been flashing warnings of any kind. No, not radiation, something else.

There was more disruption here. Blood. Tools and containers in disarray. Whatever had happened, it had happened here. No, it had started here. And it had ended behind that locked door.

It took two hours with a torch and prying tools from the machine shop to cut through the hatch to engineering. With the hydraulics compromised, she had to crank it open by hand. A gust of warm wet air blew out, carrying a hospital scent without the antiseptic. A coppery, nauseating smell. The torture chamber, then. Her friends would be inside, beaten or cut to pieces. Julie hefted her wrench and prepared to bust open at least one head before they killed her. She floated down.

The engineering deck was huge, vaulted like a cathedral. The fusion reactor dominated the central space. Something was wrong with it. Where she expected to see readouts, shielding, and monitors, a layer of something like mud seemed to flow over the reactor core. Slowly, Julie floated toward it, one hand still on the ladder. The strange smell became overpowering.

The mud caked around the reactor had structure to it like nothing she'd seen before. Tubes ran through it like veins or airways. Parts of it pulsed. Not mud, then.

Flesh.

An outcropping of the thing shifted toward her. Compared to the whole, it seemed no larger than a toe, a little finger. It was Captain Darren's head.

"Help me," it said.

Chapter One: Holden

A hundred and fifty years before, when the parochial disagreements between Earth and Mars had been on the verge of war, the Belt had been a far horizon of tremendous mineral wealth beyond viable economic reach, and the outer planets had been beyond even the most unrealistic corporate dream. Then Solomon Epstein had built his little modified fusion drive, popped it on the back of his three-man yacht, and turned it on. With a good scope, you could still see his ship going at a marginal percentage of the speed of light, heading out into the big empty. The best, longest funeral in the history of mankind. Fortunately, he'd left the plans on his home computer. The Epstein Drive hadn't given humanity the stars, but it had delivered the planets.

Three-quarters of a kilometer long, a quarter of a kilometer wide—roughly shaped like a fire hydrant—and mostly empty space inside, the *Canterbury* was a retooled colony transport.

Once, it had been packed with people, supplies, schematics, machines, environment bubbles, and hope. Just under twenty million people lived on the moons of Saturn now. The *Canterbury* had hauled nearly a million of their ancestors there. Forty-five million on the moons of Jupiter. One moon of Uranus sported five thousand, the farthest outpost of human civilization, at least until the Mormons finished their generation ship and headed for the stars and freedom from procreation restrictions.

And then there was the Belt.

If you asked OPA recruiters when they were drunk and feeling expansive, they might say there were a hundred million in the Belt. Ask an inner planet census taker, it was nearer to fifty million. Any way you looked, the population was huge and needed a lot of water.

So now the *Canterbury* and her dozens of sister ships in the Pur'n'Kleen Water Company made the loop from Saturn's generous rings to the Belt and back hauling glaciers, and would until the ships aged into salvage wrecks.

Jim Holden saw some poetry in that.

"Holden?"

He turned back to the hangar deck. Chief Engineer Naomi Nagata towered over him. She stood almost two full meters tall, her mop of curly hair tied back into a black tail, her expression halfway between amusement and annoyance. She had the Belter habit of shrugging with her hands instead of her shoulders.

"Holden, are you listening, or just staring out the window?"

"There was a problem," Holden said. "And because you're really, really good, you can fix it even though you don't have enough money or supplies."

Naomi laughed.

"So you weren't listening," she said.

"Not really, no."

"Well, you got the basics right anyhow. *Knight*'s landing gear isn't going to be good in atmosphere until I can get the seals replaced. That going to be a problem?"

"I'll ask the old man," Holden said. "But when's the last time we used the shuttle in atmosphere?"

"Never, but regs say we need at least one atmo-capable shuttle."

"Hey, Boss!" Amos Burton, Naomi's earthborn assistant, yelled from across the bay. He waved one meaty arm in their general direction. He meant Naomi. Amos might be on Captain McDowell's ship; Holden might be executive officer; but in Amos Burton's world, only Naomi was boss.

"What's the matter?" Naomi shouted back.

"Bad cable. Can you hold this little fucker in place while I get the spare?"

Naomi looked at Holden, *Are we done here?* in her eyes. He snapped a sarcastic salute and she snorted, shaking her head as she walked away, her frame long and thin in her greasy coveralls.

Seven years in Earth's navy, five years working in space with civilians, and he'd never gotten used to the long, thin, improbable bones of Belters. A childhood spent in gravity shaped the way he saw things forever.

At the central lift, Holden held his finger briefly over the button for the navigation deck, tempted by the prospect of Ade Tukunbo—her smile, her voice, the patchouli-and-vanilla scent she used in her hair—but pressed the button for the infirmary instead. Duty before pleasure.

Shed Garvey, the medical tech, was hunched over his lab table, debriding the stump of Cameron Paj's left arm, when Holden walked in. A month earlier, Paj had gotten his elbow pinned by a thirty-ton block of ice moving at five millimeters a second. It wasn't an uncommon injury among people with the dangerous job of cutting and moving zero-g icebergs, and Paj was taking the whole thing with the fatalism of a professional. Holden leaned over Shed's shoulder to watch as the tech plucked one of the medical maggots out of dead tissue.

"What's the word?" Holden asked.

"It's looking pretty good, sir," Paj said. "I've still got a few nerves. Shed's been tellin' me about how the prosthetic is gonna hook up to it."

"Assuming we can keep the necrosis under control," the medic said, "and make sure Paj doesn't heal up too much before we get to Ceres. I checked the policy, and Paj here's been signed on long enough to get one with force feedback, pressure and temperature sensors, fine-motor software. The whole package. It'll be almost as good as the real thing. The inner planets have a new biogel that regrows the limb, but that isn't covered in our medical plan."

"Fuck the Inners, and fuck their magic Jell-O. I'd rather have a good Belter-built fake than anything those bastards grow in a lab. Just wearing their fancy arm probably turns you into an asshole," Paj said. Then he added, "Oh, uh, no offense, XO."

"None taken. Just glad we're going to get you fixed up," Holden said.

"Tell him the other bit," Paj said with a wicked grin. Shed blushed.

"I've, ah, heard from other guys who've gotten them," Shed said, not meeting Holden's eyes. "Apparently there's a period while you're still building identification with the prosthetic when whacking off feels just like getting a hand job."

Holden let the comment hang in the air for a second while Shed's ears turned crimson.

"Good to know," Holden said. "And the necrosis?"

"There's some infection," Shed said. "The maggots are keeping it under control, and the inflammation's actually a good thing in this context, so we're not fighting too hard unless it starts to spread."

"Is he going to be ready for the next run?" Holden asked.

For the first time, Paj frowned.

"Shit yes, I'll be ready. I'm always ready. This is what I *do*, sir."

"Probably," Shed said. "Depending on how the bond takes. If not this one, the one after."

"Fuck that," Paj said. "I can buck ice one-handed better than half the skags you've got on this bitch."

"Again," Holden said, suppressing a grin, "good to know. Carry on."

Paj snorted. Shed plucked another maggot free. Holden went back to the lift, and this time he didn't hesitate.

The navigation station of the *Canterbury* didn't dress to impress. The great wall-sized displays Holden had imagined when he'd first volunteered for the navy did exist on capital ships but, even there, more as an artifact of design than need. Ade sat at a pair of screens only slightly larger than a hand terminal, graphs of the efficiency and output of the *Canterbury*'s reactor and engine updating in the corners, raw logs spooling on the right as the systems reported in. She wore thick headphones that covered her ears, the faint thump of the bass line barely escaping. If the *Canterbury* sensed an anomaly, it would alert her. If a system errored, it would alert her. If Captain McDowell left the command and control deck, it would alert her so she could turn the music off and look busy when he arrived. Her petty hedonism was only one of a thousand things that made Ade attractive to Holden. He walked up behind her, pulled the headphones gently away from her ears, and said, "Hey."

Ade smiled, tapped her screen, and dropped the headphones to rest around her long slim neck like technical jewelry.

"Executive Officer James Holden," she said with an exaggerated formality made even more acute by her thick Nigerian accent. "And what can I do for you?"

"You know, it's funny you should ask that," he said. "I was just thinking how pleasant it would be to have someone come back to my cabin when third shift takes over. Have a little romantic dinner of the same crap they're serving in the galley. Listen to some music."

"Drink a little wine," she said. "Break a little protocol. Pretty to think about, but I'm not up for sex tonight."

"I wasn't talking about sex. A little food. Conversation."

"I was talking about sex," she said.

Holden knelt beside her chair. In the one-third g of their current thrust, it was perfectly comfortable. Ade's smile softened. The log spool chimed; she glanced at it, tapped a release, and turned back to him.

"Ade, I like you. I mean, I really enjoy your company," he said. "I don't understand why we can't spend some time together with our clothes on."

"Holden. Sweetie. Stop it, okay?"

"Stop what?"

"Stop trying to turn me into your girlfriend. You're a nice guy. You've got a cute butt, and you're fun in the sack. Doesn't mean we're engaged."

Holden rocked back on his heels, feeling himself frown.

"Ade. For this to work for me, it needs to be more than that."

"But it isn't," she said, taking his hand. "It's okay that it isn't. You're the XO here, and I'm a short-timer. Another run, maybe two, and I'm gone."

"I'm not chained to this ship either."

Her laughter was equal parts warmth and disbelief.

"How long have you been on the *Cant*?"

"Five years."

"You're not going anyplace," she said. "You're comfortable here."

"Comfortable?" he said. "The *Cant*'s a century-old ice hauler. You can find a shittier flying job, but you have to try really hard. Everyone here is either wildly under-qualified or seriously screwed things up at their last gig."

"And you're comfortable here." Her eyes were less kind now. She bit her lip, looked down at the screen, looked up.

"I didn't deserve that," he said.

"You didn't," she agreed. "Look, I told you I wasn't in the mood tonight. I'm feeling cranky. I need a good night's sleep. I'll be nicer tomorrow."

"Promise?"

"I'll even make you dinner. Apology accepted?"

He slipped forward, pressed his lips to hers. She kissed back, politely at first and then with more warmth. Her fingers cupped his neck for a moment, then pulled him away.

"You're entirely too good at that. You should go now," she said. "On duty and all."

"Okay," he said, and didn't turn to go.

"Jim," she said, and the shipwide comm system clicked on.

"Holden to the bridge," Captain McDowell said, his voice compressed and echoing. Holden replied with something obscene. Ade laughed. He swooped in, kissed her cheek, and headed back for the central lift, quietly hoping that Captain McDowell suffered boils and public humiliation for his lousy timing.

The bridge was hardly larger than Holden's quarters and smaller by half than the galley. Except for the slightly oversized captain's display, required by Captain McDowell's failing eyesight and general distrust of corrective surgery, it could have been an accounting firm's back room. The air smelled of cleaning astringent and someone's overly strong yerba maté tea. McDowell shifted in his seat as Holden approached. Then the captain leaned back, pointing over his shoulder at the communications station.

"Becca!" McDowell snapped. "Tell him."

Rebecca Byers, the comm officer on duty, could have been bred from a shark and a hatchet. Black eyes, sharp features, lips so thin they might as well not have existed. The story on board was that she'd taken the job to escape prosecution for killing an ex-husband. Holden liked her.

"Emergency signal," she said. "Picked it up two hours ago. The transponder verification just bounced back from *Callisto*. It's real."

"Ah," Holden said. And then: "Shit. Are we the closest?"

"Only ship in a few million klicks."

"Well. That figures," Holden said.

Becca turned her gaze to the captain. McDowell cracked his knuckles and stared at his display. The light from the screen gave him an odd greenish cast.

"It's next to a charted non-Belt asteroid," McDowell said.

"Really?" Holden said in disbelief. "Did they run into it? There's nothing else out here for millions of kilometers."

"Maybe they pulled over because someone had to go potty. All we have is that some knucklehead is out there, blasting an emergency signal, and we're the closest. Assuming..."

The law of the solar system was unequivocal. In an environment as hostile to life as space, the aid and goodwill of your fellow humans wasn't optional. The emergency signal, just by existing, obligated the nearest ship to stop and render aid—which didn't mean the law was universally followed.

The *Canterbury* was fully loaded. Well over a million tons of ice had been gently accelerated for the past month. Just like the little glacier that had crushed Paj's arm, it was going to be hard to slow down. The temptation to have an unexplained comm failure, erase the logs, and let the great god Darwin have his way was always there.

But if McDowell had really intended that, he wouldn't have called Holden up. Or made the suggestion where the crew could hear him. Holden understood the dance. The captain was going to be the one who would have blown it off except for Holden. The grunts would respect the captain for not wanting to cut into the ship's profit. They'd respect Holden for insisting that they follow the rule. No matter what happened, the captain and Holden would both be hated for what they were required by law and mere human decency to do.

"We have to stop," Holden said. Then, gamely: "There may be salvage."

McDowell tapped his screen. Ade's voice came from the console, as low and warm as if she'd been in the room.

"Captain?"

"I need numbers on stopping this crate," he said.

"Sir?"

"How hard is it going to be to put us alongside CA-2216862?"

"We're stopping at an asteroid?"

"I'll tell you when you've followed my order, Navigator Tukunbo."

"Yes, sir," she said. Holden heard a series of clicks. "If we flip the ship right now and burn like hell for most of two days, I can get us within fifty thousand kilometers, sir."

"Can you define 'burn like hell'?" McDowell said.

"We'll need everyone in crash couches."

"Of course we will," McDowell sighed, and scratched his scruffy beard. "And shifting ice is only going to do a couple million bucks' worth of banging up the hull, if we're lucky. I'm getting old for this, Holden. I really am."

"Yes, sir. You are. And I've always liked your chair," Holden said. McDowell scowled and made an obscene gesture. Rebecca snorted in laughter. McDowell turned to her.

"Send a message to the beacon that we're on our way. And let Ceres know we're going to be late. Holden, where does the *Knight* stand?"

"No flying in atmosphere until we get some parts, but she'll do fine for fifty thousand klicks in vacuum."

"You're sure of that?"

"Naomi said it. That makes it true."

McDowell rose, unfolding to almost two and a quarter meters and thinner than a teenager back on Earth. Between his age and never having lived in a gravity well, the coming burn was likely to be hell on the old man. Holden felt a pang of sympathy that he would never embarrass McDowell by expressing.

"Here's the thing, Jim," McDowell said, his voice quiet enough that only Holden could hear him. "We're required to stop and make an attempt, but we don't have to go out of our way, if you see what I mean."

"We'll already have stopped," Holden said, and McDowell patted at the air with his wide, spidery hands. One of the many Belter gestures that had evolved to be visible when wearing an environment suit.

"I can't avoid that," he said. "But if you see anything out there that seems off, don't play hero again. Just pack up the toys and come home."

"And leave it for the next ship that comes through?"

"And keep yourself safe," McDowell said. "Order. Understood?"

"Understood," Holden said.

As the shipwide comm system clicked to life and McDowell began explaining the situation to the crew, Holden imagined he could hear a chorus of groans coming up through the decks. He went over to Rebecca.

"Okay," he said, "what have we got on the broken ship?"

"Light freighter. Martian registry. Shows Eros as home port. Calls itself *Scopuli*…"

Chapter Two: Miller

Detective Miller sat back on the foam-core chair, smiling gentle encouragement while he scrambled to make sense of the girl's story.

"And then it was all pow! Room full up with bladeboys howling and humping shank," the girl said, waving a hand. "Look like a dance number, 'cept that Bomie's got this look he didn't know nothing never and ever amen. You know, que?"

Havelock, standing by the door, blinked twice. The squat man's face twitched with impatience. It was why Havelock was never going to make senior detective. And why he sucked at poker.

Miller was very good at poker.

"I totally," Miller said. His voice had taken on the twang of an inner level resident. He waved his hand in the same lazy arc the girl used. "Bomie, he didn't see. Forgotten arm."

"Forgotten fucking arm, yeah," the girl said as if Miller had spoken a line of gospel. Miller nodded, and the girl nodded back like they were two birds doing a mating dance.

The rent hole was three cream-and-black-fleck-painted rooms—bathroom, kitchen, living room. The struts of a pull-down sleeping loft in the living room had been broken and repaired so many times they didn't retract anymore. This near the center of Ceres' spin, that wasn't from gravity so much as mass in motion. The air smelled beery with old protein yeast and mushrooms. Local food, so whoever had bounced the girl hard enough to break her bed hadn't paid enough for dinner. Or maybe they did, and the girl had chosen to spend it on heroin or malta or MCK.

Her business, either way.

"Follow que?" Miller asked.

"Bomie vacuate like losing air," the girl said with a chuckle. "Bang-head hops, kennis tu?"

"Ken," Miller said.

"Now, all new bladeboys. Overhead. I'm out."

"And Bomie?"

The girl's eyes made a slow track up Miller, shoes to knees to porkpie hat. Miller chuckled. He gave the chair a light push, sloping up to his feet in the low gravity.

"He shows, and I asked, que si?" Miller said.

"Como no?" the girl said. *Why not?*

The tunnel outside was white where it wasn't grimy. Ten meters wide, and gently sloping up in both directions. The white LED lights didn't pretend to mimic sunlight. About half a kilometer down, someone had rammed into the wall so hard the native rock showed through, and it still hadn't been repaired. Maybe it wouldn't be. This was the deep dig, way up near the center of spin. Tourists never came here.

Havelock led the way to their cart, bouncing too high with every step. He didn't come up to the low gravity levels very often, and it made him awkward. Miller had lived on Ceres his whole life, and truth to tell, the Coriolis effect up this high could make him a little unsteady sometimes too.

"So," Havelock said as he punched in their destination code, "did you have fun?"

"Don't know what you mean," Miller said.

The electrical motors hummed to life, and the cart lurched forward into the tunnel, squishy foam tires faintly squeaking.

"Having your outworld conversation in front of the Earth guy?" Havelock said. "I couldn't follow even half of that."

"That wasn't Belters keeping the Earth guy out," Miller said. "That was poor folks keeping the educated guy out. And it was kind of fun, now you mention it."

Havelock laughed. He could take being teased and keep on moving. It was what made him good at team sports: soccer, basketball, politics.

Miller wasn't much good at those.

Ceres, the port city of the Belt and the outer planets, boasted two hundred fifty kilometers in diameter, tens of thousands of kilometers of tunnels in layer on layer on layer. Spinning it up to 0.3 g had taken the best minds at Tycho Manufacturing half a generation, and they were still pretty smug about it. Now Ceres had more than six million permanent residents, and as many as a thousand ships docking in any given day meant upping the population to as high as seven million.

Platinum, iron, and titanium from the Belt. Water from Saturn, vegetables and beef from the big mirror-fed greenhouses on Ganymede and Europa, organics from Earth and Mars. Power cells from Io, Helium-3 from the refineries on Rhea and Iapetus. A river of wealth and power unrivaled in human history came through Ceres. Where there was commerce on that level, there was also crime. Where there was crime, there were security forces to keep it in check. Men like Miller and Havelock, whose business it was to track the electric carts up the wide ramps, feel the false gravity of spin fall away beneath them, and ask low-rent glitz whores about what happened the night Bomie Chatterjee stopped collecting protection money for the Golden Bough Society.

The primary station house for Star Helix Security, police force and military garrison for the Ceres Station, was on the third level from the asteroid's skin, two kilometers square and dug into the rock so high Miller could walk from his desk up five levels without ever leaving the offices. Havelock turned in the cart while Miller went to his cubicle, downloaded the recording of their interview with the girl, and reran it. He was halfway through when his partner lumbered up behind him.

"Learn anything?" Havelock asked.

"Not much," Miller said. "Bomie got jumped by a bunch of unaffiliated local thugs. Sometimes a low-level guy like Bomie will hire people to pretend to attack him so he can heroically fight them off. Ups his reputation. That's what she meant when she called it a dance number. The guys that went after him were that caliber, only instead of turning into a ninja badass, Bomie ran away and hasn't come back."

"And now?"

"And now nothing," Miller said. "That's what I don't get. Someone took out a Golden Bough purse boy, and there's no payback. I mean, okay, Bomie's a bottom-feeder, but…"

"But once they start eating the little guys, there's less money coming up to the big guys," Havelock said. "So why hasn't the Golden Bough meted out some gangster justice?"

"I don't like this," Miller said.

Havelock laughed. "Belters," he said. "One thing goes weird and you think the whole ecosystem's crashing. If the Golden Bough's too weak to keep its claims, that's a good thing. They're the bad guys, remember?"

"Yeah, well," Miller said. "Say what you will about organized crime, at least it's organized."

Havelock sat on the small plastic chair beside Miller's desk and craned to watch the playback.

"Okay," Havelock said. "What the hell is the 'forgotten arm'?"

"Boxing term," Miller said. "It's the hit you didn't see coming."

The computer chimed and Captain Shaddid's voice came from the speakers.

"Miller? Are you there?"

"Mmm," Havelock said. "Bad omen."

"What?" the captain asked, her voice sharp. She had never quite overcome her prejudice against Havelock's inner planet origins. Miller held up a hand to silence his partner.

"Here, Captain. What can I do for you?"

"Meet me in my office, please."

"On my way," he said.

Miller stood, and Havelock slid into his chair. They didn't speak. Both of them knew that Captain Shaddid would have called them in together if she'd wanted Havelock to be there. Another reason the man would never make senior detective. Miller left him alone with the playback, trying to parse the fine points of class and station, origin and race. Lifetime's work, that.

Captain Shaddid's office was decorated in a soft, feminine style. Real cloth tapestries hung from the walls, and the scent of coffee and cinnamon came from an insert in her air filter that cost about a tenth of what the real foodstuffs would have. She wore her uniform casually, her hair down around her shoulders in violation of corporate regulations. If Miller had ever been called upon to describe her, the phrase *deceptive coloration* would have figured in. She nodded to a chair, and he sat.

"What have you found?" she asked, but her gaze was on the wall behind him. This wasn't a pop quiz; she was just making conversation.

"Golden Bough's looking the same as Sohiro's crew and the Loca Greiga. Still on station, but…distracted, I guess I'd call it. They're letting little things slide. Fewer thugs on the ground, less enforcement. I've got half a dozen mid-level guys who've gone dark."

He'd caught her attention.

"Killed?" she asked. "An OPA advance?"

An advance by the Outer Planets Alliance was the constant bogeyman of Ceres security. Living in the tradition of Al Capone and Hamas, the IRA and the Red Martials, the OPA was beloved by the people it helped and feared by the ones who got in its way.

Part social movement, part wannabe nation, and part terrorist network, it totally lacked an institutional conscience. Captain Shaddid might not like Havelock because he was from down a gravity well, but she'd work with him. The OPA would have put him in an airlock. People like Miller would only rate getting a bullet in the skull, and a nice plastic one at that. Nothing that might get shrapnel in the ductwork.

"I don't think so," he said. "It doesn't smell like a war. It's... Honestly, sir, I don't know what the hell it is. The numbers are great. Protection's down, unlicensed gambling's down. Cooper and Hariri shut down the underage whorehouse up on six, and as far as anyone can tell, it hasn't started up again. There's a little more action by independents, but that aside, it's all looking great. It just smells funny."

She nodded, but her gaze was back on the wall. He'd lost her interest as quickly as he'd gotten it.

"Well, put it aside," she said. "I have something. New contract. Just you. Not Havelock."

Miller crossed his arms.

"New contract," he said slowly. "Meaning?"

"Meaning Star Helix Security has accepted a contract for services separate from the Ceres security assignment, and in my role as site manager for the corporation, I'm assigning you to it."

"I'm fired?" he said.

Captain Shaddid looked pained.

"It's additional duty," she said. "You'll still have the Ceres assignments you have now. It's just that, in addition...Look, Miller, I think this is as shitty as you do. I'm not pulling you off station. I'm not taking you off the main contract. This is a favor someone down on Earth is doing for a shareholder."

"We're doing favors for shareholders now?" Miller asked.

"You are, yes," Captain Shaddid said. The softness was gone; the conciliatory tone was gone. Her eyes were dark as wet stone.

"Right, then," Miller said. "I guess I am."

Captain Shaddid held up her hand terminal. Miller fumbled at his side, pulled out his own, and accepted the narrow-beam transfer. Whatever this was, Shaddid was keeping it off the common network. A new file tree, labeled JMAO, appeared on his readout.

"It's a little-lost-daughter case," Captain Shaddid said. "Ariadne and Jules-Pierre Mao."

The names rang a bell. Miller pressed his fingertips onto the screen of his hand terminal.

"Mao-Kwikowski Mercantile?" he asked.

"The one."

Miller whistled low.

Maokwik might not have been one of the top ten corporations in the Belt, but it was certainly in the upper fifty. Originally, it had been a legal firm involved in the epic failure of the Venusian cloud cities. They'd used the money from that decades-long lawsuit to diversify and expand, mostly into interplanetary transport. Now the corporate station was independent, floating between the Belt and the inner planets with the regal majesty of an ocean liner on ancient seas. The simple fact that Miller knew that much about them meant they had enough money to buy and sell men like him on open exchange.

He'd just been bought.

"They're Luna-based," Captain Shaddid said. "All the rights and privileges of Earth citizenship. But they do a lot of shipping business out here."

"And they misplaced a daughter?"

"Black sheep," the captain said. "Went off to college, got involved with a group called the Far Horizons Foundation. Student activists."

"OPA front," Miller said.

"Associated," Shaddid corrected him. Miller let it pass, but a flicker of curiosity troubled him. He wondered which side Captain Shaddid would be on if the OPA attacked. "The family put it down to a phase. They've got two older children with controlling interest, so if Julie wanted to bounce around vacuum calling herself a freedom fighter, there was no real harm."

"But now they want her found," Miller said.

"They do."

"What changed?"

"They didn't see fit to share that information."

"Right."

"Last records show she was employed on Tycho Station but maintained an apartment here. I've found her partition on the network and locked it down. The password is in your files."

"Okay," Miller said. "What's my contract?"

"Find Julie Mao, detain her, and ship her home."

"A kidnap job, then," he said.

"Yes."

Miller stared down at his hand terminal, flicking the files open without particularly looking at them. A strange knot had tied itself in his guts. He'd been working Ceres security for thirty years, and he hadn't started with many illusions in place. The joke was that Ceres didn't have laws—it had police. His hands weren't any cleaner than Captain Shaddid's. Sometimes people fell out airlocks. Sometimes evidence vanished from the lockers. It wasn't so much that it was right or wrong as that it was justified. You spent your life in a stone bubble with your food, your water, your *air* shipped in from places so distant you could barely find them with a telescope, and a certain moral flexibility was necessary. But he'd never had to take a kidnap job before.

"Problem, Detective?" Captain Shaddid asked.

"No, sir," he said. "I'll take care of it."

"Don't spend too much time on it," she said.

"Yes, sir. Anything else?"

Captain Shaddid's hard eyes softened, like she was putting on a mask. She smiled.

"Everything going well with your partner?"

"Havelock's all right," Miller said. "Having him around makes people like me better by contrast. That's nice."

Her smile's only change was to become half a degree more genuine. Nothing like a little shared racism to build ties with the boss. Miller nodded respectfully and headed out.

⚡

His hole was on the eighth level, off a residential tunnel a hundred meters wide with fifty meters of carefully cultivated green park running down the center. The main corridor's vaulted ceiling was lit by recessed lights and painted a blue that Havelock assured him matched the Earth's summer sky. Living on the surface of a planet, mass sucking at every bone and muscle, and nothing but gravity to keep your air close, seemed like a fast path to crazy. The blue was nice, though.

Some people followed Captain Shaddid's lead by perfuming their air. Not always with coffee and cinnamon scents, of course. Havelock's hole smelled of baking bread. Others opted for floral scents or semipheromones. Candace, Miller's ex-wife, had preferred something called EarthLily, which had always made him think of the waste recycling levels. These days, he left it at the vaguely astringent smell of the station itself. Recycled air that had passed through a million lungs. Water from the tap so clean it could be used for lab work, but it had been piss and shit and tears and blood and would be again. The circle of life on Ceres was so small you could see the curve. He liked it that way.

He poured a glass of moss whiskey, a native Ceres liquor made from engineered yeast, then took off his shoes and settled onto the foam bed. He could still see Candace's disapproving scowl and hear her sigh. He shrugged apology to her memory and turned back to work.

Juliette Andromeda Mao. He read through her work history, her academic records. Talented pinnace pilot. There was a picture of her at eighteen in a tailored vac suit with the helmet off: pretty girl with a thin, lunar citizen's frame and long black hair. She was grinning like the universe had given her a kiss. The linked text said she'd won first place in something called the Parrish/Dorn

500K. He searched briefly. Some kind of race only really rich people could afford to fly in. Her pinnace — the *Razorback* — had beaten the previous record and held it for two years.

Miller sipped his whiskey and wondered what had happened to the girl with enough wealth and power to own a private ship that would bring her here. It was a long way from competing in expensive space races to being hog-tied and sent home in a pod. Or maybe it wasn't.

"Poor little rich girl," Miller said to the screen. "Sucks to be you, I guess."

He closed the files and drank quietly and seriously, staring at the blank ceiling above him. The chair where Candace used to sit and ask him about his day stood empty, but he could see her there anyway. Now that she wasn't here to make him talk, it was easier to respect the impulse. She'd been lonely. He could see that now. In his imagination, she rolled her eyes.

An hour later, his blood warm with drink, he heated up a bowl of real rice and fake beans — yeast and fungus could mimic anything if you had enough whiskey first — opened the door of his hole, and ate dinner looking out at the traffic gently curving by. The second shift streamed into the tube stations and then out of them. The kids who lived two holes down — a girl of eight and her brother of four — met their father with hugs, squeals, mutual accusations, and tears. The blue ceiling glowed in its reflected light, unchanging, static, reassuring. A sparrow fluttered down the tunnel, hovering in a way that Havelock assured him they couldn't on Earth. Miller threw it a fake bean.

He tried to think about the Mao girl, but in truth he didn't much care. Something was happening to the organized crime families of Ceres, and it made him jumpy as hell.

This thing with Julie Mao? It was a sideshow.